Lian Hearn studied modern languages at Oxford University and worked as a film critic and arts editor in London before settling in Australia. A lifelong interest in Japan led to the study of the Japanese language, many trips to Japan, and culminated in the *Tales of the Otori* series. The books in the series have been sold into thirty-six countries and have been worldwide bestsellers. For more information, you can visit her website, www.lianhearn.com

Also by Lian Hearn

Tales of the Otori

Across the Nightingale Floor

Grass for His Pillow

Brilliance of the Moon

The Harsh Cry of the Heron

Heaven's Net Is Wide

BLOSSOMS AND SHADOWS

LIAN HEARN

Quercus

First published in Great Britain in 2011 by Quercus
This paperback edition published in 2012 by

Quercus
55 Baker Street
7th Floor, South Block
London
W1U 8EW

A CIP catalogue record for this book is available
from the British Library

ISBN 978 0 85738 298 6

10 9 8 7 6 5 4 3 2 1

Typeset by Ellipsis Digital Limited, Glasgow

Printed and bound in Great Britain by
Clays Ltd, St Ives plc

BLOSSOMS AND SHADOWS

In the Meiji Restoration of 1868 an alliance of young samurai and Court nobles overthrew the semi-feudal government of the Tokugawa Shōgun. So began the birth of modern Japan.

Since the arrival in 1853 of US Commander Matthew Perry with his demand for an end to Japan's isolation, these remote islands of around thirty million people divided into over two hundred and sixty domains, each ruled by its own *daimyō*, had been racked by turmoil, confusion and civil war. The central government was incompetent; the domains were deeply in debt; comets, earthquakes, famines and epidemics followed one after another; samurai fought for reform; commoners sought world renewal. Among radical loyalists a movement grew to restore power to the emperor and resist the foreigners: above all to avoid colonisation by the West. Their slogan was *sonnōjōi* (*revere the Emperor, expel the foreigners*), their preferred method: violence.

Chōshū, a powerful domain in the southwest and an old enemy of the Tokugawa, became one of the loudest in the cry for change. This is the story of a handful of its young men and women who dedicated their lives to the reform of their domain and the modernisation of their country, and in doing so changed the course of world history.

It begins in 1857.

In particular physicians are entrusted with human lives, view the naked body, speak about deeply held secrets and listen to humiliating confessions. Hold always a feeling of warmth and generosity within and speak sparingly. Strive to be silent.

From *Mr Fu's Advice to Physicians*
(Christoph W. Hufeland's *Enchiridion Medicum*,
quoted by Ogata Kōan)

LIST OF CHARACTERS

The fictional characters

Itasaki Yūnosuke	a Chōshū domain physician
Chie	his wife
Tetsuya	his son
Mitsue	his older daughter
Tsuru	his younger daughter, the narrator
Itasaki Shinsai	Yūnosuke's younger brother
Kuriya Jizaemon	a pharmacist in Hagi
Misako	his wife
Heibei	his son, Mitsue's husband
Michi	Mitsue's daughter, adopted by Tsuru
Makino Keizō	an employee in the Kuriya pharmacy
O-Kiyo	a geisha at the Hanamatsutei
O-Kane	a maidservant in the Itasaki house

Hachirō	a manservant in the Itasaki house
Nakajima Noboru Hayashi Daisuke	students of Dr Itasaki
Imaike Eikaku	an artist
Seiko	his sister
Mrs Minami	a second-hand-goods dealer in Kyōto
Yoshio Gongorō	a Nagasaki doctor
O-Kimi	his daughter
Kitaoka Jundō	one of Dr Yoshio's students

The historical characters

Sufu Masanosuke	Chōshū bureaucrat and leading government figure
Yoshitomi Tōbei	village headman and friend of Sufu
Shiraishi Seiichirō	wealthy merchant and supporter of Chōshū activists
Yoshida Shōin	teacher and reformer; his students include:
Itō Shunsuke/ Hirobumi	activist, later first Prime Minister of Japan
Katsura Kogorō/ Kido Takayoshi	activist, later minister

Takasugi Shinsaku	activist, military reformer
Kusaka Genzui	activist, Shōin's brother-in-law
Yamagata Kyōsuke/ Aritomo	activist, military reformer
Yoshida Toshimaro	activist
Fumi	Shōin's sister, married to Genzui
Shiji Monta/ Inoue Kaoru	activist, later minister in the Meiji government
Towa	a shrine guardian, admired by Shōin
Masa	Takasugi's wife
O-Uno	Takasugi's lover
Mōri Takachika	Chōshū *daimyō*
Mōri Sadahiro	his adopted son and heir
Nagai Uta	Chōshū government official
Mukunashi Tōta	leader of the conservative party in Chōshū
Tokoro Ikutarō	a doctor
Ōmura Masujirō/ Murata Zōroku	a domain doctor, later military reformer
Maki Izumi	activist

Miyabe Teizō	activist
Kijima Matabei	activist
Akane Taketo	leader of the Kiheitai
Sanjō Sanetomi	loyalist nobleman
Nishikinokōji Yorinori	loyalist nobleman
Ii Naosuke	Bakufu government offical and Tairō
Tokugawa Iemochi	14th Shōgun
Hitotsubashi Keiki/ Tokugawa Yoshinobu	15th and last Shōgun
Shimazu Hisamitsu	father of the Satsuma *daimyō*
Saigō Kichinosuke (later Takamori)	Satsuma government official and commander
Sakamoto Ryōma	Tosa activist
Nakaoka Shintarō	Tosa activist
Thomas Glover	Scottish merchant and arms trader
Nomura Bōtōni	loyalist poet and nun

PART 1

起

Ansei 4 to Bunkyū 1
1857–1861

THE FIRST WEDDING

It was the bittersweet day of my sister's wedding and everyone was crying, even me, though I did not often shed tears. The skies wept in sympathy with the steady trickle of the plum rains. It was the fourth year of Ansei, in the intercalary fifth month, four years after the black ships had arrived in Uraga Bay; a strange time, like waiting for a potion to boil: the ingredients are all mixed, the fire is intense, yet nothing seems to be happening. The more you watch the slower it is to boil.

We had arranged a large party, neighbours and relatives from Yuda and Yamaguchi, my father's fellow doctors, masters from the schools my brother had attended before he left for Nagasaki, and from the private academy where my uncle, Shinsai, had until recently been the top pupil-teacher. Several of Shinsai's friends had turned up too: the young men who had studied with him, and competed with him in sword fighting, boasting and loud expressions of loyalty to the Emperor, contempt for foreigners and exasperation with the Bakufu, the Shōgun's government.

The women of the Itasaki family – my mother, my sister Mitsue, and me, Tsuru, together with our maid, O-Kane, and my father's mistress, O-Kiyo – had been preparing food for days: red bean rice, *chirazushi*, *mochi*, tofu in many different forms, and huge whole bream. The guests brought presents, more whole fish on beds of oak leaves, sweet bean cakes, *umeboshi* and other salted delicacies, abalone and cuttlefish, and casks of sake in festive straw wrappings, of which cup after celebratory cup was poured.

Some of the other geisha from O-Kiyo's house came, and played the *shamisen* and sang, but O-Kiyo, as my mother often said, had not been blessed with looks or talent. You might have thought that was spite on my mother's part, but nothing could be further from the truth. My mother pitied O-Kiyo, who had not been able to attract a man with more influence or money than my father. Mother took O-Kiyo under her wing and treated her like an older but less well-established relative, deferring to her and dominating her in equal measure.

We did not know how our father had acquired O-Kiyo. Maybe he had inherited her from a grateful patient or won her in some gambling game. He himself did not seem to know what to do with her, and if my mother had not chivvied him into visiting her he would probably have hardly seen her. She had to practically drive him out of the house: *Isn't it about time you called around at the Hanamatsutei?*

'I suppose it is,' Father would say with no great enthusiasm. He came back having drunk too much, which made him liverish and headachy the next day, and usually regretful, for he would have agreed to give someone a free consultation or some Chinese medicine, and he was already overworked.

My sister and I liked O-Kiyo, mainly because the Hanamatsutei was a popular tea house and O-Kiyo loved to bring us all the local gossip. We were always pleased to hear her call at the door; one of us would make tea while the other sat with her on the outside veranda and watched her take out her tobacco box, prepare her pipe and light up. She would puff deeply and then begin to chat in her smoky voice.

Our house had two front entrances, one on the main street where samurai patients came, and one on the side street for townspeople and farmers. We all knew that it was the latter who paid for the house and everything in it, and O-Kiyo, but they still had to use the side street entrance and be prepared to wait while my father attended to his samurai patients, who paid for nothing if they could help it. My father, to his own great surprise, for we were not related to any of the famous medical families, the Wada, or Aoki, or Ogata, had been appointed a domain physician a few years before. He received a stipend of twenty-two *koku* a year and the right to wear two swords, though he cut his hair short in the usual style of a doctor. Our family occupied that nebulous position that physicians hold in the hierarchy of the domain. They have less respect for status than most: they see the beloved son of the domain lord die of measles or smallpox as swiftly as the peasant's child. They can do no more for the elder succumbing to consumption of the lungs than they can for the lowly *sottsu*. They see men and women at their weakest, and usually at their most grateful.

My father came from a family of rural physicians. His father had been impressed by what he knew of *ranpō* – Dutch medical knowledge – and had sent his son to Nagasaki, where my father had studied medicine with men who had known and worked with the Dejima doctors Siebold and Mohnike. It may have been this connection, or my father's impressive collection of Dutch instruments, or the plants and herbs he grew in his garden, that had led to his promotion. Or maybe it was his sake-fuelled relationship with Sufu Masanosuke, one of the most important figures in the domain government, who often stayed in Yuda with our neighbour Yoshitomi Tōbei and went with him to O-Kiyo's Hanamatsutei. This was another reason why we were all quite glad O-Kiyo was part of our family, for Lord Sufu, a man we wholeheartedly admired, had become our father's patron and protector.

Mr Yoshitomi came to the wedding, and so did another of our neighbours, Shiji Monta. His family were the Inoue who lived near us, and I had known him first as Yūkichi, but he had been adopted by the Shiji family in Hagi, where he had studied at the domain school, the Meirinkan, and had been given the name of Monta by Lord Mōri Takachika himself. He brought another young man with him, Takasugi Shinsaku. My mother and I were terribly impressed by this great honour. Takasugi was from a high-ranking family in Hagi and was already well known throughout the domain for his brilliance.

'Brilliance as a drinker,' my uncle, Shinsai, said later. He was the same age as these young men, maybe a little younger, and had a half-admiring, half-envious attitude towards them. Takasugi had already been to Edo to study sword fighting with Saitō Yakurō and would easily find a position in the domain government; Monta planned to go the following year: he was a page with Lord Mōri. They had opportunities for advancement that my uncle would never have.

Shinsai was the same age as my sister, less than two years older than me, and two years younger than our brother, Tetsuya; my grandmother was pregnant with her last child at the same time as my mother carried her second. My grandmother, weakened by childbearing at her age, did not survive long after the birth. She left her baby to my mother's care, and so my uncle grew up in our family, as close to us as another brother, yet not a brother, and not really an uncle either.

On the day of the wedding I watched him in between the rush of bringing in the trays of food and refilling the cups of sake. At first he listened deferentially to the other men as they talked about the current situation, the inertia that seemed to have gripped the entire country since the arrival of the foreigners with their aggressive demands, the need to act against them if the Bakufu would not, to protect our domain of Chōshū and defend the house of Mōri. But as the sake took hold Shinsai began to argue more forcefully, talking about the news Tetsuya sent back from Nagasaki, the Ahen wars against China, the likelihood of another war, over something to do with a ship called the *Arrow*. He did not seem to be making sense to me. China was the centre of the world, huge and invulnerable. How could it fall to a handful of English or Americans? How could it be *colonised*? I was not very clear about the difference between English and Americans, or what colonisation actually meant. In any case, the government of the Tokugawa shōgunate would surely continue to keep the peace they had maintained for two hundred and fifty years.

I saw my father's expression: talk about politics always

made him uneasy; and I saw the look that flashed between Monta and Shinsaku. They might not voice them with the same unguarded passion as Shinsai, but I felt they shared his opinions.

These are the men my story is about. It is they who broke down the old world and reformed the nation I now live in, with their dreams and delusions, their courage and stupidity, their unexpected successes and their painful failures. Now they are famous men, those who survived, and I read about them in the new newspapers and look at their photographs, with their Western clothes and short hair, or uniforms, chests heavy with medals. And sometimes the newspapers print older photographs, like the ones I would see in Nagasaki, of our leaders in their youth, posed, hands on swords, in formal attire, their faces serious and expressionless as they prepare to confront the modern world with all its confusing demands and challenges.

You would not have thought them future leaders then. Monta was small, hardly taller than a child, with a boyish look, which was deceptive for he was more daring and aggressive than most adult men. He had a quick wit and a teasing, provoking manner. Shinsaku was a little taller, lean with deeply slanting eyes in a long horse face, marked by smallpox. He seemed to keep himself apart, reserved by nature or perhaps shy, until the sake lifted his spirits too. As the day wore on he became more boisterous, and finally, in response to Monta's urging, took the *shamisen* from the geisha (he was well known to them all) and began to sing one of his own songs.

The gentle drip of the rain, the young man's voice (he

was not yet twenty), the plaintive notes of the instrument brought to the surface all the grief we knew there was no escaping. Mitsue, *oneechan*, older sister, beloved first daughter, was leaving us. My father, my mother and I all wept without restraint.

'There was no need for all those tears,' Shinsai said later when the horses had left, carrying the bride away to her new family. Mitsue's face, framed by her white headdress, was pale with nerves and anguish. She was clutching her shell box and the doll given to her for protection on the journey. Her lips were reddened with the safflower rouge O-Kiyo had brought as a betrothal present, and her nose was reddened by weeping.

Torches at the gate gleamed through the rain, and 'sending-away fires', as if for a funeral, cast flickering shadows on the departing guests.

'It's a good enough match,' Shinsai went on, 'and she's only going to Hagi after all.'

Hagi was a day's journey away, if you left at daybreak. Because Mitsue did not depart until afternoon, her new family had arranged to meet her at an inn in Sasanami, where they would all spend the night. Her husband was the son of a pharmacist called Kuriya. I imagined my sister meeting him there, exchanging the ritual cups of sake in one of the guest rooms of the inn, and then being left alone for the first night of their married life. I was glad I was not marrying young Kuriya, but I couldn't help being curious...

'You can visit her when I go to Hagi,' my uncle said, addressing me in the offhand way he used when he was disclosing something important.

'And what will take you to Hagi?' my father asked, sniffing loudly and wiping his eyes.

Shinsai did not answer immediately but kept looking at me as if he could read my mind. It made me very uncomfortable. Thoughts of marriage, the sake, the music, the young men, the moist humid air had produced a strange sensation in me, both languid and irritable, a sensual awareness which I was sure was perfectly visible to my uncle. My whole skin burned with a sudden rush of heat.

'Tsu-chan has had too much to drink,' he teased. 'She's turning red!'

'Go outside and get some air,' my mother told me, 'or you'll have a headache all night.'

The rain gave a green light to the garden. I could hear the chirping of the baby swallows in the nests below the eaves. The parents swooped in and out endlessly, feeding their young until the little ones left the nest and went out into the world to mate and raise babies of their own.

My tears fell like the rain. How unbearably sad! But somehow how delightful to be me, feeling so deeply the sadness of things!

Our cat came out of the mist, purring with pleasure at finding me there. I rubbed her head and ears. She was soaking, but unlike most cats she did not seem to mind the rain. She sat with me for a while and then her huge eyes blinked and gazed, her ears swivelled and the tip of her tail quivered. She leaped noiselessly away into the wet garden.

I could still hear them talking inside. My father repeated his question and this time my uncle answered.

'I want to study with Master Yoshida. I'm going to write to him and ask to be accepted into his school.'

'But Yoshida is under house arrest,' my father replied.

'He is still teaching though; he is allowed to receive pupils. Kusaka Genzui is already with him, and Takasugi says he will join, even though his father is against it and he may have to sneak out at night, and that friend of Monta's, Itō Shunsuke…'

'What does Yoshida Shōin teach that you don't already know?' my mother asked. It was her opinion that my uncle should study less and work more, help my father more, maybe become a pharmacist like my new brother-in-law and open a shop. Yoshida Shōin was a controversial figure in Chōshū. No one could deny his intellectual brilliance, the originality of his thinking or the depth of his learning; both Lord Mōri Takachika and Sufu Masanosuke admired him enormously, but as my father pointed out he was technically a criminal. He had tried to board an American ship in Shimoda Bay. He was, people said, desperate to know better the countries that were threatening us. He wanted to see for himself the magical technologies they had been developing while our country lay isolated under the Tokugawa rule – ships that sailed by the power of steam like tea kettles, carriages that ran on rails transporting people and goods at great speed over vast distances, and of course guns and cannons and all sorts of military developments that gave power and authority to whoever owned them.

We had been listening to Shinsai and his friends talk about these things for the last four years, so I knew too that Master Yoshida had been imprisoned by the Bakufu in Edo, and then, the following year, sent back to Hagi to the samurai prison, Noyama. He set up classes for his fellow prisoners on the teaching of Mencius, who was his spiritual mentor, salted with his own ideas for the protection and advancement of our nation.

The young men spoke of the passion and clarity of his thinking, his determination and single-mindedness; older people called this obduracy and criticised his disregard for the niceties of hierarchy and rank. They even questioned his sanity. Yet people spoke of his gentleness, his tender care of other prisoners, his unusual ability to look into the heart and soul of each individual and discern what he needed in his quest for spiritual and intellectual maturity.

I wrote *he* and *his* without thinking, for naturally almost all Shōin's pupils were young men, but my uncle told me that women also attended his classes, and in the prison there was at least one woman who had not only learned from him, but had shared her own knowledge with him. For this reason I was more interested in him than I might otherwise have been.

Shōin was released from prison in the winter of the second year of Ansei, and sent back to his uncle's house on the eastern side of the Matsumoto River. He was given permission to teach his uncle's children, then their neighbours', and so the school came into being: the Shōkasonjuku, the village school under the pines.

This was where my uncle wanted to study.

'But we need you here,' my mother said. 'We cannot lose Mitsue and you at the same time. Who will help the doctor then? Tetsuya seems unlikely to return any time soon.'

I waited to hear my father say he would not allow it, but he was silent.

The swallows flew out and returned. The chicks cheeped, fell silent, cheeped.

'Tsuru is more help than I am,' Shinsai said.

'That's all too true,' Father replied. 'But Tsuru already works tirelessly; we cannot expect her to take on your work as well as Mitsue's.'

I could hear the approval in his voice. My skin, which had cooled in the damp air, threatened to take fire again. I was not used to praise. Girls were expected to work without praise or thanks; it was our duty to do everything for our parents: why should they thank us? But my father's words warmed my heart as well as my face.

'It won't be long before Tsuru leaves us too,' my mother said. 'What a terrible thing it is to have daughters. All that hard work bringing them up for another family's benefit.' The injustice of it brought a sob to her throat.

'Well, I've got a suggestion,' Shinsai said briskly. He had obviously had enough of tears for one day. 'It is the answer to both problems. Bring a bridegroom into the house for Tsuru; look for a doctor's son and adopt him into the family. That way you replace me and keep Tsuru with you.' When my father did not respond, he added, 'She really would be wasted if you sent her away.'

Of course my father could not agree immediately. Shinsai was more than twenty years younger than he was: it would not be right to take his advice, however much sense it made. My mother normally opposed everything Shinsai suggested as a matter of principle; she had rather a low opinion of him. So it was difficult now for her to seem to agree with what was secretly her deepest wish. Then there was the question of what people would think. The Itasaki were of no very great consequence, nor were we rich, though my father's reputation was high and he had more patients than he could deal with. It was not unusual to adopt a son-in-law, but in this case there were already two possible heirs to the family, even if one showed no sign of ever returning from Nagasaki and the other no interest in medicine. My father's recent appointment and his friendship with Lord Sufu had already elevated our family to a more lofty position than we deserved in the hierarchy of the domain. We did not want to jeopardise that position by behaviour which might be considered eccentric or unsuitable.

However, we lived not in conservative Hagi but in Yuda, where the hot springs, they say, make everyone more easy-going. In the weeks following my sister's wedding it was tacitly decided that the Itasaki family would keep me at home and start looking for a husband for me, and my uncle would apply to the Shōkasonjuku to study with Master Yoshida.

My father could not bear it when his patients died, which is a drawback for a doctor as so many of them do. I on the other hand was deeply interested in the fact and the process of death, making me an ideal assistant. My father's warm nature caused him distress which in turn distressed his patients. When he was upset he had the habit of caressing his arms and patting himself. This became the background sound to death for me, the uneven exhalation of the dying and the gentle pat-pat of my father's hands on his jacket sleeves. After a time I concluded that my cold approach was more calming than his concern and helped the dying accept what could not be avoided.

I cultivated this coldness into a way of looking that enabled me to see what was truly taking place within the patient's body. Sometimes I felt as if I had microscope eyes: my father had been given a microscope when he was a student in Nagasaki, and being shown how to look through it for the first time is one of the strongest memories of my childhood. It made me determined to become a doctor myself – not that I dealt with many patients directly, apart from cases of birth and death when I was allowed to assist my father. Medicine was still the domain of men. But sometimes extreme modesty on the part of a *bushi* woman, or the extreme punctiliousness of her husband, made her reticent about being examined by a man. She remained hidden behind a screen while my father was expected to diagnose the symptoms and suggest the cure without being able to take the pulse or look at the tongue or the skin.

'I can't tell what's wrong if I can't see or touch,' he would exclaim in exasperation, and I would be sent to the other side of the screen or into the next room to act as his eyes and hands. In this way I learned how to take the different pulses, how to distinguish the healthy unimpeded life force from the blocked, how to tell from the surface of the tongue or the white of the eye what might be wrong in the organs or the viscera. By the time I was fifteen I knew the eight principal patterns and the five phases, the six pernicious influences and the seven emotions that formed the basis of *kanpō*, the old tradition that came from China, as well as the more modern teachings that we called *ranpō*, Dutch medicine. My father began taking my opinions seriously and discussing treatments with me. I helped him prepare and dispense medicine, measuring and weighing China root, senna, anise, licorice, ginseng, peony root, powdered gecko skins and earthworms, and all the other ingredients that were stored in jars and boxes on shelves that lined the front room of our house where my father, sitting on a raised tatami matted area, carried out his consultations. He was surrounded by books, most of which I had read: treatises on anatomy and surgery, pharmacology and herbal medicines, pregnancy and childbirth, eye problems, madness, skin diseases and syphilis, moxa, acupuncture and the health benefits of hot springs. Some were by Japanese writers, some were translated from Chinese or Dutch. As well as books my father had a shelf devoted to his surgical instruments, most of them hidden under silk cloths to protect them from dust, his two travelling medical chests, and a few glass jars he had procured from Nagasaki containing various pickled creatures that the neighbourhood children were convinced were dragons or mermen.

Patients waited outside on the verandas, samurai on the more elegant one overlooking the front garden, and townspeople on the narrow one at the side which gave a view of the hedge and the drying poles, draped with cotton cloths, wadding and bandages. We usually served tea to the samurai but not to the ordinary people. They brought their own snacks and they sat cheerfully outside swapping these along with symptoms, remedies and their opinions of all the local doctors. They were often quite noisy, causing my father to call out in annoyance, demanding silence.

Inside, the room smelled of dried orange peel, moxa, camphor, oil of terebinth and bay leaves, as well as the incense we burned in front of the shrine to Shinnō which stood among the ingredients on one of the shelves.

Our house was a little way from the centre of Yuda, a town which had grown up around the hot springs. There was a hot spring in our garden, which we used for our own bathing as well as for making medicines and salves. Between the road from Yuda and the mountains, which rose abruptly less than a mile away, lay both dry and wet fields; directly over the road from us was a dry field were we grew our vegetables. Beyond, a stream we called the Karasugawa divided the vegetable fields from the rice paddies. At every corner fuit trees had been planted, peaches, mulberries, apricots or persimmons; a particularly large persimmon tree marked where our land joined that of the Inoue family, whose children, including Monta, we had known all our lives.

The mountains were not very high but they had the charming irregular aspect of mountains in Chinese landscapes and were often swathed in mist. Bamboo with its slender trunks and heavy foliage grew on the lower slopes; higher up was a mixture of sweet chestnuts, cork trees, oaks and cedars, with mountain cherries revealing themselves pure white in spring, and maples deep red in autumn.

At our gate stood one of those huge trees known as gambling trees, because their bark comes off in strips like a gambler's clothes. For this reason my father's practice was often referred to as the Gambling Tree Place, a source of constant jokes and puns among his cronies. The tree was home to many birds, particularly a pair of owls who would call softly at night, a sound, along with the rustle of falling bark, that I always associate with those years before the storm.

My father's warm-hearted and gentle nature made him dislike conflict of any kind. We used to teasingly call him Sōseiko (Lord I Agree) which was the name given, not really maliciously, to the Chōshū *daimyō*, Mōri Takachika. At that time I had never set eyes on Lord Mōri, though sometimes we walked to the Hagi Ō-Kan, the road that led from Hagi to the southern port of Mitajiri, to watch as he set out on his journey of alternate attendance to the distant capital of Edo. Every domain *daimyō* had to spend alternate years in Edo, where his family lived permanently, not unlike hostages, and the processions to and from the capital were marvellous to behold: hundreds of men, and horses, the domain's banners and crests, the *daimyō* and his senior retainers in palanquins.

Lord Mōri was obliged to spend lavishly on his retinue and in the *honjin*, the special lodging places along the road, for he was one of the greatest (unquestionably *the* greatest, if you listened to Chōshū men) of the *tozama* or outside lords. These were the families who submitted to Tokugawa Ieyasu after the battle of Sekigahara in the fifth year of Keichō, over two hundred and fifty years ago – a long time, you might think, but not long enough for the men of Chōshū to forget the wrong dealt by the Tokugawa to the Mōri family, who ever since had been bottled up in the castle town of Hagi, cut off from trade routes and remote from Edo, left to brood on injustice and plan revenge.

They were only partly true, these tales told to children who liked to sleep with their feet insultingly pointing towards the east and the Tokugawa, as our brother Tetsuya used to insist we did. The elders in Hagi were said to greet their lord at New Year with the question, 'Has the time come to overthrow the Bakufu?', and so far he had always replied, 'No, it is not yet time.'

And would that time ever come? The house of Mōri still survived, its processions were still impressively lavish. We children might refight the battle of Sekigahara in play and remember it in our dreams, but our lord was the *sōseiko*, who agreed with every suggestion made to him, just like our father. It was hard to imagine him having the energy to overthrow the shōgunate.

Yet Lord Mōri shared other qualities with our father: a willingness to encourage young people and see the best in them, an ability to spot men of competence among samurai of lower rank, and a stolid conviction that if you only established modern schools with the best teachers some good had to come of it. Lord Mōri was not a clever man, and he knew it, but he used good advisors, and so achieved many clever results.

Twenty years earlier, in the Tenpō period, our domain, like so many others, had suffered several years of unseasonable weather and crop failure. There had been no rain in the planting period and heavy cold rain in the growing period. Not only rice but millet, barley and beans failed to ripen.

There was a huge outbreak of rioting, involving over a hundred villages. People were starving and the domain's finances were in such a terrible state little could be done either to help them or suppress them. The domain's income of over six hundred thousand *koku* was already pledged to merchants in Osaka in return for money to cover expenses, and according to my father the total debt of the domain far exceeded its income – and that was taking into account the cancelling of any repayment of interest.

The way to solve most financial problems, the authorities decided, was to cut samurai stipends and persuade everyone else, especially merchants, to be more frugal. I grew up believing everyone, everywhere, was poor, except for Lord Mōri of course. We were better off than most; my father at least had a profession. His patients might not be able to pay him his whole fee but they would make it up with gifts of food, or things they made like straw sandals, raincoats, umbrellas, baskets. We had enough land to support ourselves – and then there was the surprise of my father's official appointment, which made it possible to send Tetsuya to Nagasaki for further training.

The work was unending and nothing was wasted. My mother worked as hard as anyone, but she had two ways of withdrawing from the round of daily tasks. At the end of our garden beneath the old plum trees was a small collection of family graves; my grandparents were buried here and my younger brother and sister who died aged four and two in the smallpox outbreak in the first year of Kaei (1848). I had smallpox at the same time but more mildly and I survived with only a few marks, like extra dimples, in my cheeks.

The following year the domain made the decision to introduce vaccination. Kusaka Genki, the older brother of my uncle's friend Genzui, had just returned to Hagi from studying with Ogata Kōan in Ōsaka, where the practice had recently been introduced from Nagasaki. Genki was instrumental in obtaining live vaccine and persuading families to have their children treated.

My father took up vaccination with alacrity. He admired Genki greatly, and perhaps identified with him for they were of a similar age, and both had a much younger brother. The deaths of so many young children from smallpox had always distressed my father and the fact that he had not been able to save his own children was particularly painful. My mother often sighed and said, 'If only the vaccine had come a year earlier you would have a little brother and sister,' but I thought it was interesting that they had died before me and I knew their deaths had made me more precious to my parents. On the other hand, I felt I should do everything possible to ease my parents' grief and never make them regret that I was the one chosen to live. So when my mother disappeared every afternoon to spend a little time with the dead, resting her body and regathering her spirits, I happily took on her work as well as my own.

My mother's other great consolation was literature. She knew by heart all the stories from *The Tale of the Heike* or *The Great Peace*. Heroes like Yoshitsune or Kusunoki Masashige came alive in the tales she told us at night while we did our evening chores, mending and sewing. She also owned a few precious books: *The Tale of Genji*, *The Mirror of Learning*, and so on. Her favourite was *A Country Genji*, a rewriting of the Genji story, about a handsome young man, Mitsuuji, who pretended to be a playboy but was really a great warrior.

The book was old – it was in several volumes – and damaged by insects and humidity, but to us it had the aura of a holy relic. It had been banned by the Shōgun; its printing blocks had been destroyed. Just to own it was a subversive act. It was only brought out in the presence of our closest family. My mother kept it by her pillow at night so she could save it if the house burned down. It was a wonderful tale of love and courage in a world far removed from our austere everyday life.

The other book my mother loved was *The Tale of Dashing Shidōken*. When I was eleven years old she gave me a white feather fan and told me it was a magic one like Asanoshin's: with it I would be able to see distant places and watch events unfold in other cities, other countries. I believed her, and would often hold the fan to my lips and pretend I could see what was happening in the faraway world.

My father taught me how to use a microscope and encouraged me to become a doctor. My mother gave me a magic fan and unlocked my imagination.

DISAPPOINTMENT

My uncle immediately set about the process of approaching Master Yoshida. He sought recommendations from his teachers at the Shirane *juku* in Yamaguchi, from his friends, like Kusaka Genzui, who were already in Yoshida Shōin's circle, and even from Sufu Masanosuke, who had just taken over the government in Hagi. Shinsai spent his days writing letters and waiting anxiously for replies. Composing the letters seemed to require many consultations in Yamaguchi and Yuda, and even when he was at home he was distracted and careless.

One afternoon in the seventh month a messenger from Hagi, on his way to our neighbour Yoshitomi's house, arrived at our gate and called out importantly, 'Itasaki Shinsai-sama, a missive for you.'

My uncle, who was meant to be making some concoction of crushed pepper and artemisia leaves (I could tell from the fragrance), leaped to his feet, letting the bowl roll aside, spilling the contents onto the floor.

'Tsu-chan, bring a cup of tea!'

I had just made a pot for my father's waiting patient so after sweeping up my uncle's mess I poured another cup and took it out to the messenger. He was wiping the sweat from his face with a small towel.

'Ha!' he exclaimed, when he saw the tea. 'My deepest

gratitude to you, Miss.' He bowed deeply before taking the cup.

I tried not to laugh, for he spoke in such flowery old-fashioned language he might have been Mitsuuji himself. Now that a husband was being sought for me I couldn't help appraising every young man I met. This one was undeniably handsome. His unpocked skin was darkened by the sun and glowed bronze. His legs, uncovered for ease of movement, were long and muscular. No signs of ill-health were visible to my physician's eye. I imagined being married to a messenger: he would be running like the wind across the domain with urgent letters of policy. Maybe he would be promoted and run to Kyōto and then on to Edo...No, it would not work out. I would be left at home with my parents and would hardly see him at all. And he would not solve my father's problem of too many patients.

I took the tea cup from his outstretched hands and ran inside and refilled it.

When I came back my rejected lover was saying with no apparent rancour, 'If Itasaki-sama wishes to reply I am returning to Hagi in the morning.'

Ah, his heart is broken, I reflected contentedly. *How well he hides it.*

'Yes, please call,' my uncle said, gazing on the paper in his hand with round eyes.

The messenger drank his tea in one gulp, expressed his thanks most eloquently and ran off down the road, the dust rising golden around him.

We moved into the shade of the gambling tree.

'It is from Master Yoshida,' my uncle said reverently.

'Let's read it.' I hurried him onto the veranda. We could hear my father's voice explaining his treatment to a patient.

'No sake, no tobacco; avoid all foods that will overheat your system. Definitely no boar or hare.' My father's usual opinion was that moderation and exercise would cure most complaints.

'What wonderful handwriting,' Shinsai said, unrolling the short scroll and gazing at it.

I peered over his shoulder. 'Oh, he is rejecting you.'

'So he is. But how beautifully he writes!'

Shinsai continued to stare at the letter, caressing the brush strokes with his fingertips. It was as if there was room in his mind for only one emotion at a time. He had to get over the wonder of holding in his hands a letter from Yoshida Shōin before he could deal with its actual contents.

'It is because we are not samurai,' Shinsai complained later as we ate the evening meal. 'We have no status. That's why Master Yoshida cannot accept me. The school probably has the same strict rules as everything else in Hagi.'

Despite Lord Mōri's encouragement of young men of talent, there was still little opportunity of advancement within the domain bureaucracy even for the lowest-ranking samurai, the *sottsu*. Only in exceptional circumstances would their stipends increase and, since honour as well as constant scrutiny prevented most of them from accepting bribes, there was no way of ever rising out of poverty and debt. Many would never be able to afford marriage and a family. But even though everyone was always chronically short of money this was not the main issue: it was the fact that so many young men, with all their energy and intelligence, were banned from service of any real influence within the domain that rankled with them. And Shinsai was right – his situation was even worse since our family were below even *sottsu* in rank.

'Imagine a house on fire,' he said. 'You know you could save the occupants, but you are held back and told, Don't interfere; leave it to the firefighters. But the firefighters have not even arrived on the scene, and when they do their equipment is useless and they are overwhelmed by the blaze.'

'Nothing is on fire, Shinsai-san,' my mother said, trying to calm him down.

'The whole country soon will be. And I will still be pounding powders and mixing medicines. I can fight with the sword, I know about Western arms and military techniques. My brain is as good as anyone's. Yet I'm condemned to waste my days here, in the Gambling Tree Place in Yuda!'

'It's not that bad,' my father said, sounding rather offended. He, after all, had risen to some extent; he had a much higher standing and a greater income than his own father, and his practice was flourishing.

'It's fine for you,' my uncle said. 'But you are middle-aged and I am not yet twenty.'

'You would be accepted in the School of Medicine,' my father suggested, 'if you really want to go to Hagi.'

The very reasonableness of this seemed to annoy my uncle more. He stood up, said he was going to walk for a while and went out. Father sat and scowled, patting his arms, and then he went out too, saying he would walk to Yuda, and not to wait up for him. I accompanied him to the gate, thinking he must be upset if he was going to see O-Kiyo.

It was a brilliant night, the air soft and still, the stars made huge by the humidity. A three-quarter moon was turning the eastern sky silver. Crickets were chirping and rain frogs called from the stream. I was restless. I did not feel like sleeping and after my mother went to lie down I told O-Kane to go to bed, and, taking a candle to the front room, I lit the lamp there and sat down to do some sewing.

My sister had taken new robes to her husband's house and I had unpicked the old ones and washed them. Now was as good a time as any to restitch them for myself or for O-Kane. I liked sewing and had always been deft at it, a useful accomplishment for a doctor, I thought. In fact I could stitch up a wound more skilfully than my father and with less pain to the patient. Sometimes when I was mending I used to practise, pretending I was pulling together the lips of a battle wound. In reality most of the deep cuts we treated were from cooking knives or farming implements. I had never stitched a sword wound: no one really fought seriously with swords, though all men of the samurai class carried them and all learned sword-fighting techniques. My father often said my neat stitching reduced the size and ugliness of the resulting scar, but this was probably not a great concern to a warrior, who would anyway not want to be stitched up by a girl.

In Kyōto and Edo there were apparently real fights between samurai of rival domains, ambushes and brawls after drinking or insults. And of course even in Chōshū there were murders by robbers, or jealous husbands using knives or swords. Among Chōshū samurai some no doubt were ruffians and bullies like the ones we read about in books from

Edo and Ōsaka, but we did not come across them in Yuda.

I was thinking idly about all these things and taking real pleasure in the tiny stitches my needle was making, when my uncle returned.

'Welcome back,' I called quietly and began to fold away the cloth. I thought I would make him some tea.

'Don't get up,' he said as he stepped up onto the matted area. He sat cross-legged beside me. He smelled of the summer night mixed with tobacco.

'You don't want tea?'

He shook his head. 'Can you see?' he said, peering at my work. The dark cloth absorbed the stitches completely. 'Don't strain your eyes.'

Sometimes Shinsai seemed much older than me, more like the age an uncle should be, and other times hardly even as old. He often teased me in the way a younger brother might, and then he would be unexpectedly solicitous, like now, reminding me how close we were, how well we knew each other. He had always been in this house, in my life. Even though he sat outside the fall of the lamplight I could see in my mind every inch of his face: his high cheekbones and wide forehead, his thick hair as glossy as a crow's wing, his serious gaze that drew his brows together, the way his bold smile lit up his eyes.

He was not smiling now. His whole demeanour spoke of his disappointment. I tried to find something to encourage him.

'Maybe you should apply to the Kōseikan.'

The School of Medicine had been one of our *daimyō*'s pet projects and had been renovated and expanded about two years ago.

'I have been thinking about it,' he admitted. 'At least it would get me to Hagi. But honestly, I am not that interested in medicine, though I would like to learn more about Western science, their technology, how they fight their wars.'

He fell silent for a few moments. I took up the cloth thinking I might as well start on the hem.

'Really it is you who should go to the School of Medicine.'

We both smiled, knowing that it was true, knowing that it was impossible.

'You should have been born a boy, Tsu-chan.'

I sighed, not wanting to admit that recently I had been thinking that myself. My clever mind, my big hands and feet, my physical strength, all seemed to belong to some boy whose place in the world had been stolen by a girl.

'On the other hand,' Shinsai said, 'you are going to be a fine woman. I envy the man who marries you.'

Suddenly the room seemed too small to hold us. We were sitting too close to each other. I put the cloth back in the basket and stood quickly. The heat swept over my face and my heart thumped. 'First someone has to be found,' I said, trying to speak lightly.

THE YOUNG LORD

Quite early the next morning I heard voices outside. I thought it might be the messenger on his way back to Hagi and I ran out quickly to ask him to wait for a few moments while I went to fetch Shinsai.

However, I saw Hachirō, who lived with our family and looked after the garden and the fields, talking at the gate with Shiji Monta and another young man whose name I did not know.

'O-Tsuru-san,' Hachirō called, 'the young lord has come to see the doctor.'

The young lord was what everyone in our little hamlet had always called Monta.

'I'll go and call my father,' I said. 'I'm sorry, it's a little early. Won't you come up and I'll prepare some tea.'

'Maybe you can give us something to eat,' Monta said as they came forward and sat on the edge of the veranda.

Naturally I hurried off to the kitchen to see what could be spared from our own breakfast, thinking how typical it was of the young lord. He acted as if every home was his own and everyone was just waiting around to carry out his wishes. My father was still lying down; he'd come home very late, but I didn't know if it was from a sickbed or some drinking party. I told O-Kane to bring miso soup, rice, pickles and some fried eggplant, and went back to see if the medical problem was urgent enough to wake him.

Hachirō had called my uncle, and Shinsai was now sitting on the veranda, talking excitedly to Monta.

'Shinsai-san.' I beckoned to him and whispered, 'Find out what the matter is. Should I wake Father?'

'We were talking about Master Yoshida,' he replied. 'Apparently he always refuses people at first. Even Kusaka. Itō says it's because the Master cannot be seen to encourage young people when he is considered a criminal.' He spoke loudly enough for the others to hear.

'That's right,' the boy called Itō said. 'Just go to Hagi – he will not turn you away once you are there. That's what I intend to do. Only Yoshida Shōin understands the times; only he can teach us how to deal with what lies ahead.'

His eyes were glowing with enthusiasm; to me he looked absurdly young, even younger than Monta, though he was a little taller. It looked as though both had dressed with some care, in blue kimono and grey *hakama*. I wondered if this was for the doctor's benefit.

'Shinsai-san,' I said again as quietly as I could, 'is one of them sick? Is it something we can deal with or should I wake Father?'

At that moment O-Kane came with two trays which she placed carefully down; the two young men fell on the food as if they had not eaten for a week. They were starting to annoy me more and more. Neither of them looked in the least bit ill; they probably just wanted a meal on their way to wherever they were going.

'It's Itō who wants to see the doctor,' Monta said through a mouthful of rice and eggplant.

'What sort of problem is it?' I asked outright since my uncle was still preoccupied with new plans concerning Yoshida Shōin.

'He's not going to tell you!' Monta said, wiping his mouth with his hand.

'I shall go and wake my father,' I said primly, having by now formed a very good idea of what Itō's problem might be. I left them trying to stifle their giggles.

My father was up, still wearing the light robe he had been sleeping in. He was yawning, his face grey with tiredness. My mother had brought tea which he drank in quick sips as he dressed. I told him about the young man waiting to see him. Something of my disapproval must have showed in my voice: he gave me a penetrating look as he tied his sash but did not say anything. When he was finally dressed, shrugging his shoulders into the short jacket he always wore even on the hottest days, he said, 'Ask him to come up. And you'd better wait outside; we don't want to embarrass him.'

When I had shown Itō where to go I went back to the veranda. Shinsai had settled down next to Monta. I asked Monta if he wanted anything more to eat and, when he shook his head, began to tidy the empty bowls on the trays. I was dawdling more than I should – I was already behind with the morning work because of the interruptions, but I wanted to hear what Monta and Shinsai were talking about. Their enthusiasm irritated me, but it also excited me; their concern for our country stirred me; the prejudices and setbacks they faced inflamed me with a desire for justice and a new world.

'Bring us some tobacco, Tsu-chan,' Shinsai said, so I had to go inside again. I could hear Father talking and Itō responding in monosyllables, his exuberance dampened. Concern gripped me. These young men might be annoying but I couldn't help admiring them, and anyway I wouldn't wish on my worst enemy what I suspected Itō had.

I took the tobacco box and two pipes back to the veranda, and went to light a bamboo spill at the kitchen fire, taking the eating trays with me. Hachirō had joined O-Kane in the kitchen and was squatting on his heels on the step to the back garden, eating breakfast. The cicadas were already deafening and the air smelled faintly of thunderstorms.

Piles of eggplants, cucumbers and green beans which he had picked earlier lay in baskets on the floor. I sighed inwardly. O-Kane would need my help chopping and pickling the vegetables, just one more of the tasks Mitsue and I used to do together. I missed her terribly, not only for the extra pair of hands, and longed to see her again.

When I went back to the veranda the young men had prepared the pipes. I held the spill for them while they puffed and blew. The tobacco caught alight, adding its fragrance to the morning air. The trouble with smoking was it prevented them from talking, and really there was no reason for me to linger any longer. Luckily Monta was in the mood for chatting.

'So, O-Tsuru-san, Shinsai tells me you are looking for a husband.'

This was not a subject I wanted to talk about with the young lord. 'I believe my parents have spoken to a go-between,' I said. I couldn't believe how prim I was still sounding, but that was the effect Monta had on me, as though I had to keep up all my defences of good behaviour. He had a barely concealed air of danger about him; he was probably one of those boys who liked to set fire to things just to watch them burn, not malicious or cruel, just thoughtless and wild.

'I am an adopted bridegroom,' he said. 'It's a shame, otherwise I could have applied.'

I knew he was only teasing me. His family was of quite high samurai rank; there was no way he would be allowed to marry into a family like ours.

'My father is looking for a young doctor,' I said. 'I don't suppose Shiji-san would qualify.'

That made him laugh. 'Your uncle says you are very clever. He says you know more about medicine than most doctors.'

'Yes, I do,' I said. 'That's why my parents want to keep me at home.'

'I know several doctors' sons,' Monta said. 'Kusaka Genzui, Katsura Kogorō...but none of us wants to spend the rest of our lives in Chōshū, while our country goes to ruin. A *shishi* really has no time for wife and family. He needs to be untrammelled, to be free to answer his country's call at any time, to act decisively and ruthlessly.'

My uncle sometimes used this word *shishi*: a man of high purpose. I repeated it under my breath thinking how marvellous it sounded. Maybe I could be married to a *shishi*. I thought of Kusaka Genzui whom my father had befriended after the deaths in less than a year of his father, his brother, Genki, and his mother: he was only a year older than me, well-built, intelligent, altogether a fine young man. But to be married to a *shishi* would probably be much like being married to a messenger. Your husband would be constantly on the move, carrying vital messages to *shishi* in other domains, hiding out in Kyōto or Edo, evading the Bakufu's secret police. I wondered how much Monta's wife saw of her husband. He rarely spoke of her.

Anyway, even Kusaka outranked our family.

'I'll let you know if I hear of anyone,' Monta said, getting to his feet as Itō came out of the house. I wondered what my father had prescribed. *Ranpō* treatment for syphilis was with mercury, which was almost as dangerous as the disease, or with calomel or a compound of potassium, both of which were scarce and expensive. Itō was smirking with embarrassment and, I thought, relief. He tucked a small paper packet into the breast of his kimono. *It can't be too bad*, I reflected.

'We are on our way to Hagi,' Monta said after he had greeted my father. 'Itō is to study with Master Yoshida. He will put in a good word for Shinsai.'

'What about yourself?' my father enquired.

'The domain is sending me to Edo in the new year,' Monta replied. 'I am to study Western learning, and English.'

'Ah, English?' my father said with interest. 'Tetsuya has been studying Dutch, with some success, but it seems he should have been learning English all along. Are there many English schools in Edo?'

'They are proliferating but who knows how good they are?' Monta said. 'How are we supposed to judge the teachers? We know nothing about the outside world. The Bakufu has kept us isolated, like children.'

'It has failed us totally,' Itō agreed.

'We have to catch up,' Monta exclaimed. 'We are years, maybe centuries, behind.'

'We should be killing foreigners, not learning from them,' Itō cried, carried away it seemed by renewed pleasure in life.

'We learn from them first and then kill them,' Monta said, clapping his hand onto the hilt of his sword.

Shinsai was watching them with a mixture of admiration and envy.

'Will you come to Hagi with us?' Itō addressed him.

My uncle's face showed his confusion. There was nothing he would like more, but it was not possible for him just to walk out of the gate with these carefree young men.

My father seemed to regard all three with the same mixture of irritation, admiration and pity that I felt.

'If Shinsai were to follow in a month or two he could bring some more salve and pills for you,' he said. 'Tsuru could go too; we have some things for Mitsue, and for the Kuriya.'

'Do you mean it?' Shinsai was almost speechless with surprise and gratitude. I was nearly as excited myself: to go to Hagi, to be with Mitsue and meet her family…

'Then we will see you in Hagi,' Monta said, impatient to be on the road.

'Stay away from the tea houses,' Father said to Itō.

Shinsai said he would accompany them to the main road at Yuda. After they had left my father stretched and yawned.

'Was it syphilis?' I said.

'I don't think so. It was more of a localised rash. No sign of chancre, and he has no secondary symptoms. But it easily could have been. It's rife in Mitajiri and Shimonoseki. And that young man loves the geisha by all accounts.' He frowned.

'Young men will act like young men, I suppose, but they risk a life sentence.'

Syphilis was especially prevalent in the port of Nagasaki. I knew my father worried about Tetsuya; now I was starting to worry about my future husband. I would try to make sure he did not go to geisha houses. But would I be able to prevent him? I was beginning to wish I did not know so much about diseases and their treatment – and all too often their lack of any cure.

TAKASUGI SHINSAKU

Ansei 4 (1857), Ninth Month, Age 18

It is already dusk when Shinsaku slips out of his parents' house – not that it is possible just to slip out unseen: everyone always knows what he is doing at any time of day or night. The house is not large – his family, the Takasugi, may be of high rank with a stipend of one hundred and sixty *koku*, but his father is a *bushi* of the old school who hates luxury and extravagance – and he has three sharp-eyed younger sisters as well as an adoring mother. As the eldest child and only son he has been the centre of his family's attention all his life.

He does not give any explanation for leaving but nor does he lie. He has been brought up in a strict, traditional way and to lie to his father is unthinkable. Instead he retreats into a scowling silence which he has noticed keeps his family at arm's length. Lately he has spent more time wrapped in this dark disguise, but the truth is it is no longer a disguise that he can put on and off at will but one that falls on him without warning or that he wakes enveloped in. He has not yet come to dread it but it puzzles him. It is as if it steals the real Shinsaku, the one who is destined for greatness, the fearless lad who has fought all the neighbourhood boys and overcome them physically and mentally, who once threatened an old samurai who stepped on his kite, and in his place produces a replica, a Shinsaku paralysed by doubt and fear.

He is not afraid now as he walks swiftly through the narrow streets of the castle town, past the samurai residences with their long white walls and barred and latticed windows, but he is apprehensive for he is disobeying his father's wishes for the first time since he was a child and stole sweet bean paste from the kitchen. His father is a terrifying man, proud of his own integrity and capable of icy rage when his children fall beneath his high standards. Shinsaku loves him and has striven to please him all his life, studying diligently and excelling in both classical learning and martial arts. All his teachers praise him. But lately he has been dissatisfied; the subjects seem irrelevant and his teachers inflexible and old-fashioned. Neither offers any solutions to the pressing problems of the day: how to deal with the Westerners who have sailed up in their modern ships, backed by their modern weapons, demanding trade and treaties; what to do about the tottering Bakufu, a government which has become a labyrinthine bureaucracy, taking weeks to arrive at trivial decisions; who will be the next Shōgun after the ailing Iesada; how the domains of the southwest, who feel they are in the front line, will defend themselves. These are the topics that obsess him and his friends, and that they discuss endlessly in tea houses, but that is not where he is going now, though he pauses outside one house where he can hear music playing and a young woman singing. His spirits lift immediately. He loves the popular songs of the city and as he walks on he is humming this one under his breath.

Let's kill the crows of the ten thousand worlds so I can lie late with you, my love.

It refers to the commitments a geisha would have, her contracts kept at the shrine and guarded by the shrine crows. So few words summon up an image behind which lies a whole story of two lives. How wonderful poetry is, often the only way to express the complex contradictions of his feelings. He pictures the lovers: they stare intently into each other's faces; a stillness has come over them in the moment before intimacy. He shivers with the memory of his own pleasure, but that is not his purpose tonight.

Several people glance at him as they pass him. Even in the dim light he is recognisable with his long face, *more like the horse than the rider*, and his narrow slanting eyes. He could not be called a handsome young man – he himself wishes he were taller, wishes the smallpox which nearly killed him at ten years old had not left its scars on his complexion – but his face is unforgettable. Everyone knows him in Hagi – everyone knows everyone! As he calls to a ferryman to take him across the river he looks out over the estuary towards the open sea and longs to escape. The lights of fishing boats twinkle between the twinned dark of sea and sky. Above his head the heavens are spangling as the stars appear. Then the huge ninth-month moon begins to rise in the east.

Under its light he makes his way up the narrow road. The air smells of pine and deutzia and the sudden rotting odour of gingko nuts. Near his destination he turns and looks back. The moon illuminates the bay and the islands. Castle walls and wave-fringed rocks gleam fragile white. Shinsaku throws his arms wide as if he would embrace it all. How huge the world is! He wants to know it all, taste it all. Then hearing footsteps he lets his arms fall, suddenly feeling foolish.

'Shinsaku?'

'Genzui,' he replies, knowing him even before he speaks. He would recognise him anywhere: Kusaka Genzui who went to the same school, then to the Meirinkan. They played together as children, but are not friends, nor are they enemies. They have the closest relationship of all: they are rivals, always aware of each other, like dog and monkey, or more poetically tiger and dragon. Shinsaku envies Genzui for his good looks and strong physique, but he feels his own intelligence is greater, and Genzui cannot match him in music and poetry. In sword fighting they are roughly equal: Genzui is stronger but Shinsaku is quicker in reflex and strategy. However, he has the uncomfortable suspicion that Genzui is braver, mentally and physically.

Genzui speaks again. 'You are going to Yoshida's house.' It is not a question. There can be no other reason for Shinsaku to be on this road. 'I've just come from there. I'll wait for you and we can go back to Hagi together.'

Shinsaku is irritated by this suggestion and disappointed that Genzui seems to have got ahead of him and is probably already part of Yoshida Shōin's school. For this is where he is going, to the Village School beneath the Pines where Shōin, under house arrest, continues his inspired and impassioned teaching, in the home of his birth family, the Sugi.

He says nothing as they walk together up the hill. Genzui rattles on in his usual way, his ebullient self-confidence both attractive and annoying. His familiarity, too, ruffles Shinsaku's pride. Genzui is from a doctor's family; his parents and brothers are dead. He has been alone in the world since the age of fourteen. Shinsaku outranks him, yet Genzui acts as if they are equals. Not that Shinsaku wants deference from him, but he wants something, some recognition of the importance of the occasion, some acknowledgement of his defiance of his father.

It is in this confused state of mind that he is welcomed inside. Genzui, he can't help noticing, is treated like one of the family by Shōin's mother and sisters. Shinsaku's apologies for calling so late are brushed aside and he is shown into the teacher's study where Shōin kneels by a writing desk immersed in a book. He looks up as Shinsaku kneels before him.

'Takasugi!' he exclaims, his thin stern face illuminated by the warmth of his smile.

They know each other already; Shōin taught at the Meirinkan when Shinsaku was a student there, but now something has changed. Their world has tipped further out of balance; the cataclysms of the future have drawn closer. The shabby room, the dim light, the well-worn books: in this unlikely setting something happens between them. A spark ignites that will grow into a pure and passionate relationship. The teacher continues to smile and the pupil falls completely under his spell. In one of those imperceptible adjustments made between humans and history the lives of both men change course.

JOURNEY TO HAGI

The hot days of summer passed. We celebrated O-Bon, the festival of the dead. Typhoons rushed up the coast and passed over us with their usual trail of heavy rain and flooding. Then came autumn, moon viewing, chestnuts falling, and mist over the Karasugawa in the early morning. Insects changed their note to their autumn song, and flocks of migrating birds crossed the skies on their way south.

We often received letters and packages from Mitsue's new family, the Kuriya, and we replied, exchanging news, boxes of pills, information about new treatments and so on. The Kuriya pharmacy was well known: they had several of their own brands of pills and ointments and their servants, in the shop livery, often called at our house on their travels around the domain. My sister included letters to my parents but they said nothing in particular, other than commenting on the weather and expressing gratitude to her new family for their kindness to her. My parents worried about her; a daughter-in-law's life in a new family could be very hard, especially if her husband's mother was selfish or unkind, so they were quite glad to send me to Hagi to see for myself Mitsue's true situation.

My uncle and I set out in the middle of the ninth month, the best season for travelling. We hired a packhorse from Yuda, for we were taking many medical supplies with us, as well as presents for Mitsue and the family and our own clothes and belongings. Everything was stowed in baskets which hung on either side of the horse's back. The horse boy led it with a rope tied to its halter.

'If Miss gets tired she can sit on the horse,' he said, thumping the board that made a kind of seat between the baskets.

I was reluctant as I had never been on a horse, but the road to Hagi was steep and winding. We stopped at the little village of Ōda to eat the midday meal. By the time we reached the next village, Edō, my legs were aching and my feet were sore. The idea of walking up yet another mountain pass seemed beyond me. I was persuaded to let my uncle lift me onto the horse's back where I perched uneasily, gripping the rims of the baskets on either side.

The mountain forests were just beginning to take on their autumn colours of scarlet and gold and the sky was a clear cool blue. As we came over the final pass, the sea, dotted with white-fringed islands, stretched away into the haze.

We stopped briefly beneath a group of pine trees, and my uncle pointed to the oldest one.

'They call that the Weeping Pine. You cry for sorrow when you leave Hagi and you cry for joy when you return,' he explained.

The horse boy laughed as if he had heard this many times.

The horse quickened its step on the downhill slope and while it did not cry for joy, it seemed cheerful at the prospect of the journey's end.

The city lay on an island, an irregular three-cornered shape, where the Abugawa divided into the Hashimoto and the Matsumoto rivers, their separate mouths opening into the sea. On the western side rose the roofs and white walls of the castle, clear in the evening light against the foliage of the mountain behind it. Houses clustered round the port, the setting sun glinting on the tiles. Hundreds of boats filled the rivers, ferry boats, fishing craft, transport barges. The air was salty and fresh, adding to my excitement.

We crossed a wooden bridge at the narrowest part of the western river. A group of houses here made me think this was the town itself, but within a few minutes we were once more among rice fields. The rice was already harvested and drying on racks on the banks and outside the farmhouses. Even though it was after sunset men were still working, spreading rotted leaves and manure on the empty fields.

A small waterway separated the rice fields from the town centre. I learned later it was called the Aiba canal, after the indigo that was used for dyeing cloth. On our left lay a large enclosure filled with several imposing-looking buildings.

'That's the domain school,' Shinsai said. 'The Meirinkan.'

'Did Your Honour study there?' the horse boy asked.

'No, it is only for the sons of samurai. They say they will take any young man of ability, but between saying and doing there is still a huge gap. Master Yoshida on the other hand takes people of any rank. He believes in the practical application of study and acts on what he learns.'

'Do we know where we are going?' the boy said, my uncle's remarks seeming to pass straight over his head.

'Yes, of course,' Shinsai replied. 'The house backs onto this canal and is just along the next street on the left.'

The tired horse did not want to make the detour and baulked, throwing up its head.

'Let me get you down,' Shinsai said, holding out his arms, and I half scrambled, half slid off the horse's back onto the ground. I was stiff and aching all over.

Relieved of my weight, the horse snorted and blew, and then allowed itself to be led the remaining distance to the Kuriya house. It was the largest building on the street. The front was latticed, with boards announcing the name of the pharmacy in large white letters over the windows. Its smell reminded me of home: medicines, potions, oils, herbs. My uncle called at the door and began to unload the baskets from the horse's back.

There was an answering call from inside, followed by the sound of footsteps.

'Ah, it's Itasaki-san and the young lady!' A rather plump middle-aged man stepped out. 'Welcome! Welcome!'

My uncle set the basket down and bowed deeply. I did the same, guessing this was Mr Kuriya himself, my sister's father-in-law. I made the customary greetings, asking for his favour, thanking him for his kindness. He replied graciously, if rather pompously, and called for a servant to come and collect the baskets.

We were ushered into the front room, which was the shop premises. Normally the shutters were open onto the street but at this time of night they had been closed. The walls were lined with shelves to the ceiling, filled with boxes of ingredients and medicines, labelled in red characters. Along one wall was a workbench, holding knives, saws, chopping boards, mallets, grinders, pestles, mortars and alembics. At the back was a hearth where a fire smouldered. Several iron pots and kettles were lined up beside it. On the other side was a raised tatami area where a young man sat before a low desk. He was using an abacus and writing in a long notebook. At his side was a stack of small boxes and paper envelopes. He stopped his work as we went past and bowed respectfully. I thought at first he was Mitsue's husband, but Mr Kuriya did not bother to speak to him or introduce us and so I assumed he was just a clerk in the shop.

We followed Mr Kuriya through to the back of the shop and up into the living area.

'Wife,' he called. 'Our guests are here.'

His wife and Mitsue popped into the room as if they had been hiding around the corner waiting for us all day. I bowed deeply to Mrs Kuriya, while trying not to grin too obviously at my sister. She caught my eye once and then looked quickly down, her skin turning pink with happiness.

Mrs Kuriya was very slender and had a languid air about her that surprised me. For some reason I'd expected her to be energetic and hard-working. I suppose I'd imagined the thriving Kuriya business to be at least partly due to her contribution. I soon discovered from casual remarks dropped by Mitsue and from my own observations that the more the business flourished the more languid Mrs Kuriya became. The harder everyone else around her worked, the less she did. Now that she had a diligent and capable daughter-in-law she did almost nothing at all.

She was not unkind to Mitsue; indeed she seemed to be fond of her. At the evening meal she praised her constantly. 'Mitsue-san made these pickles – delicious, aren't they? Mitsue cooks rice to perfection, I let her do all the cooking now.

Mitsue-san cleaned the whole house for your arrival. I do so love the smell of a clean house.'

Mitsue looked embarrassed at these compliments, but her husband, who had joined us for the meal, was obviously pleased. When Mitsue finally sat down after serving everyone else Mrs Kuriya said, 'You mustn't do too much in your condition.' She turned to me. 'Your sister is expecting a child. Of course pregnancy is no reason to indulge oneself. It's best to keep moving as much as possible. That ensures an easy delivery. Here, my dear.' She selected a small piece of fish from her own bowl and placed it in Mitsue's. 'Eat and make us a fine grandson.'

'She is so kind to me,' Mitsue said when we finally found ourselves alone. 'I am very lucky.'

I did not want to say that I thought Mrs Kuriya was the lucky one and that I suspected she was taking advantage of my sister's good nature and willingness. I was not going to suggest that Mitsue was anything but fortunate. She liked hard work, she was already pregnant, there was plenty of food in the house. My parents did not need to worry about her, and nor did I.

Mitsue's husband was an only child. I decided the whole process of procreation had taxed Mrs Kuriya's energies to their limit. She was simply too lazy to go through it all again. Mr Kuriya's response to this situation was to treat his wife like a child, indulging her and pampering her, while he took himself off to the geisha houses several nights a week and in between times indulged himself with the maids. The energy that ran the business came from him. You could almost feel it blazing like the fire that distilled the medicines.

Mitsue's husband took after his father in looks and build.

He was talkative and liked an argument, especially after a few drinks, but he was so sure of his own opinions that my uncle did not persist in expressing his own. It was soon obvious that the Kuriya family had no very high opinion of Master Yoshida Shōin. Indeed they thought the domain authorities had been too lenient in releasing Shōin into his uncle's care and they thoroughly disapproved of his school and its pupils.

'My husband thinks Shinsai is a young hothead,' Mitsue whispered to me. 'He doesn't think he should study with Master Yoshida. He thinks it will reflect badly on the whole family.'

The Kuriya were only merchants but they were among the richest and most successful in Hagi. They liked fine things and found ingenious ways to spend their money and express their good taste without breaking the stringent sumptuary laws set out by the domain.

'Show your sister our cypress floors,' Mrs Kuriya said to Mitsue on the morning of my first day. My sister was outside, tidying up the garden according to Mrs Kuriya's instructions. She beckoned to me, and I helped her lift a section of the boards of the veranda. Below lay another floor of beautiful new cypress. Most guests never saw it, yet the Kuriya derived great satisfaction from knowing it was there, paid for by their own hard work and good business sense.

'And O-Tsuru-san, look at my robe.' Mrs Kuriya held out one slender arm and turned back the sleeve with her other hand. The outer garment was plain cotton, dyed indigo; the lining was finest silk, very pale rose pink.

'My skin is delicate,' Mrs Kuriya explained. 'Rough fabrics irritate it. I have to wear silk next to my body.'

It was not only Shinsai who came in for the Kuriya's disapproval. They were also affronted by my parents' decision to look for a bridegroom to bring into our family so they could keep me at home. Mrs Kuriya expressed her annoyance several times, without giving any reason other than that people would think it strange.

'It's not an uncommon arrangement among doctors,' Shinsai tried to explain. 'My older brother is a respected physician. A young man would be glad of such an apprenticeship; we have had students in the house before.'

'Well, we will keep it in mind,' Mr Kuriya said. 'We have a wide acquaintanceship in Hagi and I am sure the connection with our family will help you find someone.'

Mrs Kuriya sighed and looked downwards with tightened lips.

Now that my sister was a married woman she blackened her teeth every few days, preparing the iron solution for herself and her mother-in-law, and holding the mirror for Mrs Kuriya. I did not look forward to this practice. I wished I could be like the lady, in the story my mother read to us, who refused to blacken her teeth or shave her eyebrows and who was much more interested in caterpillars than in butterflies. I had always thought I was like her, and I was musing about her while I watched my sister one morning, when the young clerk from the shop came to the step and said softly, 'Excuse me, Mrs Kuriya, but is Mr Itasaki in the house?'

'I really don't know. O-Tsuru-san, where is your uncle?'

I knew Shinsai had gone out – almost certainly to the Sugi house where Master Yoshida had his school. He had taken the pills and ointment for young Itō. I had very much wanted to go with him and see the famous teacher for myself, but Mitsue had asked me to help her sort out some winter clothes and put the summer ones away, and by the time we had finished Shinsai had grown impatient and left.

'I believe he has gone to Tōkōji,' I said, which was only a slight amendment of the truth. Tōkōji was a temple in the eastern hills, not far from the Village School under the Pines, and my uncle had expressed a desire to visit it. 'What did you want him for?'

'There are some items in the last consignment…they were not clearly marked. I need to make the inventory.' He spoke hesitantly, but I liked the serious tone of his voice.

'I could help you with that, if it's all right with Mrs Kuriya.'

'If it's not too much trouble, Miss.'

'No trouble at all.' I was quite eager to see how the pharmacy was run; after a few days helping Mitsue with purely domestic chores I was missing the much more interesting work I did at home. I left the other women to their teeth-blackening and followed the young man into the shop.

I knew his name was Keizō for I had heard Mr Kuriya call him that, but I wasn't sure how to address him. Keizō seemed too familiar and I didn't know what his family name was. No one had told me anything about him; no one considered him to be important enough. In my mind I called him the Accountant, because he sat at his desk like Enma, the lord of hell, weighing and measuring, calculating and recording.

I soon realised that it was his quickness and diligence that underpinned Mr Kuriya's energy and business sense and kept the shop going. The Accountant had an extraordinary memory and a natural understanding of the properties of herbs and minerals. He could add strings of numbers in his head; he hardly needed the abacus, though he used it like a shield to retreat behind in order to give himself time to think. He could mix medicines and potions from memory with complete accuracy, though again he used scales and measures like defensive weapons.

Later he would say to me, 'People are frightened by pure intelligence, and they resent it. But they think anyone can use an instrument and that reassures them.'

It did not take long to explain the ingredients we had brought. It occurred to me that the Accountant did not really need my help at all. Maybe he had known very well that Shinsai had gone out, and had sought me out on purpose.

The thought was intriguing and once it was in my head I could not get rid of it. As I said before, I could not help assessing every man I met as a potential husband. I kept casting little glances at the man next to me as he quickly recorded the names I dictated. His writing was forceful and unusually clear. He had very nice hands, with long fingers and square nails. His eyes were interesting, gleaming with intelligence and humour. Apart from that he was quite ordinary, extremely thin, his bones clearly visible beneath the skin, especially in his wrists, his forehead rather domed, his hair already starting to recede.

Finally he caught me looking at him and a kind of embarrassment hit us both at the same time. He laid down the brush and said, 'That seems to cover it.'

I got to my feet and started examining the shelves with great interest. 'I see you have a large amount of dried earthworms,' I said. It was the first box my eyes fell on. 'Do you find them effective?'

'They are one of the ingredients of the famous Kuriya Cure-All,' he said, standing too and pointing to the stack of boxes at the front of the shop, all stamped with characters reading *Hagi Kuriya Cure-All.* There was also a basket filled with paper packets, bearing the same name, for customers who could not afford a whole box.

'What else is in it?'

'Oh, I couldn't tell you that! It's a well-guarded secret, you know, handed down from generation to generation.'

'Really?'

'Well, maybe not so very many generations since it was I who created it. But I would certainly hand it down to my son if there was ever any chance of me marrying – highly unlikely at the moment – and of course Mr Kuriya could be said to have handed it down to his son, after a fashion.'

This speech was delivered in a quick low voice, full of self-mockery.

'Does it work?' I asked.

'If you are sick it makes you feel better and if you are well it keeps you that way. What more could anyone ask for? Doesn't your father use his own Cure-All?'

'He prefers to use specific treatments,' I replied.

'The Kuriya Cure-All is very popular,' the Accountant said gravely. 'So I imagine people believe it works.'

I had the opportunity to see for myself just how popular the Cure-All was. People came into the pharmacy with many different complaints: sore eyes, stomach pains, coughs, boils and other skin problems, piles, bruises, blisters. That morning alone nearly three-quarters of them left with a specific ointment and the Cure-All. Mr Kuriya and his son both had a fine speech which they used over and over again to sell it. At one stage there was such a crowd Mr Kuriya threw me an appealing look and I found myself measuring out the powder into the paper envelopes.

'Take it in tea or warm water,' I advised my customers just as I had heard Mr Kuriya say.

I was still in the shop when Shinsai returned.

'So Tsu-chan, they've put you to work,' he said.

'She's a quick learner,' Mr Kuriya said, and then gave me permission to go and help his wife with the midday meal.

'What were you doing there?' Shinsai said as he followed me to the living rooms.

'He asked me to help since he didn't know where you were.'

'Who? The boss? Mr Kuriya?'

'No, the other man. The clerk.'

'He knew very well where I was,' Shinsai exclaimed. 'We talked about it before I left. The sly fox! Don't trust him, Tsu-chan. And I don't want you spending time with him.'

He sounded very annoyed, which made me angry in turn. My uncle often seemed to think he owned me.

'I was helping in the shop,' I said. 'It's good to learn about their medicines too. Maybe I can make a Cure-All for Father when I get home.'

'They're no more than quacks!'

I warned him to keep his voice down. I was worried that Mrs Kuriya would hear us. For Mitsue's sake we should not insult our in-laws. We didn't talk any more then but

Shinsai remained quiet and irritable for the rest of the day. He saw the Accountant's ruse as something tricky and devious, whereas I was more inclined to treat it as a joke – and a flattering one.

THE VILLAGE SCHOOL UNDER THE PINES

I had enjoyed helping in the shop and I looked forward to spending more time there. However, the following morning my uncle announced that he was taking me out with him.

'To visit Tōkōji again, I suppose,' Mrs Kuriya remarked. 'It *is* very lovely at this time of year.'

It was impossible to tell if she was being sly or not. Shinsai cleared his throat and said, 'Well, I want O-Tsuru to see the temple before she goes home – and I will not be around after today.'

Mitsue shot an enquiring look at me but I knew no more than she did. I just saw that Shinsai was carrying his belongings in a bundle.

The men were all in the shop as we walked through, the Accountant in his usual place bent over the abacus. Its rapid clicking did not stop and I did not know if his eyes followed me or not.

'Come back safely!' all three called as we stepped out into the street.

Apart from going to the local bathhouse once or twice I had not yet been out into the city. But much as I longed to explore the narrow streets and the markets, especially the fish market at the port, we did not go that way but crossed the bridge over the waterway and walked through the rice fields towards the east. It was a cool morning and white mist hung on the mountains. Around the paddies the last of the equinox lilies glowed red, and the tasselled heads of susuki grass shimmered in the weak sunshine. There were many people about, farmers taking autumn produce to market, porters with heavy loads, and even a few samurai walking purposefully towards the city in twos and threes, their dress sober, their faces serious, swords at their hips. People swerved out of their way; if they could not avoid them they gave them a perfunctory bow. Most of the samurai in Hagi worked in the ever-increasing bureaucracy, and were as short of money as everyone else – excepting the Kuriya of course.

The tide was ebbing and the exposed mudflats glistened; seabirds paddled over them or swooped into the water, their cries mingling with the ripple of the waves against the moored boats. The bridge across the Matsumoto was half bridge and half fish trap; men stripped to their loincloths stood waist deep in the water pulling up the nets where the tide had trapped the fish, and throwing the thrashing, shining creatures into buckets and baskets. The smell of fish and mud and salt was overpowering. Everyone was shouting and pushing – those who were doing a whole day's work in the short time allowed by the tide and those who simply wanted to cross the river.

The planks were slippery and narrow. Most people were laden with baskets on shoulder poles, or wooden back hods. My uncle darted nimbly between them, leaving me to follow as best I could. I thought I was sure to fall in the water; indeed I could not see how anyone stayed on the planks, but they did, and in a strange clumsy dance crossed to the other side.

Here the low-lying river bank had been built up with a dyke and ferrymen waited with flat-bottomed boats.

'We should have hired a ferry,' I said as I caught up with Shinsai.

'Can't afford it,' he said briefly.

'It's only a few *mon*.'

'It's still too much for me.'

'How are you going to live if you stay in Hagi?' Our household already sent all our spare cash to Nagasaki to pay for Tetsuya's studies, the books he needed and his surgical instruments.

'Itō's offered me a place to sleep,' he replied. 'I can eat at the school and pay for it by sharing the physical work. Maybe I can get some other work to tide me over; maybe I can pawn something.' He slowed down for a moment and turned to look at me directly. 'The main thing is, Master Yoshida is allowing me to join his classes. It's such an opportunity, such a privilege. I mustn't let anything prevent me from taking full advantage of it.'

I had never heard Shinsai speak so seriously about anything. For the first time I saw him as an adult, inspired by something other than the loyalty to family and household that had always been the strongest obligation for all of us. I suddenly saw him moving away from us, towards the future, towards a new Japan. It both scared and impressed me.

'Wait till you see Master Yoshida,' Shinsai said. 'Then you will understand. You must explain to your father why it is so important. He listens to your opinion.'

We had left the fishermen's shacks behind, and the narrow road steepened as it wound between terraced fields. The land that was not cultivated was covered with the sort of oak tree called *shi*, along with pines and cedars. When we paused to catch our breath I looked back.

'I've never seen anything so beautiful!'

The bay lay beneath us, the sea clear lapis blue, turning indigo on the horizon. Small islands jutted up from it, some no more than rocks, each with a hem of white at its foot, many scarlet-splashed with autumn leaves.

'Over there is the kingdom of Korea, and the empire of China,' Shinsai said. 'And the whole wide world. Imagine growing up seeing this every day, knowing it is all out there, yet forbidden from exploring it.'

I could not help thinking how huge the world was, and how small and defenceless our country. I thought of all the changes we had already seen; some wonderful, like the vaccines brought by the Dutch from Batavia, some more frightening, such as new diseases, new weapons, new ideas.

We walked on and halfway up the hill came to a small cluster of buildings with thatched roofs and wooden walls. Yellow butterbur flowers and sacred bamboo with red berries grew around the stone steps.

'This is the Sugi family's place,' Shinsai said. 'The school building is over there.'

I could hear voices both from the main house and from the school. The wind made that special soughing it makes in pine branches, and kites mewed in the valley. A young woman stepped out onto the veranda's edge and called good morning to us.

Shinsai went forward to introduce himself. 'I am Itasaki Shinsai. I have come to attend classes with Master Yoshida.

This is my niece, Tsuru. I wanted her to see the *sensei* for herself; I hope that will not be an inconvenience.'

He looked a little awkward as he said this, but the young woman smiled, her face lighting up.

'Everyone should have the chance to do that. Please go directly to the schoolroom, Mr Itasaki. I will bring your niece when we serve the midday meal. In the meantime, if O-Tsuru doesn't mind helping me...'

'Of course not,' I said, and followed her into the house.

'My name is Fumi,' she told me. 'I am the *sensei*'s younger sister.' She glowed even more as she said this. She was small and very slight, with a charming manner that immediately put me at my ease. She seemed about the same age as I was.

'You must be terribly proud of your brother,' I said.

'Shōin is a genius,' she replied seriously. 'But we can't help worrying what will become of him. He is not like other people, you see.'

'Surely no one will harm him. His reputation and his value to the domain must protect him. He has the favour of Lord Mōri, and of Sufu Masanosuke.'

'That's true. It's thanks to Lord Sufu that he is out of prison and allowed to teach. That's all he cares about really, to be able to continue his studies and pass his learning on to others. Even when he was in Noyama he read all the time, taught the other prisoners, and got them to teach each other what they knew too.'

'Did you visit him there? What's it like?'

Her face clouded. 'Noyama is a terrible place. Dark, over-crowded. It has a very bleak history; many people have been put to death there. I am sure it is haunted by their ghosts.

But my brother was as content there as in his own home, always cheerful, always thinking of others and trying to spare them pain.' She smiled at me. 'Do you have a brother?'

'Yes, in Nagasaki.'

'Really? Shōin went there too. He has travelled all over Japan. What's your brother doing there? Is it medical studies?'

I told her about Tetsuya and about my father's medical practice. She was so easy to talk to I even told her how my family was looking for a husband for me. She smiled more widely and bringing her mouth close to my ear said, 'My brother and my uncle are also finding me a husband.'

'Have they decided on anyone?' I asked, made daring by her confiding in me.

'Do you know Kusaka?' she whispered. 'I think it will be him.'

I felt a twinge of envy. Naturally I had known Kusaka Genzui could never be for me, but I had allowed myself to dream a little about him.

If I had known what lay ahead I would not have envied O-Fumi. But of course we had no insight into the future. We were just two young girls dreaming of marriage and children, hoping we would be good wives and wise mothers. At least, that's how I imagined O-Fumi, and I kept my own private dreams to myself.

We had started washing and chopping vegetables when a woman of about sixty years came, limping slightly, into the kitchen.

'Towa-san,' Fumi greeted her politely. 'Please don't trouble yourself. O-Tsuru can give me all the help I need.'

'Let me lend a hand,' Towa said. 'I can do little enough to repay the *sensei* for his kindness. I'm not happy sitting idle, never have been.'

I was intrigued by the old woman. From her dress and speech she was obviously very low-caste, but she had been received into the Sugi household, Fumi treated her as a guest, and she radiated a dignity and self-possession that contrasted completely with her outward appearance. I wanted to ask who she was, but felt diffident.

'How are your legs this morning?' Fumi asked. 'Why don't you sit down and I'll rub some ointment on them for you?'

The offer seemed to embarrass Towa. 'No, no, a fine young lady like you! It wouldn't be right.'

'I'll do it,' I said, drying my wet hands on a dishcloth. 'I am a doctor's daughter and assistant, so there can be nothing wrong in my doing it. O-Fumi, what ointment do you have?'

She brought a pot of salve; I put my nose to it, trying to guess what it was: a soft oil base, possibly mixed with soap. It smelled of orange peel and aniseed, with an underlying whiff of sulphur.

We left the food preparation for a few moments and went outside with Towa. She sat down on the veranda in a patch of sunshine, leaning against a post and stretching her legs out, groaning slightly.

'It's very good of you, Miss. I've done that much travelling, my poor old legs and feet are all but worn out. I thought I'd done with journeys and I'd stay put for the rest of my days, but they told me the *sensei* wanted to see me and hear my story so I came all the way to Hagi.'

Her ankles were very swollen and hot to the touch. Her knees too were puffy and red. The feet were twisted, the toes curled under. I rubbed the ointment in and began to massage firmly, trying to get the muscles to relax and lengthen.

'Have you ever had needles?'

She shook her head. 'I have a massage now and then. And I go to the *onsen* when I can.'

'The hot springs in Yuda where I live would do you good,' I said. 'My father or I could treat you with needles too. Is there any chance you could travel a bit further and come to us?'

She laughed and said, 'This is my last journey: to see the *sensei* and tell my story. Now that's done I can go home to Uemura. At least I know we will not be forgotten now. Lord Sufu and Master Yoshida will see to that.'

I could not contain my curiosity. 'Lord Sufu?'

'When he was the government official in Ōtsu he heard my story and asked the *sensei* to write the inscription for the memorial stone.'

Since the Tenpō riots it had become the custom to erect a memorial stone for villagers who had lived worthy lives or done exceptional things. But I had never heard of a woman being honoured in this way. Towa must have done something really extraordinary.

My fingers worked on her calves. I could feel her relaxing like a cat in the sun.

'I couldn't stand no one caring,' she said. 'They were all dead, all murdered by that evil *rōnin*, and no one could be bothered to do anything about it, just because we are who we are, humble shrine guardians. And then the magistrate suggested it was our fault, that we had provoked him. He killed three people, well, four really, for my poor husband was never the same, he was that badly wounded, and now he's disappeared and no one knows what became of him – all that and then to be told it was our fault!'

'Who did the *rōnin* kill?' I asked.

'His own wife – she was my husband's sister. And her father and brother when they tried to save her.'

The *rōnin*, Kareki Ryūnoshin, had gone to discuss his divorce with his former wife and her family. An argument had broken out – he was a difficult and violent man; eventually he had drawn his sword and attacked them. Because of the delay in setting up the investigation, Kareki was able to flee the domain. Towa's husband, Kokichi, took years to recover from his injuries, during which time she nursed him, took over his duties in the shrine and waited for some kind of justice. When it was obvious no one was going to take the matter any further – Kareki was after all a samurai and the victims mere shrine guardians – Towa decided to pursue the murderer herself. Leaving Uemura for ten years she followed his trail as far as Edo and Mito, even to Tōhoku, finally locating him in Kyūshū. She informed the authorities and in the twelfth year of Tenpō, the year of my birth, Kareki was arrested. He tried to kill himself, and died of his injuries a week later. His body was dispatched to Hagi where the head was severed and pilloried.

Fumi had heard the story before but tears still welled in her eyes.

'Someone had to do something,' Towa said. 'We are all human beings, aren't we? Why should *bushi* be allowed to kill without being brought to justice? We work hard, we serve the shrine – we should be murdered for that?'

'When my brother was in Noyama,' Fumi said quickly to me, 'he met a woman called Takasu Hisako. She is a musician and was part of a *shamisen* circle. She was imprisoned because some members of her circle were not of the *bushi* class: she should not have associated with them. Even worse, she was heard to say that she thought such restrictions were nonsense and that the whole four-caste system was old-fashioned and restrictive. My brother says her ideas were pure Mencius, for the sage taught that virtue can be found in any class and that men should be educated according to their ability not their rank, and that she opened his eyes to how Mencius's teachings should be applied here today, since human nature is essentially good and society must be so organised that goodness is allowed to flourish.' Fumi smiled at the old woman and said quietly, 'We see this in Towa-san.'

I continued working on Towa's legs, thinking what an extraordinary journey they had made and seeing for myself the price they had paid for the quest for revenge. Towa had not struck with the sword herself but she had pursued a criminal and brought him to justice. I tried to express my admiration and gratitude through my hands.

'You have a good touch, Miss,' she said when I had finished.

'Thank you for telling me your story,' I murmured as I stood up. I went back into the kitchen with Fumi and we finished preparing the meal.

Some of the students had their own boxes with bowls and chopsticks packed neatly away in them. These were kept in the little kitchen of the schoolhouse. I helped Fumi carry the other trays and utensils and we set them out on the veranda. By now the soup was hot, so we took that over too, with big bamboo tubs of rice mixed with millet and vegetables, sliced pumpkin and onions, and bowls of fresh tofu. Jars of pickles completed the meal. I couldn't help wondering how the household managed to feed so many students as well as themselves.

'Will you go and tell them it is ready?' Fumi said.

I walked along the veranda to the main room. The *shōji* were open and I lingered for a moment, peeping round the frame. The room was crammed with small desks at which students sat completely still, concentrating fiercely. Among them I saw my uncle, Itō, Kusaka and Takasugi. I did not recognise any of the others. The teacher was very thin with a long, stern face. His fingers, following the text of the book in front of him, were elongated and bony. He looked frail, as if a sudden gust of wind would blow him away like a wisp of straw. But his voice was clear and distinctive and so authoritative it was hard to believe it was really coming from him. His method seemed to be to ask questions and then to tease out complete understanding from the replies. The students' answers were considered, their voices deferential. You could tell how much they wanted to please him. His manner towards them was both strict and affectionate.

I knelt in the doorway and shuffled into the room. After bowing to the ground, I said, '*Sensei*, your sister said to tell you the meal is ready.'

Just then the midday bell sounded from a nearby temple.

Master Yoshida said, finishing up his teaching, 'Remember, setting life's goals is the basis of everything. Devote your talents to society, always help each other. Choose the right friends, and never stop reading the works of the masters and sages.'

Then he turned towards me and said, 'And who is the new guest in our house?' He looked at me directly, astonishing me. His eyes seemed to see straight into my heart. I felt he knew all my dreams and hopes.

'I am Itasaki Yūnosuke's daughter, Tsuru, from Yuda. Please treat me favourably.'

'You are related to Shinsai-san?'

'*Sensei,* she is my niece,' Shinsai said.

'Very good, very good.' Master Yoshida waved to the students, indicating that they were dismissed. 'Your uncle is going to join us here. I'm looking forward to discussing Western military affairs with him. It seems this is one of his interests.'

'If only we could travel overseas and see for ourselves,' my uncle said.

Itō Shunsuke had stayed in the room. 'We will one day,' he said.

'Shunsuke, I believe you will,' Master Yoshida said, smiling at him.

When I went outside Itō followed me.

'The other day,' he said quietly, 'I was very grateful to your father and you…'

'Don't mention it,' I said.

'Thanks anyway.' He made a rueful face, and rubbed his ear. 'Please thank your father too.'

'I'm glad everything was all right!' I was trying to hide my smiles and so was he.

'Please be careful!' I said, wishing I could freely discuss his symptoms and my father's medicine with him, wishing I could be a man among these young men.

I helped Fumi serve the students and then took a bowl for myself. Takasugi and Kusaka both greeted me and asked after my father, but did not talk any more either to me or anyone else. Takasugi was particularly withdrawn. I realised his moods swung violently from one extreme to the other. At the wedding he had been silent at first, then excited and sociable, now he seemed sunk in gloom. He kept glancing curiously at Towa, as though he wanted to say something to her but did not know how to approach her. For a high-rank samurai like him the presence of a low-caste woman might have been disturbing. Yoshida Shōin's teachings were disturbing too. All these young men were having their ideas of who they were challenged. I could see how confronting it might be, as well as exhilarating.

I thought I saw Kusaka's eyes follow Fumi as she went to and fro. Master Yoshida must have had a very high opinion of him to want him to marry his sister. Later Shinsai would tell me that these two young men, Kusaka and Takasugi, were considered the outstanding talents of the school.

Towa had come across from the main house with another woman, Yoshida Shōin's mother. We women cleared away the dishes while the men smoked and chatted in the sunshine. Before they resumed their studies I managed to speak to my uncle and tell him I thought I should be returning to the Kuriya house.

'Yes,' he said vaguely. 'Do you think you can find your own way?'

'Really, Shinsai-san, I don't think I should have to walk back to Hagi alone!'

'I don't want to miss a moment of the *sensei*'s teaching,' he said fervently.

'You've got your wish, you're going to be studying in his school for months.' I was suddenly really angry with him; maybe I was jealous at the opportunity he had been given; maybe it was because I had already realised how much I would miss him. 'You could at least see me home.'

Towa was standing nearby. 'I'm going back to Hagi today. I can accompany the young lady.'

'Well, that's perfect,' Shinsai said.

'So when will we see you?' I demanded before he disappeared into the classroom.

'I don't know. Tell your father I'll write. And if anyone can send any money I'd appreciate it.'

'Not a single *mon*,' I said under my breath. 'I hope you starve. It'll serve you right.' Then I tried to regather my scattered composure in order to thank Towa for her kind offer and say goodbye to Fumi and Mrs Sugi.

I left with mixed feelings, elated to have met the famous *sensei*, frustrated that I could not study with him. Even if we were in prison at the same time, he would be in Noyama and I in the commoners' prison, Iwakura. I was angry with Shinsai for abandoning me, and anxious for him in the company of those brilliant arrogant young men who I was afraid would despise and bully him. Then I began to worry about Towa, who limped slowly along beside me. How would she manage to cross the fish bridge, let alone make it all the way back to her home in Uemura?

However, once we arrived at the bottom of the hill, Towa made her way to the ferry boats where one of the boatmen greeted her with warmth, called her *Grandmother* and helped her into the boat.

'Come, O-Tsuru-san,' she said, settling herself down in the bow.

I jumped in and crouched on one of the plank seats in the middle, while the boatman worked the oar from the stern. It was even more frightening than riding a horse. The tide was full and the wind was blowing strongly off the sea. A mass of craft bobbed about in the estuary, driven by sails of all shades of brown from ochre to sand, or like ours by oars, in the hands of half-naked men who shouted and cursed each other, mostly good-humouredly.

The tides dictated life in this city, everyone dependent on their ebb and flow. Was it this that made its inhabitants so opportunistic, so quick to grab their chances with the tide of history?

We made it to the opposite bank and disembarked, slightly damp from the spray. The air was growing colder, the shadows lengthening.

'Towa-san, where will you sleep tonight?' I said as we set off through the rice fields, the boatman's farewells and good wishes echoing in our ears. I wanted to ask her to stay but I was afraid of the Kuriya's reaction.

'Don't you worry about me, Miss,' she replied. 'There are plenty of people in Hagi who will take me in.'

'You must be a heroine to many,' I said.

'Maybe to some people,' she said with quiet pride. 'Even if others don't see it.'

'Like Takasugi?' I said, ashamed of the young man's awkward coldness.

'He'll change. He's only young. He's been brought up in a certain way. But he'll come to understand that everyone deserves their chance in life, and maybe people like me can help people like him. After the great riots in the Tenpō era we all saw the energy and the strength of common folk. When farmers unite with *bushi* then we'll see change, we'll see the world renewed. Takasugi-sama will realise that one day too.'

I could not believe I had met two such impressive people in one day. When we came to the Kuriya's shop I asked Towa to wait for a few minutes.

'I'm back,' I called as I stepped inside.

'Welcome home!' The Accountant sat in the same place as if he had not moved all day.

'Excuse me, could I take a box of Cure-All? I'll pay for it later. I need to give it to a friend.'

'Help youself,' he said.

I took a box and ran back to Towa. 'Here,' I said, 'take it with tea. It's to thank you...for everything.'

She thanked me profusely, tucked the box into her robe and set off slowly down the street.

I never saw her again so I never found out if the Cure-All worked for her or not.

STUDENTS

A few days later I returned home, accompanied by one of the Kuriya's servants who was making deliveries to Yamaguchi. I arrived late in the evening. It was already the tenth month, and it was quite cold. I had walked on my own from the Matsudaya inn at Yuda, carrying my *furoshiki*-wrapped bundle in one hand and a lantern with the inn's name on it in the other. The familiar shapes of the mountains and the fresh scent of autumn, wood smoke mingled with roasted barley and sesame oil, filled me with delight. Lamps shone from inside my house, and there was a friendly rustle as a piece of bark fell from the gambling tree.

The cat was sitting at the gate looking annoyed. She mewed when she saw me as if in complaint. There was a smell of tobacco and the glow of lit pipes. Two strangers were sitting on the veranda.

'Good evening,' I said to them.

'Welcome back,' they replied. One of them tried to bow, forgetting he was still holding his pipe and nearly poking himself in the eye. The other said, in an over-familiar way, 'You must be tired after your long journey.'

I bobbed my head to them and went inside. The front room was empty. There was a scuffle of feet and Hachirō came bustling along the walkway that led to our living quarters.

'Welcome home! Welcome home!' He took the lantern from me, saying he would return it to the Matsudaya in the morning.

'Hachirō-san, who are those two men? Are they patients? Isn't my father here?'

'The doctor and your mother are in the main room,' he replied. 'And the two young masters are the new students.'

'Students?'

Without waiting for him to say any more I rushed down to find my parents. I wrenched back the *shōji* and without even greeting them demanded, 'What are those men doing here?'

My mother was reading aloud to my father by the dim light of the lamp. I did not recognise the book; it must have been a new one. I had only been away two weeks and the whole house had changed. I glared at the cover as my mother lowered it.

Her face lit up. 'Tsu-chan, you're back!'

'We missed you,' my father said.

'It looks as though you've replaced me!' I knelt on the tatami and began to unwrap my bundle, taking out the sweet bean paste and dried fish I had brought as presents from Hagi.

'Mmm, my favourites,' my father said greedily.

'I'll make some tea.' As she stood up, my mother leaned towards me and touched my brow with her hand as if I was a little girl. I thought they were trying to avoid answering my question. They both seemed uncomfortable.

'Neechan is having a baby,' I said, and Mother burst into tears. I don't know why she cried. I was the one who should have been crying, upset as I was by the presence of strangers in the house. I took myself off to make tea while my mother calmed down, and the three of us drank it and ate little pieces of Hagi *yukan*. However, I was not going to go to bed without a few answers.

'So, why did you suddenly decide to take on students?' I addressed my father.

'They suddenly started applying,' my father said. He was not looking at me directly. 'Ever since you and Shinsai went away in fact. There's a waiting list; these were the first two. They are only here on trial.'

It took a while for me to understand. I was tired and not thinking with my usual clarity. 'They are prospective sons-in-law?' I couldn't quite bring myself to say the word *husband*.

'It's good to have students,' Father said, as if trying to convince himself. 'They will pay fees, you know, and with Shinsai in Hagi I need the extra help here.'

'You might even like one or other of them,' Mother said.

'I suppose I might, but living with them, working alongside them…it's going to be a little embarrassing.'

'I'm sorry,' Father said, 'I couldn't turn them away. They came with very persuasive introductions from people who've done me favours in the past.' I noticed Father couldn't help looking rather pleased with himself. 'I hadn't realised how many young men want to become my son-in-law. Imagine! There is a waiting list!'

'Yes, it's a great honour,' Mother said. 'Maybe Tsu-chan would like to meet them now.'

At least someone remembered I had some interest in the matter too. 'No!' I exclaimed. I felt dirty after the journey and my hair was all over the place. 'I'll leave it till morning.'

'There's no hurry to make a decision,' Father assured me. 'After all, we have to make sure we get the right person, someone intelligent who will make a good doctor, who I get along with…'

I went to bed feeling as ruffled as the cat. I did not like having strangers in the house, the unfamiliar smell, the noises they made, snores, farts and coughing. The house seemed filled with too many people, yet empty because Shinsai was no longer in it.

The students were called Nakajima Noboru and Hayashi Daisuke. Noboru was the older, Daisuke the taller. They were both younger sons of the *sottsu* class, the lowest rank of samurai, who were seeking an alternative career in medicine. Noboru had studied sword fighting in Kokura, in some minor school, and this experience had given him a taste for blood. The more gruesome the case the more it interested him. He liked the idea of surgery and longed to amputate, practising on the giant white radishes which Hachirō had stacked up along the wall of the house. Swollen limbs or testicles, tumours and dropsy intrigued him, indeed anything grotesque and deforming aroused his interest, and he talked about these cases endlessly, as well as about brawls he had been in, men he had killed, crimes he had witnessed, and so on. He was small and stocky, pugnacious and argumentative, but he had a natural intelligence underneath the show.

Daisuke also talked endlessly but I never understood a word he was saying. That is, I understood each word but he had a way of stringing them together that made them incomprehensible. He was interested in ancient taboos that affected the health and was fond of quoting obscure philosophers and doctors in classical Chinese. The patients preferred him to Noboru, in fact they begged my father not to let Noboru near them in case he should chop off one of their limbs in an excess of enthusiasm, but they liked listening to Daisuke's long-winded diagnoses, even if they did not understand them.

'Doesn't he speak beautifully?' they said, and quite a few of them spontaneously felt much better.

Both young men were keen to impress my father but neither of them seemed to realise it would make more sense to try to impress me. Neither of them ever noticed that I knew as much about diagnosis and treatment as my father and they never once asked my advice, though they were quite happy to give me instructions on mixing medicines or making pills.

They were desperate to be accepted into our family. To marry me and become my father's adopted son, a partner in his practice, maybe even his heir, would give them a way out of the poverty and loneliness that awaited most younger sons. I felt sorry for them sometimes, when I wasn't resenting them. They just wanted what everyone else wanted in our creaking, constricted society: a way up or a way out.

I felt like the bamboo-cutter's daughter. I thought I could not bear to be married to either of them, but I didn't want to offend my parents by refusing them. Sometimes I would look up at the moon as it rose above the gambling tree and watch the owls gliding silently on their white-feathered wings. I wished heavenly beings would fly as silently from the moon and wrap me in a robe of feathers so that I would no longer feel human emotions.

Like the girl in the story I wanted to set impossible tasks for my suitors: not the branch from the jewelled tree or the fireproof coat of the fire rat, but maybe something like the swallows' easy birth shells or, better still, a cure for syphilis or a true Cure-All that would fight all infections.

The swallows had left for the winter. By the time they returned Mitsue would have had her baby. We were all worried about her. My father seemed to have a series of patients who had difficult deliveries, two babies were stillborn, another was seriously deformed. My mother's anxiety drove her to visit a shrine in Yamaguchi on the day of the dog in the twelfth month. She brought back amulets and *o-mamori* which we sent to Hagi with letters and prayers.

I spent my days physically occupied with all the work of the household and practice, while in my mind I pondered which of the students would be the lesser evil.

Daisuke would probably be easier to handle. Already I'd found ways to unsettle him, even to bully him. But he bored me deeply, after only a few weeks. After a year of marriage I would be ready to murder him. Also I was not sure that he had any real interest in women. He had none of the liveliness, the animal spirit, of Shinsai's friends.

Noboru, on the other hand, was impossible to bully; his skin was too thick. He, at least by his own account, had had a certain success with women, and I had to admit I shared some of his interests in death and dying, though I hoped our motives were different.

When we prepared the babies' corpses for burial he looked

at them longingly. 'Shouldn't we cut them open just to see what's inside?'

I really wanted to do that too, but Daisuke was firmly against it, telling us that there was nothing the dead could teach the living. He also warned that the babies' ghosts would haunt us if we desecrated their bodies. Father stopped the argument by reminding us that the dissection of just any corpse was illegal and that there was no surer way to alarm our patients and send them running to our competitors.

'If we are to do surgery we need to practise,' Noboru argued, but neither the living nor the dead were eager to offer themselves for the sake of his cutting techniques. Sometimes a hunter would bring an otter – otters were believed to resemble humans in their physiology – and Noboru and I would carefully dissect that, but mostly he had to content himself with winter vegetables. The thwack of pumpkins falling apart echoed through the frosty air, until O-Kane took to hiding the vegetables away.

'We'll never survive till spring if he keeps murdering the poor things,' she grumbled.

At New Year Shinsai returned for a few days in the company of Shiji Monta, who had come to see his birth family on his way to Edo. They brought news of Yoshida Shōin and the school and its pupils, most interesting to me the fact that the *sensei*'s sister, Fumi, had married Kusaka Genzui the previous month. Again I felt a pang of envy. She was married to the brilliant, good-looking Kusaka while I had the choice of the windbag or the pumpkin slasher.

'Kusaka also will be in Edo before long,' Monta said.

'How I wish I was going with you!' Shinsai exclaimed.

'You have the chance to study with Master Yoshida,' Monta said. 'Make the most of it. I'll write to you from Edo, and you must keep me in touch with what's happening in Hagi.'

Because he worked for the *daimyō*, Monta heard all the news from Edo before the rest of us. He told us now that the American envoy, Harris, had been received by the Shōgun, and that negotiations for a treaty were underway.

The water that had been on the fire for so long was at last coming to the boil, the first bubbles rising to the surface.

'Foreigners on our soil! In the presence of the Shōgun,' Shinsai said angrily.

'We are so vulnerable in Chōshū,' Monta said. 'Every foreign ship has to go through the strait at Shimonoseki. We would be powerless if they decided to invade us and settle here, as they have done in China.' He turned to me. 'Not married yet, O-Tsuru?' he remarked. 'You will be by the time I see you again.'

His excitement at going to the capital made him look younger than ever.

'Take care of yourself,' I said, and under my breath added, 'And stay away from the pox-ridden geisha of Yoshiwara.'

The weeks with Master Yoshida had changed Shinsai. He seemed more disciplined and more remote, much older than our two students, whom he treated with some disdain.

'Surely you won't marry either of them,' he said to me the morning he left to return to Hagi. I handed him an extra bundle containing more presents for Mitsue: paper dogs and other charms to ensure an easy delivery, lovingly prepared by Mother and O-Kane, some of her favourite foods, letters and books from me. He made a face of mock horror and pretended to stagger under the weight.

'I must do whatever my parents want for me,' I said. 'I am leaving it to Father to decide.'

'That doesn't sound like our Tsu-chan,' he replied. 'Surely there's no hurry. You are still so young.'

'I am seventeen now; it's quite old enough to get married.'

I had turned seventeen with the New Year – it was now the fifth year of Ansei, 1858 by the Western calendar – but because I was born in the twelth month I became two years old very shortly after my birth, so in fact I was younger than it sounded.

Shinsai's eyes seemed to soften as he looked at me. Or was I imagining it? I felt so close to him at that moment, beneath the gambling tree. I couldn't help trembling.

'You're cold,' he said. 'Go inside.'

My eyes suddenly became hot as if I was about to cry. 'When will we see you again?' I asked as I had done in Hagi.

He replied in the same way. 'I don't know. I'll write.' Then he added, 'Don't make any hasty decisions.'

It was freezing; my toes and fingers were numb, but I stood at the gate watching until he was out of sight.

CHOLERA AND OTHER FOREIGN IMPORTS

Early that same year news came of a cholera outbreak in Nagasaki; it caused many deaths there and began to spread along the highways and through the ports into the whole country. It was a terrifying disease: the common people called it *korori* – tiger, wolf, *tanuki*, for it seemed to be like those animals: savage, cunning and unpredictable. A healthy person could be in shock from the terrible diarrhoea within a couple of hours, and usually died within three days, a shrivelled husk of their former self, sucked dry of all fluids. We had no treatment for it, though there were various suggestions – the so-called Ōsaka remedy which involved huge amounts of alcohol, or the use of opium or quinine.

The foreigners' ships were blamed for bringing the disease, and their presence in our country was said to have offended the gods. People believed other disasters, earthquakes, storms and floods, were all happening for the same reason. The divine country was being polluted. Straw boats with effigies of foreigners were sent downriver in the vain hope that the gods would bear the hated intruders away.

Whatever the cause, cholera added to the anxieties of the time, and we were particularly worried about my brother, Tetsuya. My father wondered if he should send him a message to come home for a while, but before he could come to a decision, Tetsuya himself arrived, on a cold day with low grey skies that threatened snow, even though it was nearly spring. I was tired of winter. My face was chapped raw and my chilblains itched and ached at night. Everything irritated me and I was short-tempered with everyone around me.

'You need a husband, O-Tsuru,' O-Kane told me, making me even crosser. My marriage was on everyone's mind but no one dared talk about it. Tetsuya's arrival gave them all something else to think about.

My brother had decided to come home almost as soon as he heard of the first cases in Nagasaki. My father's solicitude for his patients manifested itself in Tetsuya as a deep concern for his own health and safety. In many ways he was the most timid of all our family, though he hid it beneath a confident manner. Since he had been away he had acquired a precise rather pompous way of speaking as if he had been doing too much translating from a foreign language. He dropped Dutch words into his speech from time to time, *thee drinken* and *dank je wel*, and had even brought back several items of Western clothing: a three-cornered hat, a jacket made of blue wool, and high leather boots.

'What could be more practical?' he demanded when he showed the boots to us. 'They are warm, waterproof and they last for years.'

'Rather hard to slip on and off,' my mother remarked.

'Foreigners don't take their footwear on and off like we do. They put their boots on in the morning and don't take them off until they go to bed at night.'

'Inside the house?' O-Kane was incredulous. 'How dirty!'

Tetsuya had brought gifts for us all: a European watch for Father, some blue and white dishes from Holland for Mother, glass bottles for the practice, and the famous *casutera* cake, which had grown a little stale and crumbly on the journey. The watch only told European time, dividing day and night into two sets of twelve equal parts, but it made a fine ornament and Father was very proud of it. He looked at it and listened to its *tick tick* many times a day. He said it had a calming effect.

I was fascinated by the watch, which seemed to encapsulate the uncanny precision of the Dutch way of thinking, and by the wool jacket, which Tetsuya called his *jekker*. It had a faint animal smell and its weave was close and dense. It was heavier than anything we wore – even our padded winter clothes – and like the boots it resembled some kind of restraint that you put your body into in order to hold it down. Our clothes, I thought, left us more open to the weather and the world. They did not protect us. Farmers, builders and craftsmen often injured their feet and hands with deep cuts from hoes, axes or knives that quickly became infected despite everything we tried to do to keep the wounds clean. We lost many such patients to tetanus or gangrene. My father used boiling water, hot sake, soap, infusions of herbs known to have wound-healing properties, but whether the patient survived or not seemed to depend more on the whim of heaven than on anything we did.

But no matter how practical leather boots were I did not think our farmers would ever wear them. The Tenpō riots were still fresh in people's memories. The worst riots in Chōshū had been sparked by the violation of a taboo against transporting animal hides during harvest. Leather carried an aura of danger and profanity, offensive to the gods. Those who were dependent on the gods for everything could not risk offending them.

Tetsuya was a little older than our two students and quickly became their leader. They were impressed by his studies in Nagasaki, and fascinated and alarmed by his stories of the foreigners who were beginning to arrive in large numbers, not only the Dutch and Chinese who had always been there, but English, Americans and Russians.

Now there were three extra men in the house there were more chores for me to do as a woman, and less medical work. Father could hardly call on me to help with a difficult diagnosis or advise on a new treatment; it would have been insulting to his son and his students. However, I still looked after the pharmacy, tending the garden as spring returned and sowing the seeds I had collected in the autumn.

We grew many plants for their medicinal properties, like *hakka* and *daiō*, *shiso*, hollyhocks, peonies and wormwood. Others like China root, licorice and senna we had to import, but you could find lots of valuable plants growing wild on the mountain slopes, if you knew where to look for them. One afternoon in the fifth month I went out with knife, trowel and hod, hoping to get a good supply of elder bark and flowers, wild carrot root, and *katsura* twigs. The plum rains had started but they were sparse and fitful this year, something else the foreigners were blamed for, and many days were like this one, hot and humid with no rain.

I was able to fill my back hod and was walking home past

the Inoue house when one of the maids called to me, as if she had been looking out for me.

'Miss Itasaki, my lady wants to talk to you.'

I went up to the veranda and looked into the room. Monta's older brother's wife was nursing a child just inside. I took the hod off my back, and greeted her with respect. I did not know her at all; Monta's brother was older than we were and had never taken much part in our childhood games.

'I hope all the family are well,' I said. 'Do you have any news from Edo?'

'That's why I needed to speak to you,' she said. She eased the nipple from the child's mouth. It immediately screamed in protest and waved its hands in the air, its face screwed up with rage.

'Here, hold him for a moment, will you?' She thrust the baby at me, and he wriggled and kicked even more.

'Heavens! He's strong!'

'He's a little *bushi* all right!' She could not keep the pride from her voice. 'But what a temper!'

She disappeared into the house while the baby went on screaming, and came back a few moments later with a letter. She looked around as if to check no one was watching or listening and then whispered, 'My husband's brother, Shiji-san, writes now and then from Edo. This came with his last letter; he asks us to give it to you to send on to your uncle. He did not want to write directly to the school because of Master Yoshida's somewhat irregular position.'

'I'll make sure my uncle gets it,' I said. I handed the baby back to her and took the letter, tucking it inside my robe. This was the most interesting thing that had happened since

Tetsuya's return from Nagasaki. I wondered if Monta had specifically asked for my help, remembering my good sense and my courage.

'My advice to my husband was to burn it,' Mrs Inoue said. 'Monta is too easily led; he keeps bad company. No good can come of this association with Yoshida Shōin. I would keep it secret if I were you. And let us never speak of it again.'

She took another furtive look around as if domain officials or Bakufu spies were lurking in the lush landscape, but nothing disturbed the summer tranquillity, apart from the baby screaming.

His cries stopped abruptly as his mother put him to the breast again. He sucked like a little demon. I couldn't help noticing that she winced in pain and that the breast was streaked slightly with red.

'*Okusama*, I could bring a poultice for you…' I suggested.

'Oh, it's nothing,' she replied swiftly. 'Just my little warrior attacks me so strongly.'

Social propriety struggled with medical sense within me. My face grew hot. 'Milk fever is very dangerous,' I said, louder than I had intended. 'The young lord needs a healthy mother.'

'I will seek your advice if I think I need it.' She stood, hunching over the baby, and went into the house, still clasping him to the breast.

My face and neck burned more strongly. I felt like an idiot, dismissed so suddenly, and I regretted exposing myself to her scorn. It served me right for presuming I had anything to offer a *bushi* wife. I swung the hod onto my back and went home, muttering under my breath with rage.

It took me some time to sort out my emotions as well as my harvest. I tried to calm myself and think rationally about Monta's letter. I decided I had to read it before I sent it on. I told myself it was to check the contents – I would burn it if there were anything in it that would incriminate my family or Shinsai or Master Yoshida – but even without that excuse my curiosity was so great I would have read it anyway.

Before it grew dark I slipped out to the garden to the family graves. I had picked a handful of *yukinoshita* earlier – we used the leaves in medicine or to flavour *tempura* and I'd put aside the delicate white and pink flowers. Now I laid them at the foot of the stone and prayed quickly under my breath for my little brother and sister. Then I took out Monta's letter and unrolled it.

It was sent from the upper Chōshū mansion in Sakurada. All the domains kept two or more residences in Edo called *yashiki*. They were designated as upper, middle and lower, according to their proximity to Edo castle, where the Shōgun resided, the seat of Tokugawa power. Samurai went there without their wives and families. Edo was a town of single men, serviced by a huge network of merchants, artisans, servants and entertainers. And doctors. The Edo medical schools were famous and we knew the life stories of all the great physicians and their heroic sacrifices in their pursuit of knowledge. I had never been there: I could not imagine a city so huge. I tried to picture Monta there as I read the letter.

It was dated the first day of the fifth month and began abruptly. *Lord Ii Naosuke of Hikone has been put in charge of the Bakufu and named Tairō. It is the end of any hope of reform within the government, and Ii will decide the problem of the shōgunal succession himself. Worse, a treaty is to be signed with the Americans. All Edo is in an uproar. Everyone is of the opinion foreigners should not be allowed in our land, but few dare say so outright. I am learning English but I spend more time practising sword fighting with Katsura. I hope it will be of more use to me.*

I am worried about the sensei's safety. It is becoming very dangerous to express his sort of opinions openly. People in Edo are being arrested for much less. Please do all you can to persuade him to be discreet. Keep him and yourself safe.

The letter ended with the usual regards to the family. I thought it was disturbingly outspoken. I would have expected Monta to write in a more subtle way. On second reading it seemed more innocuous; nevertheless as I put it back inside my robe I felt like a conspirator. I intended to show it to my parents and ask if we should send it to Shinsai, but as I left the graves I heard the sound of a sudden disturbance in the road beyond the house, running feet and shouting. I recognised Tetsuya's voice. I couldn't make out the words, but the note of urgency alarmed me. I thought some accident must have occurred and I hurried to help my father.

Tetsuya burst through the front door, white-faced, barefoot, his hair dishevelled. He was breathing hard as if he had run all the way from Yuda.

'There's been a fight! Nakajima Noboru's wounded.'

Father came hurrying along the veranda. He was wearing a light cotton *yukata* – he must have been to the *onsen* earlier.

'What about you?' he stammered. 'Are you hurt?'

'No, no, I ran away. I was not armed. I wanted Nakajima to run too but he insisted on fighting. They were waiting for us outside the inn. One of the girls came to warn us and lead us out the back way, but Nakajima had been drinking; he leaped up and ran outside with sword drawn, and they fell on him.'

'But who? Why?' Father said. 'Why would anyone do such a thing?'

Really there was no time to seek explanations. 'Oniisan,' I said to my brother, 'take Hachirō and bring Nakajima here. Go quickly! If he is only wounded maybe we can save him.'

'I daren't go back there,' Tetsuya said. He was shaking all over. He tore off his woollen jacket, rolled it up and looked around as though seeking a hiding place for it. 'It was me they were after. It was all my fault.'

I caught myself wondering why on earth he was wearing the jacket on such a hot night: shock imprints these tiny unimportant details on the mind.

'I'll go with Father,' I said. 'No one will attack us. But where is Hayashi-san? He could come with us to help carry Nakajima home.'

'I don't know,' Tetsuya cried. 'He ran away too. He must be hiding in the fields.'

I couldn't help feeling exasperated. One of them had had too much inappropriate bravado, the other two none at all when it was needed.

Hachirō appeared with a lantern, looking eager and resolute as though rescuing wounded samurai were something he did every day.

'I must get dressed,' Father said, patting his *yukata* nervously.

I began to plead there was no time, but at that moment there was the sound of wheels outside and men's voices calling for the doctor.

I ran out and saw two men from the Hanamatsutei with a small handcart in which Nakajima lay, in an awkward huddle as if he had been thrown down in that position and would never move from it. I thought he was already dead, but when I came closer I saw his eyes were wide open and his teeth clenched. He did not make a sound.

Hachirō had followed me with the lantern and in its light we saw the blood. Nakajima was soaked in it as it flowed from deep sword cuts to neck and waist, and oozed from superficial slashes on his hands and arms.

'Take him inside,' I said. I could see he might die at any moment from shock and loss of blood. It was only his unusual physical strength that had kept him alive at all. But if we could stop the bleeding we might save him.

The men lifted him and then he did scream.

'Kill me, kill me,' he begged. 'Put an end to it quickly.'

His words were slurred; I realised he had been drinking heavily, was actually still drunk. It was a good thing: he wouldn't realise how badly he'd been wounded and the shock would be less.

'It's all right, sir.' One of the men tried to calm him. 'You're at the doctor's now, he'll look after you.'

Like the woollen jacket, those clumsy words of compassion would stay with me for a long time.

My mother had cleared the workbench and she told the men to put Nakajima down on it. Hachirō gripped him by the shoulders while I took a pair of scissors and cut his garments away.

Father found one of the pulsing veins in the neck and pressed down on it, arresting the flow of blood from that wound. The slash at the waist was long and deep. I feared the sword had thrust right into the stomach or the liver. The wound had to be closed as soon as possible, but first it had to be cleansed.

'Kill me, kill me,' Nakajima begged again. But I did not want him to be killed. I wanted to try to save him.

Mother returned with a bowl and strips of clean cloth, and we washed out the wounds with cold water. Nakajima panted as Hachirō held him down more firmly.

'Let him rest for a moment,' Father said. 'Hachirō, bring boiling water and whatever alcohol we have. Okusan, get the needles and thread. Tsuru will stitch while the rest of us hold him still. Where is Tetsuya?'

'Here,' my brother replied from the doorway.

'You grip his ankles.'

Hachirō came back with a large flask of sake and a kettle with steam rising from it. Father, still holding the pressure point in the neck, took the sake in his other hand and poured it into the wound. He passed it to me and I did the same with the deep waist wound. Then I swabbed the other cuts, hoping the stinging would slightly distract our patient. I took the kettle from Hachirō and poured the hot water directly into the wounds.

Nakajima howled, a terrible animal sound.

'Someone find something for him to bite on,' Father said.

Mother fetched a small wooden stick and put it between Nakajima's teeth.

His eyes flickered open and his gaze found mine.

'Be brave,' I said. 'Lie still. I will be as quick as I can.'

Mother handed me a threaded needle and then held the

lamp so I could see. It was not my neatest work. The edges of the wound and the skin were slippery with blood and sake. The lamp was dim and unreliable. Nakajima shuddered and flinched beneath me. It was like a scene from a painting of hell: the sinner in the clutches of demons and I the main torturer. The gaping slashes seemed endless. I must have pierced his skin, pulled it together and tied off the knots fifty times. At one stage mercifully he lost consciousness. I wished I had a sleep-inducing drug to lessen his pain and make my job easier, and found my mind wandering to Dr Hanaoka and his datura-based solution, and to the drug called ether I had read about in foreign texts.

It was past midnight when we were finished. Mother had prepared plasters dipped in egg yolk and rose oil and we covered the wounds and bandaged them with cotton cloths. I had done the best I could – but there was so much I did not know. Would the bleeding stop now the skin was closed over or would the blood continue to escape inside the body? If the organs were pierced would that mean inevitable infection? My hands had been deft and steady all night but now I started to tremble all over. Spots danced before my eyes and I saw strange shapes in the shadows.

Mother urged me to lie down but I could not bear to leave Nakajima. If my eyes strayed from him for a moment I thought he would slip away. The men carried him to the back room overlooking the garden and laid him down on a pile of old clothes. I brought a bowl of water and cool barley tea. I wiped the sweat from his face and wetted his lips with the tea.

It was a warm still night. Mosquitoes droned around us

and I could hear the owls calling from the gambling tree. The scents of the summer garden drifted in through the open doors and the moon cast patterns of leaves and branches onto the matting.

The rest of the family went to lie down but I don't think anyone slept. The moon had set and dawn was approaching when Tetsuya crept into the room and knelt beside me.

'How is he?' he whispered.

'Still alive.'

Nakajima's breathing was rapid and shallow; his limbs twitched.

'Can he hear us?'

'I think so,' I said.

'Nakajima-kun, hang in there. You're going to make it. Hang in there.'

Nakajima's head moved slightly, as if in agreement. It gave me hope. *If he lives, I'll marry him*, I promised the gods or fate or whatever it is that hears our prayers and chooses to answer or ignore them. *I will be a good wife to him. I won't mock him or argue with him. I'll hold him at night and give him children.*

'I'm sorry,' Tetsuya said in a low voice. 'It was all my fault. But why did you stay and fight, Nakajima-kun? If only you'd run away too.'

'Oniisan, what happened?'

'We went to the inn to have a few drinks and talk to the girls. I didn't think. I forgot this isn't Nagasaki. I wore my Western clothes, the boots. We were in a private room at the back. There was a group of samurai in the adjoining room. I'd seen them when I went out to the privy. I didn't know any of them; they must have come from Hagi for some reason. Maybe they were on their way to Mitajiri or Shimonoseki. They'd heard the news from Edo that a treaty is to be signed with the Americans, and that the English will be next. They were talking more and more loudly about killing all foreigners, making bets on who would be the first to cut down a Westerner. And I was chatting about Western medicine with Nakajima and Hayashi. I think I might have been showing off a bit, talking in Dutch and describing the dissections I'd seen and so on; suddenly O-Kiyo ran in and said, "Itasaki-san, those men with swords are dissecting your boots, and they say the boots' owner will be next!"

'The girls jumped to their feet saying there was no need to worry, they would take us out the back way and we could run home. Hayashi shot off like a hare; I was about to follow but Nakajima immediately became enraged. He rushed out of the room, drawing his sword and shouting, "Do you know who those boots belong to? They are the boots of Dr Itasaki's son. Dr Itasaki, the greatest doctor in the domain. You have insulted these boots. You have insulted my teacher!"'

'Nakajima is very brave,' I said, silently commenting, *What an idiot!*

'He was very drunk,' Tetsuya explained.

'Did anyone call the town officials?' I was thinking of all the possible complications: any of the parties involved might be considered guilty and punished heavily – the samurai, who had probably vanished by now, Nakajima, if he lived, Tetsuya, the innkeeper, even Father for not controlling his students.

'I don't know,' Tetsuya admitted. 'I ran away then too. I'm a coward.'

'I'm glad you did,' I said, thinking how terrible it would be for my parents if it were Tetsuya lying here fighting for his life.

'We were not brought up like samurai,' Tetsuya said, sounding more and more miserable. 'I can't fight with a sword. I never wanted to learn like Shinsai did.'

'Nakajima's different,' I said. 'He did have a samurai upbringing. He reacted like a samurai.' It might be idiotic, but I couldn't help admiring it. Men like Tetsuya and my father were cautious; they wanted to expire on the tatami at a fine old age. But Nakajima – and Shinsai – would rather die than be thought a coward.

I noticed that the night was fading and turning to grey.

Tetsuya sighed. 'I hate swords,' he said quietly. 'I hate fighting.'

When it was fully light my mother brought me some tea. Apart from that I did not eat or drink all day, but continued to sit beside Nakajima. He seemed to fall asleep for a while, and my hopes rose, but then he grew more restless and his skin began to burn. He lost control of himself and wet the clothes he lay on. Dark blood leaked from his anus along with faeces. I saw he was dying.

I was affronted. I did not want him to die. He was my patient, possibly my future husband. But my skills had failed him. I could do nothing to help him. All I could do was watch him die.

The usual work of the day went on around us. Patients came and went, meals were prepared, cleared away. When they had a free moment members of the family came to sit beside the dying man. O-Kane brought flowers and lit sandalwood shavings to mask the smell.

Towards the end of the afternoon it began to rain. The muggy heat lessened and the room filled with the scent of wet earth. Nakajima opened his eyes and spoke with sudden lucidity, calling me by my pet name, which he had never used before.

'Tsu-chan, we did get married, didn't we? We've had a good life together, haven't we?'

'Yes.' I could not bring myself to disillusion him.

'I always said you would make a grand little wife.' He smiled in satisfaction and did not speak again. At the moment he died a look of puzzlement crossed his face as though he suddenly realised what was happening to him but did not understand why, why now; then death put an end to his questions, smoothing out his frown.

I spoke the name of Amida for him and prayed for his soul's journey. When I stood my legs were aching.

My mother had been with me for the last hour or so. She stood too, came close to me and embraced me.

'Go and eat something. Tell O-Kane to bring water and she can help prepare the body.'

I nodded without speaking and walked slowly to the front of the house. Father had just said goodbye to a patient. Daisuke, who had obviously come out of hiding, was making notes at the desk, Tetsuya was at the workbench, grinding something. They all turned to look at me. I made a gesture; I did not need to say anything. Father began patting his arms, Tetsuya gazed glumly at the grinder, Daisuke sat mouth open, pen suspended.

'I'm just going outside for a while,' I said.

It was still raining slightly, hardly more than a mist. I remembered how I had felt so pleasurably sad beneath the gambling tree on the day of my sister's wedding. What I felt now was completely different. There was nothing pleasurable about it at all. I did not dwell on the fleeting nature of existence or grieve for a young life cut short too soon. I was angry at the stupidity of it, a drunken brawl over footwear, and nauseated by the messy process of dying. My robe was stained with blood – it would have to be thrown away. And I was angry at my own failure, disappointed with myself for not managing to save my patient. Why was the human body so frail? Why was it so easily slashed and broken open? I went over and over all we had done. What did we do wrong? What did we leave undone?

At the same time I couldn't help thinking of everything that needed to be dealt with, informing the Nakajima family, and the magistrate, arranging the funeral.

My family knew me well enough to leave me alone, but after a few moments Daisuke came bustling out with an umbrella.

'You will get wet, O-Tsuru-san. You have been through a terrible ordeal. You must take care of yourself.'

He placed himself beside me and raised the umbrella over both of us. If he had stopped there I would have taken his officiousness for kindness, but he made the mistake of going on. 'I was prepared to accede to the departed colleague in the matter of a matrimonial arrangement, but now that he has been so abruptly and ingloriously expunged from our plane of existence I hope that I may be considered in the way of possibly – not immediately, naturally – but with expedience and in the course of time...'

I finally realised what he was trying to say and my anger exploded. 'I could never marry you,' I cried. 'You are a fool. I despise you. You are a coward!'

I was shaking with rage. Wanting only to get away from him, I ran out into the road.

How green the world was beneath the rain! It was the time of day when travellers would arrive if they came from Hagi; from habit I gazed in that direction and saw a distant figure.

It's Shinsai. My heart leaped. It was only then that I remembered the letter from Monta. I would be able to give it to him myself. I began to walk towards him. But as we drew closer to each other I realised this man was taller than my uncle and had a different gait. I was trembling more and more and my eyes had clouded as if with tears. I blinked and shook my head to clear them, and as I recognised the man who worked at the Kuriya's, the man I called the Accountant, I saw with acute clarity that his skull was broken. It was as if I saw through a microscope; I saw the death that lay beneath his skin. My eyes dissected him, I saw the depression in the skull bone, the blood leaking into the brain…

There has been another accident, I thought, but as I continued to stare at him, the vision faded. Of course his skull was not broken; he was not even wounded. He was whole, and normal. I must still be in shock. My eyes took in every detail of his appearance. He wore a dark indigo-dyed robe with a small white arrow pattern, looped up around his waist for ease of walking. His legs were bare and he wore straw sandals. He had been travelling through the rain; his hair was soaked and his clothes dark with moisture. He carried a small chest which he took down from his shoulder as I approached.

We gazed at each other, and it was as if a hook flew from his soul into mine. I had no defences left. Grief, failure, exhaustion had left me completely vulnerable. I was like a character in an old tale, ripe for bewitchment. I probably would have fallen in love with a *tanuki* or a *tengu* if either one had crossed my path at that moment. But the gods sent me the Accountant.

I couldn't immediately see any reason for him to be here.

He probably couldn't understand why I was standing in the road, covered in blood, staring at him like a madwoman.

'What happened?' he said. He put his hand on my arm and slowly turned me. 'Is this where you live? Your sister described it to me, the Gambling Tree Place.' He spoke slowly and calmly as if he did indeed believe I had lost my senses. 'You remember me, don't you? Makino Keizō from Hagi.'

Mitsue! Of course, her baby was due. That must be why he was here. He had brought news from Hagi.

'Is my sister all right?'

'Yes, she had a boy, a week ago. The baby is healthy. They are both fine. But what's happened here?'

'There's been a death,' I said. 'One of my father's students was attacked.'

The gambling tree shuddered in a sudden breeze, showering us with huge drops as we passed beneath it. I called out at the door and my father came to the entrance. He looked diminished and old.

'Mitsue has had a boy,' I said. 'This is Mr Makino (*so that was his name*) from Hagi.'

My father seemed stunned by this alignment of birth and death, and quite incapable of dealing with a guest. He made a curious gesture as if he had forgotten what was expected of him.

'I am sorry I have come at such a bad time,' Makino said awkwardly. 'If I can help in any way I will stay; otherwise I'll go back to Yuda for the night.'

I insisted he should stay. The only clear emotion I had was that I must not let him go. I needed him by me. 'Come up,' I said. 'I'll bring water to wash your feet. And some tea...'

'I think we all need a drink,' Father said, and went off to fetch sake.

Profound emotion had made all my senses painfully acute, as though the dross of everyday life had been stripped away and the reality of our brief human existence exposed in all its exhilaration and futility. I had not been able to eat all day but now I was ravenously hungry and I drank large amounts of sake too. We all did. We had just finished eating when someone called outside. It was O-Kiyo; she had come from the Hanamatsutei accompanied by one of the servants who had brought Nakajima home.

'I suppose the poor young man is dead,' she said when she was inside. 'He looked practically gone even before they put him in the cart. I came to tell you the magistrate is going to investigate and he'll probably want to interrogate Tetsuya-san, and the other one…'

'Hayashi,' I said, looking around. 'But where is he?' I had assumed he was keeping out of my way since my outburst, but it turned out no one had seen him. When O-Kane went to look for him she came back shaking her head.

'He's gone.'

O-Kiyo made a dismissive gesture. 'Very wise in the circumstances. As I was saying, both he and you, Tetsuya-san, will be called tomorrow to give an account of what happened.' She held out her cup and Father refilled it. 'You should leave too. Go back to Nagasaki.'

'Shouldn't he cooperate with the authorities?' Mother said nervously.

'The samurai ran away; why shouldn't he?' O-Kiyo replied.

Tetsuya sighed. 'I fled the cholera only to land in a worse situation. But isn't it better for my father if I at least tell them what really happened?'

'I'll do that. I'll say the dead man was drunk, so were the rest. There was equal blame on both sides and no one else was involved. Don't worry, we'll fix it all up. The magistrate knows that we have some important connections at the Hanamatsutei. You have to go back to Nagasaki for the sake of your studies. It's what your father wants you to do and it's in the service of the domain. Your father's a friend of Lord Sufu, but it will be much easier to exploit that friendship if you're not around when they come looking for you.'

Tetsuya left before dawn to walk to Shimonoseki, avoiding the high road. Later that day Nakajima's father and older brothers came to take his body away. They apologised to Father for the trouble he had caused, getting himself killed in a street fight, and Father apologised to them for not preventing it. Then everyone spoke of the dead man's qualities, praising the good and deploring the bad, and the words, together with the sake we drank, and the flowers and incense, stitched death up so that it was no longer a terrifying rent in the fabric of our lives but something quite natural. My grief and rage softened into another feeling, closer to pleasurable sadness, mingled with an awareness of my own vitality and, I am ashamed to confess, relief that I was not going to marry either Nakajima or Hayashi.

Finally, when the body had been removed we could set about cleansing the house, and then we celebrated the birth of my parents' first grandchild.

The Accountant was there all the time. He seemed in no

hurry to return to the Kuriya's. He made himself useful; he mixed medicines, explained to the patients why the doctor could not see them immediately, helped Hachirō in the garden, and played board games with my father.

'I suppose you will go back to Hagi soon, Makino-san,' my mother said one evening. 'I hope you will be able to take some things for the baby.' We were all in the front room; my mother and I were sorting herbs and preparing them for drying, stripping the leaves from the stems. Father and the Accountant were playing *shōgi*. Makino was a much better player and usually gave my father a piece or two, at least the left incense chariot, sometimes even the angle mover or the flying chariot.

He did not answer for a moment; he stared at the board as though considering his next move. I watched him, as I had been since he arrived. I felt he was about to take a decision and make a request. I did not know much about him, and yet I felt I knew him through and through. I could see that he did not like asking for things. He was aware of his own intelligence, and proud.

'I wondered if I might stay here, with you, Dr Itasaki. The truth is, I've always wanted to study medicine – real medicine, that is. Now that you have lost your students, and your son is not here, it occurred to me that you might need my help. I do know a little about pharmacy – well, more than a little in fact.'

'It's out of the question!' Father looked astonished. 'You work for the Kuriya. What would they do without you?'

'I owe Mr Kuriya a great deal,' the Accountant said. 'But I have weighed it all up. My desire – my calling – to become a doctor is I think greater than my obligation to my employer.' He paused and then said, 'I should not boast, but I have added my abilities to the equation.'

He took one of the foot soldiers he had formerly captured from Father and dropped it into the game. Father regarded it warily.

Mother said, 'We cannot do anything that would offend our daughter's family, Makino-san. You must see that.'

'I am not really leaving their employment, simply extending it.' The Accountant dropped another piece onto the board, Father's flying chariot. 'I could sell their products here and in Yamaguchi. I am hard-working, I need very little sleep. I do not eat much and I don't drink.'

My father looked at the board and at his embattled king, now surrounded by Makino's pieces. Then he looked at me. 'Tsu-chan, what is your opinion?'

I was being asked to choose my husband. My nerve almost failed me. All the warnings I'd heard all my life against indulging daughters and letting them have their own way flashed through my mind. I wanted to tell my father I would do whatever he told me. I wanted him to take the responsibility. But then I looked at the Accountant's hands, his long fingers. I remembered the hook. I knew if I did not choose him now I would regret it for the rest of my life. I heard myself saying, 'I think Makino-san should stay.'

He smiled at me, and moved the right cassia horse. In its next move it would take the king.

'That appears to be checkmate,' Father said.

TRANSACTIONS

My father made conditions. No one spoke about marriage for a long time. It was simply to be an apprenticeship. It would be for a six-month trial and the Kuriya family had to agree. During the following weeks my gentle father suddenly turned strict and harsh. He set many tests for the Accountant and made near-impossible demands – maybe not the fireproof fur or the jewelled branch, but almost as difficult. He expected far more from his new student than he had from the others. They had been samurai, low rank admittedly, but the Accountant was not even that. His father had died when he was a child, his mother a few years later. He had been brought up by an uncle, a small-scale merchant, who had persuaded Mr Kuriya to give his nephew a chance. His whole life had depended on the goodwill of others: his uncle, Mr Kuriya and now my father.

He bore it all patiently, never complaining, always the first up in the morning and the last to go to bed at night. When he was not working he was studying. He devoured my father's books. He seemed hardly to sleep, and became even more gaunt, his eyes hollow and glittering.

He and I studied together; we had the same desire for knowledge and I tested him on the contents of the books. We spoke of nothing else during these sessions, and we were never alone. My father hovered around us, and when he could not avoid leaving home he made sure one or other of us went with him.

I continued to go out collecting herbs and other materials. The summer landscape grew daily more lush and fertile. The rice grains swelled and ripened, fruits turned red and orange. I awoke every morning with a sense of excitement and anticipation. I was in no hurry for it, yet I knew marriage awaited me.

When I showed the Accountant my harvest, told him the names and explained the properties, the plants took on an erotic significance. The rhizomes of *shiran*, the cattail heads I brushed pollen from, peach kernels and the gallnuts from the sumac tree all began to look like human organs, and when I explained their uses – *this reduces swelling and astringes the blood, this relieves blood stagnation, this controls seminal emissions* – my face and neck became suffused with my own warm blood.

The Accountant took the plants gently in his hands and listened to my explanations. He remembered everything, not only the herbs and their properties, the various teachings of *kanpō* and *ranpō*, the human anatomy and physiology, but also the names and case histories of all our patients.

We were busier than ever that summer. The general uncertainty of the times made people unwell. There were many complaints of disorders that were caused by anxiety: stomach pains, inability to sleep, irritability, and more babies than ever seemed to be suffering from *kan no mushi*.

The festivals of high summer came and we lit lanterns around the house for O-Bon. Sitting by the family graves in the warm night, not really alone, but a little apart from the rest of the family, the Accountant and I talked for the first time about Nakajima's death.

'It seems to have been fated,' I said. 'If he had not got into that fight I would probably be married to him by now.'

'And your father would not have taken me on as his student. He would have sent me straight back to the Kuriya's house.'

He put his hands together and bowed in a gesture of gratitude. I did the same. Poor Nakajima-san! I was sorry he was dead yet I could not feel sorry for the outcome.

As the year went by it became apparent that none of us could do without Makino. He began to carry the weight of the practice. He was better than Father at keeping track of administrative details; not only did the patients trust him but he presented the bills in such a way that none of them could avoid paying. Father actually began to make more money.

I could see it presented a dilemma to him, but he did not mention it until one evening in early winter he said casually to me, 'I've decided you should marry Makino-san.'

Even though I had more or less decided the same thing at the beginning of the summer, it took my breath away.

My father peered at me, mistaking my silence. 'You don't mind, do you? I think he will make a useful addition to our household and family, and now his reputation is growing I don't want anyone else to come along and snap him up.'

'Father, you know I'll do whatever you and my mother think is best,' I said dutifully. My heart was pounding and my insides melting.

Father looked at me closely and reached out to feel my pulse. He grunted as if his suspicions were confirmed but only said, 'Then I will speak to Makino-san and we will arrange the wedding. Your mother also thinks it is a good idea.'

He must have spoken to him that night for the next morning Makino (I was never able to think of him as anything but Makino or the Accountant, or to call him by his given name) seemed transformed. He could not stop smiling.

'Well, if I've achieved nothing else in my life I've made a young man happy,' Father said, when he came in to eat the midday meal. 'I believe he even made a joke or two today.'

'You've made me happy too,' I said quietly.

'I hope so.' The two of us were alone in the room. Father said, 'I want at least one of my children to be as content in marriage as your mother and I have been.' He sniffed loudly and turned his attention to his rice bowl. 'It was much harder than I thought, letting your sister go. I still worry about her, and wonder if we made the right choice.'

'Neechan is not unhappy,' I said. 'And now she has a son…'

Father nodded. If he had any doubts about the Kuriya family he was not going to voice them. He had written to Mr Kuriya asking him to allow Makino to become his student, and though the Kuriya family had eventually agreed (on condition that the contents of the Cure-All would never be divulged), relations between our two families had become rather cool. None of us had been to Hagi since the baby was born, and though Mitsue was planning a visit home – she still had not made the traditional first visit to her birth house – it kept being postponed for one reason or another, as though her parents-in-law were deliberately preventing it.

'I don't know how they will react to this news,' Father said.

'Don't expect their wholehearted approval.' I remembered Mrs Kuriya's surprise at my parents' decision to keep me at home and adopt a bridegroom. She hadn't expected that to be her husband's employee. The more I thought about it, the more unconventional the whole arrangement seemed to be. But I didn't want to say all this to Father in case he changed his mind.

'I don't expect their approval or even their understanding,' Father said. 'But I am thinking of the future. Our country needs young men of ability and intelligence. We must seek them out in every field and give them our active encouragement.'

That autumn a huge comet appeared in the skies, adding to the ferment of unrest. My father often went to the village headman Yoshitomi Tōbei's house to meet with men like himself, intellectuals, doctors, poets. They exchanged books, pamphlets, news and ideas, and talked about renewing the world. Throughout Chōshū in the last years of Ansei everyone discussed these things. Many people disapproved of Yoshida Shōin but they could not prevent his teachings from spreading, like pollen disseminated by the wind. And one of Shōin's most vital teachings was *Give opportunities to the talented*. No wonder the conservatives in Hagi opposed these teachings so strongly. They must have thought they were facing a revival of the rebellions of the Warring States period or an epidemic like cholera. So my father's decision to give Makino Keizō this opportunity was one small example of a trend that was spreading throughout the domain, indeed throughout the whole country.

'There is no point in delaying,' Father declared. Perhaps he didn't want to give anyone the chance to express their opposition and make him lose his nerve. I was grateful, for ever since the decision Makino and I had been struck by paralysing shyness. We could hardly exchange glances, let alone any sensible conversation. There were many things I wanted to ask him; at the front of my mind was whether he had had any experience with women. What if he had gone to the gesiha houses in Hagi? I knew wives were supposed to put up with that sort of thing, but the idea troubled me. I was jealous. And I knew too much about disease. But if I couldn't even ask him what he was reading, how could I broach matters of such intimacy?

My marriage was already unconventional – there was no betrothal transaction, the bridegroom had no family, I had nowhere to depart to but would stay in my parents' house – so my father decided to celebrate it shortly after New Year, and he announced his intention to throw a large party, almost as though he was defying our neighbours.

'Wouldn't it be wiser to have a quiet ceremony?' Mother suggested.

'And look as if we are ashamed? As if we couldn't find anyone better for Tsu-chan? No, we have to show the world that we believe in the future.'

Makino was quite calm about all the preparations; he was not arrogant or conceited but he knew his own worth. He believed he had made a fair transaction with my parents. I imagined he felt he had made a similar bargain with me, though we were quite unable to discuss that. But some secret communication was flowing between us. My angular body, which I had always treated so perfunctorily, seemed to soften and swell in response. For the first time I was concerned about my physical appearance. It was a cold winter and had already snowed several times. I worried about getting chilblains, not as in previous years because of the itching, but because I thought they would make my hands and feet look ugly. We made many trips to the bathhouse at the *onsen*, where Mother and O-Kane paid special attention to my hair and skin, scrubbing me with bags of rice bran or with volcanic stones, rinsing my hair in extracts of rose and witch hazel.

The other women there exclaimed, 'So O-Tsuru-san is to be married? To a man of genius, we hear.'

If they found it all very irregular they did not say so. No doubt there was plenty of gossip behind our backs. I could just imagine their tongues going, but people's opinions have never bothered me. I was obeying my parents, my bridegroom was a man who would bring great benefits to my father's medical practice. Let them say whatever they wanted: I did not care.

As soon as the decision about my marriage was made Father wrote to Mr Kuriya to let him know, and I wrote to both Mitsue and my uncle. I had shown the letter from Monta to my parents and they had decided it was harmless enough, and we had sent it on. But I had received no answer then, nor did I hear from my uncle now.

We did not get any response from the Kuriya family either, but on the day before the wedding, in the second week of the year, Shinsai arrived in the late afternoon with Mr Kuriya's son. It had been a cold bright day, sunny, but not warm enough to melt the snow which had fallen in the night. Father had said that morning that he did not think anyone would come from Hagi. Mother and I were in the kitchen. O-Kane had just gone to take the cloths off the drying poles. She heard their voices at the gate.

'Shinsai-san is here!' she called.

Mother dropped her knife and I dropped the pestle, and we hurried around the side veranda to greet them.

As Shinsai came through the gate the sun glinted off his wet clothes and for a moment I thought I saw them streaked with blood. His face was as pale as if he had been mortally wounded. I stepped forward with a muffled cry, my hand to my mouth. I saw with detailed clarity again, as though I was examining him from a great height, like an angel with a microscope. The flesh peeled back from wounds so deep I could see the bone laid bare. Then I realised the darkness was just moisture, his pallor exhaustion. Both travellers were wet and cold, and irritable after a long day in each other's company. I had a sudden picture of them struggling through the snow while arguing about Yoshida Shōin's ideas, Kuriya pulling Shinsai out of a snowdrift when he would probably rather bury him in it. Normally this would have made me laugh, but the earlier vision of blood had left me chilled.

Kuriya remembered his manners enough to greet Mother politely, assure her Mitsue and the baby were well, and deliver his parents' best wishes. Shinsai said nothing.

The household was already turned upside down by the preparations for the wedding, and several patients had appeared with bad coughs and colds. Father and Makino were fully occupied talking with them and making up medicine. I felt it was better for the visitors not to meet Makino yet and I tried to lead them round the side of the house, but snow had drifted up to the veranda, and anyway Shinsai pushed past me into the entrance hall and Kuriya followed.

Father was in the consulting area, behind a screen, and two patients were waiting for medicine which Makino was mixing at the workbench. He was frowning with concentration and he turned to see who was coming in with a resigned smile, as though he expected more patients. He froze for a moment staring at Kuriya.

'I suppose you're handing out our Cure-All,' Kuriya said loudly. 'You ungrateful scoundrel! After all my father did for you!'

'Kuriya-san.' Makino bowed politely, finished measuring the medicine into small boxes and said to me, 'O-Tsuru-san, would you wrap these for me, please?'

I went to his side, glad of the opportunity to stand next to him.

'I agreed not to pass on the secrets of the Kuriya Cure-All,' Makino said, 'and I have kept my word. Your father gave his permisison for me to study with Dr Itasaki…'

'But not to marry his daughter! And stay here forever! Study is one thing; marriage is quite another.' Kuriya slapped the workbench with his open hand, making the boxes and scales jump and tinkle.

Makino gave the medicine boxes to the two patients who were in no hurry to leave; in fact they were waiting eagerly to see what would happen next. 'Please come back in two days: you can pay Dr Itasaki then.'

Mother escorted them through the door, and at the same time Father emerged from behind the screen.

'I must have some peace! I cannot feel this man's pulse properly...' He broke off and said, 'Shinsai!'

My uncle did not even take the time to greet my father but immediately exclaimed, 'Oniisan, have you lost your senses? You can't seriously be thinking of marrying Tsu-chan to this...this...'

'This Cure-All thief,' Kuriya put in.

'This nobody! She's far too good for him. We could have found anyone for her – possibly even a samurai's son. Anyway, she's too young. What's the rush to marry her off?'

'I'm sorry, Shinsai,' Father replied. 'The arrangements have all been made. The wedding takes place tomorrow afternoon. I hope you will stay for it; we are all very happy to see you.'

Shinsai started to say something, but Father cut him off. 'Really the decision is nothing to do with you!'

'If I am concerned with our family's standing it is.'

'Yes, indeed,' Kuriya butted in. 'It is causing a scandal in Hagi. Our family is disgraced.'

'I hardly think so,' Father said sharply.

'But he has stolen the secret of the Cure-All.'

'Nonsense,' Makino said. 'The recipe is written out. It is in the middle drawer of my old desk. Anyway, how could I steal it when it's been handed down in the Kuriya family from generation to generation?'

'It doesn't work any more. People are complaining. They say it doesn't taste the same.'

'That is hardly my fault.'

Kuriya was silent, his frustration reflected on his plump face. He pushed out his lips like a child who'd been thwarted.

Makino said, in an attempt to sound conciliatory, 'All you

have to do is make it up correctly. I'm sure your wife can do it; she must have had the same excellent training as O-Tsuru-san.'

'Surely you haven't come all this way in the snow just to give me this unnecessary advice,' Father said, addressing Shinsai. 'What about your studies?'

'You haven't heard? Master Yoshida has been sent back to Noyama prison. The whole of Hagi is in an uproar about it. Without our teacher there are no studies and no school.'

'Anyone could have seen he had it coming to him,' Kuriya muttered.

Shinsai ignored this. 'His uncle, Tamaki Bunnoshin, has resigned in protest, and eight students have been arrested. I was told it would be wise to leave Hagi.'

'Does that mean you have come home to stay for a while?' Father said.

'I haven't decided yet,' Shinsai replied.

I was shocked by the news. Since Monta's letter I had hardly thought about what might be happening in Hagi, or Edo or Kyōto. I had been absorbed in my own feelings and distracted from everything else by the Accountant's presence in our household. Now my uncle had reawakened all my contradictory feelings about him. I was delighted to see him, but I was also angry with him for turning up at my wedding, for bringing such bad news, casting ill luck over my future and disturbing my happiness with visions of blood.

Mother took control of the situation, told Father's patient to come back in two days, sent the visitors off to the *onsen*, with Father to prevent them from drowning each other, took out dry clothes and extra bedding, instructed Hachirō to bring another brazier and O-Kane to prepare more food. She even found time to tell Makino not to worry. 'Shinsai-san has never remembered to think before he speaks. Don't take any notice of him.'

But like the rest of us she was eager to hear the details of his news. At the evening meal we all had many questions. Shinsai answered them briefly; he expressed his own anger and distress, pointed out that we were lucky he was not among those arrested, and then fell silent. It was an uncomfortable meal with many undercurrents of emotions, and when it was over we were all relieved when Kuriya said he was exhausted and would like to sleep. He went off to share Hachirō's room – Hachirō always went to bed early. Makino said he had work to finish, adding, 'I imagine none of us will work tomorrow!' in a way that let me glimpse his excitement and happiness.

O-Kane cleared away the dishes and brought tobacco and pipes, before going to bed, and the four of us sat with our legs under the *kotatsu* and smoked. The old familiarity between us began to reassert itself.

'I can talk more freely now,' Shinsai said. 'I don't trust Kuriya at all. He will repeat everything I say to his father, who has contacts among all the conservatives in Hagi. It could make things worse for everyone, especially our teacher.'

He described the background to the arrest. Since Lord Ii Naosuke of Hikone had been made Tairō, the Bakufu had imprisoned and executed many of its critics. Great lords like Matsudaira of Echizen, Tokugawa Nariaki of Mito and his son, Hitotsubashi Keiki, had been put under house arrest. These harsh measures had aroused fierce resistance, and a plot had been formed with *shishi* from Echizen and Mito to assassinate both Ii and the Bakufu representative in Kyōto, Manabe Akikatsu.

'Shōin-*sensei* believes it is time to act,' Shinsai said. 'But Genzui and Shinsaku are both against it. So is Katsura. They all say it is too soon.'

'Where is Genzui now?' Father said. He sounded anxious for his old friend's son, in whom he had always taken such an interest. 'Was he arrested?'

'No, he's in Kyōto. So is Itō, and another of Shōin's students, Yamagata – you know him, I think. Shinsaku has been in Edo since the fifth month and of course Katsura is there too, and Shiji Monta. None of them will take action. They are all trying to distance themselves from our teacher. It's pitiful.'

'Presumably they have a better idea of the risks involved,' Father said quietly. 'They are far more vulnerable outside the domain.'

'Sooner or later we are going to have to respond with violence,' Shinsai said.

'Respond to what?' Mother's voice was irritated. 'Really, Shinsai-san, no one is threatening you.'

'Maybe not yet,' Shinsai replied. 'But they soon will be. And I'm ready to act. Many of us are. They cannot treat the greatest man in Chōshū like this.'

I found it hard to sleep that night. I probably would not have slept anyway, kept awake by anticipation and by the realisation that this was my last night as an unmarried girl. But now I was also worrying about Master Yoshida in Noyama.

How would that frail body stand the poor food, the lack of light and exercise, the loss of companionship? Last time Shōin-*sensei* had been able to turn his confinement to good use, keeping up his studies and teaching. But would he be able to summon up the energy and determination to do so again? Or would anxiety and fatigue reduce him to despair as they did everyone? I was afraid he would die in prison. How terrible his family must be feeling at the moment – and O-Fumi did not even have her husband to console her. I lay next to my mother. Both my parents had fallen asleep, and I listened to their gentle breathing. At least I was not leaving them the next day. A little comforted by this thought I finally fell asleep.

I woke to the sound of loud voices. Mother had placed my shell box next to the pillow and I gazed at it for a few moments. It was probably the most valuable thing I owned and it had been brought into our family by one of my great-grandmothers. Mitsue had a similar one which she had taken with her to Hagi. I was glad this one would stay here; it was so beautiful, eight-sided, black-lacquered, with gold paintings of cranes, irises, susuki grass and butterflies. Inside were pairs of shells with poems written in tiny letters for the poem-matching game.

Kuriya was trying once more to persuade my bridegroom to return to Hagi, without me but with his secret knowledge of the Cure-All. I could hear my mother's attempts to calm him down, while my father refused more and more angrily to let Makino go.

It was a *senbu* day – bad luck before midday, good luck in the afternoon. I was not usually superstitious but I was suddenly afraid that this quarrel would be a bad omen. I wanted Kuriya to leave and take all the ill luck with him. I nearly cried, looking at the shell box, wishing my sister was here with me, not far away in Hagi and above all not married to him.

The argument came to an abrupt end. Shortly afterwards my mother entered the room and knelt beside me. She was brushing tears away from her eyes with her sleeve. I took her hand and we sat for a few moments without speaking.

'He's gone,' Mother said finally.

'I suppose we should be insulted.'

'I'm more relieved, to be honest. I really didn't want him here scowling and muttering all day. But I hope this isn't going to cause bad feeling between our families, for your sister's sake.'

'Is that why you were crying?'

'That, and everything else. Master Yoshida, your uncle, you getting married…'

I wanted her to be happy on my wedding day. 'Cheer up,' I said. 'Makino-san and I will invent another Cure-All, one that really works. It will make us all rich.'

THE SECOND WEDDING

Whatever gossip there might have been, it did not prevent anyone from attending the party my father gave for my wedding. The guests began arriving after midday. Palanquins and horses were left under the gambling tree, while porters and grooms gathered under the eaves. It was snowing lightly and Hachirō lit torches at the gate and fires in the garden. The flames glowed brilliantly in the grey winter light, and the snowflakes hissed as they melted in them. O-Kiyo and a host of geisha came from the Hanamatsutei, with all the customary gifts, and more. Since I had not had a formal betrothal they brought presents for that too, white face powder and safflower lip colouring, little fragrant bags to stitch into my robes, and various amulets from different shrines, some as far away as Kyōto, to ensure a happy relationship with my husband and my own fertility.

O-Kiyo had already given me a red and white kimono which I would change into later, and she had been helping us for days, cleaning the house inside and out and preparing food. Other guests brought celebratory offerings: the bulging-eye bream or *tai* (whose name stands for *omedetai*: felicitations), kelp, dried bonito and cuttlefish, and many straw-wrapped casks of sake.

Father had presented Makino with new formal robes for

the occasion: *hakama*, kimono and *haori*. I was still too shy to look at my bridegroom directly, but in my quick side-long glances I thought he was really quite handsome.

I was wearing a white kimono for daughters are dressed like the dead, to symbolise their departure from their birth family.

'But I am not leaving you,' I said to Mother as she dressed me. 'I should not have to wear white.'

Yet we all knew that marriage is a kind of death: the end of girlhood.

Most of the guests were crammed into our main room and had already started drinking toasts and talking loudly when we heard the sound of horses outside. Everyone fell silent as my father rushed to welcome the headman, Yoshitomi Tōbei, and his companion, obviously a man of some importance, whom I did not immediately recognise.

'It is Lord Sufu,' O-Kiyo whispered in my ear. 'What an honour to you and your husband. But fancy him riding on a day like today!'

I glanced at Makino and saw he had gone even paler with excitement. Both he and I lowered our heads to the floor as Lord Sufu Masanosuke was shown to the place of honour before the alcove. Here Father had hung his most prized painting, a work by Tanomura Chikuden called *Fragrant Plum Blossoms, Unknown Shadow*, which he had been given years before when he was working in Kyūshū.

Lord Sufu gave the painting his full attention for a few moments, and then nodded in approval. After accepting a bowl of sake and drinking deeply he said, 'A most beautiful painting. And very appropriate, for your plum blossom is indeed in the shadow of an unknown future.' He held out his bowl for O-Kiyo to fill (she of course knew him well from the Hanamatsutei), and drank again, then said as if to himself, 'As are we all.'

I kept my eyes lowered, but I tried to study him without seeming to. I was tired and a little dizzy. As he raised the bowl again and swallowed I saw his throat was cut. My eyes had taken on the microscopic clarity that had come on me before. I almost cried out. It was an ominous vision to have on the day of my wedding. Then Lord Sufu laughed at something Yoshitomi said, and the blood faded. I was looking at a man who might not be in complete health, but was certainly not dying. I tried to calm myself by diagnosing him.

I knew he was less than forty years old yet he had become one of the most powerful men in the domain government. Years before he had formed a study group called the Aumeisha (the warbling-birds society) with fellow students at the Meirinkan, the domain school. This group had had a strong influence on the government and maintained close ties with Yoshida Shōin's students. Sufu believed in reform and in encouraging young men of ability over their incompetent seniors, which made him unpopular among the more conservative high-ranking samurai. Sufu himself was of medium rank.

He drank a great deal and I thought his digestion was probably very poor. Beneath his confident manner and his self-control I suspected he had a nervous disposition, and might be subject to bouts of depression which would only be made worse by alcohol. I could see he was a complicated man, troubled by many conflicts within him.

After O-Kiyo had filled his bowl two or three more times she said, 'Lord Sufu is able to take a short holiday. It is a good idea after all the hard work of the past year.'

Sufu turned his eyes to the painting again. 'It is truly a masterpiece,' he said quietly. Then he emptied his bowl one more time and replied to O-Kiyo, 'I needed to retire for a while. I have not been well, nothing serious, and...let's just say things are a little tricky in Hagi.'

I felt he was on the verge of saying more, that it would only take another bowl of sake to push him over the edge of caution and into recklessness.

I glanced at Shinsai and I noticed my father doing the same. My uncle was gazing at Lord Sufu like a man who had just encountered a snake. He did not take his eyes off him, as he also poured bowl after bowl of sake down his own throat. I knew sooner or later he was going to bring up the subject of Yoshida's imprisonment.

My father was signalling to my mother with his eyes, to move on with the proceedings before Shinsai opened his mouth.

Normally the wedding ceremony takes place in two parts, the farewells to the bride at her parents' home, and her welcome into the new family at the bridegroom's house. Since I was not going anywhere, Mother and O-Kiyo had come up with an alternative plan. Our family house would be both the bride's and the groom's, and we would make a symbolic journey from one space to another. Now they led me into one of the side rooms – the one that would be my bridal chamber – where I changed from the all-white kimono into the red and white one from O-Kiyo. Wearing a white bride's headdress I stepped into high wooden *geta* and, clasping my shell box in my arms, went out into the snow. It was falling more heavily now and O-Kane came with me, holding a red umbrella over my head.

At the same time my father and the other men, shouting and singing and beating drums, were sending Makino off through the front door.

Our paths crossed in the garden. We stood and gazed at each other, the torches flaring in the fading light, the snow falling around us. It patterned Makino's bare head and dark clothes. For a moment we alone existed there; the music, the shouts faded away and time itself seemed to dissolve like the snowflakes in the torch flames. I felt the great mystery of the union between men and women. We were about to take part in it as our parents had, and their parents, and our ancestors all the way back to Izanami and Izanagi, and as our children would, and their children.

O-Kane hurried me on, and Makino and I entered the house separately. The boxes and chests that symbolised my dowry were placed carefully in the corners of the room, and Makino and I sat side by side opposite the alcove. Now it was our turn to drink, the ritual three sips from three cups exchanged between us to symbolise that we had undertaken to be married and bound ourselves to all that marriage entails. My hands were quite steady, but I saw that Makino's trembled.

O-Kiyo had brought folded paper butterflies to decorate the flasks of sake and designate which was the male vessel and which the female. Makino drank from the female and I from the male while the butterflies lay before us, the female facing up and the male down. Makino drank first and I followed, for if a woman drinks first it is like Izanami speaking before Izanagi, an error which resulted in the birth of the leech child.

Then the sake really began to flow. Makino never cared for alcohol and tried to drink as little as possible but by the time the trays of food for the feast were served his face was as flushed as anyone's.

I could hardly eat. Excitement and drinking had made my stomach contract. The babble of conversation rose around me. I heard Lord Sufu talking loudly, and then Shinsai's voice broke into a sudden lull.

'Perhaps Lord Sufu could explain to us his reasons for the recent actions taken against Yoshida-*sensei*.'

'This is hardly the time,' Father began nervously, but Sufu himself interrupted him.

'I will explain! Gladly! I am trying to protect Shōin from himself. Better to be in Hagi in Noyama than in Edo in Denmachō. That will be where he ends up if he continues his criticism of the Bakufu.'

'You have done a terrible thing,' Shinsai said, the sake giving him the courage to address Sufu directly.

'I have saved his life,' Sufu retorted. 'I know you are one of his students. I admire the loyalty you all show to your teacher. But neither he nor you can be allowed to interfere in the politics of the domain at this crucial time.' He leaned forward and spoke confidentially. 'Chōshū and the House of Mōri must play a greater role in our country's affairs. Both the Court and the Bakufu can benefit from our good services. My colleague Lord Nagai Uta is toiling behind the scenes to act as a mediator, with the full support of myself and my faction.'

Sufu drank another cup of sake and said, wiping his mouth, 'That's why I had to get away from Hagi. I am recovering from a sudden illness by the way, if anyone needs an explanation. Delicate negotiations are going on, and Shōin starts plotting assassinations! He sends his students to Kyōto as spies and talks of raising an army to fight Edo. Ii Naosuke is not a man to provoke. We do not want to see our lords, our *daimyō* and his heir, under house arrest, or worse, because of Shōin's recklessness.'

'We will have to confront the Bakufu sooner or later,' Shinsai exclaimed.

'For your brother's sake I will pretend I did not hear that,' Sufu replied. 'Our domain policy is as it always has been, *Faith in the Tokugawa*. I will keep your teacher in Noyama as long as I can. Everyone knows what a high regard I have for him. But I will tell you this: if Lord Ii demands he be sent to Edo, Nagai will agree and then there will be nothing I can do. Shōin should have kept quiet this year and behaved with discretion. Instead he's gone out of his way to provoke the authorities and alarm Bakufu officials.'

Yoshitomi said, 'He is mad – inspired, and brilliant, but not like normal people.'

'None of us can be normal in these times,' Shinsai replied. 'Just as everyone gets drunk at weddings, so we must all now be madmen.'

He himself was really very drunk, but before the argument could go any further one of the geisha proposed some music and brought out her *shamisen*. She sang a popular song that everyone knew, and Lord Sufu put politics aside to sing the chorus with her. Then a young man who had just come back from Ōsaka gave us some speeches from kabuki plays, *The Subscription List* and *Ghost Stories of Yotsuya,* in the style of Nakamura Tomijūrō.

When he had finished, Lord Sufu got unsteadily to his feet announcing that he must leave. He departed escorted by most of the geisha, who accompanied his palanquin to the Hanamatsutei. The groom had to follow leading his horse. It was a common occurrence. Lord Sufu loved riding but was often too drunk to ride home.

The rest of the guests accompanied Makino and me to the bridal chamber, which was all of three paces, and there everyone drank more sake, made jokes and laughed, while Mother untied my sash, leaving the garment loose. Finally they stepped out of the room, Father closed the *shōji* and we were left alone.

It was dark by now. New bedding had been put out for us and lamps burned with fragrant oil. I could hear Father's voice as he called goodnight to the departing guests. I slipped out of the heavy kimono and lay down, pulling the quilt over me. The futon had been laid out so my head was to the north; normally only the dead lie like this and I had the feeling that I had in fact died. I was as cold as a corpse. I lay on my back like the female butterfly. Although butterflies usually flit around playfully and that was the last thing I felt like. There was no way I could escape. Since my birth as a girl this was what had been preordained for me. I was a woman, I would be married, a man would put himself into my body, into the clam-shaped cleft that was designed for him, and I would bring his children into the world.

Makino pulled back the covers and slid in next to me. He was as cold as I was; he was trembling and his breathing was uneven. We lay side by side for a while; then he turned and pulled me closer, pushing my underrobe back, and putting one leg between mine. Slowly we both grew warmer and I could feel the movement in him as he became aroused.

Neither of us said anything – we were too shy to speak to each other, yet our bodies, wiser than we were, seemed to know what they were supposed to do. I could feel myself softening and opening as if I longed to take my husband inside me. I reached out and touched him, astonished at how much it delighted me. He moaned with pleasure, making me want to moan in response, but I remembered the flimsy doors and flushed at what I was doing within earshot of my parents and my uncle. I tried not to make a sound but Makino brushed his mouth against my nipple. Pleasure flooded through me and I could not keep myself from crying out.

From outside came a huge crash like thunder. We pulled apart – it is considered terribly unlucky to have sexual intercourse during a thunderstorm – and then I remembered it was mid-winter and snowing. My next thought was that we were being attacked by the local *wakamonogumi*, that the young men of the village disapproved of my wedding. The crash came again, reverberating around the garden. I realised someone was beating a drum outside. Then they shouted, 'Fire! Fire!'

I recognised Shinsai's voice and heard running feet, and Hachirō call, 'Where's the fire?'

Makino was about to get up but I pulled him back to me. 'There's no fire. It's just my uncle being stupid.'

And I'd thought his time with Yoshida had taught him something! Self-discipline, for example. Drunken idiot!

'I should go out and thump him,' Makino said, surprising me with his belligerence. It made me all the more determined that Shinsai should not spoil our wedding night.

Afterwards we slept for a while and when we woke we looked at each other with a kind of surprise.

'I didn't know…' I tried to explain.

'You are…' he began, and then we gave up and let our bodies talk for us all over again.

It was weeks before we had any kind of conversation. We spent the days tormented by hunger for each other. We continued to work together, we saw patients, mixed medicines, discussed diagnoses and treatments, but underlying all our rational behaviour was impatience to return to our room and our marriage futon.

My uncle left soon after the wedding. He said he would go back to Hagi to stand by Yoshida Shōin, visit him in prison and so on. In many ways it was easier for him, not being of samurai status. As he said, he had less to lose.

It was a relief. I knew he was distressed by his teacher's arrest, and by my marriage, but I did not spare him any sympathy. He and Makino circled each other the whole time like dogs looking for a fight. Now I was married I understood my own feelings more. I had been a little bit in love with my uncle, and he with me. I suppose it was inevitable: we had grown up together, we were so close in age and so similar. But it was better for everyone if he was not around.

If I had known how long it would be before I saw him again I would not have said goodbye so lightly.

When spring came and the snow melted I began to go outside again to collect fresh leaves, buds and tubers.

'You need to show me where these things grow,' Makino said, so he came with me. We lay down together in the woods beneath the chestnut trees while the world burst into life around us and the birds called endlessly, driven by the same desire to mate and reproduce.

'You know, there was a secret ingredient to the Cure-All,' Makino confessed to me one afternoon. 'I added something which was not written down. It gave the powder a particular flavour, very subtle. It doesn't make any difference to its effectiveness. People aren't even aware of the taste, but if it's not there they miss it.'

'Why did you do that? Did you know you would leave the Kuriya one day?'

'I didn't think they valued me,' Makino said in his straightforward manner. 'I considered I was getting something of a poor deal, so I tried to balance the account.'

I was silent. I saw the extent of his calculations: how he fashioned his life. It did not shock me; in a way I approved of it. I knew he was ambitious and that he weighed up everything. I wondered where his ambition would take him – and me, now our lives were bound together.

In the fifth month of that year, the sixth of Ansei or 1859, Yoshida Shōin was sent to Edō as Lord Sufu had feared. My father heard the news from one of his patients, and came to tell me. I was not feeling well that day: my monthly bleeding had started, I had bad cramps in my uterus, and a heaviness in my spirits. It seemed curious that I had not conceived after all our activity, and I was still at the stage where I was disappointed. Later I would be relieved. I told myself it was because I did not want to bring children into such an uncertain world, but the truth was I did not want to be a mother. I wanted to be a doctor. I had recognised my husband's ambition, but really my own was as fierce: to understand disease and injuries, to cure and make whole.

I was tidying up some of my old things – I suppose I was thinking about children without realising it, and when my father came into the room I was holding the little feather fan that my mother had told me was like Asanoshin's. It brought back bittersweet memories of childhood when I truly believed it would show me faraway places and distant events. I brushed my upper lip with the feathers and was ten years old again.

I saw the teacher, his frail body trussed up in a bamboo cage, carried on poles, setting out on his last journey to Edo. I saw the Weeping Pine where his family gathered for a last glimpse of him. The porters showed more compassion than Lord Nagai, and allowed him to speak a few words of farewell. O-Fumi was there, and her mother and uncle, their faces pale with grief and despair, and I saw those students who had not forsaken him, holding each other after he had gone and weeping.

I did not see Shinsai among them. Since he left in the first month we had heard nothing of him; we had no idea where he was.

TAKASUGI SHINSAKU

Ansei 6 (1859), Autumn, Age 20

Shinsaku longed to be in Edo again but now he is here he hates everything about it. The domain mansion where he is staying, the 'upper mansion', so called because it is closest to Edo castle, is overcrowded and noisy. He hates Edo castle with an intensity that surprises him: the weighty symbol of Tokugawa power with its interminable ceremonies, its huge consignment of officials, retainers, concubines and servants, its arrogant luxuries and its obsessive secrecies. Just the sight of its long blank walls and its guard towers fills him with rage. This rage spills over into the Bakufu academy where he is supposed to be studying (as his teachers keep reminding him, it is a great honour to be accepted). It is so old-fashioned it would be laughable, if it were not for the excruciating tedium. His fellow students strike him as shallow and immature, interested mainly in finding their way to the geisha houses or in bragging contests with young men from the other domains whose mansions surround Edo castle.

Occasionally these verbal confrontations turn into brawls and then the participants, men who are hardly more than boys, are ordered to commit *seppuku* in punishment. Their pointless deaths fill Shinsaku with horror and lead him to wonder again if he is not essentially a coward. In the sword-fighting academies the teaching is all about not clinging to life, being ready to die at any moment, facing death with careless composure. But the teachers themselves have all reached middle age without throwing their lives away, and Shinsaku is determined he is not going to die before he has achieved anything or through some miscalculation or mistake. Yet avoiding death in this way is a kind of cowardice. He does not talk about this to anyone though he has questioned his teacher in an oblique way.

But this is the worst thing about Edo, the true source of his anger and despair: Yoshida Shōin is imprisoned here in Denmachō.

The marvellous days at the Village School under the Pines, the revered teacher, the attentive students, seem now like a distant dream. As Shōin grew more extreme his students became more cautious. One by one they fell away. Shinsaku cannot forgive himself for being among them, yet what else could he do? Ordered by his father and the domain to go to Edo he had to obey. He did not know his teacher would follow him there, bound and caged.

Now he visits him, when he can, taking food, books and writing materials. When Shōin was in Noyama prison in Hagi he became famous for continuing his teaching, organising the other prisoners into reading and study groups, discovering experts among them who could lecture on Chinese poetry or astronomy, but now the deprivations of his life and the inevitability of early death have drained him of all energy. A listlessness has come over him, almost a depression, though he still treats Shinsaku with his old warmth and affection. He rouses himself to talk with enthusiasm about a new insight into some teaching of Mencius, and then they will hear the evening bell from the nearby temple of Ekōin. Shōin falls silent and then says wistfully, 'It has the same note as Tōkōji.' They are both transported to Hagi, both riven by longing for their birthplace, and Shōin, in his weakened state, cannot prevent tears of homesickness.

There are many subjects that cannot be discussed, chiefly the new Tairō, now the most powerful figure in the Bakufu government, Ii Naosuke, *daimyō* of Hikone. The effects of Ii's crackdown on all opposition can be seen throughout Edo and especially in Denmachō where prisoners are interrogated and executed and in Ekōin where they are buried.

Denmachō is a terrible place yet even here the other prisoners, their headman and the jailers show compassion. Shōin has been given his own few square feet of space on the tatami just below where the headman sits. The others address him as *sensei* and seek his advice on how to reform their lives, if they should seek revenge on the informant who landed them here, whether Ebisu or Benten is the more effective at answering prayers. Everyone from the guards to his fellow prisoners knows that Shōin should not be in Denmachō, and everyone knows he is not going to get out alive.

Shinsaku is not sorry to be alone in his visits. Genzui and other former students have been ordered back to Hagi, no doubt to keep them from making some futile protest that could only end in their own deaths. Shinsaku has asked no one's permission; he is sure no such permission would be given, but Chōshū officials, like those of all domains, know when to turn the blind eye. He probably has the sympathy of most of them. So he continues to walk quite openly every few days from Sakurada to Denmachō with his offerings of paper and books, buying rice cakes or dumplings on the way, gathering snippets of things he sees and hears, what he is studying, news from Hagi, all of which he lays at his teacher's feet.

It cannot continue. Early in the tenth month Katsura Kogorō, who holds a senior position in the Sakurada mansion, comes to his room with a letter from Shinsaku's father. Katsura sits himself down with the air of intending to have a serious talk while Shinsaku reads his father's command to return home.

'I am ordered back to Hagi.'

'Yes, you must go. You have drawn too much attention to yourself. You are in danger of being arrested and we cannot afford to lose you.' Katsura says this in his usual charming way. It is impossible not to like him. He is a few years older than Shinsaku and like most of the young Chōshū men studying in Edo Shinsaku regards him as an older brother.

'We will arrange a passage to Ōsaka.'

'I must go one more time to say goodbye.'

Katsura nods. 'Afterwards I will take care of everything, I promise you.'

Everything? They both know the only promise Katsura will be able to keep is to take care of the burial.

YOSHIDA SHŌIN

Ansei 6 (1859), Autumn, Age 29

Yoshida sits up all night. It is the last one of his life and it seems pointless to sleep. He has been moved from the main prison to a single cell and the jailer has given him an old futon and a bucket, and before he left him for the night, a cup of lukewarm barley tea. Yoshida is touched by these acts of kindness. He does not need the bucket. It's as though his body knows it is going to die and is already withdrawing from its usual functions, the acts of digestion and excretion that have sustained it for its twenty-nine years of activity. Now it can hardly be bothered to draw breath – maybe he will simply stop breathing in the night, but that is not really what he wants. He wants them to execute him, for that way his death will have the greatest effect. He has to die by the sword.

He misses the companionship of his fellow prisoners. It is curious that he has always felt at home in prison. There is truth in prison; it is a concrete expression of the state of the whole country under Tokugawa rule. In other countries people are free to travel overseas, free to go to universities and study whatever they want, free to believe what they want and raise their children how they like. All this he has gleaned from books he has read and conversations he has had in his travels around the country. He remembers the Dutch sailors he met in Nagasaki, the way they welcomed him and showed him around their ship, making themselves understood in sign language, their eagerness to engage with him and give him information. Even the Americans who had refused to take him back with them to their fabled republic, how direct and forthright they had been. Their ship so powerful, themselves so confident! He even admired the decisive way they had dispatched him to the Bakufu guards for his first stay in prison.

His whole life seems to have been directed by this impulse, to break out, to escape. Growing up in the mountain village overlooking Hagi, seeing every morning that incomparable view across the sea, feeling the winds that blew from the mainland so close he could smell it, must have taught him to face, not towards Edo, the centre of Bakufu power, but outwards, away, towards the West and the rest of the world.

As soon as he was born his future was laid out for him. The second son of the Sugi family was always adopted by the Yoshida, hereditary teachers of the Yamagaryū school of martial arts. This enabled the two families to survive side by side in the stringent economic circumstances of the times. The Sugi were of high rank and held important positions in the domain bureaucracy yet their stipend could only support one marriage with descendants in each generation. The Yoshida adopted children but had none of their own.

He thinks about this now, recalling the moment when it had dawned on him. How old had he been? Maybe no more than eight or nine, already considered something of a genius, his life a seamless routine of discipline and study. He came to visit his birth family, greeted his older brother and sisters, realised they treated him with a formal deference that excluded him from their circle. They were growing up within a family; he was not; moreover he would never have children of his own.

He feels the pang still but chides himself. It is better not to have children; they will be spared the disgrace of their father's execution. In the harsh manner of the times they might have been sentenced to share his punishment. How much more painful that would be.

He loves his family deeply. They have been like a great ship to him, and his main regret is the grief his death will bring to them. Parents should not outlive their children. How will his mother bear it? How did it come to this? Why did he not simply follow the path laid out for him, teach the way of Yamaga and eventually adopt one of his brother's sons? He could have accepted the restrictions that hemmed him in, but instead he chose to break away, and here is where it has led him – to this final imprisonment from which only the sword will release him.

He has never feared death. From a young age he recognised that fear is one of the tools used by the powerful to control the weak. Cruel and flamboyant punishments are used in a deliberate way to demonstrate power and intimidate the people. But he has noticed from his study of history that this policy has a tendency to recoil: the punished and the executed live on. Their heroic lives and pitiful deaths are immortalised in legends and dramas, beads on a long necklet of subversion that can never be quite suppressed. He can only hope his death will become this sort of victory.

For three weeks he has had no visitors, since the distressing farewell to Shinsaku the same week Hashimoto Sanai from Fukui was executed. It was Sanai's death that made him realise his own was inevitable. Sanai was an educator, guilty of nothing more than demanding reform, whereas he, Yoshida, had been actively conspiring to assassinate a Bakufu official.

Sanai the rational, himself the irrational: they have both come to the same end. The thought makes him smile wryly. When corrupt governments do not respond to reasonable demands they have to be confronted with sudden acts of violence. They have to be provoked, if not into listening then into some, any, response. If all they can do is suppress and execute, that proves the poverty of their thinking, the weakness of their mandate. He believes this fervently and he has taught it to his students. Many of them have drifted away from him, not prepared to confront the double power of the domain government and the Bakufu, but he believes they will remember his teaching when the time comes.

He thinks of them now, his students whom he has loved so much. They would be like children to him were it not for the fact that he is barely ten years older than most of them. He recalls the almost physical pleasure he gets from their quick intelligence and receptiveness, from the strength of the bond between teacher and pupil, from the warmth of their admiration and affection for him. He dwells on the heady days at the Village School under the Pines, when every day more students begged to be allowed to join, the very atmosphere becoming rarefied as if they had all moved onto a higher plane where they needed no sustenance other than ideas in all their purity. He sees again the idealism and enthusiasm of his students; their faces flash before his eyes: the Irie brothers, Maebara, Itō, Yamagata, Genzui. He knows them all so well, knows their great talents and their minor weaknesses. He says farewell to each of them, entrusting the future to them.

Finally he comes to Shinsaku. Now he can admit, though he has always assiduously avoided having favourites, that Shinsaku has meant more to him than any of them. He remembers with perfect clarity the night Shinsaku came to the house, the pleasure it gave him at making such a catch when he had not even been fishing, as though a golden carp had leaped from a deep pool to land in his lap; Shinsaku, so intelligent, so gifted, complex in his thinking yet possessing the clarity of emotion of a poet. He can recall every word of their letters. They have had their differences, have argued and debated, at one time were almost estranged, but in the end Shinsaku came back to him. When it really mattered, when there was no one else, Shinsaku came back.

It is the darkest time of night. The prison around him is completely still. Sometimes the inmates cry out or curse, whether awake or dreaming it is not clear, but tonight they are silent. In the blackness he comes close to the chasm that is despair. He could plunge into it now; it will make no difference, no one will know. For a moment he feels his chest contract as though he will start sobbing. An aching sadness that it is all over floods through him. But his body is as dry as an autumn leaf, it is not going to create moisture and longing and regret now. It refuses to sob, it will not even shed a tear.

He realises there is nothing he has to do. His death awaits him. He will be escorted to it. He will not lose his way or wear the wrong clothes or use an inappropriate salutation. He will not forget his words or stumble. The fierce self-control that has driven him since childhood is loosening its grip. He is as withered as a dead tree and as peaceful.

When they come for him he greets them calmly. He reassures the executioner and thanks him for the service he is rendering. He sees the pit into which his head will fall and admires its efficient design. It is cold and his limbs tremble a little as he kneels but it doesn't matter, it is just the chill air of early morning. He is truly not afraid. His heart fills with gratitude, for the morning air, for the lack of fear, for the decisive finality of this moment. This moment. He feels the rush of air like a bird's wing, sees the kites that swoop around Matsumoto, hears their poignant mewing, and laughs at his own foolishness as he realises it is the sword descending.

LORD SUFU'S SUGGESTION

The New Year after Shōin's death was a *kōshin* year, an extraordinary year in the sexeganary cycle. It was the only year when women were allowed to climb Mount Fuji for example, and there were other manifestations of changes in the social order. Some of our neighbours went from Yuda to Ise on pilgrimage, and they came back with tales of amulets falling from the sky, visions of bodhisattvas, men and women changing clothes, putting on fancy dress and acting in strange ways while they were on the road. Mother and I promised each other we would one day go to Ise together.

'Then we shall have something to talk about over the tea cups!' Mother said, quoting from the popular novel *Shanks's Mare*.

We did not really practice the form of health care known as *kōshinmachi* – my father dismissed the belief – but our maid O-Kane had been a believer as a child and when we were younger Mitsue and I used to sit up all night with her on the day of the monkey. You had to stay awake until dawn for if you slept that night the three worms that lived inside you would escape and report your misdeeds to Taishakuten who would then punish you with some illness. O-Kane said she owed it to the doctor to keep herself healthy, otherwise she would be a poor example to his patients. It was exciting being up all night and listening to the women's stories about what happened if you ate the wrong foods or had sex on a *kōshin* night. You would almost certainly give birth to a child who would grow up to be a criminal. And even though I knew there was no real foundation for these sorts of beliefs, our patients' health was affected by them, so we had to take them into account.

The Great Comet and the cholera epidemic of the fifth year of Ansei (1858) had been seen by many as signs of the gods' anger at the presence of foreigners in our land. Nevertheless the following year Yokohama was opened as a trading port, and despite murderous attacks, the foreigners did not seem to be discouraged, but arrived in ever-increasing numbers.

After Yoshida Shōin's death Chōshū samurai were forbidden to take revenge. But the domain of Mito lay much closer to Edo, and Mito samurai also wanted revenge on Lord Ii, for the execution and imprisonment of many of their clan in the same Great Purge of Ansei, the *Ansei Taigoku*, which had claimed Yoshida's life. In that strange *kōshin* year of the seventh year of Ansei (1860), in the third month a group of Mito samurai, who had left their domain and declared themselves *rōnin*, lay in wait outside the Sakurada Gate of Edo castle, attacked Lord Ii's palanquin and killed the hated Tairō.

The era name was changed to Man'en, but no better luck came of it, and with the next New Year it was changed again to Bunkyū. My sister now had two boys; the two pregnancies so close together had prevented her from coming home, and the second birth had been, unusually, more difficult than the first. Makino and I had been married for two years and still had no children.

Our married life had settled down. Makino no longer came with me to collect herbs, and at night we were usually too tired after the long day of work and study to spend the hours of darkness making love till the cocks crowed. My inability to conceive gave a kind of doubt to our marriage: what was it for if not to produce children? For the same reason Makino's position in our household was also uncertain. Father at one time had intended to adopt him and make him his heir, leaving the practice in his and my hands. But we still did not know if Tetsuya would stay in Nagasaki or not, and though my father did not discuss it I knew he was reluctant to do anything until Tetsuya made up his mind or I produced a child.

In the end he did not have to make a decision for events overtook us. I knew my husband was ambitious – it was ambition that had made him seek out my father and marry me. During that first year of Bunkyū it became apparent that Makino was not going to be content to remain a country doctor in Yuda; my father was beginning to say there was nothing more he could teach him. I had thought I would stay in my parents' home forever, but by the end of the year my husband and I were living in Shimonoseki, or Bakan, as everyone called it in those days.

It came about through Lord Sufu. In the years since my wedding he had become even more powerful, and had been pursuing his plan of greater participation in national politics, with the result that Chōshū was emerging as the key mediator between the Emperor and his Court in Kyōto and the Bakufu in Edo. Sufu liked to keep everything under his own control and he was always on the road between Hagi, Yamaguchi, Kyōto and Edo. He was not an extremist by nature, but as the young samurai who were his favourites became more radical he did not lose sympathy with them. He shared their idealism, and became caught up in their intoxicating dreams.

Everyone knew change was coming, but no one knew what form it would take or what the world would be like afterwards. After the Mito *rōnin* assassinated Lord Ii acts of violence increased both against foreigners and between factions, especially in Kyōto where the *shishi* tried to influence the Emperor Kōmei who, it was well known, hated foreigners. The great *daimyō* went to Kyōto and Edo, conferred, quarrelled and returned to their own domains while the Bakufu government seemed paralysed, needing to placate the foreigners and control the *shishi*. It was impossible to do both, as Ii Naosuke had found out. He had opted to concede to the foreigners' demands and avoid war with them, for which the *shishi* had made him pay with his life.

Occasionally, when he was visiting Yoshitomi, or on his way to Yamaguchi, Lord Sufu would call at our house. He seemed to have taken a liking to my father and my husband, and sometimes consulted my father about his health.

'Whatever happens, bloodshed is inevitable,' Lord Sufu said to my father on one of these visits, after my father had looked at his tongue and taken his pulse, and advised him as always to try to cut down on his drinking. 'I wish it could be avoided – but how? Irreconcilable forces are picking up speed; sooner or later they will clash.'

'You have brought up a generation of warriors who, like their fathers and grandfathers, have never had anyone to fight,' my father said. 'You've taught them all the arts of war; now they are spoiling for an enemy.'

'Better the foreigners than each other,' Sufu said.

'But to pick an outright fight with the foreigners would be madness,' Father replied.

Makino nodded in agreement. Sufu eyed him over the rim of his sake bowl.

'Makino-san, what do you know of weapons and ballistics?'

'Not enough,' Makino replied. 'Certainly not enough about the sort of wounds the domain might expect if they challenge the Americans or the British.'

Sufu smiled as if pleased with this response. 'Maybe you should find out more. If Dr Itasaki can spare you, I think you should go to Bakan. That's where any attack is most likely. We are going to need battlefield doctors.'

Coming from Lord Sufu that was an order rather than a suggestion. Makino was delighted. He had already started to think of army medicine as the most likely way to advance in his career, and now he was being placed where he would gain practical skills, and had been recognised by the most powerful man in the domain.

I felt apprehensive about our move. I did not want to leave home; I liked working with my father. As long as I stayed at the Gambling Tree Place, I was more than just Makino's wife, I had my own position within the family and the practice. And I had my own power. I knew that if we went away together I would surrender some of that power to my husband. I was not sure I was able to confine myself to the wifely role that would be expected of me in the outside world.

My father was anxious too. He did not really want to lose either of us but he could not refuse a request from Lord Sufu.

If only we had delayed our departure a little longer! By the end of the year Sufu had fallen out with Nagai Uta and was ordered into house arrest, but we were already in Bakan.

PART 2

承

Bunkyū 2 to Bunkyū 3
1862–1863

SHIRAISHI SEIICHIRŌ

Bunkyū 2 (1862), Spring, Age 50

Shiraishi Seiichirō is writing in his diary. He has been keeping it for over four years, ever since he began to feel he was becoming important – not in the usual way of a successful merchant, which he is, one of the most successful in Bakan, but as something more. His residence, part warehouse, part family home, part hostel, has become a hub, a centre for information and a haven. Men arrive late at night, their faces covered, their voices low. They bring letters of introduction from Hagi or Mitajiri and they depart on ships belonging to his business contacts with funds from Shiraishi tucked carefully inside their robes.

Kazuko, his wife, does not approve though Shiraishi takes no notice of her grumbling. He is fond of her and she is a hard worker, but she has never liked being made to consider new ideas. She can read and write and use the abacus well enough to help run the business but she does not love books in the way he does. He can lose himself in the writings of Hirata Atsutane or Suzuki Shigetane for hours in the evenings while she complains about the waste of lamp oil and the need to get up at dawn. He ignores her. For one thing he thinks she must be going through the change of life, which makes all women irritable; for another, he has worked hard as an importer–exporter for over thirty years, he has made a pile of money. He is both shrewd and trustworthy, not easily cheated. He trades with most of the southwestern domains in Kyūshū and Shikoku, in particular with Satsuma and Nagasaki, and supplies the ships that sail up and down the *kitamaesen* and through the Inland Sea. He has earned the right to spend his time and his money as he likes.

He met Suzuki and discovered the books that have so inspired him when Suzuki stayed at the hostel the same year he started the diary. Suzuki is the same age as he is, a student of Hirata, a direct link with the great scholar. Shiraishi started providing accommodation almost by accident when clients were stranded by storms. Gregarious and inquisitive, he enjoys talking to travellers; he is a good listener and inspires confidences. Ever since the black ships, the foreigners are a prime topic: their demands, their vessels, their weapons. Shiraishi is considered something of an expert; he knows quite a lot about the outside world. For the first time in his life he finds young men of the samurai class seeking his opinion, listening to him. They need him – the shelter he offers, the money he so generously lends. They don't treat him with the casual scorn their fathers have for his class. They seem to respect him and like him. It is as intoxicating as the ideas they share with him. He becomes imbued with their dreams and visions. Like them he begins to revere the Emperor and to see the Tokugawa Bakufu as an illegitimate government, proved by their inefficiency and incompetence. His reading confirms the supremacy of the Emperor and the need to restore his rule so the nation is in harmony with the gods who in return will make it prosperous and invincible.

He is less sure about the demands to get rid of all foreigners. He believes commerce is a natural human activity, civilising as well as profitable, and he would like to trade more with the Western nations. Also he has a better idea than most about the military strength of America, England, France and Russia, all of whom have come sniffing around Japan. Like everyone else in Bakan he takes a keen interest in the new defences which have been constructed along the northern shore of the strait. He is not very impressed by the calibre and number of the guns, but he does not say as much.

His family comes from the southern side of the strait, from Kokura – in fact his business is known as the Kokuraya. He is rather disappointed in Kokura, who have refused requests from Chōshū to fortify their side of the strait and persist in seeing Chōshū as a greater enemy than the foreigners. His allegiance is to Chōshū now, though the port of Bakan belongs to the branch domain of Chōfu. Relations with Hagi are not always harmonious, but in the Kokuraya samurai from both domains can meet and discuss ideas and discover they have more to unite them than divide them if they share a devotion to the Emperor.

Shiraishi sometimes arranges these meetings and presides over them himself. Then he records them in his diary. He believes that one day the young men who pass through his hostel, exchanging ideas and receiving assistance, will bring in a new world. Occasionally he allows himself to dream of his own future, the honours he will receive, the prestige he will enjoy. Maybe he will hold some government position, maybe the Emperor will be told about him and his Kokuraya, and the Emperor will silently marvel that it all began here.

Today he is writing about a samurai from Satsuma, Saigō Kichinosuke, who arrived last night. It is not the first time he has stayed here. He says the Kokuraya is conveniently situated, right on the waterfront; he likes the food, and Shiraishi's wife, a large woman of the type he admires, makes him feel comfortable. Shiraishi along with everyone else in the hostel adores Saigō. The man is so much larger than life, exuberant and outgoing, yet intelligent and no doubt ruthless when he has to be. Shiraishi likes nothing more than to bring out his best sake and keep filling the bowls while Saigō relates the successes and calamities of his life, which are better than a novel or a kabuki play. He has known the most extreme hardships of exile and imprisonment yet his sheer ability has ensured his recovery. Now his fortune is on the rise again. He has not said as much, but being from Kagoshima he is interested in establishing a foothold on the main island of Honshū. He talks about trade, about buying rice and other commodities, but Shiraishi suspects he is also considering the logistics of moving troops. Saigō will be one of the bright stars of the new world, and he is Shiraishi's friend.

He has finished the diary entry and is pressing his fingers to his temples, his eyes closed, when he hears his younger brother addressing him. He opens his eyes rapidly. 'What?'

'I asked if you were all right.' Rensaku peers at him. 'You look a little pale.'

'I'm fine, I'm fine.' Shiraishi never admits to ill health or any other weakness. He expects perfect health from his body and will accept nothing less.

'Just a little too much sake with Saigō-sama, perhaps?'

'You know me,' Shiraishi replies. 'I can drink all night and never get a hangover. You have to be more careful – you do not have a strong stomach.'

Rensaku is smaller and slighter than his older brother. He is a very able accountant and indispensable to the business, but he is fussy over his health and something of a hypochondriac. Like Shiraishi he has caught the 'revere the Emperor' contagion, but not being a great drinker is a drawback and the sessions his older brother thrives on leave him with a sick headache.

'Did you want something?' Shiraishi asks.

'I had an idea in the night. I wanted to try it out on you.'

Shiraishi raises his eyebrows. Rensaku quite often has surprisingly good ideas, which Shiraishi pooh-poohs loudly and then appropriates.

'Saigō is such an amazing person. Don't you think the Chōshū men would like to meet him? Katsura Kogorō, for example, or Kusaka Genzui.'

Both men frequently stay at the hostel and both appear in the pages of Shiraishi's diary.

'I think they would find they have a lot in common,' Rensaku continues. 'Who knows what it might lead to?'

'Satsuma and Chōshū hate each other,' Shiraishi says dismissively. 'They are bitter rivals. You expect the tiger and the dragon to cooperate?'

'Kusaka is due any day now, and while Saigō is here…'

'No, it wouldn't work.'

'It was just an idea,' Rensaku apologises.

Shiraishi knows it is rather a good one. Sooner or later he will act on it, but he doesn't tell Rensaku that now.

BAKAN

Akamagaseki, Shimonoseki, Bakan: the port that overlooked the narrow strait between Honshū and Kyūshū was known by many different names. It was the site of Dannoura, the great sea battle, hundreds of years earlier, the culmination of the Genpei War in which the Taira were defeated by the Minamoto and the child-Emperor Antoku drowned, along with most of his warriors. Now it was Chōshū's busiest port, where travellers congregated, exchanging goods and information, always waiting for something: a favourable wind or the right tide, a vessel full of precious cargo or a warship bristling with foreign guns. It had seen the beginning of the rise to power of the warrior class and it would be instrumental in bringing about its end.

We stayed, on Lord Sufu's introduction and at the domain's expense, at the Kokuraya, an import–export business run by the merchant Shiraishi Seiichirō. Shiraishi was about fifty years old at that time. He was an enterprising and energetic man, and these qualities had made him wealthy. As the *sonnōjōi* movement grew in Chōshū he began to help the *shishi* with shelter, money and gifts. Our purpose was to extend that aid into medical care, using Shiraishi's contacts to import the supplies we were going to need.

Over the past few years while Sufu had been reforming

the military, warships had been purchased from the Americans and the domain's coastal defences had been built up: around Bakan were many cannon batteries. People were extremely proud of them – many had donated their cooking pots or bells from their temples for their construction – and hoped eagerly they would soon be ordered into action (if only to find out if they worked or not). Makino and I went several times to Maeda and Dannoura to inspect them. I heard words I'd never heard before: *Dahlgren, Armstrong*, and learned the sizes of the guns, described as so many *pounds*, so many *inches*, new foreign words that were as fascinating and as sinister as the weapons themselves.

We admired the batteries, and the spirit of the soldiers and their curious uniforms, but to be honest we had nothing to compare them with. We knew little about Western arms other than that they were powerful enough to have brought down the Empire of China. The soldiers assured us that their cannon were superior, since they were supremely loyal to the Emperor; their guns must work better because ours was a divine country, but this sounded to me like magical thinking. Some of the cannon were wooden replicas, just for show, and there was a lot of talk about the defences that lay behind Bakan, defences that we knew were purely imaginary.

Neither Makino nor I had ever seen a gunshot wound. We were concerned about the guns on the foreign warships, their range, the damage they might inflict, and what treatment would be required.

With Shiraishi's help Makino ordered books from Nagasaki. The famous doctor Ōtsuku Shunsai had published two translations of Western books on gunshot wounds a few years before, and once we had obtained these we pored over them. Setting broken limbs, cleaning wounds, removing bullets, bandaging, amputation: the descriptions and the occasional illustrations were alarming but fascinating.

The books came from yet another Western country: Germany. I did not know exactly where that was. I knew nothing of the world that lay beyond our land. When I thought about it I imagined ourselves at the centre, and everywhere else arranged around us in circles, the English, the Russians, the Dutch, the Americans and now the Germans, all part of an exotic world which included the lands of the Giants, the Longlegs and the Dwarfs, just like in *The Tale of Dashing Shidōken*. But Shiraishi had maps among his collection of books, and when I looked at them I realised how huge the world was and how far the foreign ships that sailed through the strait had come.

The Kokuraya was right on the waterfront and vessels loaded and unloaded there all day. I liked watching them, listening to the sailors, smelling the strange fragrances of spices from Batavia and China. Beyond the constant hubbub of the port the foreign ships went by, so close you could almost touch them. Flying their strange flags they progressed through the choppy waters, apparently oblivious to any danger from the shore. There were some steamships, their black funnels belching out smoke, but at that time most were still sailing vessels, two- or three-masted. I learned to distinguish their names: barque, brig, schooner.

Shiraishi's hostel was a hub for travellers of all types, who kept us abreast of all the latest news. In the first month of the second year of Bunkyū (1862), Ii's successor, Andō

Nobumasa, was attacked and severely wounded at the Sakashita Gate in Edo. The Bakufu was weakening before our eyes, yet for all the passionate discussions we listened to night after night, still no one had any clear idea of how to dispatch it or what to replace it with. In an effort to shore up the tottering Bakufu with Imperial prestige a marriage was arranged between Emperor Kōmei's sister, Kazunomiya, and the young Shōgun Iemochi, but this only further enraged the *shishi* in Kyōto where their violent attacks were increasing.

One day in the third month, when the scent of blossom was beginning to mingle with all the smells of the port, I was returning to the hostel when I thought I heard a voice I recognised. I peered into the inner courtyard and saw Kusaka Genzui. He was sitting on the edge of the veranda, smoking, talking to Shiraishi.

'There you are, there you are,' Shiraishi said, beckoning to me to come closer, but I hardly heard him for I was staring at Genzui. Blood poured from his throat and chest, his clothes were soaked in it and scorched by fire. Smoke seemed to swirl around us and I heard a crackling noise like flames. With my acute vision I saw Genzui dying.

I drew back behind the pillar, closing my eyes, leaning my head on the cool, smooth wood.

'Mrs Makino!' Shiraishi called. 'Kusaka-san wants to talk to you.'

I went towards them. Genzui was smiling. It was hard to imagine anyone looking more alive. His presence was striking; he had always been an intelligent and forceful man. Now grief had hardened and refined him.

I tried to smile too as we exchanged greetings, and I

enquired after the Sugi family and his wife, O-Fumi. He told me they were all well, although still grieving for Shōin.

The knowledge that they would soon grieve for him should have saddened me but with the microscopic vision came a certain coldness. Maybe this was how Genzui would die, but could I do or say anything to prevent it? And anyway, I told myself, these episodes were probably not true visions of the future, but simply hallucinations, a prolonged after-effect of the shock of Nakajima's death.

Genzui said, 'I have a message for you.'

'Come inside,' Shiraishi said, getting to his feet. 'I'll have someone bring you a drink.'

I watched him go with affection. I had been able to help his wife with some treatment and massage for menopause; they had both become fond of me, and treated me like one of their daughters.

We moved into a room at the back that looked onto the courtyard. It was late afternoon and the breeze from the sea was growing colder. It rattled the *shōji* and found its way into every corner. Showers of petals fell from the cherry tree in the courtyard. I was glad of the hot tea when the maid brought it. Genzui was drinking sake.

'I've seen your uncle in Kyōto,' he said quietly. 'He asked me to let you know he is all right, if I happened to run into you.'

'He is in Kyōto?' I might have guessed he would find his way to the capital, where so many *shishi* were gathering. 'Where is he living?'

'Here and there,' Genzui replied, grinning a little. 'We sometimes find a place for him in the mansion in Kawaramachi, or in Fushimi, and he has his own boltholes no one knows about. He's very useful to us. He can look after himself and he keeps his eyes and ears open.'

'He must be in danger there.'

'We are all in danger,' he replied. 'Even within our own domain and from our own people.'

I felt he was referring to Shōin's death and began to express my sympathy. 'You were so close to Master Yoshida, his favourite pupil, his brother-in-law.'

He barely let me finish but said, 'I have two aims; first to make sure his death was not in vain and second to avenge it.' Lowering his voice he went on, 'I wish I had been among the Mito men who dealt with Ii Naosuke, and Andō. But Nagai is mine and I will make him pay.'

At that moment I did not doubt he would, but even in Bakan, in Shiraishi's house, it was not wise to speak of such things.

'Have you just come from Hagi?' I asked.

'Yes, I've been there all winter. I was ordered back last year. Nagai does not know exactly what I am up to, but he suspects something and it unnerves him.'

'And what are you up to?'

'Last year I travelled a lot, making new contacts, strengthening old ones. I spent quite a long time with Sakuma Shōzan in Nagano. He is an old friend of my brother-in-law and another wonderful teacher, incredibly wise and knowledgeable about Western ways. Now I have been given permission to go to Hyōgo – of course that means I can return to Kyōto.'

He grinned in the same way as when he had been talking about Shinsai; danger excited him. For a moment I thought

I could see them both involved in the intrigues and conspiracies of the capital. I saw the narrow alleys, the shabby tea houses where they met…

There was the sound of footsteps outside and my husband slid back the *shoji* and entered the room. He knelt and bowed his head to Genzui.

'Dr Makino, Lord Sufu told me he had sent you here,' Genzui said. 'If war does occur with the foreigners you will certainly be needed in Bakan. But at some stage perhaps you could bring your expertise to Kyōto.'

'So you expect fighting to break out there?' Makino said.

'Yes, but not against the foreigners,' Genzui said, laughing. 'We've already had the odd sword wound. We are sure to have more, and from firearms, since everyone is buying rifles and cannon now.'

He leaned forward to pour sake for my husband. 'How many more memorials am I supposed to submit? How many more carefully written demands for justice and reform? If we saw any real signs of change we would not need to resort to the threat of violence. But people don't listen to you until you make them afraid.'

'Did Master Yoshida teach you that?' I asked.

'He taught that the cruel and arrogant should be punished,' he replied. 'Those who commit crimes against the Emperor and his divine nation must be held accountable.'

'But what gives you the right to appoint yourself their judge?' Makino asked. I suddenly saw how much he had changed since the time I first knew him as an assistant in a pharmacy. He addressed Genzui as an equal, and Genzui did not take offence.

'Our clarity of vision, our willingness to act, to die if necessary, and our loyalty to the Emperor.'

It was impossible to remain unmoved by him. Neither Makino nor I could take our eyes off him. He made a gesture that drew us closer to him and whispered, 'We are not alone; it is not only in Chōshū that the tide is turning. Early this year a Tosa samurai came to see me in Hagi. He brought a letter from Takechi Hanpeita, one of the loyalist leaders in that domain. He is quite a remarkable man; his name is Sakamoto, Sakamoto Ryōma. We *shishi* must be united throughout the nation. We cannot trust the great lords to deal with either the foreigners or the Bakufu. All the domains are splitting in similar ways. Men of high purpose, like your uncle, like me, Takechi, Sakamoto, we see that change must come, but samurai of high rank everywhere are both self-serving and timorous. They want to keep things as they are and they will not hesitate to sacrifice any one of us, as Nagai sacrificed Shōin.'

'You mention Tosa,' I said. 'What about Satsuma? Shiraishi does a lot of business with Satsuma merchants and many guests from Satsuma stay here. Not only merchants but samurai too.'

'The big man,' Makino said, 'Saigō Kichinosuke. He is here now.'

'Satsuma,' Genzui said, shaking his head. 'How can Chōshū ever trust Satsuma? Yet we can only achieve our goals if our domains work together.'

Kusaka Genzui was interested in Saigō, but I don't believe they met then, though at times only a thin *shōji* would have separated them. The mutual envy and suspicion of samurai from the two great domains prevented it.

We did not speak to Genzui again and saw him only briefly before he left for Kyōto. I wanted to send a message for Shinsai, but I did not think my husband would like it, so I said nothing. Makino promised he would come to the capital if he could, but in the end it was I who went to Kyōto, and I did not go with him.

Saigō Kichinosuke, later known as Takamori, was one of the largest men I'd ever seen. My husband was above average height but even he was not as tall. When Saigō arrived at the hostel the maids lined up to peek at him, and they all found excuses to wait on him. They were only the least of those who wanted to set eyes on the great Saigō; many people came to see him.

Mrs Shiraishi, and everyone else, gossiped about his life and I was able to piece together his story. He had worked with the Satsuma *daimyō*, Shimazu Nariakira, to reform and strengthen the domain. Lord Nariakira had died suddenly in the fifth year of Ansei (1858), and many believed he was poisoned either by his stepmother or on Ii Naosuke's orders. His half-brother's son became *daimyō*, but the real power in the domain was held by the father, Hisamitsu, who it was said never forgave a slight nor missed the opportunity to do a spiteful act. After his lord's death Saigō came under threat from the Bakufu and from the domain authorities, and had tried to commit suicide with the monk Gesshō. They both threw themselves into the sea. Gesshō died but Saigō was saved, only to be sent into exile on a remote island. But his talents were so great the domain could not do without them, and he was recalled into service.

I had glimpsed him. Had I seen his death, after defeat in battle, when he stabbed himself with his sword, his comrade decapitating him? Maybe I saw the wash of blood, the despair and the relief of death. I was becoming accustomed to these frequent visions. I learned not to let my eyes dwell on the unfortunate being before me. All men will die, and some violently. I was shown violent death. I did not understand why. It often disturbed me, as when I had seen the blood pouring from my host's younger brother, Rensaku, but I could not say anything to anyone.

Anyway I was more interested in people's present health. In Saigō's case I was sure that the size of his limbs was not entirely natural, and I suspected it was due to the sort of oedema known as elephantiasis. His attempted suicide, the immersion in cold water and subsequent lowered body temperature had also affected him badly. His feet were damaged by poor circulation. Makino had been asked to treat him and recommended leg massage and moxibustion, and gave him an infusion of longan, ginseng and angelica to warm the blood.

Then he was gone as suddenly as he came, but in the fourth month Shimazu Hisamitsu himself passed through Bakan on his way to Kyōto. I went to the *honjin* to watch his procession. I wanted to see for myself the man who everyone said would play a crucial role in national politics. He never really lived up to these expectations. Despite his undeniable intelligence he was quarrelsome and arrogant, unable to achieve anything lasting because he could never get on with anyone else.

All I saw of him anyway was his palanquin and his retinue.

But in Kyōto he acted forcefully to bring the *shishi* from his domain under control. They were expecting him to support them and expel the foreigners. In fact what he did was send soldiers to subdue them at the Teradaya in Fushimi; many of them were killed. I heard later from my uncle that he, Genzui and other Chōshū loyalists had intended to join the Satsuma *shishi*. They had had a lucky escape.

Suddenly Chōshū's position with the Court which had seemed so promising was being threatened by the rise of Satsuma. The news we got was like a game of picture *sugoroku*, snakes and ladders: one rose, another fell. In the seventh month Nagai Uta was recalled in disgrace; Genzui threatened openly to assassinate him on the road. It was not long before Genzui himself was ordered back to Hagi.

'O-Fumi-san must be happy her husband is so frequently under house arrest,' I commented to my husband. 'Otherwise she would never see him!'

It was late at night around the time of frost fall, in the ninth month. Shiraishi had told us about Genzui earlier that day and I had been thinking about him on and off ever since. The hostel was also buzzing with the news of the attack on foreigners by men of Satsuma in a village on the Tōkaidō called Namamugi. They had somehow insulted Hisamitsu and one had been killed and others wounded. They were English, and the English officials were outraged and threatening retribution. Hisamitsu had retreated to Kagoshima to consider his options, and no doubt strengthen his defences. People reacted to the news with a mixture of admiration and envy. Satsuma had struck the hated foreigners. Chōshū must not be left behind. I wondered how Genzui was reacting to the news. And Shinsai.

'Do you think people can see the future?' I asked Makino.

He yawned and stretched. He seemed as tired as I was. He had been studying all evening while I had visited a family in town. Their two young children had both died of measles while I was there. They were five and three. They say a child belongs to the Buddha until it is seven, but I could not help sharing in the parents' grief. I was depressed at how many children I had to watch pass into the next world when they had scarcely tasted life in this one.

'Everyone thinks they can,' Makino replied after considering my question for a few moments. 'Why else would you have divination and fortune-telling, auspicious days and lucky directions?'

'But you don't believe in that?' It had once been an essential part of a doctor's training, understanding the supernatural causes of ill health and knowing how to counteract them.

'No, but if our patients have superstitions, and many of them still do, we have to understand what they believe, and at the same time try to educate them to see the world differently. Why are you asking now? If you thought the children were going to die that was a medical diagnosis. Measles is often fatal. We have no cure for it.'

I thought of the parents' pathetic efforts, the images of dogs and monkeys (dog means *not here*, monkey means *go away*), the amulets from shrines, the pictures of noble warriors overcoming the measles demon, and I remembered the common saying, *Measles takes your life, smallpox takes your beauty*. I tried to put the dead children out of my mind.

'It's not that. Talking about Genzui made me think of something that happened when I saw him here. A vision of him dying. It's a bit like looking down from on high and seeing through a microscope, seeing all the little living things that you cannot pick out with your own eyes. Yet it's not life I see but death, the blood bursting out, the body dissolving.'

'You read too many lurid books.' Makino had never approved of my love of fiction. However he looked at me more closely. 'Is it only Genzui?'

'There have been others.' I did not want to tell him how many, or that he had been among them. He would probably think I was insane.

'Hmm.' He rubbed his eyes. 'Have you recorded any of them?'

'I haven't written anything down, but I can't forget them.'

'Well, make a note every time it happens. It's probably just imagination. You don't have to be clairvoyant to see Genzui's not going to die on the tatami!'

My husband's rational approach comforted me and I felt a rush of affection for him.

'Let me rub your shoulders,' I said, kneeling behind him. As my hands worked on his knotted muscles he leaned against me, and I was aware of the charge between us, our old passion returning. We did not bother to lay out the futon or even undress, but clung to each other, joining our bodies with sudden urgent desire.

Afterwards I said, 'I wonder why we do not make any children.'

'Does it distress you?'

'Not really. I've seen too many children die. And childbirth itself frightens me: so many things can go wrong. I feel lucky, to enjoy what we do together without having to fear the result. But I don't like thinking there's something wrong with me.' My monthly bleeding had always been irregular and scanty. I suspected there was a problem with my womb.

Makino laughed. 'It may be something wrong with me. Many a woman, divorced or replaced for being barren, conceives with a new man.'

'I could always try that if I get desperate.'

'We could both experiment,' he offered.

We both said, 'No!' at the same time.

'I think I'm meant to step aside and put up with you taking another wife or at least a concubine.' I seemed to remember reading something like that in *Great Learning for Women*, or some other Confucian text, written by a man naturally.

'Marriage is as much about desire as children,' Makino said. 'It harnesses the passion men and women have for each other, which I've always had for you.'

'Oh?' I feigned surprise. 'I thought you just wanted to study with my father.'

'It was the other way round. I wanted you to be my wife.'

Makino was an undemonstrative man and this was the most affectionate thing he had ever said to me.

'I don't care about children,' he went on. 'Like you I could not bear to see them die, or have you go through the danger of giving birth. At this time the work we do for our domain is more important. Without a family we can work together and go wherever we are needed.'

The house around us was completely silent in the brief time before dawn. I could hear the lap of water on the stone embankment and the creaking of boats as they rubbed against each other in the turning tide. Soon the first cocks would crow. I knew I should spread out the futon and the quilt and go properly to bed. The air in the room was freezing. But I liked lying against my husband, my arms around him. We were so rarely intimate now I did not want to waste this moment.

So we did not talk any more that night about visions of death or anything else, and by the time we thought about getting into bed it was time to get up.

MADNESS

Throughout the winter tension in the port city increased. Severe storms prevented any outbreak of actual war, but they also hindered the arrival of the medical supplies we had ordered from Nagasaki. In the second month of the following year came the news that Nagai Uta, who had risen so high in the service of the domain, had committed suicide in his home in Hagi on the government's orders. He was forty-four years old, younger than my father. Many rejoiced at his death: Genzui was no doubt among them. Nagai had never been forgiven for his role in Shōin's execution, and now he had been punished for Chōshū's loss of influence at Court to Satsuma.

I had never set eyes on Lord Nagai so I could not know if I would have foreseen his tragic end. I had made records for my husband, but I felt the hallucinations were fading. I had had no more of the graphic visions that had so troubled me since Nakajima's death, just a slight flickering as if I could see blood beginning to seep through the skin. The more closely I tried to record the experience the less it occurred, as if the act of observation exorcised whatever it was that had temporarily possessed me.

Makino did not comment on my list of names, which included my uncle's but not his own. He read it carefully and put it away with the other lists he kept. He recorded everything:

books he read, patients and their treatment, statistics of births and deaths, outbreaks of infectious diseases, cases of syphilis.

Because of these records he was aware that, along with measles and syphilis, various forms of mental illness were also increasing as a result of the confusion and extreme emotions of the times. We had several cases of unshakeable lethargy; two sufferers threw themselves into the sea. There were three brutal murders where the accused was found to be insane. Women disappeared, only to turn up miles away – they were believed to have been bewitched by foxes. Young girls refused all food and wasted away. All these unnatural events added to the anxiety of the city's inhabitants. People thronged to temples and shrines or became adherents of new religions which sprang up like bamboo shoots.

Generally the mad were confined at home and were considered the responsibility of their families. Only very severe cases were imprisoned by the authorities. Because their families were usually desperate no one minded if I tried to treat them. Even my husband was happy to leave them to me, commenting only that he thought I was wasting my time. Usually madness was seen as some obstruction of the natural force within the body; I noticed that the mad were indeed often constipated, and many books recommended various laxative treatments. I wrote to my father asking him to send me his textbooks by Kagawa and Tsuchida and I studied the various forms of madness these doctors had recorded and compared them with my own observations. During the winter I worked on devising methods to lift depression and calm excessive agitation. I found massage and certain herbal remedies to be effective, as well as bathing, especially under cold waterfalls as Tsuchida recommended. Making a pilgrimage often had excellent results, though I suspected these were due more to the exercise and change of scene than to the intervention of the buddhas or the *kami*. Talking to someone like me also seemed to bring a certain relief to my patients.

Shiraishi-san, who was a disciple of the nativist thinker Suzuki Shigetane and had a deep interest in spiritual and mental development, followed my work carefully, and soon began to recommend patients to me. I liked working with the mad, partly because I felt I was not all that sane myself and partly because they did not seem to notice that I was not a man, or if they did, they did not care. There were many cases where I could do nothing: the confusions of old age or, saddest of all to me, the dementia of advanced syphilis, accompanied as it usually was by the collapse of the nose, the loss of fingers and other terrible ulcers. But now and then I could see I made a difference. I became very fond of my lunatics, and when I reread the records I kept I thought I could discern some patterns to their fits of insanity.

There was one man I visited regularly. His name was Imaike Eikaku, he was about forty years old, and was cared for by his unmarried sister. He thought he had had syphilis, but it was in its dormant stage and so he did not show any symptoms. He was an artist, and in his manic periods he painted obsessively, mostly scenes of hell, without eating or sleeping. If he had no paper or wooden boards he painted on whatever surface he could find. Walking into his long-suffering sister's house was like entering all the hells of the afterlife. Poor frail humans, usually naked, tried in vain to escape punishment meted out by huge monsters with animal heads, armed with bows, spears and swords, smiling and chuckling as they tore the bleeding bodies apart. Eikaku diligently matched the punishment to the sin: those who had lusted after women were condemned to struggle through trees of thorns while the avaricious who had never helped anyone in their lifetime begged endlessly for water to ease their burning throats.

I liked his pictures because they reminded me of my own hallucinations, and other people liked them too. Many Buddhist priests commissioned him to paint his visions of hell for their temples. Rich merchants also collected his works. Despite his popularity Eikaku never had any money, spending everything he earned on sake or tobacco or giving it away carelessly.

'I don't want to be cured,' he said when we first met, 'for then I would no longer have my visions. But I want you to keep me from killing myself. Can you do that, Doctor?'

'I can if you do as I tell you,' I said. 'You need to be aware of the cycle you follow. You must remember to eat and rest when you are excited, and when you are depressed you should not drink.'

'Drinking cheers me up,' he argued.

'It might do, temporarily, but afterwards the depression is more severe.'

It bothered me that so many of my patients drank so much, yet how could I stop them? From Sufu Masanosuke downwards the entire domain was fuelled by alcohol. Eikaku was an extreme case, but his paintings revealed how everyone felt: on the brink of an unknowable future, on the brink of collective madness, under the unknown shadow. Large amounts of sake seemed the best way to prepare yourself, as well as help you get through the hardships of daily life. Even the wealthy could not escape the pain of the human body: aching teeth, piles, rheumatism, earaches, sore eyes, ulcers. One thing that surprised me about the mad was that they complained so little about physical pain. Not only did they seem not to feel pain as others did but they were usually healthy and strong. This was often depressing to their families who might have secretly hoped for their early release into the next world.

Eikaku's depressions came on little by little. He would gradually cease painting, finally throwing away his brushes, swearing he would never take them up again. His sister had learned not to argue with him but to put them away quietly. Sometimes he put on women's clothes, blackened his teeth and made up his face like a kabuku actor playing a courtesan.

When I asked him to tell me why, he would say something like, 'I am so hopeless I might as well be a woman.' I realised he could cope with his depression if he could dramatise it. I came one day and his sister told me he had not spoken for forty-eight hours, but simply wept, wiping his eyes on the sleeve of his brilliantly coloured kimono. When I went into the room and knelt beside him, greeting him quietly, he suddenly seized me by the arm. My flesh jumped at his grip. He stared into my face, the tears streaking the white make-up.

'Makino-*sensei*,' he said. He used female speech and addressed me as if I were a man. 'We would make a fine couple. You are a man in a woman's body. I am a woman in a man's. In a world turned upside down the only way to live is in opposites. Come and live with me and be a man.'

The idea seemed to energise him. He jumped to his feet. 'I will get you my clothes. You must put them on.' He ran to the door with dainty little steps like a geisha, and called to his sister. 'Oneesan, come and help the doctor change clothes.'

His sister came immediately, and between us we managed to calm him down. It was clear that the depression was lifting and giving way to the manic stage. Eikaku was no longer crying; his speech was animated.

'He will soon dress as a man and start painting again,' his sister said, resignedly, and went to prepare something to eat, knowing it would not be long before her brother realised he was ravenous.

The words he had spoken stayed with me. *You are a man in a woman's body.* Was that why I had no children, why I was interested in disease and death, why Makino and I were more like colleagues than husband and wife? For a moment, when Eikaku had called for men's clothes, I had been tempted to go along with his fantasy and put them on. I could feel the difference they would make to my posture and gait, and to the way other people looked at me. From that time on I began to make my dress less feminine. I wore subdued colours and adopted the kind of short jacket worn by male doctors. I tried to flatten my hair and pull it back from my forehead. I watched the gestures men made and studied the cadences of their speech. Cautiously I began to adopt them; I found men listened to my opinions more seriously and my patients were more likely to be reassured by my diagnoses and remedies.

At the end of the second month of the third year of Bunkyū (1863) I received a letter from my father asking me to go to Hagi. My sister was expecting her third child; the second delivery had been difficult and my parents were worried about her health. Our family and the Kuriya had been reconciled, and Mitsue had been home for a visit the previous year, though I had not seen her as we had already left for Bakan. We wrote as often as we could, but she had very little free time and the intervals between her letters were becoming longer and longer, so I was eager to see her. Makino did not want to go to Hagi at that time when war seemed imminent, but he willingly gave me permission, and accompanied me as far as my parents' house in Yuda.

I had written to my father to tell him what Kusaka Genzui had said to me in Bakan, that my uncle was in Kyōto and was to some extent under Chōshū protection. My parents had heard nothing more. Violence in Kyōto had been growing more intense every week. A group calling themselves Tenchū, the Wrath of Heaven, had been punishing officials and their retainers, murdering them and delivering their severed body parts over the walls of mansions and palaces. Rumours were just arriving about a strange attack on the wooden statues of the Ashikaga Shōgun. They had been decapitated, the heads displayed complete with placards denouncing their treachery to the Emperor.

'Just the sort of thing Shinsai would be involved in,' Father said, patting his arms as usual. He had put on weight since I had last seen him, and became breathless more quickly. When I first got there I realised he was growing old, but after a few moments the ability to see him as he truly was faded, and he and my mother became as they had always been, unchanged. Affection and gratitude brought tears to my eyes. How good they had been to me, allowing me to follow my vocation, never standing in my way! I wished I was still living with them, looking after them, giving them grandchildren.

'Tetsuya's teacher has offered his daughter to him,' my mother said. 'Your father has agreed and they are to be married next month.'

'Does this mean he's not coming home?' I bent to stroke the cat which was twining around my legs, purring.

'We're not sure yet,' my father replied. 'It depends on so many factors. Tetsuya doesn't want to come back into the middle of a war. You know what he's like.'

I nodded. We all knew that my brother was not physically brave; furthermore he liked his life in Nagasaki, that lively, open city where the whole world mingled.

'Of course we still hope that you and Makino-san will settle down here,' my mother said, 'when you have finished your service to the domain.'

'That's what was planned,' I replied. 'But who knows…'

I allowed myself to look at that bright future, when the war had come and gone, when the world had been renewed. I imagined Makino and I growing old together here. We would adopt an heir: one of the students who would flock to study with us, maybe even one of our nephews. But of course I could not really see ahead: the only visions I had were the useless ones of blood and death.

My mother had decided to come with me to Hagi; she wanted to make a pilgrimage to Ōmishima and see the sixteen rocks that looked like Buddhist monks. Several of her friends were also going and we set out together as soon as it was light. It was a beautiful spring morning, and the five women were in a merry mood. They were the same age as my mother, all grandmothers, two already widowed, and their age and status gave them a freedom they had never had before in their lives.

We stopped at midday at a mountain *onsen* whose waters were said to be beneficial for arthritis and women's complaints. As we soaked in the scalding water, steamy and dappled with sunlight through the new green leaves, I observed their ageing bodies, the scars, creases and wrinkles that told the story of their lives, smallpox, childbirth, hard work in sun and rain, missing teeth, burns and other injuries. Yet their wrinkles were also from laughter and nothing diminished their pleasure in their outing – unless it was distress at my childless state, which they discussed at length, advising me as to the right day to lie with my husband, what food we should both eat, which shrines we should visit, and which was the best position. Then they described their experiences of childbirth, the pain and the joy, but out of consideration for my mother and myself they did not talk about the perils, the deaths.

It was already twilight when we arrived in Hagi, the cold blue twilight of spring on the edge of the Japan Sea. The water was the colour of indigo and a chill wind blew from the northwest. The rice paddies were clamorous with newly awakened frogs, and owls were calling from the groves around the temples and shrines. The lights from lanterns and fires looked cheerful and welcoming in the gathering darkness. My mother's friends went to an inn on the edge of the castle town. They were going to explore the sights of Hagi for two days, then my mother would join them on the pilgrimage to Ōmishima, and they would return by the coast road, while I stayed with my sister until the baby was born.

Mitsue was already nearly at full-term, her body swollen and hard beneath the silk belly wrap my mother had woven for her. The two little boys were lively and demanding. Mrs Kuriya admired them enormously and was lavish in her praise of Mitsue, but she had grown more languorous than ever, and did little to help her.

I couldn't help comparing the Kuriya household with that of the Shiraishi. The Kuriya were as rich and as successful but they were self-absorbed, unreflective and conservative. I could not imagine them devoting their energies and wealth to any cause other than their own. I missed the excitement of the Kokuraya and Bakan, the coming and going of so many dedicated and enthusiastic young men. The Kuriya shop where Makino used to sit like Enma in judgement seemed empty without him; the young man who had replaced him hardly rated a second glance.

Still, Mitsue seemed content with her two sons, and she looked healthy enough, though her ankles were swollen and her skin dark in the way of pregnancy, and she said she was always tired. I did all I could to help her in the house and shop – in those days my own energy was boundless – but the Kuriya, although superficially polite, still bore great resentment towards me for stealing away the Accountant, as well as for my uncle's association with Yoshida Shōin. They supported the conservative faction within the domain government, and spoke with angry disparagement of Sufu Masanosuke. It was hard for me to hold my tongue when I heard such lies about the man who had become my family's patron, and sometimes when the atmosphere became unbearable I felt obliged to leave the house for a while.

Sometimes, as I walked along the western bank of the Matsumoto River, my thoughts turned to O-Fumi, Shōin's sister, Genzui's wife, and I wondered if I should call on the family, but a certain diffidence prevented it. On one of these days I was watching the terns and the herons fishing, and occasionally glancing up at the slopes of Mount Tatoko where the last of the wild cherry blossoms glimmered white, along with the first scarlet splashes of azaleas, when to my surprise I heard someone call my name. I looked around to see Shiji Monta walking towards me.

He greeted me cheerfully enough but I could tell something had dimmed his usual jauntiness and his eyes were bright as if he was holding back tears.

'I thought you were in Edo!' I exclaimed.

'I was called back by Lord Sadahiro; actually it was to escort Takasugi Shinsaku home. He's in rather a bad way.'

I wondered if that was what had upset Monta. I waited for him to explain further.

He seemed to pull himself together and said, 'I have just come from divorcing my adoptive family. I am resuming the name of Inoue.'

I was astonished. I didn't even know that such a thing was possible. 'But why?'

'Let's walk a little. There's a lot to tell you. I'm going to Takasugi's now – he's living up in Matsumoto. Will you come with me? Maybe you can help him. I've heard about your work in Bakan.'

I did not ask how he knew. The former *sonjuku* group kept in constant touch with each other, sending information and reports on the political situation around their network, from Hagi to Bakan and Mitajiri, to Ōsaka, Kyōto and Edo, and back to Hagi. They travelled and stayed with each other or at the houses of well-known sympathisers like Shiraishi who gave them money as well as shelter. One of these 'flying ears and long eyes' must have passed through Bakan in the last few months and thought my work with the mad worth mentioning.

Monta walked on and I followed a few paces behind him. When we got to the Matsumoto bridge he summoned a ferry boat, argued fiercely about the fare and finally clambered in.

'Even the verdicts of hell depend on money,' he muttered as I followed and crouched precariously on the planking. Now he had left the Shiji family I supposed he would be even more short of funds than usual. I was curious about the details of the rupture, but I did not like to ask in front of the ferryman.

When we reached the other side we followed the bank of the Tsukumigawa, crossed over a small bridge and began to climb the hill towards the village of Matsumoto. Monta finally slowed his gait and motioned to me to walk alongside him.

'I am going to England in a few weeks.'

This announcement left me speechless. The only thing I could think of saying was, 'But it is forbidden by the Bakufu.'

'That's why you have to keep it completely secret. I've been dying to tell someone – someone who doesn't matter. You turned up at just the right time. Now I'll be able to keep quiet about it!'

I wasn't sure he would be able to restrain himself. 'What will Lord Sufu say?'

'It is he who wants us to go. And Lord Mōri himself. They realise we have to see the West with our own eyes. The domain is giving us money; the English in Yokohama are helping us board a ship.'

'The English? What happened to "expel the foreigners"?'

Monta laughed. 'Did you hear we tried to burn down their legation in Yokohama? You should have seen us! It was just like Chūshingura, only there were fourteen of us not forty-seven. We didn't kill anyone though – actually there was no one there: they hadn't moved in yet. The English were very generous about it; we're all good friends now. I even got some money off one of them; I sold him my sword.'

I looked at Monta, trying to diagnose this extraordinary behaviour. He was in a very emotional state, but could he be called manic?

'No one needs swords now,' he said. 'What we need are pistols, rifles. Anyway, Itō and I are sailing from Yokohama. We're going to learn English – well, I speak quite a lot already – study navigation, artillery, industry, technology, all those things.'

'And sleep with English women, I suppose.' I was still smarting from being described as someone who didn't matter.

'If we have the chance.' He grinned at me. '*Skirts*: isn't that an erotic word? That's what they're called, those full wide garments English women wear. I can't imagine how you get through them though. They are like armour.'

'Is it just you and Itō-san?'

'There are five of us altogether. The others are Yamao Yōzō, Endō Kinsuke and Inoue Masaru.'

I had heard their names but had never met them.

'We're taking separate ships and will meet in Hong Kong.'

Monta spoke the name casually as if he went to Hong Kong every day. He was as contradictory as ever, I thought, as I looked at him. Hardly taller than me, he still had his boyish appearance. He was upset, he was excited, but what most occupied his mind was getting women to sleep with him.

'I wanted Takasugi to come with us,' he went on, 'but he has retired from public life.'

'What?' I could not believe it. Takasugi, of whom everyone had such high expectations, who was considered a future leader, how could he retire when the domain had such great need of him?

'He tried to persuade Lord Sufu to overthrow the Bakufu,' Monta explained. 'Sufu said, "Maybe in ten years' time." Whereupon Takasugi retorted, "Then I'll take ten years' leave!" He has shaved his head, withdrawn from the world and says he intends to be a hermit.'

'And he hasn't been punished?'

'What can anyone do to him? Put him under house arrest? He's already done that to himself! They'll just humour him until he comes to his senses. Lord Sufu is good like that; he understands Shinsaku. Anyway, he's not going to stay in retirement for ten years – if it lasts ten weeks it'll be a miracle. You know what he's like, always up and down, no moderation.'

'Not like Shiji-san,' I said.

'*Inoue*,' he corrected me. 'Compared to Shinsaku I'm a fine example of moderation, and so is Itō. Look how reasonable I'm being now. It's obvious we can't fight the foreigners without being defeated, not Chōshū, not Satsuma, not even the whole nation if we were united, which we aren't. We just aren't prepared, we don't have the weapons, the ships or the trained men. So instead of cutting down one or two foreigners with the sword, satisfying as that might be, we are going to learn about them and their technology.'

'So you can cut down more of them?'

'You know, trade may be better than war,' Monta said, 'though it probably offends my ancestors to say so. What we could all do with is more money. Merchants get richer all the time and *bushi* get poorer. When you're poor, you're weak. It's the same with countries. If your country's weak, everyone exploits you – in trade, in treaties, in everything.'

'The Shiji family must be sorry to lose you,' I said. 'Such a pillar of moderation.'

'My wife paid me the compliment of weeping profusely,' Monta replied. 'But they are lucky to be rid of me. I've been a most unsatisfactory son-in-law, never around, always getting into trouble.'

'Do you have any children?'

'There is a daughter – I suppose she is mine. I'm afraid she has hardly seen her father.'

I said nothing but Monta might have sensed my disapproval for he went on, 'It is better for us not to have family ties and obligations. We need to be free to act. Wives rarely understand this. But you know, geisha do – that's why we like them so much. I have a friend in Kyōto, Kimio-san, who knows me better than my wife ever could.' He took a mirror out of his robe and showed it to me. 'This was a farewell present from her, to remember her by. She did not cling to me or weep or want me to swear undying love for her. But when I use this mirror I will think of her from time to time. And if it all goes wrong and I'm arrested and executed like Shōin, no one will be dishonoured by it.'

We stopped outside a small house with a thatched roof. It was surrounded by cedars and the mountain rose directly behind it. A bush warbler called piercingly as we approached the veranda. Through the open door we could see into a small room, no more than four mats in size. Takasugi Shinsaku sat next to a low table, a sake gourd and a glass of Western design at his elbow. He was writing with brush and inkstone. He wore dark clothes like a priest and his shaved head made his skull look even more elongated, somehow increasing the striking effect of his unusual features. We were able to watch him for a moment before he noticed us, and he did indeed look wrapped in melancholy, but when he raised his head at the sound of our footsteps a look of pleasure momentarily lightened his expression.

'Monta!' he exclaimed, then called to his wife. 'Okusan, Shiji-san is here.'

'No longer Shiji.' Monta explained again how he had left his adoptive family. 'I've brought an old friend from Yuda to see you. You remember Dr Itasaki's daughter, Shinsai's niece?'

'You came to my sister's wedding,' I said after I had bowed my head.

'O-Tsuru is also married now,' Monta said, 'and living with her husband, Dr Makino, at Shiraishi's place in Bakan.'

'I have taken the name Tōgyō,' Takasugi said, with a perfunctory nod in my direction.

What did he mean by this name? That he was withdrawing from the world? That seemed the most likely since he took no interest in Monta's information, nor did he ask about Shiraishi or about events in Bakan. But Tōgyō meant turning to the east. Edo, the seat of Bakufu power, lay to the east. Did Takasugi mean he was waiting until the time came to overthrow the Tokugawa?

'Others are going to the west,' I said.

'Indeed,' Monta said. 'I have come to say goodbye for a while.'

Takasugi looked at him doubtfully. 'So you are really going to England? Itō too?'

'Why don't you come?' Monta said. 'It won't be the same without you.'

Takasugi did not reply but seemed to lapse again into his own gloomy thoughts.

We were still standing outside, and I was wondering if we would be invited in or not when a small rather plain woman, about my age, came into the room carrying a tray.

'Shiji-san, come up, come up,' she said hurriedly. 'You must forgive my husband; he has not been well.' Then she addressed me. 'We have not met. I am Takasugi Masa, daughter of Inoue Heinemon of Hagi. Please sit down. I have made tea.'

She managed to be extremely polite and condescending at the same time in the way of all *bushi* wives: she reminded me of Monta's sister-in-law. I stepped out of my sandals and followed Monta into the room, sitting a little behind him and Takasugi. Monta asked for sake, which Takasugi poured from the gourd. Masa gave me tea from a pot made of cracked-glaze Hagiyaki, decorated with pictures of the six wise poets.

I made a comment on the pot just to show her I knew who the poets were, and she asked me a few questions, where I lived, if I had any children, and if I liked the tea, but Takasugi remained silent, and his heavy presence made conversation hard to maintain. Monta kept signalling me to try to talk to him. Eventually I mouthed back, 'Leave us alone then!'

Monta emptied his glass in one swig and jumped to his feet saying something about the view, a waterfall, O-Masa-san must show him, no, not O-Tsuru; she was tired and had to rest before walking home, and before we quite realised it, he had hustled the surprised Masa outside, leaving me alone with her husband.

I did not say anything. I had learned from the mad that they cannot be made to talk but if they want to unburden themselves they will, as long as you allow them a silent place in which to begin. I studied Takasugi openly, changing my approach subtly from visitor to visiting doctor. It was a warm afternoon and he had no doubt been drinking a great deal, but I did not think either of these accounted for the flushed patches on his cheeks or for his shallow breathing. I could not feel his pulse points, but I was sure the pulse would be rapid and irregular. A doctor has to use all the senses in diagnosis and my sense of smell was particularly acute. Takasugi did not smell like a healthy man. Apart from the depression I suspected there was something else wrong with him. I hoped it was not syphilis, but perhaps it was *kekkaku*, the slow and always fatal consumption of the lungs.

The bush warbler called again. It was so quiet we could hear the wind in the cedars and the distant waterfall. Takasugi said abruptly, 'I have already been abroad.'

'Really?'

'I went to Shanghai. Last year. You've no idea how terrible things are there. It no longer even looks like China. Have you heard of "colonies"? The English made India a colony and now they want to do the same all round the world. Shanghai has been turned into what they call a concession port. That means the foreigners treat it as their own country. They are the masters and the Chinese are the slaves. When you remember how huge and powerful the Middle Kingdom has been and for how many centuries, that it should be subdued and humiliated by a handful of Westerners is unbelievable. What hope does our country have if it comes to war? This is what goes through my brain day and night, why I cannot eat or sleep. We are following blindly in the same wheel rut. The Bakufu does not know what to do: they can't expel the foreigners because they cannot match them in weapons and trained men, but if they don't act against them they face civil war.' He glanced at me as though he was surprised to be talking to me like this. '*Jōi*, the idea that we can expel the foreigners, is madness. That's what I learned in Shanghai. It's an unattainable dream. But anyone who says that openly runs the risk of being assassinated by the *shishi* because they have made *jōi* their cause. I understand them – sometimes madness is irresistible. Madness releases you from the need to be prudent; it gives you permission to kill for your cause. Never underestimate the power of the mad.'

He smiled bitterly, poured another glass and sipped slowly.

'I study medicine and healing,' I said, my voice firm and decisive. 'I know something about helping those who have lost their senses.'

'I hope Monta did not bring you here to heal me!' he retorted.

I smiled without replying and let another silence build up.

‘You came to Yoshida-*sensei*’s house,’ he said suddenly. ‘The day Towa-san was there.’

‘That’s right.’

‘I saw him in prison in Edo, you know. I visited him a lot. I took him books and food and read to him. But I couldn’t be with him at the end. My father ordered me to return to Hagi and I could not disobey him. That is partly why I am here. I cannot live in my father’s house. My father…he is very conservative. He is close friends with men I despise: Nagai, Mukunashi, Tsuboi. I am his only son. My family has always had the highest expectations of me, yet to follow my own principles I must go against his. He is baffled and disappointed by me.’

Again I said nothing.

‘I held Yoshida’s bones in my hands,’ Takasugi said. ‘When we reburied him. That great mind, that noble heart all reduced to whitened bones. I think about him all the time, go over and over his writings, wondering what he would advise me to do. If only he had not died. But that is what the Bakufu does. It kills those who are trying to save the country. They say they will change, they will reform, but there is no remedy for gangrene. You of all people must know that. The only remedy is amputation, to cut away the infected part.’

‘I like surgery,’ I said. ‘I like cutting.’

‘You need a steady hand. Hold out your hand.’

I held my right hand out over the table and Takasugi did the same. After a few moments his began to tremble. I was proud that mine remained motionless.

He drew his hand back with a groan of disgust. ‘I was weak even as a child. I nearly died from smallpox, never grew as tall as I should have done. Now look at me; you would not believe the hours I've spent in the *dōjo* trying to gain strength, yet at the moment I can hardly lift a sword. I am useless.'

'It is the sake,' I said. 'You should not drink; you should walk to the top of the mountain and back every day.'

'Is that your remedy for me? It's no use. I am retired. If the domain want me to take part in overthrowing the Bakufu, I'll come back. But not before then.'

A fit of coughing overtook him at that point, and he drained his glass. 'That is why I need to drink,' he said when he could talk again. 'Ever since I came back from Shanghai I have been plagued by colds and coughs.' He wiped his eyes and took a small lacquer *inrō* case from his sash. The *netsuke* toggle was a skilfully carved fox, head on paws, bushy tail curled around its body. He took out a twist of paper and shook powder into a bowl, mixing it with the tea that was left in the pot.

'What are you taking?'

'Something my wife buys from the pharmacy in town, some so-called Cure-All.'

'Come to Shimonoseki and I will make you up a better one, one that works.'

He looked at me and laughed. 'What are you doing in Shimonoseki, anyway? You know war's going to break out there? The Shōgun is going to have to fix a date to expel the foreigners, even though he knows it's impossible, and our poor ill-equipped soldiers are going to obey in some way, even though we know it's impossible. They think their samurai spirit will prevail, just like the Chinese thought their virtue would. But nothing prevails against the gun. I'll show you something I bought in Shanghai.'

He got to his feet, swaying a little, and walked out of the room. When he returned he was carrying some heavy object wrapped in a *furoshiki* of mauve silk with the Chōshū crest in white. He placed it on the table and unwrapped it. It was a handgun, a revolving-barrel pistol, the first I had seen.

'It's a Smith and Wesson, Model 2 Army,' Takasugi said. 'One of the most famous American guns. I bought a couple of them. They are expensive. But this is what we need – guns, rifles, cannon, warships.'

He showed me the bullets and how they slipped into the revolving chamber. I weighed them in my hand and tried to imagine the impact they would have on human flesh. How far would they penetrate into the body? Would they be deflected by bone? To what extent would the bone shatter?

'This is why we are in Bakan,' I said. 'To care for the wounded. My husband and I need to know about battle injuries. Lord Sufu wanted my husband to train with the military.'

'So he is Sufu's man? Well, so am I, I suppose. But if anyone should drink less it is Sufu. In Edo he was so drunk he got into a fight with the Tosa *daimyō*. I only got him out of it by declaring Chōshū punishes its own in its own way. In the end his horse bolted with him.'

I remembered my own wedding and could not help smiling, though I did not want to seem disrespectful to my husband's mentor, and the man who had always championed and protected Takasugi himself. I looked away into the garden and saw Monta and O-Masa had returned and were standing outside listening. Monta caught my eye and made a half-pleased, half-mocking grimace. But I thought I saw a flash of jealousy in O-Masa's face, and when she invited us to stay and eat with them it was with an underlying coldness that made me reluctant to accept. Luckily Monta was planning to walk as far as Sasanami before nightfall on the first leg of his journey back to Yokohama, and from there to Hong Kong and England. He declined for us both. I gave O-Masa the names of ointments that she might use in massaging her husband's temples, and suggested laxatives, exercise and warm foot baths, but I suspected she would not take my advice.

Monta and Takasugi clasped arms like brothers, tears in their eyes.

'Don't forget to check out the whisky,' Takasugi said. 'But be careful, it's a lot stronger than sake.'

'I'll be checking out the whisky and the women, don't worry. I'm not a three-cup drunk like you! And I'll bring back a couple of warships.'

'Give my regards to Shiraishi-san,' Takasugi said to me.

'I will. Come and see us in Shimonoseki.'

'Maybe one day soon,' he replied.

'There,' Monta said, delighted, as we walked back down the hill. 'I knew you would do him good!'

'The illness takes its course,' I said. 'He is coming out of the melancholy stage and into the manic one.' I had seen the same pattern with Eikaku. 'All I did was listen – but sometimes that helps, the right kind of listening.'

We said goodbye at the corner of the Kuriya's street.

'I'll write to you from England,' Monta promised.

'Take care of yourself,' I replied.

BIRTH

When I got back to the Kuriya house Mitsue was complaining of some pain, though she did not think the birth was imminent. She was more experienced than I was; she had delivered two healthy sons while I had only assisted at births with my father. He had some knowledge of the Kagawa school of obstetrics and used straps and forceps for difficult births or to remove a dead foetus, though he did not really like either technique as they often ended more lives than they saved. Both Makino and I had studied the Kagawa methods, but my husband did not attend many births. In those days it was more common for the birth to be supervised by a midwife, who used a mixture of common sense, practical knowledge and superstition to allay the fears of the mother.

In some country areas dried seahorses were given to pregnant women and 'hurry-up medicine' was dispensed in tiny amounts in cowrie shells. Spells and charms, the characters of the Ise Shrine for example, were written on paper which was then shredded and given to the mother to drink. But Mitsue was a doctor's daughter, and did not really believe in such things.

I spread out the bedding in the room we had prepared at the back of the house, helped Mitsue take off her clothes, leaving her under-kimono loose over her shoulders, and made her lie down. I put my hand on her abdomen, palpating it gently to feel the baby's shape. To my relief it was in the right position, and it wriggled under my fingers, proving it was alive. Just as I said this to Mitsue, she gave a gasp, and I felt the first real contraction. The whole belly area hardened as the wave went through it.

Mitsue panted. 'It's starting.'

I sent her husband to fetch the midwife. When I came back to the room Mitsue had sat up and was leaning back against the wooden birth board. I had brought a collection of rags and old clothes which I placed beneath her.

'I didn't wash my hair,' Mitsue complained. 'I didn't think the baby was going to come today. I had it all planned. I would wash my hair in the morning and dry it in the sun.'

'Don't worry about it,' I said. I knew it was typical of women about to give birth to concern themselves with trivial matters, cleaning, housekeeping, personal care.

Mitsue gasped again. 'I'm wet,' she said urgently.

The waters had broken. I called to the maids to bring hot water, and washed and dried my sister.

The midwife arrived. She had delivered both the boys and knew Mitsue well. She felt the belly gently, as I had done.

'This time will be easier,' she said. 'The baby is smaller and in a good position.'

Indeed, it was barely dark when the baby came in a rush.

'Ah, shame, shame,' the old woman muttered as she took it in her hands.

'What is it? What's wrong?' Mitsue cried.

I grabbed the slippery little creature from the midwife.

The cord was round its neck and the baby was blue. I thrust my fingers between the cord and the flesh trying to loosen it. As soon as I had unwound it a little, I put my mouth to her bloody little face, and blew gently into her nose, at the same time pushing on her chest. She opened her mouth, drew an astonished breath and began to cry.

I did not give birth to the child who would become my daughter, but I gave her life and I loved her from that moment.

'It's a girl,' the midwife said to Mitsue. 'Do we keep her or send her back?'

'Of course we keep her,' I said sharply, as I began to wash her little body clean from blood and birth fluid.

'Yes, we keep her,' Mitsue echoed, her voice weak but determined.

I wrapped the baby and held her while the placenta was delivered, and then gave her to her mother. She had stopped crying and when Mitsue offered her the breast she took the nipple and began to suck. She was small, but she was strong.

The midwife and I washed Mitsue; she was bleeding a little but the quick delivery had been easy on her. Her daughter had not torn her as her last large son had.

The midwife took the placenta away to make sure that it was buried properly, and Mitsue and I were left alone with the baby girl. The room was heavy with the special atmosphere of childbirth, when a woman comes so close to the possibility of death. Time seems to stand still in a moment of wonder that death has been averted and a new life brought into the world.

'What was wrong with the baby when she was saying "Shame"?' Mitsue whispered.

'Cord round the neck,' I said. 'She was turning blue.'

'Tsu-chan, if you hadn't been here the *obaasan* would have let her die.' Mitsue was filled with the stormy emotions of childbirth and tears welled in her eyes. 'You saved her. She will always be partly yours. She will be our little girl and she will always remind me of you. Now I will not be so lonely.'

'Neechan, I thought you were happy here.'

'I miss you and our parents so much. I know it's wrong of me. I am very fortunate in my husband and my new family. But I miss our home.'

Mitsue's daughter was born at the beginning of the fourth month. After seven days a small celebration was held in the house and the baby was given the name Michi. I had planned to stay for the thirty-three days after the birth in order to accompany the family to the local shrine to present the baby to the *kami*, but events in the domain sent me hurrying back to Shimonoseki. Just as Takasugi had predicted, the Shōgun had been pushed into announcing that a date had been set for the expulsion of all foreigners from Japan and Chōshū was determined to carry out this order, considering it the wish of the Emperor himself. Frenzied activity followed to prepare coastal defences and raise an army. A thousand men rushed to Shimonoseki and the government of Chōshū was moved from Hagi to Yamaguchi, since that was considered less vulnerable to attack. The domain lords, Takachika and Sadahiro, both returned.

Finally it seemed the war against the foreigners really was about to break out. I didn't want to miss out on it. I wanted to join my husband in the middle of the action.

The domain was in turmoil, one rumour following another. Many fled from Hagi and the roads were crowded. Yet the *bushi* wives left behind in Hagi came out from behind the high walls and the latticed windows of their husbands' residences and joined the townspeople building defences on Kikugahama. Everyone was singing the popular song 'Otokonara':

> *If I were a man*
> *I would shoulder a spear*
> *And march to Shimonoseki.*

It made me feel as if I myself was doing something really courageous in marching back to Bakan.

I stayed one night at my parents' house. My mother was already home after her pilgrimage and was delighted and relieved to hear of the birth of her granddaughter. I told my father about the cord; he did not make much of it, but murmured, 'You did well, Tsu-chan.' They did not want me to return to Shimonoseki, but I was determined, and I left early the following morning.

Once I was on the road out of Yamaguchi the traffic was all coming towards me. People were streaming out of the port town with their children, animals, birds and other belongings packed into handcarts or baskets. Apparently everyone had decided if the government had moved to Yamaguchi they would be safer there too.

As I approached the port I realised not quite everyone had fled. Some had chosen to stay and watch the war as if it were a *misemono* or a fireworks show. They were encamped on the surrounding hills out of the range of any guns, watching the foreign ships sail obliviously through the strait, yelling threats and warnings to them which naturally they could not hear, and would not have understood anyway.

The high road ran along the coast, past the gun batteries at Maeda and Dannoura which were manned by soldiers in their strange motley uniforms, and past Amidadera and the shrine at Kameyama. Across the Inland Sea rose the mountains of Kyūshū, violet in the evening haze. On my right, in a position that gave a good view over the bay and the strait was the temple, Kōmyōji. Usually this was a tranquil place, frequented only by monks, and cats sunning themselves on the verandas or chasing leaves under the huge gingko tree, but this evening I could hear voices raised in argument and shouts of raucous laughter. A group of over thirty men had set up camp in the temple grounds. They looked like real ruffians and my first thought was that they were bandits who had taken advantage of the breakdown of normal society to move into the city. Most of them wore their hair long, caught up in a tail like a horse, their foreheads unshaven. Many wore headbands of red or white material, some bearing the Chōshū crest, others various characters denoting 'loyalty' or 'courage'. All wore two swords.

I would have hurried by, but to my surprise I heard my husband's voice. I stopped and saw Makino coming down the steps towards me.

'You're back safely!' He took my baskets from me. 'You must be tired.'

'What are you doing here?' I asked.

'I'm trying to find someone who will discuss the treatment of the wounded – we need to set up a temporary hospital somewhere, and I thought Kōmyōji might serve. But Genzui is here with his men. They're waiting to see what happens when we attack the foreigners. Come up and say hello.'

Kusaka Genzui, his long hair held back by a white headband, was standing at the outer wall of the temple, peering through a telescope in the direction of Dannoura, the narrowest part of the strait. As we approached he took it down from his eye and held it out to Makino.

'Take a look. That's an American flag, isn't it?' He pointed to a sailing ship going briskly through the strait, carried by the evening tide and the westerly wind, the strange flag with the stripes and stars fluttering from the stern.

'Yes, that's American,' Makino agreed, then said, 'My wife is here. She has just returned from Hagi.' He turned to me. 'What news of your sister?'

'She had a baby girl.'

Genzui gave me a smile and a nod. 'Did you see my wife?'

'No, I wanted to but…'

'Please go next time you are in Hagi. She often asks after you.'

I didn't want to mention my meeting with Shiji – now Inoue – Monta. I wondered where he and Itō were now, if they had already embarked on a ship like this one, if Genzui knew they were going secretly to England. I turned my eyes to the west where the last light of the day still glimmered, reflecting with a yellow glow on the grey clouds.

'I saw Takasugi-san.'

Genzui was immediately interested. 'What's he doing?' he demanded. 'Why isn't he here?'

Again I did not know how much to reveal. Even Takasugi's illness was best kept secret, I thought.

'Will you take part in the fighting?' I said to Genzui.

He did not answer directly. He said, suddenly reminding me of the well-brought-up doctor's son he was at heart, 'You must be thirsty. Can we offer you something to drink?'

I began to protest that I was fine, but he led Makino and me to the temple entrance and we stepped up into the wooden-floored hall.

'Sit down,' Genzui said.

There were a few cushions strewn around a brazier which smouldered smokily. Even though it was nearly the fifth month it was cold inside the hall, and I was glad to sit near the fire. Genzui shouted into the shadows at the back, and a girl appeared. I was not really surprised to see her – wherever there were *shishi* there were girls, geisha or waitresses from the inns along the road, who fell in love with these young men, gave them free meals and shelter, warned them of danger, found hiding places for them, washed and mended their clothes, shared their beds. And often ended up marrying them – as Monta had said, these girls understood their lovers better than any *bushi* wife could.

This girl bobbed her head when Genzui demanded tea and sake and reappeared in a few minutes with the drinks and bowls on a tray.

'Isn't there anything to eat?' Genzui said. 'Run down to the street stall and bring back some soba and sushi. Tell him he'll be paid tomorrow.' He grinned at Makino and said,

'After all, we are virtuous samurai, employed on the business of the domain.'

When the drinks had been poured he said, 'To answer your question, of course I should be fighting – and in the front line. All of us here want that – Yoshida Toshimaro, Yamagata Kyōsuke, the Irie brothers – but we have been forbidden to take part. Mōri Noto is to be the commander and he does not want anyone who is not of *shi* rank in his forces. He thinks we will cause unrest among the samurai and undermine him. So we have been sent here to "keep a look out" – whatever that means.'

'Just sit here and watch the show,' Makino said ironically.

'Ha! They'll be sorry they didn't listen to our advice and accept our help when they get thumped. Even though they're using cannon they don't have any idea how to fight Westerners. It's what Yoshida-*sensei* was saying years ago: we should have overhauled the whole army, got rid of all those old *bushi* with their antiquated ideas, and reformed on Western lines. Now we are going to be defeated.'

Genzui looked both grim and somehow elated at the prospect. Makino's face was more serious.

'What about us? Where should we be stationed?' I asked. 'Have any arrangements been made?'

'For the wounded?' Makino said. 'That's the trouble. Even to suggest that there might be wounded sounds disloyal and defeatist. No one's made any arrangements. Western armies have what they call field hospitals set up behind the front line. I've read about them. They are equipped with surgical instruments, bandages, beds, stretchers and so on. They need a source of clean water, fires and lanterns to keep working through the night.'

When Genzui made no immediate response to this, Makino said, exasperated, 'If you can save your wounded you can return them to the battle.'

'Soldiers need to be prepared to die,' Genzui said slowly. I could almost see the conflicting elements in him. He was a doctor's son: his father and his elder brother had dedicated their lives to understanding disease and finding remedies, but he himself was imbued with the spirit of the samurai class, who despised cowardice and tried to eradicate any base instinct for self-preservation.

'Yet many of them could be saved,' Makino pressed on. 'I want you to give me a place for them: either here or at Amidadera or Gokurakuji.'

'Either of them would be better than here; they are closer to the gun emplacements.'

'At Gokurakuji they could go straight to paradise,' I said, making them both laugh.

'But we hope to keep as many as possible here in this world,' Makino said.

'I'll see what I can do,' Genzui promised.

While we had been talking several other *shishi* had wandered into the room and sat down around us. They all seemed restless and frustrated. They wanted to take part in the fighting, they wanted to attack foreigners, but they knew Chōshū faced certain defeat. Everyone agreed that an attack would break the paralysis that the whole country seemed to be gripped by, but no one knew what would happen after that. Opinions flew in the dim temple hall: the military needed reform, units of mixed status should be allowed, peasants and farmers should be armed. Some of the most vocal I knew a little – Yamagata, the two Irie boys – but I was unsettled by the flickering aura of death that shadowed so many of them. At times I thought I saw the whole hall awash with blood. The girl came back with bowls of food but I was too tired to eat. I did not want to stay with these young men whose lives would be over so soon.

Makino must have noticed how I was feeling for he said, 'My wife has been travelling all day; we should go home.'

'I'll be in touch through Shiraishi,' Genzui said as we left.

WAR

Around the time of the summer solstice my husband and I found out what cannonballs and explosive shells do to human bodies. Despite all our reading we were completely unprepared and we saw things for which we had no words.

We had moved to Gokurakuji. The priests made a hall available at the side of the temple and here we tried to prepare a place to treat the wounded. With Shiraishi's help we transported bandages, salves, scalpels and needles for surgery, buckets, kettles, firewood, and anything else we could think of.

It was well into the sixth month and very hot. We heard the guns in the morning. Makino said, 'It's started!' and we ran outside to look down into the strait.

As part of the domain's efforts to strengthen its defences Chōshū had recently acquired three Western-built warships, and two of them, flying the new red-sun flag of Japan as well as the Chōshū banners, had opened fire on an American merchant vessel, which I later learned was called the *Pembroke*. It was resting at anchor offshore in the strait, on its way to Nagasaki and then Shanghai. One shot landed in the stern of the ship, rocking it violently; the next tore through the rigging, taking away one of the masts. We could see clearly the sudden almost comical reaction of the men on board as they realised they had come under attack. Taunting shouts of *sonnō jōi* rang from the Chōshū ships, while the Americans ran to and fro like startled earwigs, waving their hands and calling out orders.

The battery at Kameyama opened fire too. The first shells fell short of the ship, sending plumes of water high into the air. The *Pembroke* had managed to start its engines and was moving out of range, fleeing towards the Bungo strait. A cheer went up from the garrison. Men were jumping and waving their hands with excitement. The air filled with the smell of bitter smoke.

'Now we have started something,' Makino said. It was a sombre moment yet I could not help feeling as proud and excited as the soldiers. Our domain, Chōshū, had been obedient to the command of the Emperor. We alone were carrying out his wishes. We were in the front line of the war against the foreigners.

Two more attacks followed. We did not know that they were different nationalities – to us they were all foreigners. In fact one was a French ship, one Dutch. Like the *Pembroke* they fled as fast as they could under the barrage from the Chōshū guns. Unluckily Chōshū had managed to offend three of the most powerful nations on earth and the fourth, England, even though not directly involved, would join forces with them to punish us.

But at that moment no one thought of the future. Everyone was too busy celebrating victory. Kusaka Genzui left for Kyōto to report the success and to encourage other domains to join us.

Makino was as usual sceptical. 'It's all too easy,' he said. 'There's bound to be retaliation sooner or later.'

'You're disappointed you don't have any interesting cases to treat,' I replied. I had expected by now to be hard at work, but we still had no casualties. The temple priest consulted Makino about his sore eyes and I treated some of the local children for various skin diseases and talked to the priest's wife about her ailments and the charms and prayers she trusted to effect a cure. We lanced a few boils, pulled a few teeth. Eikaku, who was in a pleasantly manic stage, dropped by, keen to see for himself the horrors of the new warfare. Like many mad people he seemed to be calmed by genuine crisis, as if the outside world were finally consonant with his inner turmoil. The days went slowly by. The city was quiet – so many people had fled. The weather was fine and hot, the sea calm. Even the notorious tidal flow of the straits was stilled.

After the Dutch ship fled, apart from a few brave local vessels and the three Chōshū warships, the *Kigai-maru*, the *Kōsei-maru* and the *Kōshin-maru*, which continued to patrol the coast, no shipping came through the strait until the first day of the sixth month. Then a large, fast American ship came into view, early in the morning. It had been hiding overnight behind Hikoshima, having sailed two days earlier from Yokohama.

We heard the signal guns and again ran out to watch. The ship had a purposeful air that alarmed me – it had many guns and was sailing directly towards the three Chōshū warships. The Kameyama battery opened fire but the warship had come in close to the coast and the shells passed over it and landed in the sea. Then it responded. It had no problems with accuracy or range; within moments the Kameyama battery was destroyed. The American ship then turned its attention to the Chōshū ships, which had got underway and were preparing to attack. They managed to fire their guns but then all three were hit decisively; two began to sink almost at once. At one point the Americans ran aground, and seemed to present an easy target, but the shore batteries had all been silenced and the ship managed to free itself and escape. It continued firing into the batteries and the town, seeming to hover in the water like a hawk before disappearing back to Yokohama.

The battle had lasted little more than an hour. Even though it was what we had been half expecting, the ferocity of the attack and its speed left me momentarily in shock. The guns, so accurate and so deadly, made me look at the world in a new way – they might have exploded inside my head. I wished Genzui was here, and Takasugi, to see with their own eyes the blowing apart of the fantastical illusion that was *jōi*.

Makino said, 'We must go to the battery.'

I grabbed a few things: a handful of bandages, the box of scalpels, scissors, tweezers, and, with Eikaku, followed my husband to where the battery had been. My ears were ringing from the explosions. *Explosions* – I don't think I even knew the word at that time. The only other noise I could compare it to would be the fireworks of summer festivals.

Smoke and dust hung in the air and the heavy guns were curiously awry, their muzzles pointing skywards. Of the soldiers who had manned them there was at first no trace, nor were there any cries or groans from the wounded. Then I registered the blood-spattered ground, the fragments of bone and flesh that clung to the guns, a hand flung against a fence, part of a scalp with the eyeball staring in the dust.

Eikaku said with lively interest, 'Why, they were all blown to bits!' His eyes were round with astonishment. Even in his most gruesome paintings he had never imagined the human body so taken apart, so reduced to meat and gristle.

The other batteries at Maeda and Dannoura were silent now. Birds were singing again from the wooded hills. People gathered round – other soldiers who had escaped the direct hit and were merely concussed or wounded slightly by shrapnel, and a few townsfolk who had stayed behind to watch the fighting or guard their property. An officer immediately took command and gave orders for the body parts to be collected, and the guns to be washed down, remounted and reloaded.

The soldiers, in their mixture of uniforms, some black Western style, some old-fashioned armour, obeyed their captain, but I thought they were as shocked as we were. It was their first experience of war; the last time Mōri forces had fought in a battle had been over two hundred years ago.

The priest was murmuring prayers at my side. Makino approached the captain and explained why we were there.

'We have no wounded!' the man replied angrily. 'These weapons do not wound. They pulverise!'

'How many men did you lose?'

'Eight. My best gunners.' He turned and made a rage-filled gesture towards the east where the American ship had disappeared. 'I hope we did the same to yours too!'

His shock made him exaggerate; of course there were some wounded, whom we treated that afternoon and into the night, while the heavens opened above us in a violent storm.

Four days later the Kameyama battery was functioning again, only to be destroyed the same day by two French ships which pounded it and the others into silence, with the same terrible loss of life.

Makino and I went to Maeda, collected the bodies and handed them over to the priest at Gokurakuji for burial. The soldiers who survived were completely demoralised and when the enemy actually came ashore they ran away, along with most of the remaining townspeople, who were cursing their misfortune and blaming foreigner and samurai alike.

Only one small force, under Yamagata Kyōsuke, retreated in some order and continued to resist, sniping at the French sailors. However they had little effect.

The sailors acted more like sightseers than enemy assailants. They came in rowboats, clambered up the embankment and jumped over the low fences. They looked at the six guns, and laughed at them. I hated their arrogant smiling faces beneath their silly white hats. They took photographs (another word that I did not know at the time) and posed for the camera, waving their flag and raising their hands in the air. But for all their merriment they were nonetheless ruthlessly efficient. They burned the weapons and ammunitions that were stored in the Maeda forts and set fire to several neighbouring houses as well. They did not try to harm us, but shooed us aside as if we were annoying animals, getting in the way of them carrying out their duties.

Eventually they climbed back into the boats and returned to their ships, leaving smoke and flames behind them. The two ships sailed up and back along the coast a couple of times as though challenging someone to respond. But they had done their job too well. There were no guns left. Chōshū had been defeated.

Makino and I returned the next day to Shiraishi's house to discuss with him what we would do next. He was as despondent as we were, his face grey with exhaustion. Chōshū had lost its three warships; most of its shore batteries had been destroyed and forty men had died. Shiraishi was responsible for dealing with all the practicalities: arranging the funerals, supplying provisions to the survivors, finding out if the ships could be salvaged, and keeping the hostel going as it filled up with anxious, angry young men.

Many of them came from Genzui's group at Kōmyōji. Having been excluded from the fighting they were filled with recriminations against the domain forces. I listened to them with mounting irritation as they said the same things over and over again.

'They should have used us. We would have made a difference.'

'Nothing would have made any difference. We were outnumbered and outgunned.'

'They say our gun barrels were pointing downwards and the balls rolled out!'

'What idiots!'

'But did you see that American ship? They knew what they were doing!'

'I thought we had them when it ran aground!'

'What a marvel! That ship! If we had one like that!'

Makino and I retreated to our room. I was thinking about preparing the bed. I wondered if we would get any sleep.

The depressed *shishi* would probably be drinking and arguing for the rest of the night.

'What will happen now?' I said.

'We have made enemies among the foreigners and the Bakufu,' he replied. 'I suppose there will be further retaliation.'

'But the Bakufu issued the order to expel the foreigners, following the Emperor's wishes.'

'They didn't expect anyone to take it seriously,' Makino said. 'Anyone rational would see that we cannot defeat the foreigners. They are superior to us in arms, navigation, technology.'

'So we have to let them take over our country because we are too weak to stop them?' I did not think the young men in the adjoining room would ever accept that. They would rather fight to the death. I thought about Nakajima and Shinsai. If Nakajima had been rational he would still be alive. And Shinsai would not be risking his life in Kyōto. I suddenly missed him terribly. How happy I would be if he were to appear at the door of the hostel.

'Maybe they don't want to take it over,' Makino said. 'Maybe they just want to trade and have a safe passage for their ships. Maybe if we all sat down together we could reach an agreement.' He was so rational himself he thought these things could be measured out like the ingredients for a remedy.

It was growing dark outside. The smell of the sea that always pervaded Shimonoseki seemed to intensify with the approaching night. Inside the inn lamps were being lit, and the maids ran to and fro with trays of food and sake. I heard porters shouting outside as they arrived with a guest in a palanquin, and then I heard a familiar voice greet Shiraishi. I could not believe my ears. I ran to the entrance. Before I got there I heard someone say clearly, 'It's Shinsaku!'

I pressed against the wall as Takasugi Shinsaku swept past and then I followed in his wake into the main room where the *shishi* were assembled. They sent up a great shout of delight at his appearance, and many of them bowed to the ground.

I watched him with interest. It was hard to believe this was the same man I had last seen in Matsumoto village, in the grip of melancholy. It had seemed when I left that the illness might be moving into its manic stage. Now I could see that Takasugi was, in his own mind, invincible. His whole demeanour had changed; he even seemed taller and more robust. His expression was energetic and his eyes full of purpose.

'I've been sent by Lord Mōri Takachika himself,' he said, addressing the whole room in a clear decisive voice. He paused for a moment while the significance of this sank in and then brandished the document case he held. 'These are my orders. I have been entrusted with the task of forming a new kind of troop for the domain army, to defend ourselves and our country.'

His eyes searched the room as he noted who was present. There were several old *sonjuku* students like himself. Acknowledging them with a smile, he said, 'We will put into practice our teacher's ideals. We will form a combined troop of samurai and commoners. Men will be accepted according to their ability not their rank. We will be armed with Western rifles and will drill in Western style.'

This statement was greeted with cheers of excitement. Takasugi put up a hand to silence them.

'You will be the basis of the new army,' he said, and I would swear each man thought he spoke directly to him. 'With a strong army we will have a strong and rich country, and then we will be able to confront the foreigners on equal terms.'

He sat down and took the bowl of sake Shiraishi offered. He held it out before giving a shout of 'Kanpai!' and swallowing it at one gulp.

'Kanpai!' everyone cried as they scrabbled to fill their bowls and drink.

Takasugi looked at them and they hung on that look. He said, 'There are fifteen of you here. I'm assuming you all want to fight?'

They shouted their agreement.

Takasugi went on, 'That will make three units of five men each. You are the first Kiheitai and from now on you are under my command.'

The name meant strange or special troop, and from the start had a mysterious, seductive ring to it.

'My brother and I will join,' Shiraishi said, stepping forward. His brother, Rensaku, was just behind him. I felt a twinge of unease for I knew Rensaku was one of those who would not survive their time with the Kiheitai. 'And we will take care of finances and provisions.'

'Agreed – and I'm trusting you to find us some rifles.'

'We will get them in Nagasaki,' Shiraishi promised, almost quivering with excitement.

'Shiraishi-san, I'll need you to help smooth things over

with the branch domain,' Takasugi said. Shimonoseki, which the main Hagi domain would have liked to have under its control, was in fact part of the branch domain of Chōfu, which was more often than not at odds with Hagi.

'Certainly. And perhaps you will put in a good word for me in Hagi,' Shiraishi said. His eyes gleamed as if he saw dreams of wealth and social advancement hovering before him.

Takasugi had given no sign of recognising me before, but now gazing around the room, he said, 'Where is the doctor's daughter? O-Tsuru-san?'

'I am here,' I said, stepping out from the shadows.

'We will need you and your husband. Is he here?'

'I'll get him,' Shiraishi said, hurrying from the room.

'You told me to come and see you here,' Takasugi said to me. 'And here I am!'

'I am glad to see you so much restored.'

My husband came in. He was in his night attire and had pulled his jacket on over the top of his *yukata*.

Takasugi said, 'Dr Makino, I want you to join the Kiheitai. We will set up field hospitals. I think you know something about them. I am putting you in charge. Your wife will help you.'

There was no question of not obeying him. Makino bowed without speaking, a faint flush on his usually pale skin revealing his pleasure. I imagined dreams of advancement were not far from his mind either.

Within a few days the Kiheitai had grown to sixty, far too many to fit comfortably into Shiraishi's place. Takasugi moved them to the Amidadera; by the end of the following month there were twenty five-man units. People flocked to join: lower-level samurai, farmers' sons, priests, even *sumō* wrestlers. As I came to know them I learned they had many different motives. Some were already fervent loyalists, some hoped to become samurai, some wanted advancement or adventure, some just liked the idea of fighting. All were no doubt grateful for the food and small wage provided by the domain, supplemented by merchants like Shiraishi. They would thrive on the strict education and discipline that Takasugi and the other commanders established for the Kiheitai, and over the coming months various similar troops, known generally as *shotai*, sprouted throughout the domain like bamboo after the spring rain. Not everyone liked them or approved of them, but it seemed nothing could prevent their spread.

Chōshū had suffered a humiliating defeat, and worse defeats and more painful sacrifices lay ahead, but the Kiheitai contained the secret ingredient that would save the domain from destruction.

SEPARATION

Early in the seventh month English warships attacked the Satsuma castle town of Kagoshima as a punishment for the Namamugi incident of the previous year when an Englishman was killed by retainers of Shimazu Hisamitsu. Most of the town had been destroyed and many killed, but Satsuma had fought back and forced the English to withdraw. We heard the news from merchants who traded with Shiraishi, and the Chōshū men who came through the hostel discussed it at length, with a mixture of envy, delight and grudging admiration. Both sides were seen as Chōshū's enemies, Satsuma as much as England. The idea that the two great domains of the southwest would one day form an alliance might have occurred to the astute Shiraishi at that time, but not to anyone else.

The other constant topic of discussion was the situation in Kyōto. The leading Chōshū elder in the capital, Masuda Danjō, had put forward a request to the Emperor to lead out the country's military forces against the foreigners, and hundreds of loyalist *shishi* and *rōnin* in Kyōto had launched a new wave of violence to persuade the Court to make up its mind.

Everyone wanted to go to Kyōto. They didn't know what they would do there or who they would fight; it just seemed essential to be there. It was like a legend from the olden days: the Emperor leading his loyal subjects in battle against the hated invaders. I could imagine it as a painting: the horses, the banners, the warriors in their armour. But then I remembered the guns that had pounded Shimonoseki. Being the Son of Heaven would not prevent the Emperor being torn apart by shrapnel as surely as the lowest rank soldier. But I did not voice this opinion for there were many who believed the Emperor had divine protection and that to say anything different was tantamount to treason.

Makino took to his new position with enthusiasm and threw himself into the work, but I noticed that since the bombardment of the Maeda and Kameyama batteries he had become more critical and irritable with me. He had usually deferred to me in all sorts of ways – in diagnosis, treatment, and making up remedies – but suddenly he began to question my judgement, find fault with my practice, and in particular undermine me in the presence of others. It was nothing worse than the way most men treated their wives in public, but I was not used to criticism and it rankled.

The night before we were due to move to the Amidadera to join the Kiheitai he was more difficult than ever, bad-tempered and sarcastic. I tried to approach him in bed, wanting to regain our old closeness, but he said he was tired, and turned away from me. The next morning, as I was arranging for the maids to help me pack up our clothes, Makino said, 'Put your things separately. I think you should go home to your parents.'

'I'm coming with you to work with the Kiheitai.' I did not take him seriously; I was wondering if we should transport all the medical supplies with us or leave some at the Kokuraya, using Shiraishi's godown as a central storage house. I was a little tired and distracted; it was the end of the seventh month and very hot.

'Wife, I mean it. You are to go home to Yuda.'

Makino never called me *wife* unless speaking of me to a third person. And he never gave me orders. I told the maid I could manage without her and she left reluctantly. No doubt she would have preferred to stay and witness what was going to happen. Everyone knew everyone else's business in the inn, and I was already a source of considerable gossip, for working as a doctor, for being childless, for my interest in the mad.

'What do you mean, go home to Yuda?'

Makino did not look at me directly but said, 'It is no place for a woman.'

'The Amidadera? I'll bet there are any number of women there. Where there are *shishi* there are geisha!'

'On the contrary, they have the strictest discipline and women are not to be allowed in the temple precinct.'

'I don't count as a woman anyway. I'm a doctor and your wife.'

'Let's not argue about it. I am going alone.'

'You can't just send me home!'

'I am sure your father will be glad to have your assistance again.'

I felt as if I had been hit in the belly. He had literally winded me. I could hardly breathe and I was afraid if I did draw breath it would turn into a sob. I did not want to cry above all.

Outside a street seller was crying, 'Fresh tofu! How about it?' and I could hear the rhythmic shouts of the men unloading cargo at the docks. Cries of seagulls, rattling of masts and rigging, lap of waves, the wind…

'Is it because I don't have children?'

'If you had children you wouldn't be able to come with me anyway.' He added more gently, 'It doesn't mean I want a divorce.'

'Divorce? You've been thinking about divorce?'

'No!' He tried to explain more but I was enraged now, and frightened. I knew how ambitious Makino was. He had used me already to get a foot on the ladder that would lead him upwards. The opportunity to work with the Kiheitai was another step up. I suddenly saw that he would jettison me if I stood in the way.

'If you send me home it's as good as divorcing me. I'll never come back to you. Is that what you want?'

'Calm down…'

'Takasugi himself said I was to help you. Go and ask him if I am to go home or come with you. I'll do whatever he says.' I stood with arms folded, prepared to wait until I heard.

'He has gone back to Yamaguchi. He's no longer commander of the Kiheitai.'

I stared at Makino, hardly able to believe it. Yet it was typical of Takasugi's erratic career. 'Is he all right? When did this happen?'

'A couple of days ago. They're trying to keep it quiet. There was some kind of confrontation with the Senpōtai, a government troop based in Kyōhōji, insults and taunts. In the ensuing clash at least one man died. Takasugi was ready to take his own life, as the senior officer, but Miyagi Hikonosuke accepted responsibility instead and committed suicide yesterday.'

He turned pale as he said this, then admitted, 'I had never seen a man slit his belly before.'

I had never seen it either, and could not help feeling a pang of envy. I wished Miyagi-san had not felt obliged to kill himself and I regretted that his life had been cut short but, all the same, I would have liked to see how he died. From a purely medical point of view I was interested in how much strength it took to make the cut and what layers of tissue had to be penetrated before the abdomen was opened. Presumably Miyagi had a second waiting to decapitate him as soon as was honourable...Normally I would have questioned Makino but now I kept silent.

'I don't think of myself as particularly squeamish,' he said, 'but ever since the foreign bombardment I've been plagued by bad dreams. I can cope with my reactions if I am alone, but not if you are with me. My fears for you are far greater than my fears for myself.'

That made it sound wonderful. Makino was a caring husband who only wanted to protect his wife. I could see clearly how he had weighed up the arguments in his usual way: the only trouble was he had not entered my opinions or desires into his calculation. 'I don't want to be protected,' I said loudly. 'I don't need you to look after me. I want to look after the wounded. Who's the new commander? Let me approach him.'

'It's Yamagata.'

I did not know Yamagata well. He had been a pupil at the *sonjuku* at the same time as Shinsai. He was of very low rank but he made up for it by his dedicated and disciplined approach to military matters. He was not likely to treat me favourably. I pleaded, aware of how pathetic I sounded, 'You need me. How can you do it on your own?'

'It won't work,' he replied, losing patience. 'Can't you see that? Anyway there'll be other doctors. I'll be part of a team. It's going to be hard work. This isn't just treating farmers and old women for sore eyes or colic or piles. These men are soldiers. They are not in the least refined or cultured. They are rough, many of them are bullies. They taunt and bully each other as well as rival troops; they settle differences with the sword. They would not shrink from forcing anyone they hold guilty into suicide.'

Beneath the impatience I sensed his anxiety. 'You're afraid they'll bully you if your wife comes with you?'

'It just makes it all so much harder,' he said. 'But I'm not going to argue about it any more. I'm your husband. I'm telling you you are not coming. You are to go back to your parents.'

'If I go home I will never come back to you,' I repeated.

'Don't say things you may regret later.' He had become calm and rational again. 'I don't want a divorce, but if you decide you do I will respect your wishes.'

Because I hated him so much at that moment I gave in. I began to separate my clothes and possessions, my hair combs, face powder, tooth-blackening bowl, my books and instruments, my medicine box. When I had finished I helped my husband pack up all the medical equipment we had so carefully gathered together, neither of us saying a word. He went to call the porters to carry it to the Amidadera. I had no idea what I was going to do. It made sense (it was the Accountant's plan so naturally it made sense) to go home to my parents. My father would let me work with him and my mother would be glad of my company. I loved my home and I longed to go back there and be with my family. But to be sent home by my husband because he did not want me to work with him after I had been his way into the profession, after I had taught him most of what he knew, was so humiliating.

Thinking of Makino as the Accountant made me want to cry. I was angry and sad at the same time. My pride was terribly wounded. I realised how unbearable saying goodbye would be. I did not even want to look at him again. I decided to go and see Eikaku to give him the news and make my farewell to him. I would stay there until I was certain my husband had left. Remembering I would need some money I took half of the coins and domain-issued notes that Makino had hidden away, telling myself that I had earned them as much as he had, and being scrupulous to take only half.

I left by the back entrance, instructing the maids that I would be back in a little while to arrange transport of my boxes and baskets. I felt my face grow hot under their false expressions of sympathy.

Eikaku lived a short distance away on the slopes of Sakura mountain, behind Myōrenji, close enough to hear the monks chanting and the gongs and bells of the temple. His sister came to the door and said apologetically, 'Makino-*sensei*, I'll tell him you're here. But I must warn you, he has refused to see anyone for several weeks, ever since the attack in fact.

He has been painting like a madman.' She stopped short, put her hand to her mouth. 'Well, he is a madman!'

We both laughed. 'I just came to say goodbye,' I explained.

'Oh! Where are you going?'

'I'm not sure yet.'

'Some special work for the domain, I suppose.'

'Not really.'

She gave me a shrewd look and told me to come in. I slipped my feet out of my sandals and stepped up onto the tatami. All the screens were open for the autumn day was warm. A smattering of sardine clouds in the southwest suggested a change in the weather. It was the time of white dew, two weeks before the equinox. Scarlet autumn lilies bloomed in the garden and crow vine straggled over the crumbling walls. The plaster had flaked off, revealing the straw-flecked mud within. The whole effect was neglected and sad, reflecting my mood. I was glad Eikaku's garden was not perfectly maintained.

I heard him respond angrily to the interruption, and his sister explain why she had dared approach him while he was working. A long silence followed, then heavy footsteps. Eikaku came rushing into the room. He was unshaven, his hair was unkempt, his clothes dishevelled and paint-stained.

'Where are you going?' he demanded. 'You can't come and interrupt my painting to tell me you're leaving me. I won't be able to work at all.'

'My husband wants me to go home to my parents.'

'And when have you ever done what your husband tells you? You're not a woman to go meekly home just because your husband says so. Anyway, what does he mean by it? Surely he needs you?'

'He's been assigned to the Kiheitai for an indefinite period; he says it is not possible for me to work with them.'

'Ha!' Eikaku exclaimed. 'That's a different matter. I can just see you examining those ruffians asking them what their shit looks like and if they've had sex with a syphilitic prostitute. Your husband's right. You would bring shame on him. They'd taunt him without mercy and lose all respect for him as a doctor.'

He delivered this speech with great speed and fluency, then sat down heavily, crossing his legs and running his fingers through his hair so it stood on end. 'Oneesan!' he shouted. 'Bring tea for the doctor.'

I was disappointed that he did not take my side, but I was thirsty, Eikaku's sister made very good tea, and I had anyway still not decided where I was going to go so I sat down too, more politely, tucking my heels under me and smoothing out my kimono.

'Now don't go all prim on me,' Eikaku said. 'You know I'm right. Your trouble is you always want to be the one who's right. You don't like anyone else knowing better than you. You're just like a man!'

'I wish I were a man,' I said, remembering the song the women had sung in Hagi. 'The world is changing; why shouldn't women be allowed to change too? Men are preparing for war, but what are they fighting for? People like Shiraishi-san believe it is to renew the world; what will the world be like when it is made new?'

'It will be just like it always has been,' Eikaku replied with an air of triumph. 'Men will dominate women. The strong will eat; the weak be meat. It was like that in the days of

Nobunaga and Hideyoshi, and it will be like that in our grandchildren's time.'

'Neither of us is likely to have grandchildren,' I said.

'You will go back to your husband soon enough.'

'What if I don't?' I spoke quietly, thinking aloud.

'In this life you were born a woman. Maybe next time round you'll have the good fortune to be born a man. I'll pray for you.'

He was making me so angry I was about to stand up and leave, but at that moment his sister returned with bowls of tea on a tray. She knelt beside me and handed one to me, murmuring to be careful because it was hot. Then she gave a bowl to Eikaku which he emptied in one gulp.

'You will burn your mouth,' I said.

'Doctor, don't leave me. I need you to look after me.'

As I sipped my own tea I wondered if his complete self-absorption was a symptom of his illness, and found myself thinking of Takasugi. He had also shown a disregard for anyone else's feelings or needs. Was it the mania that caused the inability to see from another's point of view, or was it the other way round? Or, more likely, was it just part of being a man?

'Well, answer me, say something!' Eikaku was irritated by my silence.

'You hardly need me. You seem quite well now. Is your painting going well?'

'I struggle,' he replied. 'I devote myself to it, it tears me apart, but I keep on struggling.'

I was glad to see he was pleased with himself, so different from when he was in the grip of depression.

‘Come and look at what I am doing.’ He put the cup down abruptly, tipping it over and spilling the last drops of tea on the matting.

‘Dr Makino has not finished her tea,’ his sister said, dabbing at the liquid with her hand towel.

‘She has, she has,’ he retorted, urging me to get up and follow him through the neglected garden to the small detached building he used for his painting.

All the screens were open to give the greatest amount of light, which showed up the paint-stained walls and tatami. It was clouding over and the wind had picked up, a hot moist wind like the ones that preceed typhoons.

Two large boards lay on the floor, half-finished paintings. One was an overall view of the gunboats in battle, the American warship delineated in black, the Chōshū vessels flying the red-sun flag and the Mōri crest. Flashes of red fire and puffs of white smoke radiated from their decks. Tiny figures manned the guns, brandished rifles, spears or swords – or were hurled skywards. I was amazed at Eikaku's almost perfect recall of the scene. The other picture was equally clearly remembered – the shocking carnage at the Maeda battery. The body parts seemed to come to life: hands still moved, eyes still saw. The whole scene was awash with blood. It had a strange and compelling aura about it, as if the explosions still echoed, the screams of the dying were just fading. It made me shiver.

‘Isn't it wonderful?’ Eikaku said. ‘I used to have to try and imagine hell. Now I've seen it with my own eyes.’

‘I've never seen anything like it,’ I said truthfully.

He contemplated his work with pride for a long moment.

Then without warning he began to undo his sash and pull off his clothes.

'Get undressed,' he said.

'Certainly not!' I backed away from him, wondering if I should call for help or run away. 'Eikaku-san, stop it. What are you thinking of?'

He had got down to his loincloth and was beginning to unwind it.

I said loudly, 'I'm warning you, I'll scream if you go any further!'

'Don't be silly. I'm not going to rape you. I just want you to try something. It's an experiment.' He held out his under-garments to me, and his kimono. 'I want you to change clothes with me. Put these on.'

I stood motionless for a moment and then began slowly to unwind my sash. It was a strange feeling to release my body from its constriction in the presence of a man not my husband. I slipped my arms out of my robe, and under-kimono, finally stepping out of my red underwear. The moist wind flowed over my body and I noticed with detachment my nipples were hardening. I stood naked. Eikaku was the same.

I stared at him levelly and he regarded me in the same way.

'Ugh,' he groaned. 'The human body is disgustingly ugly, isn't it?'

I took up the loincloth and began to wind it around me, between my legs. Eikaku put on my red underwear, preening a little. His under-kimono was white, the outer one dark blue with a white arrow pattern. Neither was really clean, and the outer one was spattered with paint. I could smell Eikaku's sweat on them as I tied the sash – it was narrower than mine and much more comfortable.

When I was dressed he looked at me in a critical fashion, then left the room and came back with a jacket like the one my father wore, a pair of *hakama* and a headcloth.

'You can wear the *hakama*, but first we'll cut all your hair off.'

'You mean shave my head like a nun?'

'Like a monk,' he corrected me. 'You are a man now.'

'Eikaku-san,' I tried to protest.

'Don't argue, *sensei*. You know you are a man inside. Don't you feel free now?'

I wasn't sure how I felt. I was trembling with a mixture of excitement and fear. It seemed like years since I had left my husband and all my belongings at Shiraishi's. Eikaku had unbarred a gate into another life. I just had to step over the threshhold.

Eikaku said, 'I could shave your forehead and put the back hair in a top knot.'

My mouth was dry. I could not bring myself to speak. I put my hands to my head and drew out my hair combs. My hair was stiff and heavy as it fell over my shoulders.

Among his tools and paints Eikaku had shaving equipment and scissors. He caught up my hair in a tail and without hesitating cut off at least half its length. I couldn't help gasping, which made him smile. Then he tilted my face upwards and with a sharp knife shaved my forehead and scalp. He pulled the back hair up and tied it neatly.

I put on the *hakama* and fastened them around my waist.

They made my legs feel long and free. I slipped my arms into the jacket.

'All I need is an *inrō* and a *netsuke*,' I said, turning around and patting my new clothes in a gesture like my father's. I suddenly felt like my father. My face settled into an expression like his, and my body assumed his posture.

'I will get you both,' Eikaku promised.

'Now it's your turn,' I said, finding my voice had dropped to a lower timbre as if naturally. His forehead may once have been shaved but the hair had all grown back. I piled his rather greasy hair up on his head, securing it with my combs. He had put on my kimono but had no idea how to tie the sash. I showed him: it was my turn to smile when he complained I was pulling it too tight. Then I blackened his teeth with ink and shaved off his eyebrows.

When we were transformed we stared at each other solemnly. The whole process had been partly childlike and playful, partly erotic. I was tingling from head to toe, and longing for my husband to embrace me. Putting on men's clothes had not stopped me feeling like a woman in that respect. Or maybe I was experiencing something of the blind urgency men feel. I had put it on with the clothes.

'Let's just stay like this,' Eikaku whispered. 'This is the best feeling, the most creative, the desire before it is consummated.'

'We are not going to consummate it,' I said in my new male voice.

'Doctor, you must not be so prudish if you are going to be a man.'

'Some men can be very prudish,' I said, thinking of Daisuke.

'But it doesn't suit you.'

'Do you have a mirror?' I asked. I wanted to see what sort of a man I had become.

He walked out of the room with his practised woman's gait and came back in a few moments with a make-up stand which had a fairly long glass mirror.

'This is where I do my face,' he said, tilting the mirror so I could see.

A small serious-looking young man stood before me. The hair and the clothes suited my heavy jaw and large features. As a girl I had never been beautiful, but as a man to my eye I had a certain appeal. I smiled and saw my blackened teeth.

'That looks grotesque,' I said. 'It spoils the whole effect.'

'The black will wear off in a couple of weeks,' Eikaku reassured me.

'A couple of weeks! What am I going to do till then?'

'Stay here of course. You've got to practise being a man. How to talk like a man, how to walk and sit and eat. All those things.'

I stared at him. I suddenly realised how far this game had taken me. There was still time to pull back. I would have to cover my head until my hair grew again, which would be hard to explain to my parents when I got back to Yuda, but otherwise nothing had changed. I could simply take off Eikaku's clothes, put on my own, and resume my old life.

But I didn't. My old life had suddenly come to an end. I was no longer anyone's wife. I had nowhere to go. And besides, it began to rain heavily, making it impossible to leave the house.

IN MITAJIRI

Around the time I was transforming my clothes and my gender in Shimonoseki another violent change was taking place in Kyōto. Emperor Kōmei, though he hated foreigners, had apparently decided he had no intention of personally leading an army against them. He had grown tired of the violence of the Tenchūgumi in the streets and of being pestered by extremist nobles within his own Court. Chōshū was the main supporter of the loyalists in the city and the Court, and suddenly it seemed that Chōshū was not only responsible for the unrest but had grown altogether too powerful. Their old rival, Satsuma, together with the Aizu domain, moved swiftly, with the Emperor's approval. Chōshū was relieved of its duties at the Sakaimachi Gate, its forces were ordered to leave Kyōto, and the young nobles were exiled.

'They had to flee in the rain,' Eikaku reported. He went to the tea houses in the port every day to hear the latest news, not in my clothes, which he kept for wearing in the house, but in his own, covered by a straw raincoat, for it had been raining every day while a strong typhoon had blown over the town. 'Now the storm is over they've all come to Mitajiri.'

Mitajiri was the port at the end of the Hagi Ō-kan where the domain lords embarked for Ōsaka on their alternate attendance progressions to Edo. Like Shimonoseki, it was a hub for travellers, from Kyūshū and Shikoku, a station on the *kitamaesen* trade route that encircled Japan.

'Who have all come to Mitajiri?'

'Seven Court nobles and hundreds of *shishi*,' Eikaku replied. 'Shall we go and take a look at them? I might take my paintings and display them at the Tenman Shrine.'

Like Takasugi and many Chōshū samurai Eikaku was a fervent believer in Tenmanjin, Sugawara no Michizane, the Heian scholar and philosopher, exiled unjustly by the Emperor. The Mitajiri Tenmangu was a popular and powerful centre of Tenmanjin worship in Chōshū.

'They all probably need medical advice,' he added, persuasively. 'After having to escape in the rain. Nobles are not like you and me, you know. They are delicate like flowers or exotic birds. Poor things! How they must have suffered! Yet it is they who are truly loyal to the Emperor.'

Even now I don't understand why I did it. I suppose partly because Eikaku talked me into it, partly because I did not know how to go back to the woman I was before, but really there is no true explanation. It was an irrational act, like the attack on the foreign ships perhaps, but sometimes you have to act without reason, on instinct, to break a deadlock, blow apart an intolerable situation, make something happen.

Eikaku's sister had arranged for my luggage to be collected from Shiraishi's, and I had sent him a note to thank him for everything. I told him I was going home to my parents for a while, but I wrote at the same time to my parents to say Makino and I were going to Ōsaka. I was deliberately vague about why and for how long. I went through my baskets and put together the things I would take to Mitajiri with me: my medicine box, needles, surgical instruments, a couple of textbooks for reference, writing tools to record cases and treatment. I was both excited and apprehensive. I revelled in the feelings my male attire gave me – energy, freedom, confidence – but to venture into the outside world as a man among people who might easily recognise me was much more of a challenge.

I'd always been embarrassed by my broad hands and feet, and envied Mitsue her slender, delicate form. But now I was thankful for them. My voice deepened and I used masculine forms of speech unselfconsciously. Eikaku's sister addressed me as a man, on his orders, and I began to treat her differently. I did not leap to my feet with offers of help. I let her wait on me. I put my needs and desires before hers as a matter of course. I was a man: I had an importance that a woman would never have.

The other motive that drove me was that I wanted to resume practising as a doctor. When I thought of the opportunities my disguise as a man opened up to me, excitement overrode my misgivings. Mitajiri beckoned seductively: noblemen, *shishi* from many different domains, *daimyō* and their retinue, as well as merchants, sailors and other travellers. A whole world of male patients lay spread before me. I would be able to examine them and discuss their symptoms with them. Luckily I had a good supply of mercury with me.

Mitajiri lay a short day's journey away to the east. Eikaku disliked the confined space of the palanquin, so we hired a packhorse and boy, and walked behind them. They had come in the opposite direction the previous day. The horse trotted briskly, eager to get home. We had to stretch our legs to keep up, since Eikaku would not allow the paintings out of his sight. The weather had cleared after the storms, the equinox had passed and the time of cold dew was approaching. There were many people on the road and, it seemed, a new rumour for every one of them.

Sufu Masanosuke had resigned; the Chōshū lords were planning to march on Kyōto; the warships sunk by the American ship had been salvaged and rebuilt; the Kiheitai were being disbanded in punishment for their quarrels with the Senpōtai and other regular forces; the conservatives, Tsuboi Kuemon and Mukanashi Tōta, were going to take over the domain government…and so on and so on, each rumour cancelling out the last.

The road followed the coast, then turned inland through Ogori to join the Hagi Ō-kan. We climbed to the Sabayama pass and stopped at one of the tea houses to drink tea and eat soba with mountain vegetables. I was hardly tired at all. To stride out in men's clothes felt so different from the last journey I had made back from Hagi. We were in no hurry so we sat outside and smoked a pipe of tobacco, while the horse grazed and the boy dozed. As I looked out over the mountains at the city of Hōfu, half hidden in the distance, and at the Inland Sea, I thought of my sister and my niece, hoping they were well, wondering when I would see them again.

As we descended the slope we passed a newly constructed gun battery, with stone walls and earth embankments. We stopped to talk to the soldiers and they told us it had been built to protect Yamaguchi when the government had moved there in the fourth month. Eikaku took great pleasure in describing the battle at Shimonoseki and the destruction of the batteries at Maeda and Kameyama, making the soldiers shift nervously and finger their collars until their officer came out and ordered us to move on.

'He's afraid his men will take flight and run away!' Eikaku sniffed, turning back to look at the guns, committing them to memory. There were two Dahlgrens, and four Japanese-made thirty-pounders.

'How did our domain learn so much about artillery so quickly?' I wondered aloud.

'Never underestimate human ingenuity when it's a question of learning new ways to kill someone,' Eikaku replied.

We passed through the bustling little town of Migita and crossed the Sanami River by a wooden bridge which led directly into the shrine town that lay in front of Tenmangu. It was crowded with people, both townsfolk and travellers. A large *honjin* displayed its name 'Kōbeike' on wooden signs and entrance curtains.

Now I could smell the sea and hear all the sounds of the port, hammers and saws, cries of street sellers and seabirds, the wind in the rigging of the tall-masted ships. Mitajiri had always been the base of the Mōri fleet, and both war and merchant ships were built and maintained here.

The sun was sinking to the west and the sea breeze growing colder as we came to the front gate of Tenmangu. Here Eikaku spoke to one of the priests; they unloaded the pictures and our belongings from the horse. Eikaku set off carrying the pictures; the boy shouted goodbye as the horse trotted swiftly homewards. I squatted down on my heels next to my boxes.

The light had faded to dusk and lamps were being lit in the surrounding houses and stalls when Eikaku returned.

'We can stay the night here. Tomorrow we'll go and see the nobles. They are staying near the port at a tea house called Shōkenkaku.'

Eikaku could not bring himself to donate the paintings to the shrine (he was still far too possessive of them), but he allowed the priests to display them in one of the halls. They were the first depictions of the battle that anyone had seen and they attracted a great deal of interest. In fact throngs of people came to Tenmangu to see them, and then they prayed to Tenmanjin, bought charms and amulets and made donations. The head priest, who was an old friend of Eikaku, knew his moods and admired his talent, declared himself delighted with this arrangement. He accepted me for what I looked like and did not ask any questions.

Before we left we had decided I would be a member of the Imaike family, a nephew or a cousin, and Eikaku made a licence for me from the domain school of medicine in Hagi, the place where I had always wanted to study, the place Shinsai had rejected. Of course the document was a fake and I was taking a terrible risk using it, but I wasn't in the least bothered. I felt I deserved the licence for I had studied just as much as any pupil there and had probably practised a great deal more. And it was part of the game I was playing, just one more piece of the fantasy Eikaku and I had created.

It didn't take me long to find patients. People will always

sniff out a doctor. First one of the young priests saw my medicine box and asked for something for headaches. Next an old man requested a massage to ease his rheumatism. No one expected to see a woman so they did not see me, Itasaki Tsuru or Mrs Makino. Instead they saw Imaike Kōnosuke, graduate of the Kōseikan.

Eikaku had to rescue me from a throng nearly as large as the one that formed around his paintings. I put the coins I had received inside my money purse (I didn't charge the priests but everyone else offered to pay and I accepted), packed away my medicine box and entrusted it to Mr Headaches, and followed Eikaku through the huge shrine gates and down the hill towards the port.

Here the streets were a maze of inns, tea houses and shops selling all kinds of produce, especially the salt Mitajiri was famous for and every variety of seafood. Street vendors pushed among the crowd, shouting their haunting refrains for eggs, octopus, sweet potato, tofu. We stopped and bought octopus in rice balls dripping with thick sesame-flavoured sauce.

The Shōkenkaku was the largest of the tea houses, rising among a cluster of roofs all glistening as the morning sun burned off the dew. The sea beyond was silky smooth, veiled in haze. Its imposing roofed gate stood open; we could see through to the inner courtyard where about fifteen men were taking part in sword practice. They looked extremely fierce and determined. Their hair was drawn up on top of their heads like Kusaka's men and several wore white or red headbands. Four men stood at the gate, fully armed with rifles as well as swords. Two wore old armour that looked as if it had been lying in a storehouse for two hundred years. The others wore trousers and helmet-shaped hats.

We stopped a short way up the street. 'They are not going to let us in!' Eikaku exclaimed.

I thought that was probably a good thing, given his excitement and the warlike appearance of the *shishi.* I could see misunderstandings arising as surely as the morning sun. The results would be stained with Eikaku's blood, and mine too.

'Let's go back to the shrine,' I said, but Eikaku had his mind set on seeing the nobles and he was not to be dissuaded. He approached the guards and began to talk in his high agitated voice, explaining that he was a famous artist, a follower of Tenmanjin, they could see his works at Tenmangu.

Their hands went to their swords. Eikaku was armed only with his paintbrushes and was oblivious to any danger. I also went up to the guards and was beginning to say, 'He really is a famous artist. Please forgive him for speaking to you so strangely. His genius makes him unlike other people,' when another man came to the gate from the inside. I turned to enlist his help and saw my uncle, Shinsai.

SHINSAI

I was sure Shinsai recognised me at once but he gave no sign of it, nor did I reveal that I knew him.

'This man is a doctor,' Eikaku said, introducing me to the guards. 'From the school of medicine in Hagi.'

'I was on my way to look for a doctor,' Shinsai said smoothly. 'How fortuitous. Let them in.'

'Just the doctor or the crazy one too?' asked one of the guards.

'I would like to be allowed to paint the noble personages,' Eikaku said, assuming a submissive demeanour towards Shinsai, who did seem to carry some authority with the *shishi*. He was dressed in a pale blue kimono and grey *hakama*, with a dark blue *haori*. He wore two swords, and his hair was considerably neater than the guards'. I did not want to stare at him directly, but he seemed to fill my vision as though nothing else existed.

'You can come in too.' Shinsai nodded to the guards, who stood aside and let us through the gate.

'Prince Nishikinokōji is not well,' he said to me as we walked around the courtyard. The men did not waver from their training for one second.

'I am very sorry to hear it.' If Shinsai was going to pretend not to know me I would not be the first to break the illusion.

'I can examine him but I don't have anything with me. I would have to go back to Tenmangu.'

'If you think you can help him we'll send a messenger for your things,' he replied.

We did not go in through the main door of the tea house but followed the veranda around to the back where the most spacious and luxurious rooms gave on to a beautiful garden, with a small waterfall, a pool filled with cream and gold carp, and several maple trees just beginning to turn crimson.

We stopped at the entrance to one of the rooms and Shinsai slid back the *shōji*, calling out in a soft voice. Inside a young man was lying on a futon, supported by a back rest. Next to him sat a man of about the same age – I put them both at under thirty. The man lying down was extremely pale and looked lethargic, the other anxious and agitated. They both had white skin and fine regular features, and a similar attenuated air as though they were barely equal to the realities of the world.

'This is Prince Sanjō,' Shinsai whispered, and all three of us bowed to the ground.

Sanjō Sanetomi was the most famous of the young men from aristocratic families in Kyōto who allied themselves with the loyalists and exasperated the Emperor by insisting he get rid of the foreigners. Apart from their excitable natures and extremist tendencies they had other things in common with the *shishi*. Whatever talent or ability they had would never be recognised in any meaningful way, and they had no role to play in society apart from the restricted Court positions suitable for their rank and age.

When Aizu and Satsuma seized control of the palace

gates in the eighth month Prince Sanjō and six of his associates were barred from the Court. They sought refuge in Myōhōin in Higashiyama, and were spirited away in the pouring rain to Chōshū when the *shishi* fled the capital. Now they found themselves in Mitajiri, part hostages, part trophies. I couldn't help feeling sorry for them. The Shōkenkaku was as spacious and luxurious as any lodging place in the port city, but it surely could not compare with the palaces and mansions of Kyōto. Even their rank could not protect them from the weather, from sickness, or more seriously from assassination. The *shishi* might protect their trophies now, but they would dispose of them as quickly if the nobles disappointed them. Prince Sanjō's closest friend, Prince Anenokōji Kintomo, had been murdered a few months earlier. No one really knew the motive though plenty of rumours flew around to explain it, the most plausible being he was suspected of abandoning the principles of *jōi*, because of his association with the reform-minded Bakufu official Katsu Kaishū.

'I did not expect such a swift return!' Sanjō exclaimed when he saw Shinsai.

'Yes, I was lucky enough to meet this young doctor outside the gate,' Shinsai replied. 'He studied with my older brother and, I believe, at the school of medicine in Hagi. His name is…'

'Imaike Kōnosuke,' I said, raising my head and bowing again.

'Imaike Kōnosuke,' Shinsai repeated.

'I hope you can help the prince,' Sanjō said, addressing me directly in a very gracious way. I saw he had a warm-hearted, gentle nature that seemed a marked contrast to the *shishi* who surrounded him.

'What are his symptoms?' I asked, shuffling forward on my knees so I could examine the sick man. I was thinking there were probably all sorts of formalities that I should be observing, and hoping that the princes would forgive me, given their unusual circumstances. I murmured an apology and lifted his wrist to feel the pulse.

'He is fatigued all the time; the journey exhausted him. He complains of having no feeling in his limbs, particularly his legs.'

The pulse was slow and uneven. I asked for permission to listen to his chest, and placed my ear against his silk robe. I tried to visualise the interior of the chest cavity. The heart was certainly beating in a strange rhythm. When I palpated the abdomen it felt swollen and pulpy.

'He has all the signs of *kakke*,' I said. It was not an illness that we often saw in Chōshū. For some reason it was more prevalent in cities, particularly among the nobility and higher ranks of samurai. It was thought to be caused by the climate or possibly some infection, though doctors agreed it was not virulent like measles or influenza.

'What can you give him?' Prince Sanjō asked, turning even paler. *Kakke* invariably led to heart failure unless its advance could be slowed.

'I can prescribe some powders,' I said, thinking about what diuretics I had in my medicine box. 'Sometimes a change of diet seems to help. Maybe the move away from the capital will be beneficial.'

It would be years before my hunch that *kakke*, known as

beri-beri in the West, was caused by a deficiency in the diet would be proved scientifically.

The sick man turned his face away from us. The weakness of being ill often makes even adult men cry easily and I thought Prince Nishikinokōji was weeping now with homesickness and despair.

Eikaku was drinking in the scene, his eyes popping, his hand twitching as if he were already drawing. We had to practically drag him away and then he begged to see the other five noblemen. Shinsai good-naturedly led him to the adjoining room and allowed him to peek in from the garden.

While Eikaku was committing every last detail to memory, Shinsai said to me, 'Shall we walk back to Tenmangu together and I will bring back whatever you recommend?'

'That might be best. If there is anything else I need we can go to a pharmacy. And there is a herb garden at Tenmangu, I believe.'

He didn't say anything more then. I sensed he had become the sort of man who knew when to keep silent, how to keep secrets. He looked older and thinner, and he held himself like someone prepared to take action at any moment, either to evade danger or to grasp the opportunity to attack. I felt as if my whole body radiated heat. I will never forget that moment when I stood next to him dressed as a man, and he treated me as a man. I did not want it to end, but all too soon Eikaku declared in a loud whisper that he was ready to start painting – and of course I had my patient to attend to.

Eikaku was single-mindedly obsessed with the idea of painting the seven nobles and did not realise Shinsai knew me. Shinsai continued to treat me as a stranger. When we got back to Tenmangu I retrieved my medicine box, took out the powders I thought would be suitable, *kudzu*, *shinan-otsuki*, and gave them to him.

'I will try to get some red peppers – maybe they grow them here. And if someone can direct me to the pharmacy…In the meantime the prince should take these with barley tea.'

'Do you need money?' Shinsai said, taking the paper envelopes.

'I have enough. You can pay me back. But do the nobles have any money?' I pictured them fleeing with only the clothes they were wearing.

'The domain is taking care of their expenses,' Shinsai replied. 'You will be paid too. Bring whatever you can to the Gyōtenro this afternoon, and ask for me. I'll be there after midday.'

'You have not yet told me your name…'

'It's the same as always, Itasaki Shinsai.' A quick look, amused and conspiratorial, flashed in his eyes.

The priest I had dubbed Mr Headaches showed me the small garden behind the shrine, but it did not contain much of any practical use, being mainly shrubs and plants for various ceremonies, *sasaki* and so on. Then he directed me to the pharmacy, which was in the centre of town near the port. On my way I walked past the inn called the Gyōtenro; it seemed a busy place, full of guests, and I felt obscurely disappointed as if I'd hoped to meet Shinsai somewhere quieter where we might be alone.

The pharmacy was called the Hirotaya, and as I approached the open shopfront I was immediately reminded of the Kuriya place in Hagi. I recalled every detail of the evening

I had first stepped inside and seen the Accountant. The smell of the medicines brought back the day he had asked me to help him with the inventory. How angry Shinsai had been! I had chosen Makino as my husband partly to put myself beyond Shinsai's reach. And my husband had sent me away right into Shinsai's path.

The owner of the shop came out when he saw me looking over the baskets of seeds, dried roots, chopped leaves and powdered spices. There were some rarities I had hardly ever seen before: tusk of narwhal, horn of rhinoceros, bear bile and ambergris. He tried to patronise me, then browbeat me into buying his made-up remedies, but when I let him know I had graduated from the Kōseikan his manner changed. He called to the shopgirl to bring tea and we sat on the step and talked at length about *kakke* and its various remedies.

It brought home clearly what I had been realising slowly. Now I had become a man I was no longer invisible to men. They took account of me and took my opinions seriously. It was as if something had been missing all my life and it was only when I found it that I became aware of having lacked it before.

It was well past midday when I left the shop with various powders, dried grapes and bellflower root, with ginger and cassia, made up to my specification, and some ingredients for herbal teas. It had been a clear bright morning but gradually the sky had become overcast, and as I headed back up the hill I felt the first drops of rain. The wind had grown colder and was blowing from the northwest, a winter wind.

The inn smelled of grilled fish and stewed octopus but I was not hungry. My stomach was fluttering with excitement or dread, I was not sure which. I spoke to the landlady, asking for Itasaki-san, and she shouted to one of the girls to go and find him.

A few moments later he appeared, shouldering his way through the crowd.

'Doctor,' he greeted me.

'I've got the medicines you wanted,' I said. 'I just need to explain the doses.'

'Let's go somewhere a little quieter.' He went to the landlady and whispered in her ear. She nodded in agreement.

Shinsai came back to me. 'There's a room upstairs. She'll make sure no one disturbs us.'

At the side of the inn was a small building with an earthen floor. It was used for storing pickled vegetables and had a strong odour of salt and spices. At the back, half hidden by a huge vat, was a ladder that led steeply upwards into a narrow space which had been matted and furnished with futons, folded neatly in the corner, a ceramic brazier, and a lamp. There was one barred window looking out onto the street, but the shutters were drawn across and the room was dark, only a little light filtering up from below.

Shinsai went up first and I followed, ignoring the hand he held out to help me. We stood a little distance apart, not speaking. I could hear my own blood.

Shinsai said, 'I always told you you should have been a man.'

I didn't say anything for a moment. For a start I didn't know how to address him. I was certainly not going to call him *uncle*.

'What's this place used for?' I said finally, looking around.

'Hiding people who are not supposed to be in Mitajiri. *Rōnin*, spies, *shishi* who are in some sort of trouble with the authorities. The owners support the Emperor and hate the Tokugawa.'

'I'd better explain the prince's medication,' I said, in my pedantic doctor's voice.

'Later,' he said and took the pharmacist's parcel from my hands. 'We'll go to the Shōkenkaku later.'

I suddenly felt my legs growing weak and I sat down, taking some time to arrange my sandals neatly on the wooden step. Shinsai sat down next to me on the tatami, cross-legged. I badly wanted to smoke but my pipe and tobacco were still at the shrine.

'How long have you been in this disguise?'

'A few weeks. It was Eikaku's idea. He is one of my patients – he is not really very sane. He said I was a man in a woman's body and if I dressed as a man I would discover myself. And you know something? He was right.'

'But where is your husband?'

'With the Kiheitai. He is an army doctor now. He didn't think I should go with him. He told me to go home. I warned him if he sent me home I would consider myself divorced.'

'So you turned yourself into a man and ran away! Really, Tsu-chan!'

'I think it is better if you don't call me that,' I said. 'It started as a game. I liked how I felt. I didn't want to stop. If I have to go back to being a woman it will kill me.'

'It's dangerous,' he said, adding, 'Addictions are.'

'Well, it's difficult finding somewhere private to piss and

I haven't worked out how to use the public baths yet, but it's not really dangerous. You're the only person who's seen through me so far. That's only because you know me. I wouldn't get away with it in Yuda or in Hagi, but hardly anyone knows me here.'

I said all this in the men's speech Eikaku had schooled me in, making the appropriate expressions and gestures.

Shinsai laughed. 'It's uncanny! Even though I know who you are, you play the part so well I keep forgetting you are not a man.' His voice became quieter and more teasing as he said, 'Maybe I should check.'

The space between us seemed vast, even though the room was so small, and I did not think he would be able to broach it, but his hand reached across and slipped inside my robe. Beneath the lined kimono I had bound a cloth around the top half of my body to flatten my breasts.

'Oh,' Shinsai said in surprise when he encountered this. 'It seems you really are a man!'

'Try a little lower,' I suggested, as he placed his other hand on the back of my neck and pulled me towards him.

I could pretend he had forced me. He was much stronger than I was and no one would hear me if I screamed. But he did not. After that moment when he held me against him, and I felt relief wash over me as if I had come home, he pulled back and looked in my face.

'We should stop now.'

But I was beyond being able to stop. I was in a dream with no power over my actions. It was I who sought his mouth with mine, I who tore at his clothes. I took him as fiercely as he took me, realising we had always desired each other. We had been forbidden to each other by our relationship, but here in Mitajiri with the world falling apart around us we were suddenly freed from its old rules and expectations.

What can I say? It was like sleeping with myself. I was both man and woman. I became him, and when it was over and we had fallen together into the ecstasy that is near death, I was more myself than I had ever been.

That was just the first time of many that day. Our lust, denied for so long, once it was allowed to emerge was insatiable. Now and then I surfaced from the lake of desire and thought about the sick nobleman or Eikaku, then Shinsai's lips would graze my neck, my breast, and pull me under again.

At one stage we paused long enough to spread out the futons and lie under the quilts. Rain fell heavily against the window shutters and wind whistled up the ladder well. Heat radiated from Shinsai's body where I was curled against him.

'You know I've always loved you,' he said.

I could not believe he was talking of love, Shinsai so cynical and unsentimental. Even my husband had never said he loved me, nor I him. Love was for people in plays and books, and was almost always a disaster.

'It's true. I realised years ago I was in love with you. You've no idea how much I've suffered, knowing I could never have you, seeing you married to someone else.'

I said, 'I love you too. I think I always have.' So this was what love was, this mysterious possession that drove men and women to acts of complete madness.

Later Shinsai went out and returned with bowls of noodles and a flask of sake. We talked about what we would do, and laughed a lot. I was happier than I had ever been in my life. Shinsai told me about his life in Kyōto, how dangerous the capital had become, how the Bakufu police force, the Shinsengumi, had been created to control the streets and contain the outbreaks of violence, how they were even more feared than the *shishi* and the townspeople had become impatient with the way they extorted money and provisions from them.

'When will you go back there?' I asked, knowing that he would not stay away for long.

'In a few weeks, I suppose. I'll see how the situation here develops, and keep Genzui informed about it. Then I'll go back and discuss it with him. I think you should come with me.'

'I think I should too.'

'You can certainly help us as a doctor. And in a way it's safer for you there, if you continue as a man. No one knows you. There are many places where it's still possible to disappear. And…'

'And?'

'I'm not going to let you go now. We've plunged into the water, we must go where the current takes us. Who knows what will happen to us? Life is so brief we should taste everything it offers before it's over. We face death every day in Kyōto.'

I did not tell him then or ever that I had seen how he would die.

While we stayed in Mitajiri Shinsai was busy looking after the nobles' accommodation and helping to keep the gathered *shishi* under control. Maki Izumi, a former Shinto priest from the domain of Kurume, had emerged as their leader. He was then about fifty years old, much older than the young men who were flocking into Mitajiri every day to join the loyalist cause, yet just as idealistic and inexperienced in either government or warfare. Listening to them as I did when I was called on to treat their ailments, I was both moved and alarmed by their blind devotion to the Emperor and their irrational commitment to driving out the foreigners. Even my descriptions of the bombardment of Shimonoseki, together with Eikaku's paintings which everyone went to study, could not open their eyes to reality. Talk in the tea houses and inns buzzed around and around: Chōshū must regain its position with the Court; to accept defeat by Satsuma and Aizu was to lose face in an intolerable way; all Kyōto was waiting for Chōshū to act; they all loved Chōshū for the domain's loyalty to the Emperor; you should have seen how impressed people were when our soldiers confronted Satsuma; how magnificent and fearless are our young men!

There was a delicate balance that had to be maintained. The men at the Shōkenkaku were energetic and courageous. They had left their families and fled from their domains, they were exiles and outlaws with nothing to lose. Maki and his officers kept them under strict discipline, with a rigorous daily programme of military training and classical studies, but they were still a dangerous, volatile force, swift to take offence and easily swayed by emotion.

'It's like having a wolf as your guard dog,' Shinsai said one day. 'He frightens off intruders but he's just as likely to turn on you and tear your throat out.'

We were in the shrine at Tenmangu watching Eikaku put

the finishing touches to his painting of the seven nobles fleeing through the rain. Each one was immediately recognisable. They wore straw rain capes and wide-brimmed black hats, and huddled in a group like plovers on the shore. Around them soldiers with lanterns urged them forward. You could sense their uncertainty and apprehension.

'Now you have finished that – and it is magnificent – maybe you can do some more forgeries for us,' Shinsai said. 'Imaike and I are going to Kyōto and if we take some famous remedies with us it will help our finances.'

'But what am I going to do without Dr Imaike?' Eikaku said, looking downcast.

Shinsai ignored the question, explaining instead how he wanted the flyers to look as if they were from the celebrated medical town of Isa, and I gave him the names of the ingredients we would use.

'We are finally quacks like the Kuriya,' Shinsai said cheerfully, and went off to make preparations for our journey. Eikaku looked at me mournfully.

'Do you know what you are doing, Doctor?'

He had said nothing about my relationship with Shinsai. I did not even know how much he had perceived, how much he knew already. When he was painting he was blind and deaf to the rest of the world. He had been filled with energy and good spirits ever since we had been in Mitajiri, but now the painting was finished he was likely to start the descent into depression again.

I felt guilty about leaving him, but I hid it with anger.

'It's none of your business what I do! I am a free man.'

He smiled a little ruefully. 'You truly are no longer a

woman. Well, I created you. I cannot blame you if you act as I told you to.'

'That's right,' I said harshly. 'You will have to look after yourself.'

Eikaku had a natural aptitude for forgery and created many flyers for our famous remedies. Then luckily some news came from Yamaguchi that seemed to cheer him up even further. The Sufu government, which had been forced to resign after Chōshū's fall from favour in Kyōto, was reinstated by the Kiheitai, and the head of the conservative party, Tsuboi Kuemon, ordered to commit suicide. In his usual contrary way Eikaku admired Kuemon deeply and was touched by his fate. It inspired him to paint Kuemon's portrait as Sugawara no Michizane in exile. Once he had been gripped by inspiration his spirits usually became more buoyant, and I felt I could leave him. Mr Headaches, by now much in my debt, promised to look after him, and anyway he did not lack friends and supporters in the town. I only hoped the loyalists would not take offence at the subject of his painting and feel obliged to erase it with Eikaku's blood. But that was a risk everyone took in those days of madness.

In the time before our departure I noticed how effective Shinsai was and what a high opinion others had of him. I could see that he received the same envious, admiring looks he used to give men like Genzui and Takasugi. There were other glances too, now he spent so much time with me.

'They think you have taken a male lover,' I said.

'They've already formed the opinion that I don't like

women,' Shinsai replied, smiling. 'Since I never go with them to the brothels or the geisha houses.'

'I don't believe you,' I teased him, relieved all the same.

'It's true. I've never felt desire for any other women. I think I had to suppress my feelings for you so I suppressed everything else.'

He was twenty-five years old at this time and I was twenty-three. We were no longer children, to be carried away by infatuation, but adults. Yet, we were carried away as if by contagion.

I had become busy too. I had been wise to bring mercury, for syphilis was rife in the port. There was little understanding of the disease. When the symptoms of the first stage subsided the afflicted not only assumed they were cured, but believed they were immune from further infections. I tried to suggest abstinence but I had little hope of my advice being followed: most of my patients expected to die gloriously in battle long before the second or third stages of syphilis manifested themselves.

My patient Prince Nishikinokōji improved slightly. I was able to reduce the dropsy in his legs and stomach with the diuretic powders, massage and needles. However, all the young noblemen suffered from inactivity and uncertainty. They were not so much guests as prisoners, whose guards thought they knew what was best for them, filling their heads with wild schemes for campaigns against the Bakufu and plots to take control of the Emperor. Their world had been turned upside down and they were flying like kites with cut strings, at the mercy of the wind. They began to agitate for action as much as the most reckless of the *shishi* – anything to get them back to Kyōto and back in the Emperor's favour.

Just before we left for Kyōto in the tenth month, one of them, the most frustrated by the situation, Prince Sawa Nobuyoshi, was persuaded to take part in a doomed campaign which became known as the Ikuno incident. It came right after the Tenchūgumi uprising in Iga. Both movements contained elements of peasant unrest and both were explicitly anti-Bakufu. Both petered out; the leaders were killed in battle or executed and Prince Sawa fled ignominiously back to Mitajiri. But these outbreaks were seen by the *shishi* as harbingers of the future struggle, and their demands for action became louder.

'It's a question of waiting for the right time,' Shinsai argued. He was in touch with Genzui and Katsura in Kyōto and with the Kiheitai leaders throughout the domain. Letters flew to and from Mitajiri by swift messengers or by ship. Genzui, Katsura and Takasugi were still favoured by Lord Sufu and all had positions in his government now. Each of them counselled patience. But the Shōkenkaku group would prove to be beyond anyone's control.

PART 3

転

Genji 1 to Keiō 1
1864–1865

KYŌTO

Shinsai was employed by the domain in some clandestine way and we travelled with their permission, at their expense and under their protection. This still counted for something, even though Chōshū had fallen from favour, for many still sympathised with their cause and most common people supported them. We boarded a ship in Mitajiri and followed the coast through the Inland Sea east to Ōsaka. Here we stayed in the domain residence for Ōsaka was the centre of Chōshū's trading activities, and the domain had many contacts with the city's wealthy merchants (and owed most of them a great deal of money).

Despite people's anxieties about the political situation and their fear of war, trade went on, fortunes were made and lost, new commodities discovered, new fashions launched. Ōsaka seemed like a vast city to me, coloured more brightly than anywhere I had seen, decorated with signs and banners. I could have spent days exploring it. Every kind of shop operated there, selling everything from charcoal, rice, cakes and tobacco, to metal ornaments, sushi, cloth and medicine. Everyone seemed to be talking at the tops of their voices all the time. I listened to the conversations, trying to understand the unfamiliar accents and dialects, storing up new words as eagerly as I tasted new foods. It was thrilling to walk alongside Shinsai, not several paces behind, as women were supposed to, discussing ideas and plans.

On one of our walks through the city, not far from the Tosabori River, we passed a long white building with dark latticed windows.

'That is the famous Tekijuku,' Shinsai said.

'Ogata Kōan's school?' I felt I should go down on my knees in reverence. Dr Ogata was my father's hero, and I had heard him talk about the school all my life. I knew that Ogata had died earlier that year: he had been summoned to Edo to be the head of the new school of medicine, and though he had not wanted to leave Ōsaka he had been unable to refuse. But the stress of his new position had been too much for his already fragile health. He had only been about fifty years old, but his legacy was immeasurable, especially in setting up smallpox vaccination centres.

'Do you want to go inside and look around?'

I did and I did not. Thinking about Ogata made me think of my father. He had always said he followed Ogata's teachings of 'compassionate action'. Life is only life, there are no divisions. Our lives are a gift of this life force and should be spent in the service of others. As I stood and gazed on the unpretentious building and thought of the man who had lived and taught there, I saw in a moment of painful clarity my own life, my lack of compassion, my selfishness, and I felt ashamed.

'Let's go to the theatre,' I said. I wanted to smother these uncomfortable feelings, for if I gave in to them I would have to go back, back to being a woman, back to being a wife. I wanted to go forward, with Shinsai at my side.

Ōsaka had many theatres, and I had never seen a live performance of kabuki. I could not wait to immerse myself in one and forget my father and Ogata Kōan. We went into the Nakanoshibai in Dotonbori and saw *Ghost Stories of Yotsuya*, a strange grotesque story that reflected my own perverted state. Perhaps the young man who had recited from it at my wedding had unwittingly laid a curse on me. I revelled in the play. The character of Iemon was evil, and yet he had an energy that was compelling and seductive. I felt he captured the essence of our time, speaking deeply to our fears and uncertainties, preying on them. The theatre was one of the most modern in Ōsaka, with a revolving stage, a trapdoor and many special effects. It was a thrilling experience.

We left Ōsaka the following day, taking a flat-bottomed river boat up to Fushimi where we stayed at the inn called the Teradaya not far from the Chōshū Fushimi mansion. It was in this inn, a year and a half ago, that Satsuma loyalist *shishi* had been attacked and killed by their own clan.

'I was here at the time,' Shinsai told me when we had retired to a small room at the back of the inn. 'There were two or three of us here from Chōshū.'

'What were you doing here?'

'Keeping an eye on things. Genzui told me to hang around and pick up information. I was living in Fushimi then. The Satsuma lads thought their *daimyō* was coming to back their demands to expel the foreigners and restore power to the Emperor. Instead he got rid of them.'

He was silent for a moment, then said, 'It was terrible – not that so many died but that they knew they had been betrayed. It was a lesson for us though. Every domain will turn on its own people if it feels its security is threatened, no matter how just our cause may be.'

'How did you get away?' I did not need the magic fan for the scene to come to life before my eyes, the slashing of swords, the shouts of anger, the screams of the dying.

'The landlady ran in crying, "Satsuma is coming. It's not looking good!" I was in this room waiting for Genzui and some other Chōshū men. I slipped out the back, over a couple of walls and met Genzui on the way. We went back to Kyōto that night and hid in the Kawaramachi mansion for a few days.

'Satsuma and Chōshū have always been rivals, but to overthrow the Bakufu they will have to come together. Many people realise this and are working to make it happen. There's a Tosa man who often stays here, Sakamoto Ryōma.'

'Genzui mentioned him once to me,' I said. 'They met in Hagi, I think.'

Shinsai smiled. 'I have been mistaken for him. People say we look alike. He believes Satsuma and Chōshū must unite. He is on good terms with many in both domains.'

'Did you join in the fighting that night?'

The inn was falling silent around us as night deepened. It was bitterly cold, though it was not yet the winter solstice. I moved closer to Shinsai, seeking the warmth of his body.

'No, we were completely outnumbered. And it would have been a pointless death.'

'But you've fought before?'

'Yes.'

'And killed people?'

'Of course.'

'Is that how you won respect?'

He laughed. 'What do you mean?'

'I just noticed people respect you and they are a little afraid of you. It's one of the things that's changed about you since you left home.' I ran my fingers over his arm. The muscles were hard like iron. There was not a trace of fat on him anywhere, yet his skin was silky to touch. I thought about his body, the blood vessels that lay blue beneath the skin, the heart beating steadily beneath my ear, the lungs that pumped in and out the breath I could feel on my hair, the muscles and nerves that controlled each action, that had obeyed the command to kill.

'When I'm asked to do a job I get it done,' Shinsai said. 'So I believe I am trusted as much as anyone.'

'But do you like it?'

'Tsu-chan,' he began to say, but I put my hand over his mouth.

'I told you not to call me that.'

'I shall never call you anything but Imaike-kun from now on. I like fighting. I always have done. If killing comes at the end of it, it doesn't bother me. I'd rather kill than be the one dying on the ground.'

'How many people have you killed?'

'Maybe eight, ten – and three wooden statues.'

'So you were involved in that! We suspected you would be.'

Shinsai laughed again, and began to caress me in a way that put an end to any talking.

Afterwards though I was tired I did not fall asleep directly. Thoughts ran through my head. Wicked Iemon loved to kill and audiences loved to see his wickedness. Nakajima had been fascinated by death and murder in all their most grotesque forms. Eikaku painted humans suffering torments in hell at the hands of terrifying spirits and demons. I had my own blood-soaked hallucinations; I had seen many people die and though I would have preferred to save them I was interested in their manner of dying. And Shinsai liked killing…What strange and complex relationships flowed between individuals and their bodies and sex and death.

The next morning when we were eating our breakfast of rice, miso shiro and pickled radish, O-Tosei, the landlady, gave Shinsai a bundle of letters.

'These came for you, Itasaki-san.'

'Thank you,' he said, laying them aside on the tatami. We sent our boxes and baskets ahead, but he carried the letters himself as we walked, passing the huge shrine to Inari with its red *torii* and white fox statues, from Fushimi into the city. I also took a bundle with the medical flyers and samples in it, hoping to be able to do some business on the road.

It was a frosty morning, the last of the susuki grass white-rimed and glistening in the vermilion sun which was partially covered by mist so that its round shape was clearly visible. I thought it like a symbol of our country, united under the Emperor and under the red sun. The city lay between steep wood-covered hills; on the lower slopes a few bright leaves still clung to the bare branches. Higher up, around the dark cedars swathes of mist hung like grey banners. The road followed the course of the river, lined most of the way with a single row of buildings, behind which lay rice paddies, all bare and brown. As we approached the city the houses became more numerous and more densely packed together. A cloud of smoke from cooking fires hung over them and a fresh rich smell rose from the streets. Many people walked in the same direction as us, farmers carrying baskets of winter vegetables or strings of dried persimmons, fishermen with their catch packed in moss and ice, workman dressed in shabby jackets and leggings, porters and packhorses, samurai in winter capes walking in pairs, occasionally an official in a palanquin. All the domains had been building mansions and barracks in the capital and many were still under construction.

'That's Myōhōin,' Shinsai said, pointing out a cluster of buildings set back from the road, half hidden by cedars. 'Where we hid the nobles.'

'So you travelled this road with them?'

'We cut through the woods behind Tōfukuji and came through the lanes to Fushimi.'

'You must know your way around.'

'I do. I've been here over four years. Ever since your marriage.'

'Why didn't you ever get in touch? We were all worried about you.'

'Let's not talk about why,' Shinsai replied.

By now we were in the city itself. We passed another large temple precinct, Kenninji, and shortly after turned off the main road into a maze of streets that lay between the river and Higashiyama, and, as Shinsai would show me later, between the Shijō and the Sanjō bridges. He was his usual relaxed, good-humoured self, but I noticed that he was constantly alert to everything around him.

'Are we being followed?' I said in a low voice.

'I don't think so. But we'll stop and drink something before we go to the lodgings.'

Every second shop seemed to be a tea house, all offering different specialities of the district, of the season. We went into one and ordered tea and *mochi* with sauce. I took out my tobacco case, lit a spill from the brazier next to us, and smoked a pipe while we were waiting. Shinsai watched me critically.

'Am I going to pass here?' I said.

'There is something not quite right that might give you away,' he replied. 'But there are many strange people in the capital. As long as you keep out of the way of the police forces, the Shinsengumi, the Mimawarigumi.'

I was a little nettled by his remark. I had gained much more confidence in my disguise and was fairly sure no one would guess I was a woman. The tea came and we drank it slowly. All the while Shinsai's eyes flicked around the cramped smoky room and the street beyond the curtains. Even inside it was chilly. I had just picked up the long sticks to turn the coals in the brazier when a sudden silence fell over the room. I turned to see a man step into the doorway.

He wore dark *hakama* over a dark blue kimono with a light blue *haori*, patterned in white on the sleeve. He did not say anything but he exuded an air of threatening authority. Several customers were attempting to hide their faces by rubbing them with hand towels or burying them in their tea cups. Shinsai reached over and took my pipe, filled it and lit it, inhaled the smoke, breathed it out. I simply watched him, not speaking.

The man gazed at each person in the room then turned abruptly. On the back of his *haori* was a single character which read *makoto*: sincerity.

'Shinsengumi,' Shinsai said quietly as conversations began again around us.

'Did he know you?'

'I don't think so. As far as I know I have escaped their notice. But it's impossible to be sure. Of course, Genzui and Katsura are both well known to them, but their position with the domain protects them.'

When we left the tea house the same man was standing at the end of the street.

'Just walk past naturally,' Shinsai muttered.

But I knew he was going to stop us and I wanted to prove I could get away with my role as a man under any circumstances. Before we reached him I paused, unwrapped the bundle I was carrying, and took out the flyers Eikaku had made for us. When the guard stepped into our path I put one in his hands. 'From the famous town of Isa, the remedy for all your aches and pains. Guaranteed to relieve suffering from colic, headaches, toothaches and piles, stones and gravel in the urine and many other complaints.'

I heard my own voice as if it were someone else speaking, some eager young lad from Isa, complete with accent.

'I can give Your Excellency a free sample, but if your friends want some – and they will – it will cost them two *mon*.'

'Quacks!' he exclaimed, but he took the envelope and put it inside his robe, allowing us to walk on.

'There,' I said to Shinsai, when we were out of earshot. 'I fooled him completely.'

'I forbid you to become consulting doctor to the Shinsengumi,' Shinsai said, leading me through the alleys in a twisting path.

'Maybe I could poison them,' I replied. My heart was beating fast, but with excitement not fear. 'Anyway, he is not a well man. I'll bet he has blood in his urine and pain in his kidneys. He won't last long.'

At the end of the next street Shinsai told me to wait for a few moments while he checked the lodging place. I watched him enter a small narrow building between a second-hand shop and a soba house. He came out and beckoned to me. I followed him inside. The house had a curious smell that I could not identify.

'This is my little hideout,' he said, as a woman came through a doorway that joined the building with the one next door. 'And this is Mrs Minami, who runs the second-hand shop and is my landlady. Dr Imaike Kōnosuke,' he said to the woman. 'He was a student of my brother.'

The narrow building seemed to serve as a storeroom for the shop and was crammed with ceramic pots, bamboo containers, old umbrellas, chests and boxes. Mrs Minami was rather large and plump, with a good-looking face like the *kami* Benten. There was something quite inspiring and reassuring about her as if she were indeed one of the gods of good fortune. I was to discover that she had a generous nature, which involved her in good works in the neighbourhood. She adored the Emperor and was interested in the teachings of Hirata Atsutane.

'Welcome back,' she said, beaming at Shinsai.

'Dr Imaike will be staying for a while,' Shinsai said.

‘Is he looking for patients?’ she replied eagerly.

‘I certainly am, and I would be honoured to treat you with no charge,’ I said in my Isa accent.

‘Oh, listen to the way he talks! How charming!’

Our fast-budding friendship was interrupted by a customer calling from the shop door and Mrs Minami left us with many apologies.

Shinsai led me through to the back room.

‘It’s not much,’ he said. ‘But it’s very private. And it has an escape route.’

At the end of the room was a tiny courtyard, and a wall, beyond which was a large building. The smell was stronger here. I wrinkled my nose, trying to identify it.

‘It’s the public bathhouse,’ Shinsai said. ‘Like Mrs Minami the owners are loyalists and are ready to help us. I keep clothes there. We’ll get a set for you too, women’s clothes. If there’s a raid you go over the wall and leave through the bathhouse front door as someone else.’

‘Go naked over the wall?’

‘You could keep your loincloth on so you don’t bang your parts.’

‘I don’t have those parts,’ I said.

‘Don’t remind me,’ he said, grinning. ‘Our landlady will be back soon.’

Sure enough she appeared at that moment with bowls of tea on a tray, and we chatted for a while, mainly about her health, the remedies she used and what I thought of them. She left after pouring a second cup of tea which we drank while Shinsai looked at the letters he had picked up at the Teradaya.

I gazed around the room at the furnishings and Shinsai's few possessions – a clothes stand, a sword rack, boxes with spare clothes and piles of books along the walls, a small desk, an unlit brazier and a lamp. I warmed my hands on the tea bowl and let the steam flow over my face.

'This is from Inoue Monta,' Shinsai said.

'From England?'

'It must be.' Shinsai handed the envelope and the letter to me. The address was to Itasaki Shinsai at the Teradaya, Fushimi. I couldn't believe it had come all the way from England. I looked at Monta's flowing handwriting and thought I could hear his excitable voice.

'What does this say?' There were some lines at the top of the letter I could not read.

'University College, London.' Shinsai spelled it out. 'That must be where they are studying.'

'Shinsai, can you speak English?'

'I've been trying to learn a bit. I can read it. I don't know about actually speaking it.'

He went on to read the letter aloud.

It's impossible to describe what London is like. You cannot imagine it until you see it. It is built out of bricks and stone and steel. All the windows are glass. You feel as if you are in prison when you are inside, and always watched by people when you are outside. The streets are paved and are lit up at night by gaslight. Very dirty because of all the horses. Trains run everywhere above the ground, powered by steam, on iron tracks, and there are plans to put them underground as well. Inoue Masaru fell in love with Paddington Station – he had some kind of revelation there and is going to bring railways to our country. Itō has fallen in love with a series of English misses. He finds their blue eyes and gold hair irresistible. He will have to come home without one, though. We are meant to be studying analytical chemistry with Dr Alexander Williamson but really we are just trying to learn English and understand this society.

The voyage over? Well, I won't bother telling you too much about it. Itō was seasick most of the time, nearly fell overboard while trying to relieve himself. The waves washed his arse for him, just as well as he had dysentery. I learned a lot about navigation by swarming up and down the rigging with the other sailors, and being shouted at – Jonny, this and Jonny, that! I had a much better grasp of English by the end, including most of the common curses (you have no idea how many and how descriptive).

Sometimes I think I must have died at sea and am now in a special hell reserved for those mad enough to believe we could ever force the foreigners to leave Japan. Even if every son of Yamato laid down his life we still could not defeat them.

It's hard to explain the confusion of my feelings. People are kind to us, though they suspect we are really savages, and they are very generous. There is so much here which impresses us, and makes us envious and depressed. How did England become so powerful? How will our country ever catch up?

Itasaki-kun, jōi *has to be abandoned. If our domain continues to provoke the foreigners they will crush us completely. Please do your best to explain this at every level. We must avoid any confrontation that will lead to a war we cannot win. I repeat, cannot win.*

We eat beef and drink so much milk we'll probably forget Japanese and end up mooing like cows. We cut our hair in a smart Western style, and wear coats, trousers and even leather shoes. There are many drinking places here and we drink beer, gin and whisky. You probably think I have turned into a European. But I still love my country above all, even though we have no railways or telegraph, or anything else that makes a civilised nation. I will be back soon to rectify all this.

Till then, Inoue Monta.

'How brave they are to go to such an unknown land,' I said. The letter had made me both excited and rather envious of Monta's experiences.

'I agree with everything he says.' Shinsai folded the letter and put it away in its neat envelope. 'But the desire to fight is so strong now in Chōshū I don't know if it can be halted.'

THE FIRST YEAR OF GENJI

In the weeks following our arrival in the capital I walked its streets and alleys until I knew my way around as confidently as Shinsai. Often he came with me, showing me his secret routes, pointing out tea houses frequented by Aizu or Satsuma men. I listened to every snatch of talk and every rumour. I engaged all sorts of people in conversation as I handed out flyers and heard accounts of symptoms. Mrs Minami arranged for me to use a room in the neighbourhood shrine, where I consulted with patients.

I walked through Higashiyama and visited the great temples of Chion'in, Tōfukuji and Kiyomizudera, marvelling at their history and their treasures. At Ishiyama, where Lady Murasaki was said to have begun *The Tale of Genji*, I bought an amulet for my mother, wondering if I would ever see her again to give it to her. I went to the Imperial Palace and looked at the famous gates of Sakaimachi, Hamaguri and the rest, and then, through the weaving and dyeing quarter of Nishijin, to Kitano Tenmangu, where I lit incense and prayed to Tenmanjin-sama for Eikaku, Takasugi and all the young men of Chōshū.

I went to the riverbanks where beggars and other homeless people gathered beneath the bridges at Nijō, Sanjō and Shijō. I saw all kinds of illness and suffering, and the plight of these vagrants became even more pitiable as the true winter cold set in. By the end of the year the capital was covered in snow, austerely beautiful but even more cruel for the poor.

At the New Year, in some wistful attempt to change the nation's fortunes, the era name was changed to Genji. It was to be the worst year in Chōshū's history, and for me the saddest of my life.

Mrs Minami was kept busy trying to relieve the sufferings of the poor and she often came to beg some powders or pills from me, which she would then offset against the rent or repay with a bowl of noodles or *o-den*. We were eating one of these warming meals one evening early in the new year when she returned sooner than we expected – for she always brought tea at the end of the meal – to say someone was waiting at the soba house with a message for Shinsai.

'I'll go and take a look at him,' Shinsai said, swallowing one last mouthful of *o-den* and getting up. He was gone for a long time and I was just wondering if I should prepare myself for my flight over the wall when he returned to say it had been Kusaka Genzui.

'He wants me to go to Ōsaka with him and Katsura tomorrow. You can come too.'

'Genzui will recognise me,' I said. 'He's known my family for years and I've seen him several times at Shiraishi's.'

'I told him who you are. Someone had already informed him about a young doctor from Isa and he was curious. He knows all the medical families in Chōshū. I didn't think we'd be able to deceive him, and anyway I didn't want to.'

'What about Katsura?'

'He doesn't know you, does he?'

'I've been in the same place as him – maybe on one or two occasions. But I've never spoken to him.'

'Let's see if we can fool him!' Shinsai exclaimed. 'It'll be a laugh.'

'I don't want to go, it's too difficult.'

'Come with me,' Shinsai pleaded.

'Does Genzui know about us?'

'What about us?' Shinsai said, teasing me.

'You know…'

'You mean this?' He ran his hand up my leg making my whole body tingle. 'There is nothing to know. Everyone knows I have no interest in women. You are just carried away with dreams of serving the Emperor. You ran away to Kyōto dressed as a man and I am keeping an eye on you until I can send you home.'

'Is that what you told Genzui?'

'Something like that.' His hand moved higher.

I slapped it away. 'We shouldn't be together.'

'It's too late to say that now,' Shinsai said, resuming his caress, and of course it was, far too late.

Before we slept I asked, 'Why are we going to Ōsaka?'

'Takasugi is bringing Kijima Matabei to talk with Katsura and Genzui. They hope to persuade him to calm down and be patient.'

Kijima Matabei, a brilliant swordsman and a close friend and associate of Lord Sufu, had become the leader of one of the largest and most belligerent of the *shotai*, the Yūgekitai. I was not worried about him as I had never met him, but Takasugi was a different matter.

'Takasugi will certainly recognise me.' I had told Shinsai

about my visit to Takasugi with Monta and about the forming of the Kiheitai at Shiraishi's place. 'And he is quite likely to tell my husband.'

'You no longer have a husband.' Shinsai was almost asleep. I listened to his breathing grow quieter, and then lay awake for some time wondering what I should do. I liked my life how it was: I lived by day as a man doing work that interested me, and by night as a woman with a man I adored. But I had to admit it was a fantasy, only possible because the world we lived in was being turned upside down. When I looked into the future I could not imagine how our life could continue. Maybe we could run away to a place where no one knew us, maybe we could go to England like Monta.

Now Shinsai had put the challenge to me to deceive Katsura I felt I could not refuse it. The idea excited me. I would go to Ōsaka. Katsura would not see through my disguise and nor would Takasugi.

When I fell asleep I dreamed I was in a strange country where the houses were made of steel and glass. I walked among them looking for something. I could not find it; worse, I could not remember what I was looking for.

Snow still lay thick in Kyōto when we left, but by the time we arrived at the coast the last traces had disappeared and in Ōsaka there was even a hint of spring in the east wind. It was already late afternoon and growing dark. We did not stay at the Chōshū residence this time but in an inn not far away in the Dotonbori area where we had been to the kabuki theatre. Even though Takasugi, Genzui and Katsura were all now officials of the domain, they were in Ōsaka unofficially and in Takasugi's case without permission. After securing somewhere to sleep for the night we went out again to a geisha house in the area.

Takasugi was already there with Kijima, but we sat apart from them until Katsura and Kusaka Genzui arrived. They came separately – they never travelled together for fear of attack – and both wore cloths wrapped around their heads to hide their features. The girls clustered around them, taking their outer garments, their jackets and swords, and making a great fuss of them. They were popular in the geisha houses, especially Katsura, who loved women and spent freely. He was a tall young man, very good-looking with smooth unmarked skin and regular features. He was about thirty at that time, several years older than Takasugi and Kusaka, both of whom obviously looked up to him. He had become the top pupil at Saitō Yakurō's dōjō in Edo and had been promoted through the ranks of bureaucracy in the domain. He was a capable man, but people said he owed his success to his popularity and charm rather than to any outstanding talent.

Kijima Matabei was by far the oldest, at least fifteen years older than Katsura, probably in his mid-forties, I thought. He looked even older; his hair was turning grey and his face was lined. He was a big man, a renowned swordsman and horseman, respected and admired by many in Chōshū.

Genzui looked around, saw Shinsai and beckoned us over. He made no sign of knowing me but introduced Shinsai to Kijima. The others of course knew Shinsai already, Takasugi from the *sonjuku* and Katsura from the last few years in Kyōto. Shinsai mentioned my name as Imaike Kōnosuke.

Takasugi gave me a brief puzzled look but from then on

ignored me. He did not look well; he coughed frequently but said it was nothing, he had perhaps caught a slight cold on the boat from Mitajiri.

The geisha came with flasks of sake and a *shamisen* but Katsura, after a quick flirtation, waved them away. They took the *shamisen* but left the sake, frequently returning with refills.

All the men drank heavily, Shinsai maybe slightly less than the others. I tried to keep up and drink as much as a man should. I was nervous and smoked several pipes too. Soon my head was swimming as I attempted to follow the argument.

Kijima wanted to return to Kyōto with troops to win back Chōshū's position by force. The others were all against it, though Takasugi, who a year ago had gone into retirement in protest against Sufu's refusal to fight the Bakufu, was the most sympathetic. Katsura was completely opposed. Genzui did not reject the idea outright but insisted the time was not right, that Kijima and the Yūgekitai had to be patient.

'As I told you on the way,' Takasugi said to Kijima, 'if these two, who know the situation in Kyōto better than anyone, were in favour of your scheme I would support you. I am as keen to fight as you are but we cannot just launch an attack without carefully considering what happens afterwards.'

'Afterwards!' Kijima said scornfully. 'A samurai does not think about *afterwards*. The trouble with you, with all you young people, is that you think too much. You read too many books. How can you fight with such lukewarm ideas? Our lord has been disgraced. We, as his vassals, must be prepared to die.'

Shinsai said, 'If I may also speak, Chōshū cannot fight on two fronts. We have already had one disastrous engagement with the foreign powers. Dr Imaike was there; he saw the destruction at Maeda and Dannoura.'

Takasugi glanced at me again, frowning slightly as Shinsai continued. 'I have had a letter from Inoue Monta from London, the capital city of England.'

Kijima's eyes narrowed. 'What is Inoue doing in England?'

'He went there to see for himself what it was like. The domain gave him permission. His advice is to avoid war with the foreigners at all costs. There is no way that we can win.'

'Inoue says that? He must be in league with the English! Anyway I'm not arguing about fighting the foreigners. First things first. Let's restore our lord's position in Kyōto, then we can follow the Emperor's wishes and throw the foreigners out.' Kijima smacked the tatami with his palm.

'We will achieve nothing by bringing troops to the capital,' Katsura said.

'It is too early,' Genzui added. 'This current attempt at an alliance between the *daimyō*, the Bakufu and the Court will collapse shortly. None of the great lords can agree and they will all soon retreat to their domains and soothe their wounded vanity. The Emperor does not trust Satsuma, and the people of Kyōto dislike Aizu for bringing in the Shinsengumi. We only have to be patient and wait for Chōshū to rise again.'

'Someone should teach Satsuma a lesson,' Takasugi muttered. 'Get rid of Shimazu Hisamitsu for a start.'

'I'd like to see him dead,' Shinsai agreed. 'He should pay for the betrayal at the Teradaya as well as for our domain's unjust treatment.'

'But Chōshū and Satsuma need to be allies, don't they?' It was almost the first sentence I had uttered. Luckily the tobacco smoke had deepened my voice. 'Unless the great domains unite we cannot hope to achieve our purpose.'

'It goes against the grain, but the doctor is right,' Katsura said. 'However, it is hard to trust Satsuma.'

'I don't mind fighting Satsuma,' Kijima exclaimed. He was spoiling for a fight with someone and he was not going to back down easily. Tempers rose as the argument went on and everyone drank more.

In the end Kijima agreed to go back to Chōshū and persuade his troops to delay any action. The prospect seemed to depress him, and when Takasugi called to the geisha to bring the *shamisen* he stood up and said he was tired and was going to bed. Katsura also rose unsteadily to his feet and, with a longing look at the geisha (one of them really was very pretty), said he would make sure Kijima returned safely to his lodgings and boarded a ship home in the morning.

'Will you go back to Chōshū with him?' Genzui asked Takasugi after they had left.

'Not tomorrow. First I have to deal with Hisamitsu.' Takasugi's voice was slurred, and I realised he was very drunk. He took the *shamisen* up from his lap and began to play. Looking at the pretty geisha he sang a love song I'd known since I was a child. For a moment we all indulged in nostalgia for our distant birthplace, but halfway through the song he transferred his gaze to me and after another line broke off and said, 'I know who you are. You're the doctor's wife.'

I didn't say anything, wondering whether to confess or brazen it out.

Genzui said swiftly, 'Don't give it away, Shinsaku. The doctor is useful to us like this.'

Takasugi was shaking his head in a parody of amazement. 'You really fooled me. I just remembered your expression from when you came to see me.' He turned to Genzui. 'She did me good, you know. She's as good as a real doctor.'

'I am a real doctor,' I said loudly. 'Is there any reason why I can't be a doctor?' Lowering my voice, I went on, 'I am not the doctor's wife. I am the doctor!'

'Is that why you dress as a man?' Genzui asked.

'Why shouldn't a woman be a doctor? Why do we always have to pretend to be inferior to men? You are doctors' sons,' I addressed Genzui and Shinsai. 'And so is Katsura-san. Any one of you could have become a doctor, and you did not want to. Isn't it unfair that a woman should so desire it and not be permitted?' Hearing my own voice I realised I was very drunk too. 'You want to renew the world; that's what everyone longs for. In the new world will women have the same freedom as men? Isn't that what Yoshida Shōin would have wanted?'

'Wonderful! Wonderful!' cried the geisha, clapping their hands and pouring us all more sake. The pretty one came and sat down next to me.

'I like you,' she said. 'Man or woman, I don't care.'

Takasugi shouted with laughter. 'If you're going to be a man you have to know how to behave with women. Let's give you a lesson!'

I was enjoying myself, but the sake was affecting my bladder.

'I need to piss,' I whispered to the girl. She giggled at my speech but stood up and taking my hand led me to the privy at the back of the tea house and showed me where the girls went to relieve themselves.

When I came out she had brought a bowl of water and a towel for me to wash my hands. She set the bowl down and pulled me close to her, kissed me on the mouth, and caressed my face.

'You are wonderful,' she said. 'I wish I could be like you.'

At that moment I did not know if I was man or woman. She was a very small girl so she made me feel large and dominating. Our forms seemed to merge together in an entirely pleasing way. Of course I was completely drunk.

'What do you usually do? About relieving yourself?' she said curiously.

'I've learned to hold on until I'm in private. Sometimes it's a problem. Itasaki creates a diversion or distracts any other men around.'

'Is Itasaki-san your lover?'

'Yes, but don't tell anyone.'

'It's like a play,' she said, her eyes glowing. 'What about your husband – do you have a husband?'

I told her about Makino, how he had ordered me home to my parents.

'So you ran away? I wish I could.'

There was nothing I could say. I knew her life was probably harsh and unfair. She ran the risk nightly of contracting a disfiguring and eventually fatal disease. She was owned by her house and promised to clients. Unless someone wanted to redeem her and marry her she had no escape. If she fell pregnant the child would be aborted.

'What's your name?'

'They call me Ume here.'

The men were shouting for us to return. I wondered if

they ever thought about a new world for geisha and prostitutes, what their plans for the future were, what sort of world they would create when they had overthrown the old one. Kijima had accused them of thinking too much about *afterwards*. I was not sure that they thought about it enough.

I never saw Ume again but I have never forgotten her.

INOUE MONTA

Genji 1 (1864), Spring, Age 29

Monta looks at the cup of tea thrust in front of him with dislike. There is something deeply depressing about English tea; it is too strong and bitter to drink black, but adding milk gives it a sourish taste. Since he has been living in England he has learned a lot about the history of tea: it has caused the rise and fall of empires; it drove the English tea clippers to become the fastest ships in the world; whole forests have been cleared to create plantations for its bushes; men have stolen and murdered to bring it back to the addicted population. He thinks the end result should be more palatable. He yearns for the delicate flavours of Japanese tea, just as he craves rice – he has been given rice dishes here but one is made with milk and sweetened and the other, a curious hotchpotch of smoked fish and eggs, is only eaten at breakfast.

The English eat a lot of potatoes, and bread. He doesn't mind that; you can get used to bread. And meat is often the tastiest part of any meal. He is also very fond of ham with eggs, which was the first meal he ate in England, at the docks. Its taste is mingled forever with his amazement, not only at the huge black immensity of London, but also that he could make himself understood in English and could understand what was said in reply. All that study in Edo was good for something after all.

Fresh fish is another thing he misses, and sushi, soba, *mochi*, *dango*. His mouth is watering. He drinks the tea manfully but it tastes even worse after the dishes of his imagination.

Itō, sitting opposite him, is reading the newspaper, the London *Times*. They have fallen into a routine of meeting every morning in this tea room near University College where Itō is enrolled as a student in analytical chemistry. Monta somehow avoided enrolling though he sometimes attends classes. Neither of them is very clear what analytical chemistry is, but the professor who has taken them under his wing, Dr Alexander Williamson, teaches it. Itō is living in his house, Monta not far away in lodgings in Hampstead Road.

Sometimes Monta has an inkling of how important chemistry is. It symbolises the analytic approach of the West, the extraordinary ability to break things down into their component parts, to understand them in detail and manipulate them. London, all of England, seems to be in a fever of breaking things down, breaking them open, extracting their power and using it to construct new marvels. The air that stings their eyes and throats is solid with inventiveness. Who cares if the thick fogs they call pea-soupers blanket London during winter so that the days are scarcely lighter than the nights? England is undergoing a Revolution. It is in the grip of Progress, and it is extending its power all over the world.

He thinks of his own country, half asleep under the Tokugawa rule. He knows his people are as inventive and as clever as the English, as well as being hard-working and capable of great sacrifices. They just need shaking out of their slumber. As the English say, they need a good kick up the arse.

These picturesque English expressions make him laugh now he can understand the language better, like the street slang that amused him when he first arrived in Edo. He has always sought out the lowlife, in seedy taverns, illicit gambling dens and cheap brothels – the same places that exist in every city in the world as far as he can tell from his limited experience of Edo, Shanghai, Hong Kong and now London. There are two or three public houses in the vicinity where he and Itō are well known; they have been adopted like mascots or pets. The English treat them with patronising kindness, ply them with liquor and teach them vulgar phrases: *go to buggery* and *kiss my arse*. Luckily his Chōshū upbringing has given him great stamina where alcohol is concerned and he is pleased to hear his companions declare he could drink any one of them under the table, despite being such a little fellow.

He feels tiny here – even most of the women are taller than he is – and vulnerable without his swords. He is in his late twenties, but being unarmed and surrounded by people of large stature, along with his cropped hair and his uncertainty with the language, reduces him to childhood again. It has its advantages: he never makes anyone angry – the English are so certain of their superiority they are tolerant of foreigners – and Englishwomen can be quite pleasingly curious. Itō takes advantage of this shamelessly, and has enjoyed several flirtations with respectable young women, as well as encounters with girls of the street, but Monta has been more circumspect – or perhaps less brave.

The room darkens suddenly as clouds cover the sun and rain begins to fall heavily. It is officially spring and the flowers in the London parks and gardens would be beautiful were they not so beaten down by wind and rain, but it is still cold, a damp insidious cold that makes his bones ache. His cheap shoes have holes in them from the miles he walks every day, and his feet are permanently numb.

Itō is coughing again; he has had the cough all winter. Monta studies him with affectionate concern. He is a few years older and treats Itō like a younger brother whom he has to protect and sometimes chastise. He takes out a couple of small cigars – they both smoke them in preference to pipes now – and passes one across the table. He's heard it said that tobacco is bad for the lungs, but in his opinion it is better than any medicine. Itō calls for a light, takes a deep puff and returns to the newspaper.

His brow is furrowed with concentration as he mouths the words under his breath. They both read the paper every day – Professor Williamson recommends it. Monta enjoys the whole process, buying the newspaper from a boy on a street corner, unfolding it inside the tea room, letting his eyes float in the unfamiliar direction, horizontally from left to right, imagining others watching and admiring. 'Look at me,' he thinks. 'I am reading English!' Though truthfully he only understands every third word.

'Chōshū is in the newspaper,' Itō says, folding back the page so Monta can read the article. It is only short but he reads it through two or three times to make sure he has understood it.

An alliance has been formed between the nations of Great Britain,

France, Holland and the United States of America to punish the Prince of Choshiu – that is Lord Mōri – *who last year opened fire on various ships of Western nations passing through the straits at Shimo no seki.*

'They are going to attack Chōshū,' he says in alarm.

'Punishment for *jōi*,' Itō says. 'Our people are going to learn it's not that simple!'

Itō is smiling as if it is all a big joke, and of course it is: the idea of Chōshū with its puny batteries and antique rifles thinking it can take on the might of Britain and other Western powers is risible, like a small boy threatening a bunch of warriors with a toy sword, but the outcome, Monta knows, will not be a joke, at least not for Chōshū or for Japan. He has heard enough about *gunboat diplomacy*, about *teaching the natives a lesson*. He recalls the stories he's been told about the Opium and Arrow wars, when incidents like this one were the excuse for major attacks on Chinese territory, resulting in the destruction of the Summer Palace and the loss of sovereignty over Hong Kong and Shanghai.

'We have to go back!'

Itō looks dismayed, recalling no doubt the horrors of the journey over, the seasickness, the storms, the gruelling work (they thought they were travelling as passengers but were taken for seamen and with their poor English could not explain the mistake).

'What can we do?' he says, tapping the newspaper. 'It's all been decided. We can't stop them now.'

'We have to try. We must prevent the attack. We can talk to the English in Yokohama, to Parkes or Satow. We can explain what *jōi* really is, a lot of noise directed against the

Bakufu, that they mustn't take it seriously. Maybe we can offer compensation, we can get them to negotiate…'

'We burned down their legation,' Itō points out.

'That was just a…I don't know…just a prank! None of it's really directed at foreigners. They're just an easy target.'

Monta sees this clearly now. The main target is, has always been, the Bakufu. Attacks on foreigners are simply a way of destabilising the government, applying pressure, embarrassing it, pushing it closer to its inevitable collapse.

Often they speak in English for practice, but this conversation has all been in Japanese. Now Monta lowers his voice, even though no one around can understand them. Ever since he met Ernest Satow he's half expected all Englishmen to break into fluent Japanese and astonish him.

'We need to explain that it is the Bakufu that is the problem. Whatever Chōshū does is just a symptom. The English will support us – we can't do anything without them.'

He is seized by a vision. It is so lucid it makes him tremble. With English weapons and know-how Chōshū can overthrow the government. They will make Japan like another England, with the Emperor as head of state as Queen Victoria rules over the British Empire. He knows that Satow, and Parkes under Satow's influence, already view Chōshū with some favour. Since he's been in London he's understood more clearly the rivalry between the Great Powers. The newspaper speaks of an alliance between France and Britain, but while they may present a united front against the natives, behind the scenes each is involved in intrigue and manipulation to further their own interests. He has heard the French are in favour of propping up the Bakufu and there are rumours they will supply them with arms and technological assistance. To counter this the British need their own power base, and Monta is determined it will be in a secret alliance with Chōshū.

No one else can make this happen. It is clearly his mission; it is for this that Sufu Masanosuke sent him to London. Only he can act as a three-way negotiator between the domain government, the English and the *jōi* hotheads. He takes a deep breath and finishes his tea in one gulp.

'We must leave immediately.'

Outside the window horses harnessed to cabs and carriages trot to and fro in the rain. The sound of their shod hooves on the cobbles, the shouts of the drivers, the splash and rumble of the wheels fade from Monta's consciousness. In their place he sees the wooden houses and temples, the stone-walled castles, the forested mountains of his homeland. He is not going to let them be assaulted by foreigners. He has no doubt that his country will be broken down and rebuilt, but if anyone is going to do that, it will be him and his colleagues.

ATTACK AT THE IKEDAYA

Kijima Matabei returned to Chōshū only partly convinced that he should not lead the Yūgekitai to Kyōto. Takasugi abandoned the idea of assassinating Shimazu Hisamitsu and also went back to Hagi. We heard later that he was charged with leaving the domain without permission and imprisoned in Noyama as a punishment.

'What did I tell you?' Shinsai said. 'The one man we can trust to keep us out of trouble and the authorities lock him up for a trivial misdemeanour.'

We had resumed our life of selling medicines in the street, treating patients, and spying. The capital grew more tense as the weather warmed up. Rumours of plots and intrigues abounded. Every whisper held a conspiracy. In the third month reports came from Kantō of a rebellion in the Mito domain, one of the centres of Tokugawa power, right on Edo's doorstep. Mito was the birth clan of Hitotsubashi Keiki, the guardian of the Shōgun Iemochi, and his most likely successor.

The rebels called themselves the Tengutō and included some of the most respected men in Mito. They had genuine grievances and attracted many farmers and merchants to their cause. It would be months before they were suppressed completely.

Despite being distracted by the Tengutō in Kantō the Bakufu's position in Kyōto was becoming stronger. As Kusaka Genzui had predicted, the alliance with the great lords had come to nothing, leaving the Court with no other ally but the Shōgun's government. However, nothing was straightforward. The Bakufu now took up the slogans of the *jōi* party, partly in order to win popular support, and maybe partly to reassure the Emperor. The Shinsengumi were as fervently anti-foreigner as the *shishi* they pursued through the alleys and tea houses of Kyōto.

In the sixth month Shinsai received a letter from Genzui, who had been in Chōshū a few weeks before, telling us the news from the domain. Despite opposition from Takasugi, Yamagata Kyōsuke and others, preparations for action were going ahead, and at least three troop contingents were being readied to march on Kyōto.

Like Takasugi, Lord Sufu is also opposed to this, Kusaka wrote. *Takasugi's voice is not heeded as he is still in prison, and Sufu is increasingly overlooked and ignored. He attracted considerable criticism for visiting Takasugi in Noyama. He rode his horse up to the gate shouting for Shinsaku, threatening the guards with his drawn sword. Needless to say he was drunk at the time. His supporters maintain that this has never interfered with his diligence or judgement and that Sufu drunk is still wiser than most people sober, but many are arguing that he should be punished. My opinion is that Lord Sufu is depressed by the inevitable progression of events and his loss of power to control them.*

'He drinks too much, that is why he is depressed,' I said when Shinsai read this to me. I couldn't help smiling at the picture of Sufu on his horse shouting outside the gate of

Noyama while Takasugi languished inside, like his beloved mentor, Yoshida Shōin. I wondered how Takasugi was coping with prison life, if he was using it as an opportunity to catch up with his reading as Shōin did. I hoped it would not push him back into depression and I worried about what it would do to his precarious physical health.

'Where is Genzui writing from?' The letter had been handed to Mrs Minami by a customer in the soba shop.

'There is no address,' Shinsai replied. 'Somewhere in the capital, I suppose. I know he is back from Chōshū.'

There were *shishi* and *rōnin* in hiding all over the city. In Kawaramachi, just across the Kamogawa from where we lived, there were many inns and tea houses where they were concealed or where they met in secret. Increasingly the police forces were searching the streets and raiding buildings, arresting suspects and torturing them to uncover anti-government activities. The two groups had much in common – maybe that was why they hated each other so bitterly. The Shinsengumi leaders were as frustrated as the loyalists at the Bakufu's inability or lack of will to expel foreigners. Nevertheless, they were sworn Tokugawa men and were fiercely loyal to the shōgunate.

One of Mrs Minami's associates was a second-hand goods dealer who had a shop on the Takasegawa, the canal that linked the Kamogawa with Fushimi. He bought from her the larger objects that she did not have room for and in return passed small items on to her. He also dealt in saddlery. His shop was called the Masuya and everyone knew him as Kiemon. He had become useful to Shinsai for delivering messages and pieces of information. The Masuya had become quite a centre for *shishi* on the run and for stockpiling weapons.

It worried Shinsai that Kiemon was taking increasing risks and becoming too well known. At the end of the fifth month and early in the sixth several people were arrested who had some connection with the Masuya. Shinsai did not know any of them well and did not think they would have any information on him, but if they did they would certainly reveal it sooner or later at the hands of the Shinsengumi.

We both became more tense and cautious. Any call at the door of Mrs Minami's shop, especially after dark, set us on our feet ready to make the dash over the wall.

Shinsai was aware of the wild plots being bruited about – to assassinate Lord Matsudaira Katamori, the Aizu *daimyō,* Protector of Kyōto, to set fire to the capital on a windy night, penetrate the Imperial Palace in the confusion, capture the Emperor and carry him away to Chōshū. This last one had been around for several years. Both he and Genzui tried to calm the plotters and urge them to be patient, but you might as well have counselled patience to a wild boar.

Early on the morning of the fifth day of the sixth month, the eve of the Gion festival, Mrs Minami came rushing into our room with the news that Kiemon had been arrested.

'They raided the Masuya!' The words came tumbling from her mouth. 'They found guns and letters, all sorts of vital information. And they have taken Kiemon away.'

Shinsai and I exchanged a look, both knowing what lay in store for him.

'He will talk,' Shinsai said. 'He will betray everyone.'

Mrs Minami's face suddenly seemed to lose its plumpness as the blood drained from her skin.

'You will be all right,' Shinsai tried to reassure her. 'You've only dealt in old goods, not arms or secret documents. Even if they search your shop they won't find anything. Act normally. Do the same as you do every day. That way you will avoid suspicion.'

She nodded and went slowly back to the shop.

'I'm going out to see what's happening,' Shinsai said to me. 'I'll try to find where Katsura is. If I'm not back by this evening, go out and meet me under the Nijō bridge and we'll come back here together.'

He went swiftly around the room gathering up letters and documents which he gave to me, telling me to burn them. Then he took his swords from the rack.

'You should be armed too,' he said. 'We have never talked about that.'

'I have no idea how to fight,' I replied.

'You may need to kill yourself,' he said quietly.

At that moment it dawned on me that I might never see him again. 'I'll kill myself if anything happens to you. I'll cut my throat with a scalpel!'

'The only reason to kill yourself is to escape capture,' he said. 'Otherwise you must live. There will be many who will need doctoring.'

He looked as if he would say something else, but he did not, and we parted without saying goodbye, without touching each other.

It was warm and humid though the plum rains were over. After I had made a small fire outside and burned the papers, I did not know what to do with myself. It was hot in the stuffy little room, yet whenever I considered going outside I recalled the Shinsengumi man who had stopped me when I first arrived in the city. Then I had been recklessly confident. Now I was afraid. I lit my pipe and smoked for a while and took up one of the textbooks I had brought from Shimonoseki, trying to immerse myself in the study of human anatomy, but every sentence and every illustration reminded me of the frailty of the human body and its profound susceptibility to pain. And I ran out of tobacco.

Shortly after midday I heard footsteps outside, making my heart plunge, but then I heard Shinsai greet Mrs Minami. When he came into the room he was pale, sweating from the heat.

'I found Miyabe Teizō. There is some scheme going on.'

Miyabe Teizō had escorted the seven nobles in their flight to Mitajiri and Shinsai knew him well.

'Teizō should have more sense. He claims they are just discussing a plan to colonise Ezo and that's what Kiemon's supplies were for. He even suggested I should go with them! I can't persuade them to disperse and flee. They are determined to stay in the capital, even if they don't go through with this ridiculous plot. Yoshida Toshimaro is among them. We studied together at the *sonjuku*. He says they are going to hold a meeting tonight at the Ikedaya.'

The Ikedaya was a large inn further north along the Takasegawa, not far from the Chōshū mansion.

'They are mad to go there!' I exclaimed. 'Everyone knows it's a Chōshū haunt. Kiemon especially must have known that.' I used the past tense as if he were already dead. In fact he survived the torture which made him betray so many and would be executed the following month during the fighting at the Forbidden Gate. But that lies ahead in my story.

'Yes, it's certain to be raided,' Shinsai said. 'I must find Katsura. If anyone can order them to desist it is he. I will just rest for a few moments. It's so hot.'

I unrolled the futon so he could lie down and brought a bowl of water from the well in the yard. I laid a cold towel on his forehead and wiped his hands, wrists and feet.

'Where will Katsura be? Is he in hiding too?'

'According to Teizō he's living in the Tsushima mansion. I'll go there.'

I lay down next to him. Neither of us spoke, nor did we touch. Yet I felt that our souls, the essence of who we were, merged and became one. That sounds too poetic, maybe we just fell asleep, but time seemed to stand still and the world receded until we were drawn back by the sound of drums beginning to beat for the festival.

'We could go to Ezo,' I said dreamily. 'Forests and bears…'

'And snow,' Shinsai said. He stretched and began to get up. 'It's always winter there.'

'We would wear bear skins. No one would know us.'

After Shinsai had left again I straightened my clothes and my hair and went out to buy more tobacco. It was late afternoon and the streets were beginning to fill with people dressed in light cotton *yukata* and carrying lanterns. The shops were decorated with lanterns too, as well as streamers and banners. The thronging crowds, the lights and the bright colours reassured me. The images of betrayal and torture that had plagued me faded and I began to enjoy myself. We had great festivals in

Chōshū but nothing as magnificent as this one, which combined the wealth of the Kyōto merchants and the skill of their craftsmen to create the huge, astonishingly beautiful floats.

While I was buying tobacco I ran into Mrs Minami and she took me to each district to view the floats as they were readied for the processions. We stopped often to drink sake with her many friends. Everyone was determined to have a good time, yet there was something frenetic about the merriment that became more intense as the night went on.

By midnight I had had enough and my bladder was bursting. I went back to our lodgings where I could use the privy. Shinsai was not there, nor had he left any message. I set out again for the Nijō bridge.

The bridge was a gathering place for beggars, vagrants and the homeless. The festival was a good time for them as people gave generously to beseech or to thank the gods. It had brought all the street performers to the riverbank too. Acrobats, fire jugglers, basket jumpers, top spinners were all displaying their skills in the light of blazing fires and red and white lanterns. The flames turned the water to gold with their reflections and waterbirds called harshly, disturbed from their roosts by the clamour.

I waited for a long time, gazing up at the quarter moon, wondering if Monta in London was looking at the same moon. My spirits had been lifted by the sake and the crowds but now they were plummeting into dread. I felt something terrible had happened, but I did not know what to do except wait there for Shinsai.

He finally appeared out of the darkness, breathing hard as if he had been running or was wounded.

'Are you hurt?'

'No, I didn't take part. But there's been an attack, at the Ikedaya. It's a disaster. All are dead or arrested. Let's walk.'

We left the riverbank and began to make our way back to our room. The streets were still filled with people and no one paid any attention to us. Shinsai went ahead and checked that all was clear while I waited on the corner. He came into the doorway and beckoned to me.

'Did anyone escape?' I said when we were inside. I was thinking of the wounded, wondering if we could help them.

'Yoshida Toshimaro got away, but then he went back. He's dead now.'

'What about Katsura?'

'I don't know where he went,' Shinsai said. 'I spoke to him at the Tsushima residence. He said he would go to the Ikedaya and tell them to disperse, that they were inviting attack.'

'Didn't they listen to him?'

'I don't know. I didn't see him after that.'

'You don't think he's been killed?'

'I doubt it,' Shinsai said with a trace of bitterness. 'He knows how to avoid trouble.' He looked round the room. 'We can't stay here. Mrs Minami has too close a connection with Kiemon. We'll leave as soon as it's light.'

It was barely an hour till dawn. We did not sleep. Every sound made us start. At one point Shinsai said, 'I actually went there too. To the Ikedaya. I spoke to Yoshida. He wanted me to stay. I wanted him to leave. We quarrelled about it. He called me a coward. I should have stayed and fought with them.'

'Then you would have died with them.'

'Better to be dead than a coward.'

Better to be alive, I thought, but I did not say it.

At daybreak we went out into the streets, taking a few possessions in satchels and my medicine box, and mingled with the crowds. Many had heard about the affray and turned out to watch the Shinsengumi go back in triumph to Mibu. The soldiers carried their swords in their hands, many were still covered in blood. Outside the Ikedaya corpses lay with their bellies slit, their guts trailing. They were already swelling in the heat and starting to reek, attracting clouds of flies. People gazed at them with mingled horror and pity, but no one spoke. Once the soldiers had passed by silence descended on the whole city.

From the Ikedaya we went to the Chōshū mansion. The guards knew Shinsai and let us in. In the dust outside the great gate, though the bodies had been removed for burial, there were still pools of blood from those who had fled but had died or killed themselves before they could reach safety.

Eleven loyalists died at the Ikedaya and many more were arrested and would be executed later. In the following days Aizu soldiers and the Shinsengumi scoured the city for *shishi* and *rōnin*.

I did not feel very safe within the mansion. I was nervous all the time about being unmasked. It took all my energy to maintain my disguise in that world of men. Luckily the mansion was crowded with fugitives and everyone was too preoccupied with the attack and its aftermath to pay much attention to me. The deaths of so many were greeted with outrage and a desire for revenge. Those who supported bringing troops to Kyōto saw it as an opportunity to further their cause. Even Genzui, who had been opposed to this policy six months earlier, began to feel there was a chance of success in a bold attack.

By the end of the sixth month three contingents of Chōshū troops under the command of domain elders had gathered outside the city: Fukuhara Echigo at Fushimi, Kunishi Shinano at Tenryūji and Masuda Danjō at Otokoyama. At night their campfires flickered on the hillsides to the south and west. Kijima Matabei and the Yūgekitai were with Kunishi.

The presence of so many soldiers under the Chōshū banners increased the level of anxiety in the city, from the townspeople who began to pack up their belongings and prepare for flight all the way up to the Bakufu. Their most senior representative in Kyōto, Hitotsubashi Keiki, sought to negotiate with Fukuhara, demanding the withdrawal of his forces to Ōsaka, but Fukuhara replied they were only there to wipe out the false accusation made against their lords and were behaving as any good vassal should. Some domains, especially Aizu and Satsuma, demanded Chōshū be punished, but others and many in the Court felt something close to admiration for the undeniably loyalist domain.

It was almost the opening of autumn but the heat showed no sign of abating. Cicadas shrilled monotonously and even the nights were unbearably hot. The whole city stank of rotten food, waste and death. Inside the mansion the atmosphere was chaotic, packed as it was with Chōshū samurai and sympathisers, refugees from the police and other hangers-on. Many complained of colic and loose bowels brought on by the heat. I was irritable, desire tormenting me as much as the swarms of mosquitoes that plagued us at night. Shinsai was equally restless, still going obsessively over the events of the night of the attack at the Ikedaya. He had lost all trust in Katsura, who never explained why he had failed to warn those who died.

'He said he went there, found no one there and remembered he had some matters to discuss in the Tsushima mansion, about trade with Korea. But why didn't he wait for them? What if he thought he'd be better off without them? Maybe he wanted to get rid of Miyabe and the other firebrands. Do you think he left a message for them, saying everything was fine and they were to wait for him? That would explain why they were unarmed, in the upstairs room with their weapons downstairs, so completely unprepared.'

I had no answers to these questions and nor did anyone else. The innkeeper was arrested, tortured and killed. Everyone who survived was imprisoned in Rokkakugoku and inaccessible. But it was not the first time the domain had allowed others to purge their troublemakers, nor would it be the last.

It was the second such betrayal Shinsai had witnessed. Once again he had survived when so many had died. I could see he felt ashamed and guilty about it. His dead schoolmate had taunted him with cowardice, and he was desperate now to fight. He was tired of waiting and temporising. I could feel him spinning away from me. The whirlwind that had hurled us together would now tear us apart. Our individual madness had been overtaken by the madness of the times.

TENNŌZAN

At the end of the month we learned Kusaka Genzui had arrived in Yamazaki, a few hours' walk to the south, and Shinsai decided immediately he was going to join him.

'And fight alongside him?' I asked as we prepared to leave. We planned to slip out by a back entrance with the farmers who came every morning to sell vegetables, and join the crowds of refugees fleeing the city.

'Of course. If it comes to fighting. Well, it almost certainly will. The confrontation has to come sooner or later. It would be wiser to leave it till later, but it cannot be put off for much longer.'

'It will be a disaster to fight now,' I said. Even after listening to the men around me argue, discuss and explain for nearly a month I still could not understand what was driving our domain to behave so recklessly, like a spoilt, headstrong boy, determined to attract attention, even if that attention turned out to be severe chastisement.

Shinsai said, as if reading my mind, 'It's because they – we – sense a weakness. It's irresistible. You have to keep testing that weakness to see if it will give. You must have noticed it among groups of men, here or among the Kiheitai. All that taunting and jostling, trying each other out.'

'I hate all that.'

'It's what men do, what clans and countries do.'

'No one does it to you.' In the same way as in Mitajiri, within the mansion the other men gave Shinsai a lot of leeway. They respected him.

'That's because the first time anyone tried it in here I had to show I was not weak. I've been tested plenty of times. I've had a lot to prove: I'm the youngest son of a country doctor, not even a samurai by birth. Chōshū is testing the Bakufu by responding to the insult of last year and to the incident at the Ikedaya, another taunt in our direction. We have to respond or display our weakness by submitting.'

'And then the Bakufu will be offended and have to respond,' I said. 'And so it goes on and on.' But I was thinking that weakness was like an infected wound for which there is no cure but knife or fire.

'Until someone wins decisively, yes,' Shinsai agreed.

Shinsai went to tell the compound's director, Nomi Orie, that we were going to join Kusaka Genzui, and he gave us letters to take with us. We also took the flyers and my medicine box to give us some cover if we were stopped on the road, but we did not need them. The streets teemed with people pushing handcarts filled with their belongings, carrying children and baskets on their backs, desperate to get out of the city before the battle began. In their inconsistent way the police and the Shinsengumi let them go without stopping or searching them. Maybe they were more concerned with people entering the city than with those escaping.

We walked south in the direction of Fushimi, the same road that we had travelled on six months before. Then it had been so cold; now the heat was stupefying. Neither of us said much, saving our energy to lift one foot after another. At the edge of the city we turned towards the west, passing the eastern precinct of Honganji and following the Shikoku highway in the direction of Yamazaki. The countryside was lush, the rice just beginning to ripen in the paddies. Bean flowers on the banks, purple and white, attracted so many bees you could hear their humming from the road. Farmers were working in the vegetable fields, occasionally straightening up, hands on their backs, to watch the stream of people going past. Then they would turn and gaze towards the city, its roofs of hundreds of temples and mansions, thousands of houses, glistening in the morning sun. For how much longer would it look so peaceful, this thousand-year-old home of the Emperor, the place where he performed the sacred rituals that linked humankind with the gods and ensured the safety of the country?

It was late afternoon when we arrived at the temple, Hōshakuji, where one of the Chōshū contingents was stationed, nominally under the command of the domain elder, Masuda Uemonnosuke, also called Danjō. The temple, sometimes known as Tennōzan, the name of the sacred mountain behind it, was set in beautiful grounds with a long stone stepped path leading up to an imposing gate, a three-storey pagoda and many halls where the six hundred or so Chōshū soldiers were billeted. Horses were tethered under the trees stamping their feet and swishing their tails irritably in the heat. The smoke from cooking fires mingled with the smell of incense, and priests in Buddhist robes hurried to and fro looking harrassed and fretful at the invasion.

Yet there was an air of discipline about the encampment, the same discipline that the Shōkenkaku group had initially embraced in Mitajiri. Indeed Maki Izumi, the former Shintō priest from Kurume, was one of the commanders. Martial arts practice was just ending and the weapons were being packed away. As well as swords and spears many men had rifles, and there were two small field cannon mounted on wheels.

Kusaka Genzui was cleaning one of the rifles.

'Itasaki-kun,' he greeted Shinsai, 'you know something about Western guns. What do you think of this?'

Shinsai took the rifle, looked at the mechanism, squinted down the barrel, then held it up to his eye as if taking aim.

'Not bad,' he said. 'British made, Enfield, I suppose. Minié-type bullet. Should be very accurate.'

'Let's hope so,' Genzui replied. 'We spent all those years perfecting our sword fighting, but any future battles will be decided by this.' He looked around at the motley army, its soldiers clad in a mixture of traditional armour and Western-style uniforms, some wearing makeshift helmets, most in headbands. The military practice over, they were assembling in groups, sitting in neat rows on the ground while their commanders read to them from manuals on the theory of war.

'They are such idealists,' Genzui said as he led us out of earshot. 'They believe nothing can prevail against their loyal samurai spirit.'

He addressed me, with a shadow of a smile, surprising me by remembering my assumed name. 'Imaike, we've had a couple of cases of measles. Can you take a look at them?'

'I hope you've isolated them.' The last thing an army wanted was measles running through it. Two years ago the Satsuma army had carried the infectious disease into the capital. So many people contracted it business and political activity came to a standstill for weeks.

'We have; they're in a small hut outside the temple grounds.'

'Have you had measles?' I asked him.

'Yes, as a child. I've never felt so ill since!'

I remembered suddenly that Shinsai and I had had measles at the same time. I must have been eight and he ten. I recalled the long nights, the delirious dreams, the thirst.

The soldiers showed all the same symptoms, high fever and painful watering eyes. The hut they were in was tiny and very hot, but at least the light was dim. Childhood measles was very dangerous, and I'd found even in adults it could lead to pneumonia and other complications. I had a little powder left for reducing fever, which I gave them in some tea, along with a solution to ease the pain in the eyes. I warned them sternly about getting up too soon and told them on no account were they to rejoin their comrades for they would be putting the whole troop at serious risk. I had little hope of them heeding my advice though. Their desire to fight was far more burning than the fever and the rash.

When I returned to the temple Genzui and Shinsai were sitting on the veranda of the main hall, drinking tea. I sat down next to them to listen to the end of their conversation.

'We heard you were in favour now of bringing soldiers to Kyōto,' Shinsai said to Genzui.

'There seemed to be a moment of opportunity,' Genzui replied. 'The great lords had all left the capital, the Court had only the Bakufu, Hitotsubashi grows in power every day and he is open to negotiation. It all depends on what support we can get from other domains. I am in favour of having troops here; it strengthens our hand. But I'm not sure we should actually attack anyone. We must stick to our simple demand: that the injustices of the last year be rectified.'

'But by bringing these men here – Maki, Kijima, the Yūgekitai, the Shōkenkaku group – you are riding a tiger!'

'We'll see.' Genzui laughed. 'I am going to the city tomorrow to find out who, if any, will join our cause.'

Shinsai joined the other men in their days of drill and study while I looked after my measles patients and talked to the priests about the local herbs and the beneficial properties of the various hot springs. One of them told me that figwort, whose leaves are good for the eyes, could be gathered on the mountain, and a couple of days later I went out to see if I could find some, as well as mushrooms to give some variety to our meagre meals of millet and barley. The arrival of so many men in the district had put a severe strain on local farmers and food was strictly rationed. It was as hot as ever, even the turn of the moon bringing no relief, and the cries of cicadas fell like showers around me. The air smelled of cedar leaves, fading morning glory straggled along the path, and crow gourd was already ripening.

I walked slowly, taking note of various landmarks, here a Jizō statue, there a narrow stream bubbling out from a rock. The air was still but now and then a branch waved or a leaf began to twirl as though the wind were shaking it even though there was no wind. It made me think of *tengu* or other mountain spirits and I suddenly had the sensation that someone was watching me, that I could feel his breath on my neck. I turned and saw Shinsai walking silently towards me.

We did not speak but, clutching at each other, half ran, half stumbled into the forest. We fell together to the ground, tearing at our sashes to loosen them, to get at each other's bodies. Nothing mattered except that we should be joined. All the frustration and desire of the last few weeks combined in an arousal stronger than anything I had ever experienced, and I could tell Shinsai felt the same. My driving lust was like a man's, seizing its pleasure, refusing to be denied. It was not enough that I came as soon as he entered me, in a shudder that I could not have prevented or delayed, that overwhelmed my whole body. I wanted to be inside him as he was inside me, to be him completely, to hold him forever, his soul, his entire essence. I had not thought we would ever lie together again, and now I could not bear him to leave me, as though this would truly be the last time and I wanted it never to end.

There was so much we might have said to each other, but we did not speak until the evening bell sounded from the temple when the sun had lowered and the air grown a little cooler. Then Shinsai said, 'We must go back.'

I sat up and began to rearrange my clothing, then gathered up the few leaves of figwort I had managed to collect. 'I didn't find any mushrooms.'

'Just something better that springs up in the dark,' Shinsai said, as cheerful and bawdy as if we had the rest of our lives together.

When we got back to the temple we found Genzui involved in a heated discussion with Maki Izumi. It seemed his efforts to garner support in Kyōto for Chōshū's cause had been fruitless. All the commanders were to meet that evening at Otokoyama for a council of war.

Masuda Uemonnosuke had set up his base at the Hachiman shrine of Iwashimizu in Otokoyama on a steep mountainside where the three rivers join to form the Yodogawa. It was only a short walk from Tennōzan and was one of the most famous Hachiman shrines in the country. Lord Masuda it seemed was a devout worshipper and possibly put more faith in the god of war than in his soldiers.

The commanders, twenty or so in number, met inside one of the halls. Some of them had ridden from Tenryūji and Fushimi and their horses were tethered outside. Shinsai and I had walked with Genzui; we were not invited in but sat on the veranda where we could hear everything that was said since most of it was shouted loudly.

Kijima Matabei had just started speaking. Shinsai said quietly, 'The carvings under the roof are by Hidari Jingorō. Did you know, they say he carved a woman so beautiful he fell in love with her? She came to life and he gave her a soul by showing her her face in a mirror.'

'It's a pretty story.'

'Then he spent the rest of his life trying to stop her finding fault with him.'

'That's not true!' I nearly forgot myself and smacked him.

'No, I made that last bit up.' He put his lips close to my ear. 'I could carve you because I know every inch of you, inside and out.'

The heat rushed through my body again. I moved away from him slightly, and tried to compose myself to listen.

Kijima had finished his plea for immediate action. For a few moments no one responded, then Genzui replied. He began by explaining the position in Kyōto where the Bakufu was assembling troops from various domains which far outnumbered the Chōshū forces. He did not think the support they had hoped for from sympathetic domains would be forthcoming.

'You have come with sword and spear…' he addressed the gathering.

'And rifles,' Shinsai muttered.

'…to cleanse the name of the house of Mōri, but your humble entreaties would hold more sway with the Emperor than force of arms. Furthermore, we should wait for Lord Mōri Sadahiro, who is on his way to Ōsaka with more men. If you will only be patient, maybe fall back to Ōsaka, wait for Lord Sadahiro, the Bakufu will negotiate.'

His voice was drowned out by Kijima, shouting that the evil surrounding the Emperor must be driven out, that the time for waiting was over, that they must act before the noble heir arrived.

'We are not well enough prepared,' Genzui said bluntly. 'We don't have enough troops, nor have we planned what will happen afterwards.'

'You are a coward,' Kijima replied, and into the ensuing silence announced, 'I will eradicate this evil with my own hands.'

The floorboards shook as he rushed out of the hall. He did not recognise us as he went past. I doubt if he even saw us. Blind to everything but his own conviction and his own glory, he snatched the reins of his horse from the groom, mounted and galloped off into the gathering darkness.

Kijima carried a lot of weight among the others, because of his advanced years and his long history of service to the domain, but Genzui had a better grasp of the situation in Kyōto. He began again to argue logically and persuasively, but Maki Izumi interrupted him, agreeing wholeheartedly with Kijima and winning the support of the other commanders.

Even to us, listening from outside, the moment when the opinion of the gathering was won over was clear and painful. For Genzui it must have been devastating. If only he had been able to prevail, if only recklessness and wild enthusiasm had not seized almost all the leaders, if only…

But the dice had fallen. The gamblers would lose and be stripped. We walked back to Tennōzan with him, no one saying anything. It was almost nightfall. When we approached the temple Genzui spoke suddenly. 'Imaike-kun, you know my wife, I think. Please tell her about this meeting and how we came to fight in Kyōto.'

'Of course.' I could tell he did not expect to survive, and indeed I was aware of death all around him, waiting to move into his bloodstream and bones and undo everything that held him together, alive.

'You must stay here,' he added, 'and afterwards go back to Chōshū and tell her.'

'Surely I should come with you and care for the wounded.'

'There will be no wounded,' he replied. 'If we are wounded we will die by our own hand. And our bones will bleach in the grounds of the palace.'

No one slept that night. The orders were to march before dawn. The men were excited at the prospect of joining battle and the temple teemed like an ants' nest with their activity. Kusaka said he would make a final effort to present an entreaty directly to the Emperor through Prince Takatsukasa, one of the nobles who was still sympathetic to Chōshū, but no one expected the day to end peacefully.

There was no question of Shinsai not going. I did not even attempt to persuade him. I hardly spoke to him. I could not cling to him or press my lips to his for one last time. When he left with Maki and Genzui, the torches flaming, the horses prancing, the men marching in disciplined order, their rifles on their shoulders, their swords at their side, their spears like a hedge of bamboo grass, I simply lined up with the priests and bowed like them. The commanders wore armour with tassles of purple silk and carried lacquered bows. Over their heads fluttered white flags inscribed with the names of Hachiman and Tenmanjin.

Shinsai looked at me once and I said, 'Take care of yourself,' not expecting him to hear, and he called something back. It might have been *Let's meet in Ezo!* but I couldn't be sure.

When the light from the torches and the last sounds had faded, a strange silence settled over the temple, making it seem empty and uncanny. As the sun rose the priests returned to their everyday routine, but I did not know what to do with myself or where to go. I went to check on my patients but of course they were not there; they had left with the others as I had half expected. I sat down on the floor of the tiny hut and felt my eyes grow hot as if I were going to cry. I could not remember when I had last cried. Now I found myself thinking, what if I were to cry now? But it seemed like a womanish sort of thing to indulge in and the feeling soon passed. In its place came a terrible sense of loss as though one of my limbs had been brutally amputated. I saw again Shinsai covered in blood and I knew he was going to die with Genzui.

Leaning against the wall of the hut I fell asleep for a while. I woke up because the room was so hot. It was still only mid-morning. I talked to the priests about preparing a place for the wounded and they agreed to set aside a small hall. I gathered together what I could find or beg from them – some old bedding, cloths and rags – but I was succumbing to a sort of paralysing fatalism and I did not really expect anyone to return. The priests kept up a continuous chanting of sutras for protection, but I did not think any bodhisattva, not even Lord Shaka himself, could save the Chōshū army, not even Hachiman.

Now and then I thought I heard gunfire. Crows cawed and kites mewed overhead while the cicadas did not cease their stridulation. In the middle of the afternoon when I was outside smoking a pipe, I realised the smell of burning was far greater than my little wad of tobacco warranted. One of the priests came out and stood next to me, gazing northwards.

'The capital is on fire,' he said.

Ash drifted on the air and fell like petals. Above the city rose a cloud of smoke. Dread invaded me. The inactivity, the waiting seemed intolerable. One moment I thought I would rush to Kyōto to see for myself what was happening, the next I was seized by an instinctive urge to flee back home, back to Chōshū. But I did neither; I just stayed on the veranda, staring at the flames.

KUSAKA GENZUI

Genji 1 (1864), Seventh Month, Age 24

Genzui has been hit by a bullet in his left shoulder but he is not aware of any pain, just a gradual diminishing of strength until he can no longer reload the Enfield with which he has been firing sporadic shots through the bars of the window of the Takatsukasa mansion. It doesn't make much difference as they have barely any ammunition left. He thrusts the rifle towards Terajima Chūzaburō, who is still as far as he can see unwounded, and feels for his sword. The hilt is slippery with blood; he realises it is his own.

He has not yet given up, even though he has known from the start their chances of success were small and the assault was ill-timed and under-prepared. Kijima and Maki have to answer for that, though he does not really blame them. You might as well blame typhoons for tearing trees from the ground and ripping the roofs of houses. It is the way storms are, the way these men are, and he loves them for it. They are like a pair of fierce old guard dogs always ready to fly at someone's throat.

Last night perhaps he was less forgiving, knowing they faced defeat and that he would die by his own hand rather than retreat, seeing how much more he might achieve and how far he had fallen short of his expectations. He did not sleep but sat on the temple veranda, remembering the dead: his teachers, Yoshida Shōin, executed in Denmachō, Umeda Unpin, dead in prison, and Sakuma Shōzan, so recently assassinated. And then all the friends who have passed on before him. Takechi Hanpeita is foremost in his mind, his brother in violence. He recalled the threats and the murders, the pledges signed in blood, the attacks on person and property and the old restlessness stirred in him. He could not sit still, rose and paced around the gardens, the tension in his body and soul would only be released by action, by fighting, by going towards death and taking others with him. When dawn came he knew it would be his last but he did not feel regret. Now his short flamboyant life returns to him in flashes like musket fire, and he feels it has all been worth it; he would not change any of it. If he had the chance to go back he would act the same way all over again. It is the way he is; not that he has always liked his own character and been at ease with himself, but he believes no one can change who they are, no matter how much monks might struggle, with their prayers, fasting and other rigorous practices. You are born a particular person and that is what you remain all your life. If there is rebirth, and to Genzui that seems quite practical and possible, then presumably you have another character and act differently. He will find out soon.

He has never expected a long life; somehow he has never expected to grow up. For so long he was a child among adults, his parents elderly, his brother twenty years older than he was. And he continues to feel like this: in the face of the domain government, the Bakufu, the foreigners, he is a child, irresponsible, inexperienced. This is the frustration that drives him to the violence that gives him release. Death means nothing to him. Ever since his grief-filled fifteenth year when his father, mother and older brother, Genki, died within months of each other, he has felt death walk close behind him, its breath on his neck. He despises death for taking Genki and not him. Despite the efforts of his father's and brother's many friends who vied with each other to support and encourage him, despite the favour of Shōin who chose him as a husband for his sister, since then he has not really cared if he lives or dies. He has come close to death many times, has had many lucky escapes, but he never feels a sense of relief or gratitude. Rather he is angered by death's bumbling efforts, by its inconsistency and clumsiness. It makes so many mistakes, always taking the wrong people – just like the Shinsengumi! He allows himself to feel the seductive luxury of hatred for the Shinsengumi, for Aizu and Satsuma, for the Tokugawa Bakufu.

But even hatred cannot take away his exhaustion and his thirst. He wonders dispassionately how long they have been here, how long they will be able to hold out. The nobleman and his family all fled once they opened the mansion to Genzui and his men. Satsuma and Aizu troops now surround it. Genzui's plan was to wait here for reinforcements as the other contingents fight their way from Fushimi and Tenryūji, but it is clear now that no one else has got this far, and they will not be coming now. There will be no rescue. There is no way out.

No more mad drinking bouts, no more women, no more wife…

Terajima calls to him and he approaches the window again. They both jump sideways as bullets smash into the wall. They grin at each other. Through the window Genzui sees piles of straw and wood, shutters pulled from windows, tatami wrenched up, bamboo buckets and rakes, men with blazing torches, preparing to set them on fire.

'They're going to grill us like eels,' Terajima says. He is younger than Genzui, maybe not even twenty, and is trying hard not to show fear. For a moment Genzui regrets it is not Shinsaku here with him at the end. Their lives have been so shaped by rivalry it would have been fitting if they had died together, but Shinsaku is in prison in Nomura and will outlive him.

The fires catch; the men outside shout in an ugly baying. Beneath it he seems to hear his brother's voice, calling his childhood name: *Hisasaburō*.

'We must not be captured,' Genzui says to Terajima, who nods, his eyes wide. 'If we die in here our bodies will be burned, they will not get our heads.' His voice is low and encouraging; he smiles slightly as he realises he sounds like Genki.

There is a sudden hush from the men around. He does not know if they will follow his example; he hopes they will but there is no time to make sure. The room is full of smoke now and the flames are roaring, fanned by the fierce wind that has been blowing since noon. Another hail of bullets rakes the walls.

'We'll stab each other,' he says to Terajima, 'in the throat. It's quicker and surer.'

He wonders briefly if any will live to bear witness to the

way he dies, but it doesn't matter. Terajima throws aside the rifle. They both draw their short swords and loosen the armour around their necks. They clasp each other's shoulders like brothers and gaze into each other's eyes.

'Now,' Genzui whispers, and the two swords move, each stroke clean and deep. The blood jets from them, mingling in one stream, as they fall together.

Hisasaburō!

At nightfall a young boy came bounding up the stone steps shouting, 'The soldiers are coming back!'

I leaped to my feet and ran to the gate. A small group came straggling towards the temple. I could not believe there were so few of them. The blood was pounding in my ears so strongly I thought I would lose consciousness. Six hundred had left that morning. How could less than twenty have returned?

I had to remind myself I was a man and a doctor and stop thinking like a woman with a woman's heart. Most of the men were wounded, and were covered in blood and soot. I recognised one of the men who had measles and a futile anger rose in my stomach.

Two of them were holding up their leader, Maki Izumi. I grew even angrier. He had sided with Kijima and pursuaded the commanders to attack. How could he appear like this, defeated but still alive? How dare he return when Genzui and Shinsai did not?

We brought the men into the hall and began to wash and cleanse the wounds, cutting away cloth and the ludicrous armour. I tried to assess the severity of the wounds, but I soon discovered most of them were superficial and not life-threatening. The severely wounded had already taken their own lives as Genzui had said they would.

When I came to Maki he tried to push me away. 'Don't waste your efforts, Doctor. We are dead men.'

I knelt beside him. I wanted to know what had happened.

'Kusaka is dead,' he said. 'He was wounded by gunfire. He and Terajima cut each other's throats.'

Even though I had known it would happen, shock punched me in the chest, and for a few moments I could not breathe.

'And Itasaki?' I whispered.

'He was with Kusaka when he died. I don't know what happened to him after that. We were in the Takatsukasa mansion. We fought our way as far as that. We held out against Fukui, Kuwana, Hikone...Our men were like tigers but Aizu and Satsuma outnumbered us.'

He recited the names of the domains in a sonorous voice as though he saw himself and his men as heroes in an ancient ballad. 'Then they set the mansion on fire on Hitotsubashi's orders. We had to retreat through the flames. We will make a last stand here and then we will die gloriously.'

I had a little opium to ease the pain of the wounded, but I decided not to waste it on Maki Izumi. Bit by bit, from him and the other survivors, I pieced together what had happened outside the Imperial Palace in the attack that became known as the Kinmon no hen, the Forbidden Gate Incident, or the Hamaguri gomon no hen, the Incident at the Clam Gate, so-called because it closed as tight as a clam, impossible to force open.

The youngest of the three Chōshū elders, twenty-three-year-old Kunishi Shinano, had set out from Tenryūji and advanced on the city from the west. At Kitano the contingent had been divided into two; Kunishi and his men overcame soldiers of Chikuzen to reach the Nakatachiura Gate. Kijima Matabei and the Yūgekitai drove Aizu back from the Hamaguri Gate but were in turn forced to retreat by Satsuma and Kuwana. Kijima had died there, shot from his horse in a hail of gunfire. Kunishi was in flight.

Fukuhara Echigo left from Fushimi and fought his way up the Fushimi highway, getting as far as the Tanba bridge. Here he was wounded and had to retreat. Masuda, who had been at Otokoyama, had never even left the shrine. He had spent so long praying to Hachiman for help, the fighting was over before he could set out.

All three elders took what remained of their forces back to Chōshū, defeated and disgraced. By the end of the year they would pay for their blunder with their lives.

Maki however refused to flee homewards. Two days later he and his sixteen men took to the mountain, Tennōzan. Before long they were surrounded by Aizu and Kuwana troops. They had little ammunition left and many were wounded. All seventeen committed suicide rather than surrender.

I did not hear of this until later, for the day Maki left the temple I came to the decision I had to return to Kyōto. My purpose was simple: I was going to look for Shinsai. I did not believe he was dead, despite my vision of him before my marriage, despite the deaths of so many. Refugees had already started to flock to the temple, the priests working frantically to provide them with food and shelter. No one noticed me slip away with my medicine chest on my back.

The road was crowded, some people fleeing with all the possessions they had rescued from the flames, some equally burdened but heading back home again, for the fires had now been extinguished. The devastation they had caused was terrible. Whole swathes of the city had been reduced to ashes, tens of thousands of houses, as well as nobles' palaces, domain mansions and temples, including Tenryūji where Kunishi and Kijima had had their base, all destroyed. From the Imperial Palace in the north to Shichijō Avenue in the south, from the Kamogawa in the east to the Horigawa in the west, virtually the whole of the city centre had gone.

I went first along the Takasegawa, picking my way carefully through the still warm ashes to the Chōshū mansion, thinking perhaps Shinsai was hiding out there, but that too was burned to the ground. I learned later that Nomi Orie had set fire to it himself before seeking shelter in a Buddhist temple. Soldiers stood around it, keeping souvenir hunters and other looters away.

I was gazing at the ruin in shock when I realised I had come to the notice of one of the guards. He was staring at me as if he knew me. I suspected he might be the Shinsengumi man I had given the sample medicine to, though I couldn't be sure. I felt a sudden sense of terror. I wished I had not accosted him so boldly in the street. I should never have drawn attention to myself. For the first time it occurred to me that I might be in danger. I was thinking very slowly that day – I knew objectively it was one of the effects of shock but knowing it did not help speed up my brain – and it took me a few minutes to come to the unthinkable reality: that Shinsai might have been captured alive and tortured.

My mind shied away from the horror and looked instead at practicalities. It was time for me to become a woman again. I would go back to Mrs Minami's, get rid of my male attire and go naked over the wall to the bathhouse where my woman's clothes and my old self were waiting for me.

Not daring to look back I walked slowly away from the ruined mansion towards the Sanjō bridge. It was late afternoon, thunderclouds were gathering on the horizon and it was very humid. I could feel the sweat trickling down my chest and round my belly, yet even the heat made me shiver. Once I had crossed the bridge I walked more swiftly, ducking through the alleys as Shinsai had taught me and approaching our old lodgings from the east, the opposite direction from the Chōshū mansion.

The street was empty, the soba house closed. But the door at the side of Mrs Minami's shop was not locked or bolted. It slid open as it had always done, sticking slightly and creaking. I went in as quietly as I could, hoping our landlady had not given up all hope of our return and let the room to someone else. It was empty apart from a few things Shinsai had left behind: his books, an old kimono hanging on the rack like a ghost. I pressed the cloth to my face and breathed in his smell. I was shivering more than ever and my eyes hurt. But I had no time to lose. I undid my sash and took off my male clothes, my doctor's jacket, the kimono Eikaku had given me, the long cloth that bound my breasts and my loincloth. I folded the cloths and put them in the cupboard with the futon; the jacket and robe I threw over the rack. At least our clothes were together.

I went to the side door, slid it open and came face to face with Mrs Minami.

She screamed as if she had seen an apparition, and I must have looked like one: a naked woman sporting a man's hairstyle.

'Don't make a noise,' I whispered. 'Don't be afraid. It's me, Imaike. I'm sorry, I was disguised. I am really a woman.'

'So I see,' she said, regaining her composure. She pushed me back into the room and closed the door. 'But where were you planning to go like that?'

'Through the bathhouse. They keep clothes for me. I've got to dress as a woman again, then I can leave the city.'

'The bathhouse is closed. They've gone away. Everyone closed up because of the *dondon* fire.'

'*Dondon?*'

'That's the noise it made. Guns going off all day *dondon-don*. And it spread so fast *dondondon*. We were lucky it didn't jump the river.'

'I can't go back in the streets as a man. I think someone was following me. Has anyone come here?'

'Not yet. But where is Itasaki-san?'

'I don't know.' I didn't want to talk about Shinsai. 'He went with the Chōshū soldiers, with Kusaka Genzui.'

'They say Genzui killed himself.'

'So I heard.'

'Do you think poor Itasaki is dead too?'

'I don't know. I suppose he is.' I hoped he was now; it would be far better than being captured. 'Otherwise he would have come to find me.'

Mrs Minami seemed on the point of asking more personal questions but then she sighed. 'What a terrible business. Guns going off in the Imperial Palace, domain soldiers fighting each other, all those young men dead, half the city burned.'

She noticed I was shivering. 'I'll get some clothes for you. Wait here.'

She came back in a few moments with women's clothes and helped me put them on, underwear and a light summer kimono patterned with peonies. She tied the broad obi around my waist and I felt a huge weight descend on me as I was restored to female appearance. She looked at me critically. 'What about your teeth? And the hair looks all wrong. I don't know what we are going to do about that.'

'Better cut it all off,' I said.

'Yes, that's the only solution, I'm afraid.'

She went to find scissors and came back looking anxious. 'There are guards in the street.'

She made me kneel down on a cloth and chopped my hair from my head. Then she threw a scarf over my cropped hair, bundled up the cloth, swept the clothes from the rack and pulled me into the shop.

'Go and sort some goods. I'll put these in with the stock.'

The guards called out at the door and Mrs Minami told them to step up. One of them came in and gave a cursory look round the shop. He saw an old woman doing the accounts at her desk and a younger one unpacking ceramic cups from a box.

'Just checking,' he said.

'Are the fires still burning?' Mrs Minami went to the door and looked towards the west.

'No, all out now, the rebels all defeated. Gone scurrying back to Chōshū, the cowards.'

Mrs Minami waited in the doorway under the eaves until the patrol had gone. I had unpacked and packed the same cups about six times.

'Where will you go?' she said.

'I suppose I'll go home, back to Chōshū.'

'It's best,' she agreed. 'It's not safe here.' She told me Kiemon was dead – summarily executed along with over thirty other prisoners when the jail was threatened by the flames.

I was restless to get going – I did not want to bring her into any more danger, and the place had too many memories for me. Also an idea had just struck me, that Shinsai would be waiting for me under the Nijō bridge where we had met on the night of the Ikedaya attack. I did not even have anything to eat or drink, though I had taken nothing all day. Mrs Minami gave me some new straw sandals, some rice cakes and a few coins, saying they would pay for the clothes and books, and I reluctantly left my medicine box with her, though I took out the scalpel and wrapped it up inside my satchel.

She promised not to sell it but to keep it until I came back for it. I thanked her for everything and went out into the street.

It was early evening with an eerie metallic light. The sky was covered with thick clouds and lightning flashed in the distance. The air smelled of rain and ashes. Plumes of smoke still rose from smouldering buildings. There were people everywhere on this side of the river, camped out on verandas, under eaves, huddled together with their belongings, bedding, children, pet birds and insects in cages, even goldfish and carp in glass bowls. Every now and then men hurried past carrying bodies wrapped in straw mats or pushing carts laden with corpses. Dogs followed them with raised noses. I could barely prevent myself from ripping off the mats to search for Shinsai's features, and I thought how Eikaku would have loved this scene straight from hell.

All along the bank of the Kamo River refugees sat and gazed at the destroyed city. Those who could squeeze in found some shelter under the bridges at Shijō and Sanjō. People were shouting out names as they searched for the missing, and I found myself shouting too as I pushed through the throng.

'Shinsai! Shinsai!'

But the only response was the alarmed cries of waterbirds disturbed from their roost and the thunder rolling in the hills.

When I came to the Nijō bridge it was equally crowded. My legs were giving way and my head was swimming. I felt as if I had been walking for months. It was growing dark and I knew I could go no further that night. I found a space under the bridge, high up near its endposts where you had to bend double below the planks. I settled down here, my back against one of the pillars.

My companions in this open-air riverside inn were the usual beggars and vagrants as well as many others made homeless by the fire. I slept, or rather dozed, sitting up, the scalpel hidden in my hand, starting awake every time someone new arrived, peering at them in the dim light, hoping against hope that Shinsai would suddenly appear out of the darkness.

Just a little way from me, further down the bank, sat a man who looked familiar. He was dressed in rags and had a cloth wound around his head, but I kept thinking I knew him from his outline and his attitude. I figured he must be a fugitive of some sort – despite his clothes I was sure he was not a beggar. In the early morning a young woman in the elegant attire of the pleasure quarters came to distribute food. She made sure he got plenty to eat though she gave no sign of recognising him. I guessed they knew each other well, probably intimately.

Now I could see more clearly I noticed his feet. They were long and slender, white skinned beneath the dirt, hardly the feet of a beggar. He felt my gaze and turned towards me. It was Katsura Kogorō.

His eyes narrowed; he was trying to place me. He moved a little closer to me and held out the last rice cake.

'Here, you look hungry. Take it.' He spoke in a rough dialect. I couldn't help being impressed. Apart from his white feet his disguise was flawless.

'Thank you,' I said, 'I'm not hungry. Anyway, I have some food with me.'

'We've met, haven't we?' he said, putting the rice cake into his mouth and chewing.

I didn't reply directly but said, 'I'm looking for my uncle, Itasaki Shinsai.'

'He was with Genzui, wasn't he? He must be dead.' He swallowed and added, 'Like so many. They should have listened to me. They have signed the death warrant for our domain.' There were fewer people around now and he had reverted to his own way of talking.

'Does anyone know the names of the dead yet?' I asked.

'It's all too confused still. But what are you doing in Kyōto? Your family live in Yuda, don't they? And isn't your husband with the Kiheitai?'

'You know everything about me,' I said. *Except that I met you as a man and you did not know me then.*

'I've been meaning to come and visit your father.'

'It's too great an honour,' I murmured automatically, appalled by how quickly I had become a subservient woman again.

'Sufu Masanosuke told me about your father's painting,' Katsura said.

I had no idea what he was talking about. Then it came back to me: my wedding day, Lord Sufu sitting in the place of honour and saying something about the unknown shadow hanging over my marriage. How right he had been! I remembered my wedding night and Shinsai's outrageous behaviour and my heart cracked with love and pity for him, making me want to howl.

'By Chikuden,' Katsura said, oblivious to my grief.

'*Fragrant Plum Blossoms, Unknown Shadow*,' I said after a moment.

'That's the one. I'd like to see it. I admire Chikuden greatly. In fact I own several of his paintings. Maybe your father would sell it to me. You might ask him when you are back in Chōshū.'

The conversation seemed so unlikely I wondered if I was dreaming. The only charitable explanation was that he was in shock himself and could only dwell on trivialities.

'Are you going back now?' he went on when I made no response.

'I suppose so. But first I must find out what happened to my uncle.'

'I am sure he died with great courage,' Katsura said. 'He has always been extremely helpful to us and will be remembered for his loyalty. Let me know when you hold the memorial service and I will make a point of attending if I am in the domain. When you get home, apart from the painting I have another favour to ask of your father.'

'Of course, anything,' I replied though actually I wanted to kill him. What was he doing hiding out, being fed by a geisha, talking about paintings and courage and loyalty while men of his domain had sacrificed their lives? How had he escaped? Why had he not joined in the fighting? Maybe they had all been wrong-headed, but at least they were not cowards.

Runaway Kogorō, I said inwardly, foreseeing the nickname that would haunt him.

He said, 'I will have to go into hiding for some time. Please ask your father to take special care of Lord Sufu.'

'I hardly need ask him. He admires Lord Sufu enormously.'

'Someone is going to have to take responsibility for this disaster. It should not be Sufu – he advised against it constantly. Your father should make sure he is watched at all times lest he try to take his own life.'

I wondered if Katsura would feel the same obligation but it seemed unlikely. I did not want to be near him any more and I badly needed to relieve myself. I put my satchel on my back, bade him a brief goodbye and went to find one of the buckets set out for public use. It was a relief to be able to urinate freely, but as I set off along the riverbank with little womanly steps I missed the stride I had had as a man.

TOKUGAWA YOSHINOBU (HITOTSUBASHI KEIKI) (1837–1913)

Genji 1 (1864), Seventh Month, Age 27

Hitotsubashi Keiki has draped himself over the sleeping woman next to him as if hoping to be absorbed by her. He has never been able to sleep alone but tonight one woman hardly feels enough. He wants to be surrounded by women, entangled in their hair, buttressed by their breasts and thighs. His whole body aches, his ears are still ringing from the clamour of battle and his throat is raw from smoke. Even his earlier orgasms were more painful than pleasurable, like tears stinging dried-out and inflamed eyes.

Ash and smoke pervade the whole city and a dull sound rises from it as if it is groaning. He has been moved from his own palace to temporary accommodation on the western side of the Horigawa. Further west around Arashiyama buildings are still smouldering, including one of the Chōshū camps, Tenryūji; on the eastern side the fires are more or less under control. But so much of the city has burned. At least one of the conflagrations was started on his orders when he saw the Chōshū soldiers had been allowed to set up a base in the Takatsukasa mansion right alongside the Hamaguri Gate. He recognised the potential strength of the alliance between Chōshū and the Court. His anger and irritation had come boiling to the surface. Let those thoughtless princes be called to account for keeping such company! Let their palaces burn!

The rebels are nearly all dead now and those left alive will pay with their heads. His forces, the domains of Aizu and Satsuma and all those loyal to the Tokugawa have won the day and the Chōshū soldiers are in flight. But now it is all over he is riven with shock at the audacity of the attack. Chōshū's various motives – to restore the good name of Lord Mōri, to regain the influence they had enjoyed at Court – are just a smokescreen for their one true aim: to overthrow the Bakufu. This attempt has failed but he can't help being impressed by the courage of the Chōshū soldiers, their discipline and their weapons. The fact that they dared bring an armed force into Kyōto, into its very heart, up to the gate of the Imperial Palace, fills him with alarm. He knows the attack was half-hearted, that Chōshū only deployed a small part of its military power and that he and the government have had a lucky escape. Others may be celebrating victories – the Shinsengumi's raid on the Ikedaya, the rout of Chōshū at the Forbidden Gate – but he sees these as minor skirmishes in what is going to be a protracted war, a war over the future of Japan, one that he would very much like to win.

He has been reading lately about the French Revolution and the years of terror that followed it. He has no doubt that if Chōshū were to win a decisive victory a great many heads would be separated from their bodies – the sword is as effective as the guillotine – and his would be one of the first.

Chōshū must be punished and he must act quickly while the domain's support among the people and among other domains has been weakened by this brazen attack and the destruction of the city. Chōshū has always been popular for its devotion to the Emperor and its hostility to foreigners. Chōshū men spend money freely, endearing themselves to the townspeople of Edo and Kyōto. The violent attacks of the last few years have not diminished this support, possibly because Katamori's police force, the Shinsengumi, have been so much more violent as well as extortionist and the hostility of the city's inhabitants has rebounded onto them. There is no doubt the Shinsengumi are a brave bunch and completely loyal to the Tokugawa, yet the rumours he hears about them give him nightmares. On the other hand, any one of the Chōshū men he half admires is likely to attempt to assassinate him, another nightmare in itself.

He dislikes both the Chōshū lords, old Takachika with his actor's face and his slow wits, and the slippery Sadahiro who fancies himself a general but hasn't the guts to fight. He finds their claim to some special relationship with the Emperor ridiculous and it offends him that the Chōshū residence in Kyōto is considered beyond the rule of the Bakufu. What is the good of having a police force while Chōshū provides a haven for rebels and outlaws? At least that will no longer be a problem as the mansion has burned to the ground.

The woman beneath him murmurs and shifts in her sleep. He tightens his hold on her, desiring to catch her slumber. He moves her so he can slide his hardening member into her, feeling the comfort of her buttocks against his thighs. He does not want another climax, he is too tired. He just wants to feel safe. She sighs and pushes back against him, arching her back so he can penetrate further, then, knowing him and his needs, lies still, matching her breath to his.

For a moment he is on the brink of sleep. His thoughts come randomly, disconnected images flow one after the other, but just as relief begins to soften his muscles, another scene jerks him awake with its stark clarity – the execution of three hundred men from his birth domain of Mito, after the Tengutō insurrection.

They were on their way to Kyōto to plead their cause with him and before the Emperor. Like Chōshū their outward parade of loyalty had won them considerable sympathy. He knew the man who had become their leader, Takeda Ko'unsai – he had been a favourite of Keiki's father, Nariaki. If he himself had not been adopted by the Hitotsubashi family, part of his father's long-term scheme to see him made Shōgun, he might have stayed in Mito, even through the joint twists of death and fate might have become *daimyō*, would certainly have done a better job than his useless half-brother.

The mistakes made in his homeland sicken him. How much blame can be laid on his father's domineering and, Keiki has to admit, erratic character? Nariaki's drastic reforms and political ambitions split the domain into bitterly hostile factions and made enemies throughout the Bakufu and the various branches of the Tokugawa family. His father's ambitions nearly brought an end to Keiki's own life during the Ansei purge, and put him under house arrest until Mito men took revenge on Ii Naosuke, murdering him outside the Sakurada Gate of Edo castle.

It was a snowy day, he reflects, longing for snow now for

its coldness and purity, feeling sweat sticky in his armpits and groin, making the woman's skin slick. It is the seventh month, the capital's usual stifling heat made worse by the fires and the smoky air. The Tengutō began their celebrated trek to the capital through the snow-covered ranges of the Kiso valley. How pitiful their end has been! He would have spared them if he could, but he is not ready to confront the Mito government; he already has more than he can handle in Kyōto. There is something about dramatic events that is made more poignant by snow, like a scene in a kabuki play, snow falling from above, against red lanterns…he is drifting into sleep again.

But a niggling voice keeps him awake: *might have been* daimyō, *might have been Shōgun.* Is his whole life to be wasted waiting in the wings? He is twenty-seven years old and feels he is in his prime. All his life he has been prepared for positions of influence and responsibility. Now as guardian to the young Shōgun, Iemochi, for whom he was passed over in the political struggle around the succession to Iesada, he has become one of the most powerful men in the Tokugawa government, and if Iemochi dies without children there really will be no other choice for Shōgun but him. He will become the fifteenth Shōgun; his only fear is it will be too late to save the government. He will be Shōgun, but will there still be a shōgunate?

He knows he is suited to the position in every way but one: he is not sure that he really wants it. He can't hide from himself the fact that he has been happiest in recent years while under house arrest. It was a relief not to have to deal with the great lords, impossibly self-important and sensitive, their minds a jumble of feudal precepts and their own self-serving, half-baked conjectures. As for the Court nobles, they are even more irritating, with their impractical idealism and their complete ignorance of the real world. The endless repetitive ceremonies and formalities, the impenetrable intrigues that were conducted at all levels…how can any man deal with all these slithery, tangled threads of a government that has built a maze around itself so complex it can no longer find the way out?

He thinks now of his ancestor, Ieyasu, and the other great unifiers of Japan, Oda Nobunaga and Toyotomi Hideyoshi, of the various bloody and determined acts by which they achieved their ends. He does not see such resoluteness in himself or in any of his contemporaries. Lord Ii, the Tairō, was perhaps the last man to act decisively and ruthlessly. Since his death no one has had the courage. Do any of them want power enough to grasp it relentlessly and pursue it to the end? None of them is prepared to make the sacrifices needed or to spill the necessary blood.

If troubles at home are not daunting enough there are also the dangers abroad. None of them really knows how to deal with the foreigners. The clamour to expel them has to be heeded, for those shouting loudest have shown themselves to be extremely dangerous when ignored. But the foreigners cannot be expelled without provoking them into war, and without their prior cooperation in matters of arms and technology such a war can only be lost. He feels he could negotiate with them if only he was given a free hand. He is modern in a way his contemporaries are not, capable of staying afloat in the turbulent waters of the new world. He knows he is popular with the British and the Americans and especially the French. It has been reported to him that they praise his appearance – he is handsome in their eyes – and his intelligence. They find him approachable among the devious and inscrutable officials they have to deal with. He suspects the French consul, Roches, is negotiating delicately towards some sort of offer of alliance. It appeals to him; he likes the French much more than the British – he considers Parkes an ill-mannered bully and Satow a double-dealing spy. And he has even been compared to Napoleon Bonaparte, the French Emperor, which he finds flattering.

Keiki has obtained books about Napoleon and has studied the engravings that illustrate them. His attendants tell him there is a distinct likeness between the young Frenchman and himself. He decides if he ever leads his army into battle he will have a uniform made like Bonaparte's, and while he is imagining the breeches and the jacket he finally falls asleep.

HOME

I came home to Yuda in the eighth month, just in time for another brief war. Not that I saw anything of it; it was a second assault by the Western powers on the batteries at Shimonoseki, partly in revenge for Chōshū's attacks the previous year on foreign ships, partly to open up the strait again for the merchants of Yokohama and Nagasaki who were complaining about their diminishing trade. It was known as the Four Nations War and ended in complete defeat for Chōshū, but I did not hear the details until almost the end of the month, when Inoue Monta called at our house.

My parents were shocked when I arrived in the evening, having walked that day from Mitajiri – shocked and relieved and then very angry. As I passed through the gate and under the gambling tree I was shaking with hope and dread that Shinsai might be there, but of course he was not. My parents knew that I had not gone to Ōsaka with my husband as I had told them, for Makino himself had come looking for me, embarrassed and ashamed at having to admit I had run away.

'But why?' my father kept asking. 'Was he cruel to you? Did he hit you?'

I could hardly remember why, and I found it impossible to explain. I was afraid that if I started to explain I would tell them everything. I was filled with guilt, and with a grief so fierce that I would have killed them with my own hands if it meant I could live with Shinsai again. I had treated so many mad people I recognised the symptoms. I knew I was losing my mind yet I was powerless to follow the good advice I had handed out to others. I looked back at my simplistic ideas with contempt. I had told my patients not to drink, but I drank all I could get my hands on and smoked until my throat was raw.

'What happened to your hair?' my mother asked, tears in her eyes. I had had my head shaved completely as soon as I had the opportunity and now I looked like a nun. Shaving the head was one of the lesser punishments for adultery and of course my parents could not help suspecting I had run away with a man, but they were reluctant to probe too deeply and anyway I would never tell them who that man was.

The feeling of my bare scalp seemed to mean something and I would spend hours running my hands over my head trying to pin it down but I could never quite capture it. It began to haunt me. I slept fitfully and could not eat. After his anger subsided my father saw I was in danger of a complete breakdown and tried to interest me in medicine once more, discussing his patients with me, asking me to help make up remedies and telling me the latest news from the medical community in Nagasaki. But my passion for medicine seemed to have been left behind with my male clothes in Kyōto. Nothing interested me any more. I was in the grip of a fugue so powerful I can understand when I look back why people call such states 'fox possession'.

Possibly my father met Monta somewhere and asked him

to come and cheer me up. Anyway, he called at the house one afternoon when the Four Nations War was over (the fighting only lasted half a day). He had been involved in negotiations with the English, both beforehand to try to prevent combat, and afterwards.

'Itō and I read about the likelihood of the attack in *The Times*,' he said. 'Can you imagine, Chōshū in the London *Times*?'

I had no idea what he was talking about since at that time I had never seen a foreign newspaper, only the illicit placards that carried news and opinions and the sort of pictures Eikaku painted. On the surface Monta had not changed; he still seemed the young lord, brash, self-confident, irrepressible and reckless, but as he spoke I felt he had grown more serious. He had been all the way to England and back, he had seen the world. He wore ordinary clothes now and his two swords, but his hair was cut short like a child's.

'We knew Chōshū didn't stand a chance against the Western alliance so we came rushing home to try to prevent it.' His eyes sparkled as he spoke. 'The English actually sent a flagship to bring us from Yokohama – they're really very decent. When we landed we were in greater danger of being killed by the local people. They had no idea who we were with our short hair; they couldn't believe we were speaking Japanese! Then I couldn't get back to the English in time – I got delayed by the *shotai*, who wanted to attack immediately. They were ready to attack me by the end. So the foreigners grew tired of waiting and opened fire. They had seventeen ships – American, Dutch, British and French – and twice as many soldiers as us. Next morning they came ashore, destroyed or carried off the rest of the guns, burned a few houses and waited for our side to capitulate.'

'Were there many dead?' my father asked.

'About twenty of ours. I believe about eight or ten of theirs. Your son-in-law was there, Dr Makino. He's been taking care of the wounded.'

Monta glanced at me but I did not know what response to make. Of course I knew Makino was my husband, but he meant nothing to me. It had not occurred to me to wonder if he was involved in the fighting, if he was alive or dead.

'The funny thing is,' Monta went on, 'now it's over we're all the best of friends. Itō and I know one of the British diplomats; he speaks quite good Japanese.' He laughed. 'Itō made a dinner for him in Shimonoseki, English style, with a table and chairs, and knives, and an extremely tough boiled chicken. His name is Satow.'

'He has a Japanese name?' my mother said in surprise.

'Strange, isn't it? It sounds the same but it's not. Anyway, he likes our people of Chōshū. He says we're good fighters and he respects us. I suggested he should help us in our struggle against the Bakufu.' He lowered his voice. 'We need to buy better guns and the English will sell them to us.'

'What about the peace agreement?' Father said. 'Did Chōshū have to make huge concessions?'

'No, thanks to Takasugi. The best thing about the whole affair was the domain government had to let him out of prison to lead the mission. You know he was in Noyama for having left without permission earlier this year? The English are very fussy about who they deal with – it has to be someone of very high rank. Actually they demanded Lord Mōri Takachika – of course that was quite impossible; we made the excuse he had sequestered himself because he had offended the Emperor. Takasugi was magnificent. He couldn't have been more lordly. He took the name of Shishido Gyōma – Lord Shishido adopted him temporarily – and was dressed in the most sumptuous clothes. He managed to get out of conceding any territory to the English. He's been to Shanghai and he was determined no part of Chōshū should become a concession port. He declared we were only acting on Imperial and Bakufu orders and we had documents to prove it. The English wanted a huge sum of money as an indemnity but now they are going to have to seek it from Edo! We just agreed to dismantle the guns and treat foreigners well and so on.'

He was grinning with satisfaction. My father poured some more sake and after drinking it Monta made an effort to look more sombre.

'Is there any news of Shinsai-san?'

'None,' my father said. 'We know only that he was in Kyōto with Maki Izumi and Kusaka Genzui. Since they are both dead and we have had no word, we must assume the worst.'

I wanted to say of course Shinsai was not dead, he was in hiding, like Katsura, he was in Ezo…but when I thought of speaking I began to shake. Everyone was looking at me, Monta with uncharacteristic compassion.

'I hope O-Tsuru-san recovers her health soon,' he said to my father.

'Let's talk about more cheerful matters,' Mother said, a

desperate note in her voice. 'Tell us about your adventures in England.'

Monta told us about the houses with their many storeys and stairs and banisters, set in squares around beautiful gardens, the cobbled streets which made sandals totally impractical, the horses and carriages, the railways and steam engines.

'So many people wear black,' he said. 'They look like flocks of crows in the streets. And they wear black top hats and carry black umbrellas. Their country is ruled by a queen, you know? Queen Victoria.'

'Do women take part in the government?' Father asked.

'No, but they have a great deal of influence. Men listen to their opinions and seem to take them seriously.' Monta frowned and said ruefully, 'It's always difficult relating to their women. You never know if you are being over-polite or over-familiar.'

Father asked several questions about hospitals and the state of medicine in England. Monta told him about the development of nursing, under the influence of a woman called Florence Nightingale, who had learned from her experiences in the Crimean War and was reforming hospitals. Then he described the various ailments he and Itō had suffered, mainly coughs and colds, and the treatments they had received: poultices, balsam fumes, opiate mixtures, laudanum.

'We ended up eating lots of roast beef,' he said. 'It is meant to be good for the health. There is another side to London, though. Many people are desperately poor – they live in slums far worse even than in Edo. They have the same diseases we have here, possibly worse: cholera, typhoid, diphtheria, and more than their share of evil people and wrongdoers.'

'They say Edo is more lawless than ever,' Mother remarked.

'Ever since alternate attendance ended the city has emptied,' Monta replied. 'Merchants have no business, and people are starving. There are gangs of outlaws terrorising entire districts. The price of rice has soared. Storehouses are being attacked and broken open. If we don't have a change of government soon our country is doomed.'

However, the likelihood of Chōshū effecting any real change seemed more remote than ever. The foreign ships returned to Yokohama, leaving the domain government to deal with that defeat and the aftermath of the disaster in Kyōto. The Bakufu acted swiftly to punish Chōshū and restore its credibility as the dominant military power in the land. Raising soldiers from over thirty domains, it assembled a huge army of over fifty thousand men and brought them to Chōshū's eastern border.

Rumours flew wildly as to what Chōshū's punishment would be: Lord Mōri and his son were to be executed, Chōshū was to lose half its territory, Shimonoseki would be ceded to the Bakufu... The conservative party counselled total submission; the *shotai*, who had so far managed to avoid being dispersed, naturally wanted to fight it out. Sufu Masanosuke, who had guided the domain policy for six turbulent years, walking the narrow line between reform and extremism, now had to try to save the house of Mōri from complete disgrace.

One evening in the middle of the ninth month O-Kiyo, my father's geisha, brought Lord Sufu to our house.

'He is very depressed,' she whispered to my mother and

me as we prepared sake and a few side dishes. 'Maybe the doctor can help him.'

I recalled what Katsura had said to me under the Nijō bridge. 'I suppose he is going to kill himself,' I said.

My mother looked shocked at the dispassionate tone of my voice. 'Tsu-chan,' she began.

'Heaven forbid,' O-Kiyo said. 'He must be prevented.'

'Tsuru has been a little down herself,' my mother confided.

'She should go back to her husband. Women are not made to live alone.'

This advice from O-Kiyo made me angry. I poured myself a bowl of sake and drank it in one gulp, then picked up the tray and hurried to the main room, where Father and Lord Sufu were sitting, Sufu in front of the alcove where the Chikuden painting had hung. It had been replaced now with one suitable for the season. It had been a brilliant day, just after the full moon of the ninth month. A few chrysanthemums stood in front of the picture, filling the room with their scent of autumn. The doors were all open to catch the beauty of the waning moon and the stars, but the air was cold and a brazier burned between the two men.

I knelt on the floor and set the tray down. My father poured sake while I studied Lord Sufu. He had lost a lot of weight and his face was haggard. I remembered how I had seen the blood running from his throat – now it was clear that death had its hand on him. He had been under house arrest when the troops set out for Kyōto and had opposed the attack from the start. As Katsura said, he could not really be held responsible. Yet it was his government that had been in favour – the elders who led the expedition were close friends, colleagues or members of his society, the Aumeisha. Those who had died in Kyōto were associates like Kijima or protégés, like Genzui.

'I've been in Iwakuni,' Sufu said to my father. After thanking me briefly he took no further notice of me. He did not seem aware of my scrutiny. I could see he had already drunk a great deal; he was at the point where the urge to unburden oneself becomes overpowering. 'Lord Kikkawa is going to intercede for us.'

My father nodded. 'That must be a relief to you.'

Kikkawa Tsunemoto, head of the branch domain of Iwakuni, was conservative and old-fashioned and had kept aloof from the reformist and loyalist activities of Sufu's Justice Party. In this he was the opposite of the branch domain of Chōfu, whose lord, Mōri Sakyunosuke, continued to support the reformist movement even after the fall of the Sufu government, giving the loyalist *shotai* a haven in Chōfu and Shimonoseki.

'Masuda, Kunishi and Fukuhara will have to be sacrificed,' Sufu went on. 'Lord Kikkawa has been in Yamaguchi and will go to the Bakufu representatives next month to offer them the elders' heads.' He drank deeply. 'I tried to spare Kunishi – he is so young – but Kikkawa argued it was not possible. Yamaguchi castle is to be razed and the remaining nobles who fled from Kyōto are to leave the domain and go to Fukuoka. These are the terms Kikkawa will offer to Tokugawa Keishō, who is in command of the Bakufu army. Saigō Takamori from Satsuma is assisting him.'

'Satsuma will have no mercy on Chōshū,' my father said.

'Saigō will demand the execution of the commanders who

survived,' Sufu said. 'Shishido Kurōbei, Sakuma Sahei, Takeuchi Masabei, Nakamura Kyūryō.' His voice broke and tears formed in his eyes. 'I would gladly die in their stead – well, I will die soon anyway – but my death alone will not satisfy Edo or Satsuma.'

'You must not add your death to so many,' my father said. 'What good would it do? And the domain needs you more than ever now.'

'I can achieve no more,' Sufu said. He sighed and drank again. 'My rank is too low.'

'It's a lot higher than mine.' Father was getting drunk too.

Sufu leaned forward and said confidentially, 'I've risen as high as I could hope, but there are always many above me who outrank me, who hold their posts through hereditary privilege. I've struggled for years with their incompetence and dullness. Now, my good friend, I am finished. I just have to end it all with honour.'

SUFU MASANOSUKE (1823–1864)

Genji 1 (1864), Autumn, Age 41

Sufu Masanosuke has known for some time that he is going to kill himself but certain arrangements have had to be made first. It has been a frantic few months since the disaster in Kyōto, and as usual he has had to see to everything himself while all around him express their horror, make excuses, blame each other and rake endlessly over the events of the last year to explain why everything went so horribly wrong and to come to terms with the disgrace not only of defeat but of being judged enemies of the Emperor.

He still can't believe so stupid an attack actually happened. Sometimes it seems like a bad dream from which he will soon awaken, but at this moment in the still autumn night he is all too awake; his head is pounding, his throat dry, his heart flapping like a fish inside his chest. Someone is going to have to accept responsibility, and even though his wife keeps trying to persuade him he is blameless as he was under house arrest at the time, he is not going to shirk his duty.

He will not be alone. The three elders who led the expedition will be allowed to commit suicide while their captains will be executed. He thinks he has limited the number to seven, but the conservative faction who have taken over the domain government are in their usual self-righteous and vindictive mood and will seize the opportunity to eradicate as many reformers as they can. Luckily Shinsaku cannot be held accountable since he was already in prison, and Inoue and Itō were not yet back from England. Katsura has disappeared: Sufu is not worried about him, knowing his talent for keeping out of trouble. He is probably hiding out somewhere and will return when everything has settled down.

He hopes he can save as many of the *sonjuku* group – he likes to think of them as Shōin's lads – as possible. They are going to be the future. Once again he thinks of those who died in Kyōto: old Kijima, loyal and belligerent, Maki Izumi, and worst of all the brilliant and gifted Kusaka Genzui. How can he live in this world without Genzui? He feels he has failed him; he should never have let things get so out of control. This is what his enemies criticised him for, that he was playing with fire, trying to ride the tiger. He liked the company of the young *shishi*. He was flattered by their respect and affection. He could not resist drinking with them, accompanying them to the geisha houses, writing poetry and singing. He encouraged their ambitions; he helped them travel, sent them to Kyōto, Edo and beyond. Nothing wrong with that, except he had not known where to stop. If only he could turn back time.

He is lying in the guest room of Yoshitomi Tōbei's house outside Yamaguchi. His wife is next to him; he knows she is not asleep. She is afraid that if she closes her eyes he will kill himself before she opens them again. Yoshitomi is the same – they all watch him day and night. It's proving to be much harder to kill himself than he thought it would be.

Whatever happened to the samurai code of honour? His family and friends should be making it easy for him instead of holding him back, clinging to him, weeping and carrying on. It's shameful! His wife even persuaded Yoshitomi to take away his swords and hide them. Not that that will stop him. He knows where the knives are kept in the kitchen; he has checked them out under the pretence of discussing sashimi with Yoshitomi's cook.

He is irritated and touched that his wife still cares for him after years of marriage, years of his bad behaviour. What an admirable woman she is. She has never questioned or reprimanded him, never acted coldly towards him even after the most excessive bouts of drinking, the most flagrant affairs with geisha and other women. He feels absurdly grateful to her and he hopes she will realise his death is absolutely necessary and that she will not mourn for him extravagantly or pine away without him.

Yet he still wishes another woman were lying here beside him, the last girl he fell in love with, in his usual foolish way. He would like to take her in his arms and lose himself in her one last time. Perhaps he has been a fool and a drunk as his enemies say. How does he reconcile the two sides of himself? Why does the impeccable bureaucrat, the highly competent administrator (he has never suffered from false modesty) turn into the uninhibited, inebriated pleasure seeker, and more mysteriously how does he turn back again, morning after morning, and resume the highest responsibilities of government?

Why did he drink so much? Has it caused him to make mistakes? He tries to tell himself his life has not been without merit. He has risen as high in position as his rank permitted; he has had the ear and the trust of his *daimyō*. He has had many intimate friends from all walks of life, he has loved a number of women and ridden some fine horses. He has been adored, admired and hated, has been occasionally a hero, and mostly a fool. And now he has had to arrange the suicide and execution, accept the deaths, of some of his closest associates and friends.

His main achievement in the last few weeks has been enlisting Lord Kikkawa's support. Sufu is aware the austere and conservative Iwakuni *daimyō* has never approved of him, but past feelings have been set aside in the face of the greater tragedy of the looming destruction of the House of Mōri. Sufu knows that the Chōshū heir, Sadahiro, is as culpable as anyone, yet it is unthinkable that he should pay for his ambitions. It must be made to appear that he was not involved, nor his father, Lord Mōri, that the attack was the work of a rebellious faction within the domain and the perpetrators are all being duly punished. Kikkawa grasped all this quickly, perhaps relieved that Hagi is back under conservative control, perhaps settling some old scores of his own. Sufu can't let himself think about this. It is shocking enough that the three elders must take their own lives, but it is a small price to pay to preserve the existence of Chōshū and its *daimyō*. He contemplates briefly the tangled feudal structure of the domain like the underground root system of a sweet potato. You can follow the spreading fibres, never knowing which one will produce a tuber. Lord Mōri is the visible part of the plant, showy and leafy and seemingly useless but in some way indispensable, transferring the light of the sun to those beneath him. He, Sufu, is just one of many tubers. It does not matter much if it is time for him to be harvested. But if Sadahiro were a sweet potato he would offer little nourishment. He has never ripened properly but remains green and attenuated. Sadahiro is a little too impressed by his position as the Chōshū heir. He soaks up the admiration and flattery, is addicted to the deference and attention.

But Sadahiro is no longer his concern. There is no more to be done. His political life is over and if he does not kill himself his enemies will surely execute him. Besides he does not want to live when so many of his friends are gone. He has never lacked courage but he cannot face the grief and shame that lie ahead. His heart makes another plunge, then starts racing. He badly needs a drink to settle it.

As soon as he sits up his wife speaks. 'What is it? Do you want something?'

'I'm just going to get some sake.'

She doesn't make a fuss or remonstrate that it is not good for him, just gets up quickly saying, 'I will heat some for you.'

He opens his mouth to tell her not to bother but the idea of warmed sake is suddenly very appealing. A detached part of himself finds this curious since he is about to die. A man's will may come to a stern decision, but the body continues its humble existence to the very end, seeking pleasure, avoiding pain.

His wife returns with a lamp and sake on a tray. Setting them on the floor she kneels beside him and pours him a cup. The fumes rise into his face as he drinks. The liquid soothes his throat and now he can feel the warmth as it hits his stomach and seeps into his veins. What a comfort it is and how wonderful the first cup always tastes!

His wife refills the cup and he gestures to her that she should drink too. She bows her head gratefully and sips a little. There is something very poignant about their companionship in the silent darkness. Sufu feels he could almost compose a poem if he had time and if he could control the tears that begin to well in his eyes. She is crying too, the wetness trickling down her cheeks.

The sadness is insupportable. Why does she not take herself away so he can kill himself? He wants to shout at her, order her to leave him, but his pity traps him. There is nothing to be done but refill his cup and empty it. However, after the initial burst of comforting warmth the sake is letting him down. It is not silencing his erratic thoughts but making them more insistent.

He hears voices outside and thinks at first he is hallucinating. It is the dead of night, surely hours till daybreak?

Yoshitomi is up; he hears footsteps, the door being unbarred, the voices louder.

Inoue Monta attacked, gravely injured, dying…

His wife cries out and Sufu feels the shock tear his chest apart. Monta, whom he had believed to be safe? Monta, dying? And all the young dead seem to gather before him. Under their gaze he weeps with guilt, regret and shame. He must not outlive another one of them.

'Go and find out what has happened,' he tells his wife, and she in her confusion takes her eyes off him and leaves him long enough for him to stumble to the dark kitchen and locate the knives by feel: here they are, waiting for him.

He takes one and runs, quickly, quickly for no one must stop him now, through the back door and into the garden.

He smells the autumn night, the vegetable leaves he tramples in his haste, the soil, muddy under his bare feet. The moon has set and the stars blaze, but he cannot see them through his tears. The knife in his hand is like an old friend that will take away the unbearable pain of his life.

He hears them calling his name, the last thing he hears, apart from the sudden gurgle of his own blood.

TEARS

Just before the end of the month as we were getting ready for bed, someone came to the gate, banging on it and shouting for the doctor. Hachirō opened up and came running in to us, ashen-faced and gasping. 'He says the young lord has been attacked.'

The young lord? Monta?

My father seized his medicine box and his instruments. 'Tsuru, come with me. We may need you.'

The farmer who had brought the news was waiting at the gate, holding a lantern.

'Where is he?' my father demanded.

'We took him to his brother's house. I found him in my vegetable field. He was hidden under the pumpkins in a ditch. I heard samurai looking for him, shouting out, trampling the crops. They fairly slashed him to bits.'

'But he's still alive?'

'Alive enough to call out for water. I wrapped him in a mat and put him in a basket and carried him to the Inoue house.'

We hurried down the road and along the track through the fields. Lamps gleamed in the house and we could hear shouts and screaming. Great splashes of blood on the threshold showed where the wounded man had been carried inside.

They had laid him down on a futon and were trying to

staunch the blood. Monta was unrecognisable, his whole face opened by the sword cut, the white bone gleaming in the redness. He was calling out to his older brother to kill him and put an end to the pain. His brother actually had his sword in his hand and looked ready to put it against Monta's throat, but their mother was trying to prevent him, crying out that he would have to kill her first.

The night that Nakajima had been brought home similarly wounded rose in my mind. The memory of his horrible death made me begin to shake. My father was trying to inspect the wounds without causing more pain. He said quietly, 'Tsuru, I don't think any organs have been pierced. If we can stop the bleeding and sew him up there's a good chance he'll pull through.'

'Kill me now,' Monta screamed. 'Show some mercy!'

'Get sake and hot water,' Father said to one of the maids, and he began to open up his case of instruments. 'Tsuru, thread the needle for me. Maybe you can even do some of the stitches. Your hands are more deft than mine.'

I took the needle and thread and went over to the lamp but my hands were shaking uncontrollably.

'Hurry up!' my father said.

I dropped the needle. It fell off the edge of the matted area and through a crack in the floorboards. I could see it gleaming but there was no way I could reach it.

My father turned, saw what had happened and swore. I had never heard him swear before.

'Maybe I have another,' he said faintly and began to rummage among his instruments. At that moment someone else came into the room.

I knew him by sight: his name was Tokoro Ikutarō. He had recently opened a practice in Yoshiki village, not far away. He was in his late twenties and had the reputation of being skilled in Western medicine. Even though he was much younger than my father he did not hesitate to take control. Touching Monta gently and murmuring, 'Be brave, be brave,' he took out a scalpel and began to cut away the clothes. When he opened the under-kimono a mirror fell out, its glass face cracked. It was the one the Kyōto geisha, Kimio, had given to Monta.

'Lucky, this might have saved your life,' Tokoro murmured, for the mirror had taken the full force of a sword blow to the heart.

The maid came back with boiling water and sake. When Monta was naked Tokoro carefully washed the wounds, then said, 'I need a needle – anything will do – a tatami needle if you've got one – and thread.'

'I have thread,' my father said, producing it.

The maid came back with a matting needle. Tokoro dipped it in the hot water and threaded it unerringly. My father knelt next to him and cut each stitch as Tokoro tied it, while Monta's brother, having put his sword away, held the suffering man still.

There were six wounds that needed stitching, but despite the blood none had opened an artery nor gone deep enough to touch the vital organs. Tokoro worked swiftly and skilfully but it still took hours. There were over fifty stitches in all. Several times Monta seemed to lose consciousness from shock and pain but mostly he was awake, neither complaining nor moving, simply panting and sweating. I was amazed by his courage and tenacity.

When Tokoro had finished the last stitch he asked Monta's mother to bring clean cloths and lay them over her son's face and body. 'It seems to help relieve the pain,' he said. He bent forward and whispered to Monta, 'You were brave. You are going to live.'

His mother was wiping the tears from her eyes when she came back with the white cloths and covered her youngest son as though she was preparing his corpse for burial.

At that moment I began to cry too. I had rarely cried in my life but now I could not stop. I did not sob or cry out. I simply wept, the tears flowing from my eyes as if from a spring. I wept all that night, soaking my night robe and covers, and I wept even more the next morning when we heard the news of Lord Sufu's death.

My tears did not cease. I could have gathered them in bottles. They flowed throughout the tenth month while the Mundane Views Party took over government and Mukunashi Tōta returned to power. Leaders of the Justice Party were arrested. In the eleventh month the three elders committed suicide as ordered and their heads were delivered to Tokugawa and Saigō. Their four commanders were beheaded in Noyama.

The weather was bitterly cold, sleet and snow already falling. I cried sitting with my feet under the *kotatsu* while the cat purred on my knee and licked the salt tears that fell on her fur.

My parents were terrified I would try to take my own life and they did not let me out of their sight. There were days when I would have welcomed death to put an end to my grief, but I never really sought to kill myself. I knew at some level that I was passing through a phase, that one day it would be over and my life would go forward again. I had been wounded but not fatally.

Inoue Monta survived the assassination attack, though he had a long and painful recovery throughout that winter. Around the end of the eleventh month my husband went to see him with Itō Shunsuke; after the visit, leaving Itō with his old friend, Makino came to my parents' house.

I could hardly refuse to see him. The moment I set eyes on him my tears dried up. I did not know if it was because I did not want to weep in front of him, if I was still angry with him, or if he had in some way brought me consolation. He did not seem changed in any way. My parents tactfully left us alone together, but for many moments I could think of nothing to say and nor apparently could he.

Finally he said, 'Imaike Eikaku sends you his regards.'

Hearing my assumed surname made me jump. 'Is he well?' I replied, trying to sound calm.

'He had a bad period when he came back from Mitajiri, but he is recovered now and painting again. He would like to see you, I think. He's been worried about you.'

When I said nothing Makino went on, 'So have I.'

'I am sorry to have caused everyone so much anxiety,' I said.

Makino frowned and stared at the floor. He was clenching and unclenching his right hand nervously. 'O-Tsuru-san, I want you to come back to me.'

I could see how much it cost him to say this, but I replied ungenerously, 'You were the one who sent me away.'

'Maybe I was wrong to do that. I'm sorry.' He paused for a moment and then asked, 'Where did you go?'

'I can't tell you that. If you promise never to ask me that again, maybe…'

Makino raised his eyes to mine, as if making some complex calculation involving emotions, and plunged on. 'I want you to be with me. I've missed you. I realised how much I've learned from you. Come back; we can work together.'

'I'll never be a doctor,' I said. 'I'm a woman – and anyway my hands shake now.'

I held out my hand but it was as steady as it used to be. The shaking had disappeared with the tears. I quickly put my hands behind my back.

'I could do nothing for Lord Sufu. If I'd been a man of high rank I might have saved him. And Inoue Monta: I could not even thread a needle. I am so ashamed.'

Makino said gently, 'All of us have our failures. We do the wrong thing, our patients die, we don't do enough or we do too much. But we have successes too. Inoue is recovering. Tokoro certainly saved his life. You have helped Eikaku and, I've heard, Takasugi too.'

I shook my head, but a little crack opened up in the hardness around my heart.

'I've been thinking,' he went on. 'We might adopt a child. Maybe one of your sister's girls.'

'A girl?' Most adoptions were of boys to bring an heir into the family. Mitsue now had two girls, the second one born only a few weeks ago. I thought of Michi, whom I had saved at birth.

'I've learned so much since you've been away. Why shouldn't girls have the same opportunities as boys? I'd like to bring up a little girl in the way your father brought you up and educate her to take part in our new world.'

At that moment I recalled the night when Makino had played *shōgi* with my father and had dropped his captured pieces on the board, enumerating his qualities and why my father should take him on as a student, and possible son-in-law. Now he had dropped another winning piece into the game. *He has come to know me so well*, I reflected, *he knows my secret desires*. My heart opened a little more.

'I need time to think about it,' I said.

'I must return tomorrow. I hope one night will be long enough.'

There was a little awkwardness when we went to bed as it was not clear to anyone where Makino should sleep. He was still my husband and he had every right to share my bed. But I wanted to spend the night alone. I had been sleeping alongside my parents since I came home, giving my poor mother many sleepless nights, since she woke every time I did, and if I got up followed me around the house, but this night I went to the room where Makino and I had slept after our marriage and spread out my futon there. As I left Makino gave me one look and when I did not return it said he would go in Hachirō's room. Eventually we all settled down for the night. It was some relief to me not to be weeping any more and I fell almost immediately into a deeper sleep than I had had for weeks.

I dreamed about the day I had walked through Ōsaka with Shinsai. I had been beside him but he had gone ahead and disappeared. While I was looking for him I came to the

Tekijuku, Ogata Kōan's school, and in the logic of dreams I assumed he was inside. I walked into the building, remembering how I had not wanted to enter it before and glad to have the opportunity. The building seemed empty; of course, it was being closed down, but then I discovered someone in one of the rooms. I knew it was Dr Ogata, which surprised me as I had heard he was dead.

'I'm glad you've come,' he said. 'I wanted to talk to you. It's a shame you were never one of my students.'

'Now it is too late because you are no longer in this world,' I said, as gently as I could in case he did not know. 'And too late for me, anyway.'

'It is never too late,' he replied. 'You must carry on.' He looked at me and nodded, smiling, and I felt his deep compassion and his commitment to healing. A sudden wave of gratitude mixed with shame swept through me and I woke up abruptly. The room was freezing, full of shadows and draughts. I could hear the wind in the roof.

I had a visitation, I thought in surprise. I was excited and honoured that Dr Ogata should come to me. *It is never too late*, he had said. *You must carry on.* It seemed like a promise to me. I was barren, but I would have a child. I was a woman, but I would be able to practice healing. My ambition had been lofty, to be equal to men and practise alongside them, but I realised if that was not possible what mattered was the healing. If I could not work as a doctor I would be a nurse. I would be like the Englishwoman Florence Nightingale. I would do all I could to help my husband and further his career.

I did not want to forget the dream so I got quietly out

of bed and went to light a lamp in the kitchen and get a dripper of water. As I was carrying them back to the room I saw Makino's form appear in the doorway.

'I heard something,' he whispered. 'I just came to see if you were all right.'

'I had a dream,' I said. 'I wanted to write it down.' I set the lamp down and beckoned him in. He sat on the floor while I quickly wet the inkstone and wrote the words of the dream.

'I saw Ogata Kōan,' I said. 'In the dream.'

'Kōan? Did he speak to you?'

'Yes, yes. Everything's going to be all right.' I was shaking with excitement.

'You're shivering,' Makino said. 'You should get back into bed.'

'Stay with me,' I whispered.

'Do you want me to?'

'It's so cold.'

We slipped together under the quilt and I put my arms around his thin, familiar body. We did not make love, but we held each other, taking warmth from each other, until morning.

NOMURA BŌTŌNI (1806–1867)

Genji 1 (1864), Autumn, Age 58

In the early dawn Bōtōni hears the cries of the geese as they fly southwards, and when she jumps up and runs to the door to catch their fluttered wing beat, for it is one of her favourite sounds, she sees the valley below Hirao-san is filled with mist.

Autumn is here, she thinks with a tremor of mingled delight and pain. Soon cranes and shelducks will pass overhead on their way to their place of wintering. Somewhere inside her mind the *waka* begins to uncoil: wing beats and mist: herself a young girl in the moment of waking and leaping up, an old woman by the time she reaches the veranda.

As she blows up the embers to boil water to make tea the poem takes its form and hardens. Later she will write it down but first she will sit with her cup of tea and watch the sun as it comes over the mountain and strikes the opposite slope. The past seems very close to her this morning. Perhaps her husband visited her in a dream. She is filled with sorrow that the dream has vanished, leaving only the slightest intimation of his presence. She misses him most at this time of day when they used to drink tea together. It is five years since he died, joining their four daughters in the other world, leaving her alone with the birds, the trees and the poetry.

Suddenly she sees herself at seventeen, returning to her father's house after six miserable months of marriage when she was made ill by homesickness and loneliness. She recalls perfectly the all-enveloping relief she felt to be home among her books and her family, to be able to return to her studies and her writing.

What a child I was. She experiences again her gratitude to her father who allowed her to return home, arranged the divorce from her first husband and encouraged her to study *waka* with Ōkuma Kotomichi. *How many other girls were as lucky as I was? How many were able to meet and marry a man like Sadatsura, to sit at the feet of the same teacher, to enjoy so much together, the poetry, the love of nature and literature and the unspoken passion? Truly we shared one body and one soul.*

Sadatsura retired as head of his family and they lived for most of their married life in this isolated little cottage on Mount Hirao outside Fukuoka. After his death she shaved her head and became a nun, taking the name Bōtōni (her childhood name was Moto), but even as a nun she has more freedom than most women. She has no husband, no children and no elderly parents. All these losses have caused her to weep streams of tears but they have also set her free. She has plucked flowers from the surface of the water even when her reflection in it is dark.

The grief for her husband, her children, her troubled stepson who took his own life dissipates just as the mist changes in colour from the grey of a dove's wing to a luminous pearl-white, then suddenly the pine trees and cedars appear in the valley below her and the mist is gone. Thrushes are singing their lonely autumn song for their young who are fledged and flown. A weasel scampers across the garden leaving a trail of paw prints in the dew.

'Good morning!' she calls as its bright sinuous shape disappears between two rocks. 'Does this mean I will have a visitor today?' The thought sends a little flicker of excitement through her. Three years ago she travelled to Ōsaka and Kyōto with her teacher Ōkuma Kotomichi and saw for herself the unrest in the country and the turmoil in the capital. Like Chōshū across the water her domain of Fukuoka is in the grip of an internal power struggle between loyalist reformers and conservatives who support the Bakufu. In Kyōto she met up with an old acquaintance of her husband's, Hirano Kuniomi, who had become an ardent loyalist and she became convinced of the necessity of reform and the restoration of Imperial rule. Since then her mountain retreat has become a hiding place for Fukuoka *shishi* on the run from government officials. Poor Hirano died in the Ikuno uprising, over a year ago. He is another of the departed for whom she prays every day. It's for his sake and for all those who have already died in the struggle and for the Emperor and for the nation that will be reborn that she does her part. She prays, she fasts, and she offers a place of shelter. In this way she sees herself as a thread, a knot, in the great net of loyal hearts that is being woven across the country.

The weasel did not lie. Before midday she hears the sounds of footsteps on the the garden pebbles. She lays down the brush with a premonition that the early-morning poem will never be written. Going to the door she sees Nakamura Enta, a friend of Hirano's, a messenger between the Fukuoka *shishi* and those in Chōshū. With him is a young man she has never seen before. Nakamura introduces him as Tani Umenosuke and it seems like a sign, for the misty valley, *tani*, has occupied her mind all morning and *ume*, plum blossoms, are her favourite flower.

She does not ask any questions – the young man barely speaks; he looks exhausted. Nakamura tells her they fled from Shimonoseki at night across the sea and have been walking since dawn. But it is not just exhaustion, Bōtōni thinks, that has cast such a darkness over him. He is in the grip of grief, verging on despair. She remembers her stepson and fears this young man may kill himself.

Not in my house, she vows.

First he must bathe and eat and sleep. She believes in caring first for the body's needs. She treats all the young men who pass through her house as if they are her sons. With a mother's words and touch she bathes and feeds him. Tani argues briefly that he is not tired but she spreads out the futon and persuades him to lie down and within moments his eyes have closed. The mountain air of Hirao-san always has this effect.

Nakamura, impatient as always, does not take the time to rest. He has important business back in Fukuoka. He tells her before he leaves that the young man's real name is Takasugi Shinsaku. He is a poet and a loyalist. He was in prison during the fighting at the Forbidden Gate when two hundred died from Chōshū, among them Kusaka Genzui. Released from prison to negotiate with the English he then came under threat from the new conservative government in Chōshū.

She watches Nakamura's stocky form disappear down the mountain path. He walks jauntily as if afraid of nothing, but none of them knows when chance will turn. What has happened in Chōshū could just as easily take place in Fukuoka, and where will she or Nakamura or any of them flee to then?

There is some bond between them as if they were lovers in a former life. Over the days he recovers his spirits; they talk about politics and poetry, they exchange verses. Often she feels his eyes on her face as if he finds her beautiful. Even an old woman can feel the spring, she writes. Fragment by fragment he relates to her the story of his life, his childhood in Hagi, his studies at the Meirinkan and the Village School under the Pines, and in Edo. He tells her about Noyama prison, his mentor Sufu Masanosuke who killed himself less than a month ago, and his friend Inoue, still fighting for his life. They speak of Yoshida Shōin and Kusaka Genzui, and they pray together for the souls of the dead.

'I should have died too,' Shinsaku says, and Bōtōni replies, 'I have often wished for death, but if we are alive we can still serve our country. Even in winter when the branches are covered by snow the plum blossoms are still fragrant.'

Within a week he is recovering. She can see the desire to act building within him, a powder keg waiting for the spark. His lethargy has given way to impatience. Every day he walks through the mountains, then practises sword play on the level ground in front of the house. She likes watching him, his face serious and still, his sleeves tied back with cords, a headband round his hair.

Nakamura Enta returns with news from Chōshū. Even Enta's habitual cheerfulness is dimmed. The punishment demanded by the Bakufu for the uprising in Kyōto has been carried out. The elders are dead, their heads dispatched to Hiroshima; their staff officers have been executed in Noyama.

Enta has their names written down but Shinsaku does not need to read them. They are already engraved in his heart. Later he tells Bōtōni he has known these men all his life. Others from Sufu's government are still in prison. 'They will not get out alive,' he says.

He tells them he had hoped to challenge the new government using the *shotai* before he fled from Chōshū, but when he came through Shimonoseki, Yamagata Kyōsuke, on whom he had depended, had declined to give any support.

'I've had many conversations with Yamagata at Shiraishi's,' Enta says. 'He is no coward; he strikes me above all as a pragmatist. If he judges the time is right he will fight, but not before.'

'I cannot wait any longer,' Shinsaku replies. 'The next step will be to disband the *shotai*. Then we lose our main advantage. The time may never be this right again!'

'It is the hour to throw yourself into the fight,' Bōtōni says. She gives silent thanks to heaven that the news has come now when Shinsaku will be inflamed by it, and not when he first arrived.

'Yes, I will return to Chōshū as soon as possible.'

'All the ports are being guarded and ships searched,' Enta warns him.

'Then I will go in disguise.'

Bōtōni keeps a stash of clothes for this very purpose – farmers' clothes, *haori*, *juban* and *momohiki*. The *momohiki* hang loosely around Shinsaku's slight frame but she is able to alter them to fit him.

How strange, she thinks as her fingers work slowly in the lamplight, *if our country's future is stitched up in a pair of farmer's trousers.*

CIVIL WAR

I returned with my husband not to Shimonoseki but to the neighbouring town of Chōfu where Yamagata Kyōsuke had established the headquarters of the Kiheitai. Makino had gained some standing as an army doctor. He had been present during the Four Nations War when Shimonoseki had been bombarded for the second time and had treated Yamagata when he was wounded in the arm. He told me how much he admired Yamagata's orderly retreat and the courage of the snipers who continued to harass the foreigners even when they were outnumbered a hundred to one. There was no question now of anyone teasing or taunting him. He had gained the respect of the men. There were many in the Kiheitai and the other *shotai* who were like him, intelligent, competent, ambitious. Village headmen's sons, schoolteachers, struggling merchants, they had joined up because they saw a way out of their constricted lives.

Since the change of government in Hagi they had been ordered to disperse, but they did not want to be disbanded and sent back to the narrow world they came from. However, their leaders were reluctant to disobey a command from what was after all the legal government, especially when Chōshū was still surrounded by the Bakufu army.

The town was filled with restless men, arguing the rights

and wrongs of the situation. Many had fought in Kyōto. They had lost their leaders and burned for revenge, but they were also demoralised by the defeat. Others had nowhere else to go, having fled their own domains. Chōshū was their last hope and their last resort.

Into this volatile mix came Takasugi Shinsaku, on fire with his own determination to confront the conservative government.

I happened to run into him outside the Kakuonji, where the various *shotai* were encamped. We had moved in there and Makino had resumed his medical duties. I helped him, but even though I had got over my tears and shaking, I was still not really well. I had been moved by my dream of Ogata Kōan, and I clung to its memory, but the reality was difficult for me. My spirits were low and I had very little self-confidence. For that reason I would have passed Takasugi by without speaking to him, but he recognised me and drew me aside into the enclosed garden.

'So you have returned to the world of women?' he said teasingly.

'Please don't say anything about that time to my husband,' I replied.

'You have returned to him too?'

'What else could I do?'

He was studying my face. 'When you came to see me in Matsumoto I felt as you do now, as if I had no ability to influence anything and my life was worthless.'

'At least you are a man,' I said. 'Multiply your feelings by ten and you will know a tiny part of what women feel.' Then because that sounded so self-pitying I added, 'But I am determined to do what I can, even as a woman, to help my husband, to serve our domain, to renew the world.'

'I have been staying with a remarkable woman in Chikuzen,' he replied obliquely. 'Her name is Nomura Bōtōni. She writes poetry and believes in our cause of restoring a better government under the Emperor. She also wants to renew the world. You remind me of her.'

'I would like to meet her,' I said. He spoke of her with such warmth my curiosity was awakened, and I was flattered by his comparison.

'So have you any news of Itasaki?' he asked.

'Nothing.'

'I heard he disappeared after the Kinmon affair.'

'That is all I know.'

'So many have been lost,' he said. 'When I heard that Sufu was dead and the others executed I knew I had to come back and fight. After my teacher, Yoshida-*sensei*, was executed I vowed I would destroy those responsible for his death. Now I have even more comrades to avenge.'

I thought of the armies surrounding Chōshū, of the ruthless government in Hagi. What did Takasugi think he could do against them? I was afraid he had entered the manic stage of his cycle, but I envied him. At least he had escaped from the grip of depression.

'Well, don't forget your own advice,' he said. 'Take lots of walks and don't drink too much!'

He was laughing as we parted. Curiously his words had lifted my spirits. What a strange man he was, so often brooding and melancholic, over-sensitive and arrogant, yet capable of the kind of recklessness that others love and want to follow.

And, unlike most of the *shishi* I knew, interested in women's ideas and minds, not just their bodies – though he was certainly interested in them too.

That night the commanders of the various *shotai* met at Kakuonji. Takasugi wanted to move against the new government, using the *shotai*. But the other leaders could not come to an agreement.

It was a bitterly cold night. The wind from the sea blew through all the cracks and chinks in the old temple's walls, rattling the *shōji* and the shutters. Smoke from the braziers in the hall made my eyes sting. My throat was raw from smoking too much tobacco. Everyone seemed to be suffering from coughs and colds, making their already frayed tempers more irritable.

Akane Taketo, who was the overall leader of the *shotai* at the time, had just come back from Hagi. He had been trying to secure the release of the Justice Party officials who were under arrest. He was an intelligent man, he had studied with the monk Gessho, with Yoshida Shōin and Umeda Unpin, and had always been in favour of mixed-rank forces. Now he sought a reconciliation between the two sides of government, arguing that while the whole country was under threat from foreigners there had to be one strong unified government, within both the domain and the nation.

He spoke calmly and reasonably and I could see that most of those present were persuaded, but Takasugi was having none of it.

'Reconciliation between two such differing parties is

impossible. Are the wolf and the tiger to be reconciled? No, they fight until one destroys the other.'

Somebody else suggested that all decisions should be put off until the fate of the remaining five nobles had been decided. The Bakufu had demanded their return but they were still in Chōfu, in Kōzanji, and no one knew what was to become of them. The one I had treated, Prince Nishikinokōji, had died from *kakke* a few months earlier. The *shotai* had been protecting the nobles for over a year and did not want to give them up. Everyone began talking at once about what the nobles meant to them or alternately how much trouble they had caused.

Takasugi said nothing but drank more and more heavily as his expression grew darker. Finally he exploded. 'I am Takasugi Shinsaku, samurai, hereditary retainer of the house of Mōri. If you accept the views of Akane, who's nothing more than a farmer from Ōshima, there's no hope for you. I'll go and inform Lord Mōri myself and then I'll slit my belly in his presence!'

But nothing he said could persuade the leaders. I couldn't help feeling he might have chosen his words with more care. Insulting Akane was not going to persuade him or win over the others.

'Akane might not exactly be a farmer, but he's almost certainly a spy,' Makino said gloomily after the meeting had broken up. 'Reconciliation with Hagi means the *shotai* will be disbanded. And that will be the end of your friends, Itō, Inoue, Takasugi… the only reason Hagi's not coming after them now is because they are protected by the *shotai*.' He was frowning in the particular way he had when a calculation turned out to be wrong, but not all the numbers had been figured yet.

Two days later Takasugi took matters into his own hands. Dressing carefully in armour laced in red, blue and green, wearing a pointed and peaked helmet he rode through the swirling snow to Kōzanji. There he greeted Sanjō Sanetomi and the other noblemen, telling them that the brave spirit of Chōshū was about to be revealed to them. With eighty men, including many from the Yūgekitai, Itō Shunsuke and his little troop of *sumō* wrestlers, and one small cannon, he went on to Shimonoseki, where he took over the domain trading depot in the early hours of the morning, commandeering its money and stores. His troops made Ryōenji their headquarters, and the following day Takasugi took eighteen men in a small boat and sailed to Mitajiri, where after negotiating with the head of the naval office he took the three Chōshū warships and sailed them back to Shimonoseki. Suddenly he had demonstrated how he could control the southern coast of the domain.

I did not witness these astonishing events first hand as Makino had decided, reluctantly for he admired Takasugi greatly and thought he was right, that his loyalty lay with Yamagata, so we stayed in Chōfu. But when the news came the effect was like a thunderbolt. Almost immediately the *shotai* set out to march towards Hagi. Makino and I packed up our medical supplies and prepared to accompany Yamagata and his men. There was no argument this time over whether I should go or not, and if anyone questioned my right to be there I decided I would repeat what Monta had told me about the most famous woman in England, Florence

Nightingale. I wondered how many of the eager troops with whom we crossed the mountains in the twelfth month had heard her name, or even knew that the emperor of distant England was a woman, Queen Victoria.

The nobles Sanjō Sanetomi and Shijō Takauta travelled with Yamagata's troops – they had declared they wanted to consult with Lord Mōri in Hagi – but when we came to the village of Isa in the district of Mine news came that they were to be sent with their companions to Chikuzen and so they turned back. The rest of us settled down in Isa.

This was the town I had pretended to come from when I was Imaike Kōnosuke, and even though I had never been there before, in a curious way I felt as if I belonged there. It was famous for its many and varied remedies. It was a region where strange stones and fossils abounded; the locals called them dragon bones and all were believed to have healing properties if they were ground up, boiled, dissolved, infused, steeped and mixed with each other.

The trade in medicines had made many in the town wealthy, and one of these rich merchants gave over his residence to Yamagata and Ōta Ichinosuke, the *shotai* commanders, as a headquarters. Many young men from the district had already joined up and, like Yoshitomi Tōbei and Shiraishi Seiichirō, their fathers and uncles supported us with food and funds.

It was nearly the end of the first year of Genji, which had been so disastrous for our domain. The days were short and dark; snow lay on the mountains and icy rain fell with sleet in the valleys. The *shotai* maintained their now traditional strict discipline; their days were filled with drill and study; looting, gambling, drunkenness and other crimes common to soldiers everywhere were strictly forbidden. Makino and I spent our time discussing remedies with the local pharmacists and dealing with petty ailments, colds, sore eyes, ear infections. We prepared surgical instruments, needles and thread, saws and knives for amputations, strong pliers and tweezers to extract splinters, vinegar and sake to cleanse wounds, cloth for bandages, salves and ointments. Makino had seen two campaigns and I had witnessed the aftermath of the fighting in Kyōto. We had a far better idea now of what sorts of wounds to expect.

Isa lay halfway on the road between Hagi and Shimonoseki. The *shotai* had effectively cut off communication between the two cities but news came to us from both directions. From Hagi came the shocking reports that the seven officials of the Justice Party who had been held in Noyama prison had all been executed. People said it was the government's immediate response to Takasugi's actions in Shimonoseki and Mitajiri. Shortly afterwards the government army, composed of regular soldiers and the *shotai*'s old enemy the Senpōtai, was dispatched to the village of Edō, ten miles or so to the northwest of Isa. Their commander, Awaya Tateuki, sent a message to Yamagata just before the New Year, demanding that the *shotai* give up their arms and disperse.

Yamagata replied that they would certainly obey but they just needed a little more time. Awaya did not seem to know what to make of this reponse and for the next few days both sides just waited.

We celebrated the New Year with the troops at the Isa shrines and temples, grateful for the spiced sake and rice cakes provided by our hosts. The town was quiet on the first day of the year as everyone rested after the frenzied activities of stocktaking and cleaning before the year ended, but the second day was lively, with all the stores open for the first sales and celebrations with lion dancers and acrobats. A few days later we heard that Takasugi had made another attack on Shimonoseki.

'He is in a fury after the news of the executions,' the messenger added. 'He has sworn he will never share the same sky with the murderers.'

It was obvious that the *shotai* had no alternative now but to fight. Takasugi was on his way north with more troops. Yamagata did not wait any longer. In the early hours of the morning on the seventh day of the month about two hundred *shotai* forces, armed with rifles, bayonets, cannon, swords, bows and arrows, spears and pistols marched to the government army's camp at Edō. They delivered a written declaration of war, denouncing the crimes of the Mukunashi government, and immediately attacked. The government army, taken by surprise, was completely routed, and fled through the mountains. They regrouped at nightfall at the pass at Naganobori, on the edge of the Akiyoshi plateau.

The *shotai* had meanwhile decided not to try to hold Edō, which was surrounded by mountains and difficult to defend. They moved back to the little village of Ōda where they set up camp in the Kinrei shrine, establishing a line of defence, the Kiheitai on the right, the Hachimantai and the Ochōtai in the centre, the Nanentai on the left. At the back of the wooden building we prepared the field hospital under the huge cedars while Yamagata and Ōta both cut their hair and prayed for victory before the shrine to Hachiman.

In the first skirmish of the civil war at Edō the *shotai* lost only three men and injuries were surprisingly light, perhaps because their opponents were taken by surprise, but on the tenth day the two forces fought three more serious battles at Naganobori, Kawakami and Ōkitsu. This time the government forces, boosted by reinforcements from Hagi, had the upper hand, and inflicted heavy losses on our men – eleven dead and many injured.

Several houses were set alight and the flames lit up the sky while we cared for the wounded that night, extracting bullets and splinters, setting broken limbs and cleansing and stitching wounds. It seemed we had hardly finished dealing with the injured before another desperate attack took place at the Nomimizu pass, but the *shotai* had laid landmines and the government army was driven back with serious losses. Ten men died at the pass alone. The survivors retreated as far as Akamura, where they encamped in Seiganji near Hibariyama.

Even though the old plum trees in the shrine grounds had their first fragrant blossoms it was still numbingly cold. I went from house to house in the village to beg for quilts, coats, old rags, anything to keep the wounded warm. I gathered firewood wherever I could find it, going deep into the forest to look for dead trees to maintain the fires.

We did not know then how to set broken bones where the bones had pierced the skin. Our only recourse was amputation. Makino did two amputations of injured limbs, and despite the terrible conditions both men survived. I admired his skill and dexterity, the way he calculated all the factors, made a decision and followed it swiftly. If the limb was sawn through slowly the patient was likely to die of shock, so the textbooks told us. Makino was fast. The sheer volume of the injuries meant I had plenty to do, mainly extractions of bullets and metal from shrapnel and huge slivers of wood from where shells had exploded inside houses, ripping the walls apart and turning everything into a missile. One man died before I could pull one such splinter from his eye. It had pierced his brain.

I was amazed by the courage of the wounded. Whether samurai, merchant or farmer, none of them complained; they hardly even screamed or groaned. The ones who died went quietly, seemingly without fear, whispering the name of Amida. I pitied them because they were so young. The ground was too hard to dig in, so the bodies were burned and the ashes stored in the shrine, but who would tend their graves and worship their spirits, for they left no wives or children?

PROMISES

The day after the battle at Nomimizu Takasugi arrived from Shimonoseki with more of the *shotai*. I was at the back of the shrine by the makeshift kitchen helping a man with a broken arm feed himself, when I heard the sound of horses and a great cheer from the soldiers.

'What's happening?' I called to Makino, who was kneeling further along the side veranda. He looked up, then leaped to his feet.

'Takasugi is here!'

I put the bowl down and hurried to the front of the shrine. Takasugi was just dismounting from his horse. His face was alight with triumph as he greeted Yamagata and Ōta, congratulating them on the victories, commiserating with their losses.

'Just one more decisive blow,' he said, 'and the road to Hagi will be open.'

He paused on the way into the shrine and called to me. When I approached him he studied my face. 'You are better!' he said. 'You see, war suits us. We need violent action to sweep the dust and dirt away.'

He thanked me for my hard work, and walked on. I had hardly been aware of it until then, but in fact I was better. Despite the cold, the fatigue, the danger, I had come alive again. I noticed the plum blossoms like stars, the smell of frost, the beauty of bamboo crowned by snow. I stood for a moment, revelling in the freedom from depression, then Itō Shunsuke came into the shrine grounds accompanied by another man whom it took me a few moments to recognise. His face was disfigured by a long scar, still showing the red stitch marks.

'Inoue-san!' I exclaimed.

Monta and I gazed at each other for a moment.

'You see, I have lost all my good looks,' he said, grinning.

'I think you look more handsome than ever,' I replied. 'But why are you here? Are you well enough to fight?'

'We had to kidnap him,' Itō explained. 'He was under house arrest.'

'I was expecting orders to come from Hagi at any moment that I was to do myself in,' said Monta.

'His brother told us he couldn't very well just let him go, but if we came with enough men he would have no alternative but to hand him over to us,' Itō said.

'So they came with a whole troop, the Kōjōtai,' Monta said, 'and now I'm its commander. At last we have a chance to fight, to try out all we've learned.'

'And do you still have your *sumō* wrestlers?' I asked Itō.

'You can bet I do! Mukunashi's rabble will run at the sight of them. They are terrifying. One of them is the same size as three of me.'

They both looked extremely pleased with themselves.

'O-Tsuru-san, you couldn't find us something to eat, could you?' Monta asked.

I was so glad to see him alive I wasn't even angry. He

might have lost his boyish looks but he was still the young lord!

The next day the newly strengthened army attacked Akamura, completely defeating the government army. By the sixteenth day of the month the *shotai* were at Sasanami, just a few miles from Hagi. I had eaten tofu there with Shinsai a lifetime ago. Takasugi wanted to advance all the way to the castle town, but the other commanders were reluctant. They had lost many men, it would mean another difficult march through the mountains, more snow was threatening; it would be more prudent to return to Yamaguchi and consolidate their position. They also did not want to seem to be attacking Lord Mōri. Better to wait for him to decide on a change of government as now seemed inevitable.

To my disappointment, Takasugi was persuaded to withdraw. I wanted us to advance all the way to Hagi. The closer we came to the city the more pressing grew the memory of my promise to Kusaka Genzui in Tennōzan. I wanted to go to his wife, O-Fumi, as he had asked me, and tell her of his last night in this world. But I could not voice this to anyone as none there knew I had been in Kyōto at that time – only Takasugi knew of my secret life.

We returned to Ōda the day after the battle, bringing the wounded back to the temporary hospital in the shrine. Preparations were underway to march to Yamaguchi, but I did not want to go south. I wanted to go north to Hagi.

Towards the end of the day when the light was fading and the trees stood dark against the wintry sky, Takasugi came to talk to the wounded. He did not really have the common touch, unless he had been drinking, but his gruff awkward approach seemed to please them.

'Are they well enough to travel?' he asked, and Makino replied he thought they were and carts had been prepared to transport them.

'You've done well,' Takasugi said.

'There is so much more we need to learn,' Makino said hesitantly. 'Especially in field medicine.'

'In every area it is the same,' Takasugi replied. 'We are so far behind we need to gallop to catch up. Everything has to be done in haste without time for reflection. We need more weapons for a start…'

'Both arms and medicine can be got for a price in Nagasaki. The English will sell to anyone who has the money,' Makino said.

'You should go to Nagasaki. We can arrange that. Your wife would no doubt also like to go there. She would be interested to hear there is a woman doctor there, Siebold's daughter. Maybe she can learn from her.'

He turned to leave without waiting for a reply. I followed him, thinking it would be the only chance I had to speak to him privately. 'Takasugi-dono, I need to go to Hagi. I promised Kusaka-san I would tell his wife…'

'You saw Kusaka before he died?' Takasugi stopped dead. His face had lost all colour.

'Yes, I was at Tennōzan. I was at the meeting when Kusaka opposed the attack.'

'But he went anyway,' Takasugi said, his eyes bright in the torchlight.

'He marched at the front like a hero of old,' I said.

'You must tell his family this. But it's too dangerous to travel by road to the city now.' He was silent for a moment, frowning. 'I'm thinking of sending a warship to Hagi, just to demonstrate who controls the coast. You can go with them. By then Lord Mōri will have decided in our favour. Tell your husband you are fulfilling a request for me.'

The *shotai* sang as they marched back to Yamaguchi: *shi ga areba hippu mo.* I went with them and helped my husband settle our patients in the new *shotai* headquarters in the domain school. There was a lot of nursing to be done and I did not think Makino could manage on his own, but to my surprise when I broached the subject he was keen for me to go to Hagi.

'Will you ask your sister about the little girl?' he said quietly. Often in the middle of the busy days and long nights caring for the injured and the dying I had thought fleetingly of the child that we would adopt one day and now I realised with gratitude that Makino had also had her in his mind. So it was with his permission and his blessing that I left with Itō Shunsuke for Shimonoseki, where we boarded the *Kigai-maru* and sailed around the coast to Hagi.

The *Kigai-maru* (named for the *kigai* year of Bunkyū 3 – 1863) was a two-masted brig built in England. She had been holed and sunk by the American warship *Wyoming*. I had seen that during the first bombardment of Shimonoseki. She had been refloated and repaired, her sides and hull were patched and scarred and inside the wood showed signs of worm holes and other insect damage, but she dealt bravely with the winter seas, tacking up the coast against the north-westerly winds. She had ten guns.

Itō told me English boats were all called 'she'.

'That's because they are like women – fickle, difficult and irresistible.'

I smiled, thinking the *Kigai-maru* was like me, almost defeated, almost overcome, but restored and ready for life again. She gave me hope for our domain too. Surely the worst was past and the tide was turning.

The water ran white-flecked, deep green beneath her prow, the masts creaked and the sails sang in the wind.

'What are English women really like?'

'Beautiful! But you know, it's hard to work out how to relate to them. The English lords treat their women like porcelain queens. They wait on them and defer to them. They have a saying, "Ladies first". Men and women walk arm in arm, even hand in hand. But they have a huge number of prostitutes too. They call them fallen women. Many work on the streets like the women of the hills in Edo. They are treated very badly.'

'Worse than in Edo?'

'I thought so.'

'I hope Itō-san was careful.'

'Love is like war. There comes a point where being careful has nothing to do with it.'

I was hardly one to disagree with him. I thought I should change the subject. 'Inoue said you had a terrible voyage.'

He laughed. 'I thought we were going to die. But we learned a lot.'

Watching him as he gave orders to the sailors I thought how much he had changed since he came to my father for treatment all those years ago.

'You know, O-Tsuru-san, I think the way – the good way – the English treat their women is something we should emulate. It's interesting being in mixed company, men with their wives and daughters. The women are educated, they give their opinions freely.' He looked sideways at me and added, 'You'd love it! You should go there.'

I could not imagine travelling so far away to that other world.

'Didn't you feel lonely? Homesick?'

'Of course, often. And embarrassed a lot of the time too – not knowing how to act or even how to dress. People wear black a lot, it makes the city look so grim. Everything is much heavier, much more solid. The buildings are massive, they press down on the earth. Even the air is thicker. The factories are unbelievable. When you see London you understand why England has such a great empire. The secret is in the roast beef. It makes you strong. So we ate lots of it.' He patted his stomach as he said this and laughed again.

'You don't get seasick any more?'

'Not in these calm seas. You should see what it's like going round the Cape of Good Hope.' He waved his hand vaguely towards the west. 'Seas like mountains all the way round Africa.'

I did not feel sick either; I enjoyed the motion of the ship. We rounded the cape at Kawashiri and turned towards the east, passing Ōmishima with its rocky islets and the sixteen buddhas my mother had visited, and coming with the wind behind us now into Hagi harbour.

I had never seen the city from this side, nestled between the twin rivers, sheltered by the mountains all around, the castle rising proudly on the western side of the bay, its flags and banners fluttering in the wind.

Itō ordered the port guns to be prepared, put the ship about and had them fire a salvo in the direction of the castle.

'That'll give them something to think about,' he said in satisfaction, as he brought the *Kigai-maru* out of range of the shore guns.

Of course the cannon only fired blanks as Lord Mōri was in residence in the castle and Itō did not want to show disrespect to his *daimyō* or cause any actual damage. The *Kigai-maru* flew the Chōshū flags; her mission was to restore rightful government, not to overthrow the Mōri family.

We could see people on land running about in great excitement, shouting and waving their arms, but the shore guns remained silent and there were no signs of resistance.

Itō judged it safe enough and sent me ashore in a small boat with three men who were instructed to bring back information on the situation in the city. As I was to find out later there had been many developments in the brief power struggle between the two factions, but the mood of the city, and the domain as a whole, was swinging against the Mukunashi government and in favour of Takasugi and the Justice Party.

My companions were surrounded as soon as they landed, but it was clear they were in no physical danger. I left them to deal with the demands for news and slipped away from the port, through the familiar streets, to the Kuriya pharmacy.

It was the end of the first month and though the days were lengthening it was already twilight. Lanterns glowed outside eating places and the smell of food cooking hit my nostrils. The Kuriya house was lit within, the orange light spilling out onto the street for the shopfront shutters were not yet closed.

I'd been able to bathe in Yamaguchi and I'd discarded my blood-stained kimono, borrowing an old one as well as a cape and scarf from the caretaker's wife at the school, but as I called out at the door I was aware of how disreputable I must look with my cropped hair. My arrival was unexpected and I could tell from Mitsue's face that she immediately thought I had come with bad news from home.

I reassured her quickly, 'They were all fine when I last saw them.'

She said, 'But they've heard nothing about our uncle.'

'No, nothing at all,' I replied as I was becoming accustomed.

The Kuriya family welcomed me warmly enough, despite my appearance, but were astonished and alarmed when they heard I had been with the *shotai*. They had supported Mukunashi's party, being by nature conservative, and were now extremely worried that their side was going to be replaced with radicals like Takasugi. Everything I had to tell them added to their fears.

'Why did you come?' Mitsue whispered when we finally found ourselves alone. She was nursing the new baby and Michi was already asleep under the quilt, her cheeks pink, her breathing steady. The little boys slept with their grandparents, their father joining them in the larger room while Mitsue was up so much of the night with the baby.

'To see you,' I said lightly.

'Tsu-chan, you disappear for months and you turn up looking like an apparition just when everything's in turmoil. You could have chosen a better time to visit!'

'I also want to see Kusaka Fumi,' I said.

'Genzui's wife?'

'Yes, he gave me a message for her before he died. I wasn't able to give it before...I have not been well, I don't know if our parents told you. Then I had the opportunity to come to Hagi, so I took it.'

Mitsue absorbed all this in silence. The baby sucked and snuffled, lost the nipple and gave a little cry. Mitsue gently eased the nipple back into the tiny mouth.

'Genzui died in Kyōto,' she said finally.

'Yes, I was in Kyōto. Don't ask me any more. I went to Kyōto, and after the fighting at the Forbidden Gate I came back. That's when I was not well. Then my husband came to our house and asked me to join him. He has been an army doctor with the *shotai* for some time now.'

'Yes, we knew that,' Mitsue said. 'My husband often remarks on it.'

The baby had fallen asleep. My sister laid her carefully down on the futon, drawing the quilt over her. Something about the way she gazed at the two girls reminded me of Makino's suggestion.

'My husband wants to make a request of you,' I said. 'Will you think about it? There's no hurry, just when you feel ready.'

Mitsue looked at me questioningly. Then realisation came into her eyes. 'He would like to adopt one of the boys? I'm sorry, their grandmother would never agree to it. Maybe if Makino-san's status was higher, if he were even of *sottsu* rank – but they would never give one of their grandsons to a former employee.'

'What about one of their granddaughters?'

'Surely your husband does not want a girl?'

'He specifically said he would like a girl. I don't seem to be able to have children but we both agree we would like to bring up a daughter, educate her properly.'

Mitsue stared at me. 'Would you take Michi?'

'I have always felt she somehow belonged to me,' I said. 'Since I prevented her dying at birth.'

'It would be the answer to all my prayers. This child is so clever, much smarter than the boys were at that age. I can't tell you how I've agonised over her future. I don't want her to have the sort of life I have. She deserves so much more.' Mitsue flushed and said, 'Don't think I am complaining. I have no regrets…'

'I understand,' I said. 'But will the family agree?'

'I am sure they will.'

'As I said, think about it. We are probably going to Nagasaki this year. I don't think we could take her there. But after we return, in a year or two.'

We slept that night side by side as we used to in our parents' house in Yuda.

I set out the next morning for Matsumoto, taking a ferry boat across the river, remembering how I had made that journey with Shinsai, recalling his excitement at the prospect of joining Yoshida Shōin's school. How many of those students had died already, at the Ikedaya, at the Forbidden Gate, and in the mountains around Ōda and Edō? The wind was cold, blowing off the sea, but there were signs of spring, violets and aconites flowering along the roadside, plum blossoms in the gardens, and swollen leaf buds on tree branches. Water flowed everywhere as the mountain snow melted and birds were singing their first tentative melodies.

I called at the door of the Sugi–Yoshida house and the teacher's mother came out. She looked aged by grief. She did not recognise me or remember my name but she told me her daughter, Fumi, was in the school building.

'I will walk across if it is all right,' I said.

'Yes, please do.'

I could hear the sound of children's voices reciting the words of some classic work. Despite the cold the doors all stood open. I came to the veranda and looked in. O-Fumi was kneeling on the floor following the recitation from the book in front of her. One of the children became aware of me and faltered, the rest followed, fell silent and then began to giggle.

O-Fumi jumped up when she saw me. At first she did not know me either; she stared at me, puzzled, and then recognition dawned in her eyes.

'You came here before – the day Towa-san was here. And your – your uncle, wasn't it – was a student of my brother's?'

'Yes. Itasaki is our family name. My husband's name is Makino. I am sorry to intrude on you; I don't want to awaken your grief but...well, Kusaka-san asked me to come and see you.'

She gasped and swayed, grabbing the veranda post for support. Then she regained control and, telling the oldest boy to take over the class, stepped off the veranda and slipped into her sandals.

'Walk with me a little.'

I was already wishing I had not come. 'Are you all right? I'm sorry.' She had gone very pale.

'Yes. Forgive me. It's just that I forget he is dead and when you spoke, for a moment I thought he must be alive. He was away so often, you know. Some days it is just as if he is still away and will return soon.'

'I saw him just before he died, and I promised I would tell you how they came to fight.' I told her about Genzui's last days at Tennōzan, about the council of war and how he was overridden, and repeated his parting words to me. She listened with dry eyes as if she had already wept too much.

'He was the bravest and most honourable man I ever knew,' I concluded. 'Like your brother, twenty-one times a valiant samurai!'

She smiled a little. 'We are very proud of them both. And their sacrifice – the sacrifice of so many lives – will surely not be in vain. Now the government will change again. You may not know, the Peace Assembly gathered at Kōkōji are appealing to Lord Mōri to stop this civil war. They are all highly respected men. He must listen to them. We believe my uncle will be recalled to office. And Takasugi, and Katsura.'

'Your brother's students have all excelled themselves,' I said.

'They are fulfilling his dreams. What about Itasaki-san?'

I was so tired of answering this question! 'He left with your husband. That is the last we know of him.'

'I am very sorry. But your family must be proud of him.'

I bowed my head in agreement but did not reply. I found myself following a waking dream in which I went with Shinsai to the Forbidden Gate on that last day. I fought at his side and like Genzui and Terajima we stabbed each other when we knew all was lost, and died there together. I envied

O-Fumi, because she knew her husband was dead. At least he had been her husband, at least they were *bushi* and she could find comfort in the ideals of her class.

Ashamed of myself I took my leave as soon as possible. I went back to the Kuriya house unsettled and angry. I wished I had not gone – what had I hoped for? I had fulfilled the desires of the dead, but did the dead care one way or another?

If you are dead, Shinsai, tell me, give me a sign! But there was no answer, nothing that I could read any meaning into. My impetuous journey now seemed foolish. I wished I was back in Yamaguchi with the *shotai* and my husband.

It would be several weeks before I managed to make the journey back. Itō's broadside from the *Kigai-maru* had helped persuade Lord Mōri that the government must be changed, but the negotiations took some time and not everyone submitted peacefully. There were skirmishes between the *shotai* and the Senpōtai, assassinations of Peace Assembly envoys and fresh threats of an outbreak of war. But by the end of the second month Lord Mōri and the new government had moved back to Yamaguchi, the *shotai* were brought under control to form the basis of a new army and the roads between the two cities became safe for travellers again.

I spent my time at the Kuriya house helping in the pharmacy once more, and playing with Michi, discovering for myself what my sister had told me. She was a child of unusually high intelligence, already talking fluently. I thought her ability alarmed her father and grandmother for she was much brighter than her brothers. I left her with a real pang of sorrow and promised I would rescue her when I returned from Nagasaki.

WAITING

Everything achieved by the Bakufu the previous year in the first attempt to punish Chōshū had been undone by Takasugi's incitement of the *shotai* and the war within the domain. The radical Justice Party was back in control of the government, the *daimyō* and his heir were far from penitent, and the forced suicides, executions and other punishments had hardened the temper of the entire domain against the shōgunate.

In the fourth month the Bakufu announced a second expedition against Chōshū, calling for *daimyō* from all over the country to provide troops and weapons. The first expedition had been settled without fighting by Chōshū's submission, but there was no question of submitting now. Even the branch domains who in the past had had their own quarrels with Hagi were driven into unity by the threat from outside. Under the new government the domain was preparing to fight for its life.

It took the Bakufu a long time to assemble its new army; it would be over twelve months before the two sides exchanged fire. During that time not only was Chōshū frantically rearming but there were also negotiations going on for the unbelievable to happen: an alliance between two arch-enemies, between the tiger and the dragon, an alliance with Satsuma against the Tokugawa.

Makino and I still intended to go to Nagasaki, despite the uncertainty hanging over everyone. Takasugi had gone there in the third month, planning to travel on to Shanghai, mystifying his colleagues who had expected him to play a major role in the new government. I could not help wondering if he was not repeating his usual pattern, running away from the success his manic behaviour had achieved. Inoue and Itō had also gone into hiding – all three were still under constant threat of assassination, this time from samurai in Shimonoseki who resented Hagi's plans to open the port to foreign trade.

'Crabs in a bucket!' my father exclaimed when he heard this news. 'Each one struggling to preserve its own little life while trampling down its fellows!'

Indeed, so confused and turbulent were those times we often seemed no more than helpless creatures struggling not to be consumed.

I had gone home to Yuda to say goodbye to my parents and as usual our talk was mainly of events in the domain. Father had heard that Katsura Kogorō was returning to Chōshū to take up a high position in the government. He had been in hiding ever since the disaster at the Forbidden Gate; people were amazed and delighted that he was still alive.

'Maybe this means we should not give up all hope for Shinsai,' Father said. 'Perhaps he is also in hiding somewhere.'

'He could come home at any time,' Mother said brightly, trying to cheer him up, for my father had taken Shinsai's disappearance very badly and grieved for him deeply.

I sat for a moment saying nothing. I pictured the scene outside where summer was transforming the landscape. I imagined the dusty road and Shinsai walking along it, passing through the gate and under the gambling tree. I felt his ghostly presence so strongly my skin crawled. To change the subject I said, 'Murata Zōroku is going to be asked to reform the army, so I heard in Yamaguchi.'

'Murata.' Father sniffed. Murata Zōroku, later known as Ōmura Masujirō, had a medical practice in a village not far from Yuda and Father knew him quite well. 'He'll do better in the army than as a doctor.'

'Dr Murata is a very clever man,' Mother reminded him.

'He's clever, but he doesn't like his patients. I'm glad for their sake he's going to deal with soldiers instead.'

'Dr Murata studied in Nagasaki, didn't he?' I said.

'Yes, under the famous Pompe. You'll meet many of his pupils, and Siebold's too.'

'Takasugi-san told me Siebold had a daughter and that she is a doctor.'

'That's correct,' Father replied. 'Murata knows her well. I believe she went to Uwajima and is greatly favoured by Lord Date.'

'Oh, I hoped she would be in Nagasaki and then I could meet her.' I was a little disappointed.

Father said maybe she returned to Nagasaki from time to time and that Tetsuya would certainly know how to get in touch with her, for the family my brother had married into had close connections with Siebold's old Narutaki school. Then his thoughts returned to Shinsai.

'Katsura may come here,' he said. 'Then we could ask him if he's heard anything.'

I was about to reply that I thought he would be far too busy when I remembered the conversation I had had with

Katsura under the Nijō bridge. He was in fact quite likely to call on my father to see the Chikuden painting and my father would fall for his compliments and hints and give it to him. This thought made me extremely angry. It made me relive that intense and anguished time after Shinsai's disappearance. I resented Katsura for being alive, for hiding out for so long when Genzui and the others had sacrificed their lives and Shinsai was almost certainly dead. I decided I would retrieve the picture from the storehouse and take it with me to Nagasaki. I would give it to Tetsuya's new family or throw it into the sea rather than allow it to fall into Katsura's hands. Why was I so hostile? I did not really understand my own feelings. I just kept seeing the dying – their gaping wounds, their courage, their tears of pain – and Katsura's white feet beneath his beggar's disguise, and the elegant clothes of the woman who brought him food.

So when my belongings were packed up and sent to Shimonoseki *Fragrant Plum Blossoms, Unknown Shadow* was hidden inside one of the baskets, wrapped up in a silk kimono that had been my grandmother's. Of course I did not take it without my parents' permission. I asked for it, thinking I would say that Tetsuya had hoped to inherit it or that I wanted a memory of home to take with me, but my father did not demand any reason. He simply gave it to me, saying he hoped it would in some way ensure my safety. My illness had made my parents unnaturally nervous about me; they wept when Makino came for me and we had to say goodbye. Their faces were distorted by the fear they would never see me again. They had already buried two children, but both of them were to be spared the grief of outliving the rest of us.

Makino and I went to Shimonoseki and stayed once again at Shiraishi's Kokuraya. Shiraishi was unchanged – a few more grey hairs and wrinkles but as hospitable and generous as ever. We had much to talk about: our time with the *shotai*, the campaign in the mountains around Ōda, our plans for Nagasaki, but as usual the hostel was overflowing with visitors and our host had to keep excusing himself to deal with the various guests and their demands.

The second evening we were there – it was the intercalary fifth month, eight years since my sister's wedding, and had the strange feeling such months always had of the days going past but time standing still – Shiraishi came in, full of excitement that he lost no time sharing with us.

'Don't tell a soul, but something very important is taking place right now, just down the passage. History is being made! Under my roof!' He paused for dramatic effect and then whispered, 'Katsura-dono is here.'

My own first guilty reaction was that Katsura had followed me to take possession of the painting.

'Shiraishi-san, please don't tell him I am here,' I began, but my husband had other ideas.

'We should see him,' he said. 'He is going to be a very powerful figure. He can help us with his influence, maybe even with money.'

'I already told him about you,' Shiraishi said, a little annoyed at my unenthusiastic response to his news. 'He wants to meet you.'

'My husband will go. I am rather tired,' I said.

Makino stared at me, frowning. 'He is an old acquaintance of your father. It would be rude not to come with me. And why would you not want him to know you are here?'

During the months we had been together again my husband and I had not grown closer. We worked alongside each other well enough but we did not talk intimately any more, nor had we resumed our marital relations. We were too busy, too tired – but if the fire of passion is burning such things are irrelevant. The truth was there was no desire between us any more. I was not free from physical and emotional yearning, and I don't suppose my husband was either, but we did not turn to each other. If he was seeking comfort elsewhere I did not know about it. He had kept his promise not to question me about my absence. Now I thought I saw in his expression something I had overlooked: jealousy.

Could he really think I had disappeared with Katsura? Then I remembered little things that I had hardly noticed: his unease when I was alone with Takasugi, his displeasure when Inoue and Itō joked with me. I felt a wave of pity for my rational husband succumbing to the irrationality of jealousy and for the first time in months a kind of tenderness welled up in me. He had made a request of me in Shiraishi's presence and I could not refuse without shaming him, so I followed him, careful to stay a couple of steps behind, down the passageway to the rooms that were reserved for guests of high status. Apart from his hereditary position Katsura was now one of the leading officials of the domain.

The spacious room looked out over the garden. It was around the time of the plum rains and the trees and shrubs dripped with moisture. The azaleas were in flower, looming red in the lamplight. There were already several men there whom I knew by sight. They had all passed through Shiraishi's place at one time or another. Katsura sat at one end of the room, near the open *shōji*, far more elegantly dressed than the last time I had seen him, but I hardly looked at him. My eyes fell on the man next to him and my heart stopped. For a moment I thought it was Shinsai. Almost immediately I realised of course it was not him, but there was a resemblance. Like Shinsai this man was tall, and his head was the same shape, his hair looked similar. He sat knee to knee with Katsura, their heads close, their voices low. The lamps sent a flickering light across them and made their shadows dance.

Katsura glanced towards us as we stepped into the room. Shiraishi said, 'We must not disturb you, but this is the doctor I was telling you about, Makino Keizō. He and his wife are on their way to Nagasaki.'

'I hope I can be of service to you there,' Makino said.

'Please wait,' Katsura said. 'I would like to speak with you.' He did not address me but I was conscious of his eyes flicking over me. I wished I had not come, but I could not very well escape now he had seen me, and I wanted to hear for myself anything he might say about me. I prayed that he would have more important things on his mind than our last meeting in Kyōto.

As Katsura continued talking and the other man replied in a Tosa accent, I realised who he was: he had to be the *rōnin* Sakamoto Ryōma. I remembered Genzui talking about him in this very place. Shinsai had told me he was sometimes mistaken for Ryōma, and it was easy to see why. I could not hear Sakamoto's words, but his manner was impressive and I could see that Katsura found him persuasive.

After a few more whispered exchanges Katsura raised his

head and with his usual warmth of expression drew everyone in the room into the conversation.

'Saitani-san is returning to Nagasaki,' he said to Makino. 'He may be able to help you contact merchants who import drugs and medicine.' Turning to the so-called Saitani (Saitani Umetarō was the name Sakamoto used at that time: his ancestors were called Saitani when they were still merchants in Tosa) he said, 'Makino-san is one of our most promising young doctors. He helped set up field hospitals in our recent campaign and is going to Nagasaki to study at the Western hospital established by Pompe.'

Makino bowed, obviously flattered by this warm introduction. It was typical of Katsura's phenomenal memory. He never forgot a name or any little piece of information he was told. And this was despite the copious amounts of sake he consumed. It had made him an effective spy and would make him an even more effective politician.

For once I was happy not to be noticed or mentioned. I bowed as well, then sat demurely as a good wife should, a little behind my husband, my eyes lowered.

'Come and look me up in Nagasaki,' Ryōma said, getting up to leave. 'I usually stay at Kosone Eishirō's prawn shop.'

'Prawn shop!' one of the samurai scoffed after the sound of Ryōma's footsteps had faded away. 'That Tosa prawn is a bit fishy, I think!'

'I have a great regard for him,' Katsura said, though he joined in the laughter. 'And he has some very interesting ideas.'

He did not go into details then; after several more flasks of sake the other men suggested a visit to the geisha house. Katsura said he would join them in a little while.

The men staggered to their feet and left noisily. A maid appeared, trying not to yawn (it was approaching midnight) and refilled the sake cups. I asked her to bring some tea.

'Shiraishi, Sakamoto wants me to meet Saigō Takamori,' Katsura said. 'He believes we cannot waste any more time. Satsuma and Chōshū must become allies.'

'He talks a lot of sense,' Shiraishi replied. 'Sakamoto is a practical man and he understands about trade. The more trade between the domains the better, in my opinion. Satsuma and Chōshū are both powerful, but they squander half that power squabbling with each other.'

'Can anyone from Satsuma be trusted?' Katsura said. 'It was Saigō after all who was responsible for the terrible punishments last year.'

'Maybe it's Saigō you have to thank that the punishments were not even more extreme,' Shiraishi suggested. 'And hasn't he declined to join the new campaign against Chōshū?'

'The domain samurai will never accept such an alliance,' Makino observed. 'They hate Satsuma as much as Aizu: *satsuzoku aikan* – Satsuma bandits, Aizu villains – that's what you hear everywhere.'

Katsura frowned. 'You may be right. They'll take a lot of persuading.' He remained silent for a few moments, wrapped in his own thoughts. 'Sakamoto's not the only matchmaker,' he said finally. 'There's another Tosa man, Nakaoka Shintarō. He's gone off to tell Saigō to stop in Shimonoseki on his way to Ōsaka. If he agrees we'll meet this month – here if you can arrange it.'

'Certainly,' Shiraishi said. 'Saigō has stayed here before. It can all look quite coincidental.'

'Both Tosa men are in some danger at the moment,' Katsura said quietly. 'The conservative faction have regained control in that domain as they did here last year. Takechi Hanpeita is dead, ordered to commit suicide in prison. Sakamoto knows he can expect no support from Tosa. He's safe for the time being in Nagasaki, but he and Nakaoka need help from both Chōshū and Satsuma.'

'Sakamoto will be a useful go-between in the matter of weapons,' Shiraishi said.

'I've seen Nakaoka all over the place,' Katsura commented as he poured more sake. 'He was at Mitajiri for a while and he's always popping up in Kyōto. Did you ever run into him when you were there?'

This remark did not seem to be addressed to anyone in particular. After a moment Makino answered, 'I have never been in Kyōto.'

'Oh,' Katsura said, surprised. 'I saw your wife there. I thought perhaps you had accompanied the Chōshū army.'

'I stayed in Shimonoseki,' Makino said, speaking very precisely.

Katsura looked at me. 'But you were in Kyōto. We met under the Nijō bridge and spoke about the painting. Did you ever find your uncle, by the way? You were looking for him, I remember.'

'We believe he is dead,' I said, speaking as precisely as my husband. I was aware of his emotional turmoil that equalled my own. We sat like two squat alembics on the fire, boiling away some noisesome distillation. I could almost see the steam escaping from him.

'My condolences,' Katsura said. 'I'll go and visit your father when I am back in Yamaguchi.'

'He would be honoured,' I said, thinking I could see an acquisitive gleam in Katsura's eyes. Little did he know the painting he desired was no longer in Yuda but packed away in a nearby room.

I had to admire my husband's self-control as he talked for many long minutes about the situation in Nagasaki, the opportunities for learning and trade and the need for Chōshū to rearm. Then Katsura grew restless, recalling the geisha house no doubt, and Shiraishi ushered us away.

'Katsura really drinks too much,' I said when we were back in our room. I picked up a fan from the chest and began to fan my face which had suddenly become very hot.

'So you were in Kyōto?' Makino voiced each word as clearly as before. 'With Shinsai?'

'We happened to be there at the same time,' I said. 'That's all.' I could see him struggling against a knowledge he really did not want to possess.

'Don't go any further,' I said.

The calculations passed visibly across his face: the scandal, the pain caused to my parents, the loss to himself, the humiliation.

He said, 'I should kill you.'

'If you were a samurai you would. But you aren't – and nor am I. Anyway, nothing happened, and now Shinsai is dead.' For the first time I believed this was true.

He pulled me towards him, staring into my face. I thought fleetingly of all the ways in which he might kill me: the scalpels that lay within reach, the poisons he knew so intimately, the simple objects, a sash, a cushion, a pestle that could strangle, smother, bludgeon my defenceless body.

'Nothing happened?' he repeated. His grip tightened.

'Nothing,' I said, my heart beating faster at the lie as well as with fear.

He so much wanted to believe me. I felt again the same surge of pity for him, for all men really, with their needs and jealousies and weaknesses. What pathetic creatures humans were. How could we hope to change anything when our ideals for a better world were always betrayed by our own lies and illusions?

Just as it had the day Nakajima died, when I had watched the Accountant walk towards me in the rain, some deep feeling sparked between us. Lust swept through us both, lust with its remarkable capacity to rise at the most unlikely yet the perfect moment. My husband wanted to kill me and I had truly thought he might, but instead we fell to the ground, pulling at each other's clothes, grasping and clawing at each other like animals until he thrust himself hard up inside me and we both came at the same time, and both wept in a mixture of need and release and shame and pity.

Afterwards Makino said, 'Since Shinsai is dead there is no point in speaking of any of this again.'

I did not reply, but in my silence another transaction in our marriage was concluded.

We postponed our departure, partly because Makino was eager to witness the meeting and partly because the plum rains persisted. However, in the end Katsura did not meet Saigō at this time. The great Saigō changed his mind and did not stop in Shimonoseki. Katsura was angry, his pride took a blow, but unlike many Chōshū samurai, rationalism and pragmatism always overruled hurt feelings with him. Sooner or later he would meet Saigō and he would deal with Satsuma. In the meantime he returned to Yamaguchi to oversee the reform of the military with Murata.

The rains finally ceased and we were able to board a ship to take us to Kyūshū on the first stage of our journey to Nagasaki.

PART 4

結

Keiō 1 to Keiō 3
1865–1867

NAGASAKI

Even though it was hardly wider than a river I had never been across the strait to Kokura. I gazed over the side of the boat at the deep blue water, the white crested waves, and thought of the Battle of Dannoura in which the Heike met their final defeat. The infant Emperor had perished beneath these same waves – and the surviving Heike princesses and noblewomen had been forced to sell their bodies or starve. The Shimonoseki geisha claimed to be descended from them. The thought made me smile.

From Kokura we would walk the rest of the way along the Nagasaki highway, hiring packhorses to carry our luggage, and occasionally men to carry us. The Nagasaki highway had been used for hundreds of years – it was said that Ieyasu himself had ordered its construction when Nagasaki was established as the only port open to trade with the West. Along this road had travelled the *daimyō* of Saga, Fukuoka, and Kurame with their elaborate two thousand-strong processions on their alternate attendance journeys to Edo, and the Dutch *kapitans* had followed the same route and stayed at the same *honjin* when they made their yearly visits to the Shōgun. The journey took seven days and there were a number of posting inns along the way – all of them suffering hardship. Alternate attendance had ended three years earlier and it was many years since a Dutch *kapitan* had travelled to Edo, probably not since Siebold's day.

Siebold himself would have travelled on this same route. His eyes would have taken in the same sights as mine, the huge camphor trees with their inky shadows, the fertile valleys, every available space terraced, edged with tea bushes, the bamboo forests that gave shade on the steep climb to each pass, the many statues of Ebisu, the white foxes of Inari, the headless Jizō in little mountain shrines. Siebold would have drunk at the cool spring that gave Hiyamizu pass its name. Maybe he even bathed as we did in the hot springs of Ureshino, said to cure syphilis, scabies and rheumatism.

We left Ureshino early in the morning of the fifth day of our journey, hoping to get as far as Ōmura that night, but a sudden rainstorm forced us to take shelter at Yunoda and then we had to wait at the Hirano crossing for the water to subside. The river raced high between its steep rocky banks, but the locals assured us it fell as rapidly as it rose and we would surely get across before nightfall. The horse boy gave the horses food and water and my husband and I sat on the veranda of one of the tea houses – it was called the Crossing Pine, I think – and drank tea from Ureshino and ate broiled eel.

I was lighting my pipe and thinking how pleasant the tobacco tasted in the fresh mountain air when someone coughed nervously behind me and a man's voice said, 'Surely it is O-Tsuru-san.'

I turned and saw a thin shabbily dressed young man, with a shaved head. He was wearing a doctor's coat and clasping the strap of a travelling medicine chest. It took me a moment to recognise him, and before I could say anything he went on with some diffidence, 'Of course there is no reason at all why you should recall a person of such insignificance and no doubt our last meeting was so distasteful to you that you have erased me from your memory...'

'Hayashi-san!' I exclaimed.

He smiled with exaggerated delight, his eyes nearly disappearing into the creases of his cheeks. I had hardly given Hayashi Daisuke a moment's thought since he had disappeared from my parents' house after Nakajima died.

He introduced himself to my husband, who raised his eyebrows at me but indicated to Daisuke that he should sit down with us. The maid came with fresh tea; Daisuke took out a small illustrated guidebook and after consulting it ordered *tamago sōmen.*

'It's a speciality here,' he said, showing the page to Makino. 'I like the sweets in Kyūshū – they are made with sugar and egg. It's the influence of the Portuguese, you know.'

We didn't know, so Daisuke filled in the interval by telling us the history of the different foreigners in Nagasaki: Portuguese, English, Dutch, Chinese. The Portuguese and English were long gone, though the English had reappeared now there was so much money to be made from selling weapons. The Portuguese had left behind all sorts of convenient things: firearms, bread, *tempura*, sponge cake...

'And this,' Daisuke said, licking his lips as the maid returned with the sticky yellow sweet strands of egg that did indeed look like noodles.

We all had a taste. Makino did not care for it, having no liking for anything sweet, but I thought it was delicious and ordered another dish.

'I hope your parents are well,' Daisuke said while I was tucking into it.

I replied that they and the whole household were in good health and then said, 'But where have you been all this time? It must be seven years…'

'I went to Ōsaka first, and for the last three years I've been in Nagasaki. I studied at one of the private schools there and then I was fortunate enough to work with the Dutch teacher, Pompe, at the hospital he established. That was just before he left.'

He had finished eating and now took a travelling medicine pouch from his robe and extracted a large brown-coloured pill from one of its compartments.

'My stomach is delicate, you may remember,' he explained, 'so I always travel with a supply of medicine.'

'What's in it?' Makino asked.

'Oh, you know, mainly *daiō*, some licorice, mint. It's called the Shōgun – it's very strong.'

'Not such a good name for it in these days,' Makino joked.

Daisuke looked alarmed. 'Be careful. Nagasaki is run by the Bakufu and there are spies everywhere.'

'It was just a joke,' I said. While I had been eating the sky had darkened again. Now thunder rolled and it began to rain heavily. We were obviously not going to cross the river that night. Makino went to enquire about lodging – there were several other travellers in the same predicament, but the owner of the Crossing Pine said he would find a space for us and could give us soup, rice and grilled fish.

The portions were small but there was plenty of sake to go round and it turned out to be a merry evening. Tea-house owners had to be competitive to stay in business – we'd already experienced a hundred different ways of enticing a customer – and Mr Crossing Pine's speciality was his skill as a storyteller. He described the great processions of the *daimyō* and the *kapitans* as if they had gone past just the other week, and told tales of all the exotic creatures that had crossed the river on their way from Nagasaki to Edo – elephants and giraffes, tigers, sloths, orangutans, parakeets and peacocks.

'And camels,' he said, grinning in our direction. 'As affectionate as this young couple, snuggling into each other all night long. They say mandarin ducks are devoted, but your camel beats your duck every time.'

We had no opportunity for any affectionate behaviour as we slept in a room with Daisuke and two others. We did not bother unpacking our bedding but slept under our robes, using the pillow blocks provided by the tea house. It was a warm night, humid after the rain, and the old mosquito net kept out a few larger moths but did nothing to stop the clouds of mosquitoes whining and biting all night. I was glad to hear the cocks crow.

We left at first light. The flighty river had dwindled to a trickle and we crossed with dry sandals. At the domain border between Saga and Ōmura there was a guard post, manned by a solitary official and a handful of foot soldiers. He looked at our papers but did not search our luggage and waved us on without delay.

'They are more concerned with weapons coming out of Nagasaki,' Daisuke remarked as we descended the pass. He kept up a continual commentary on the towns we went through, the tea houses, the shrines, the views, this famous ancient pine tree, that miraculous healing spring, consulting his guidebooks from time to time but mostly speaking from memory. The words poured out of him in his lengthy convoluted sentences, each one as aggravating as last night's mosquitoes.

'I can't take this any longer,' Makino muttered at the foot of the climb up to the Warabi pass, and he signalled to the porters, pushed me into one palanquin and climbed into another himself. I took off my hat and veil, wiping the sweat from my face with my towel as the men took off at a brisk trot. Despite the heat and the unpleasant motion I revelled in the silence, which was broken only by the rhythmic shouts of the bearers.

But we couldn't afford to take palanquins all the way, and Daisuke made sure he caught up with us.

'I bet you're glad you didn't marry him,' Makino whispered to me that night as we lay side by side in another stuffy, mosquito-filled room.

'Now you know why I married you,' I teased him.

'I suppose I should be grateful to him. He made me seem like a good proposition. Though I don't know if you still think so.'

A kind of shame swept over me. 'I do,' I said in a low voice. For the first time I asked myself if Makino felt the same. Suddenly I saw what it would be like to lose him, not to war or disease, but if he did as he was entitled to – left me, divorced me. I did not want that to happen. I wanted us to grow old together, like my parents.

I will try to be a better wife. That was my resolve as I lay awake listening to the mosquitoes whining and the men snoring.

On the last morning of our journey Daisuke was delayed.

The Shōgun had finally taken brutal effect and he could not leave the privy.

'They should call that pill the Tairō,' Makino said in my ear. 'It's a great purgative.'

'You're in a good mood,' I commented, panting as we climbed, sure this final pass was the steepest yet.

'I'm excited about getting to Nagasaki. I suppose it's something I've always dreamed of.'

I felt the same. Nagasaki glowed in my imagination like some paradise of the West, a place of knowledge and learning. On the road we had passed many pilgrims going to Ise or making one of the many other sacred journeys, but we were also pilgrims, drawn to the shrines of medicine and science.

Finally we stood at the top of the Himi pass and gazed on the city, spread out below us. The afternoon sun glistened on the tiled roofs and the masts of ships, as thick as a forest of pines, in the harbour. Many different-coloured flags fluttered in the breeze.

'That must be Dejima,' Makino said, pointing at the fan-shaped island. The neat two-storey buildings with glass windows and green-painted frames and shutters looked inexpressibly foreign and exotic.

There were many bright red Chinese temples too, reminding me of Shimonoseki. As we descended the hill into the town there was the same tang of the sea, and all the other smells of a port town, the fish, raw and cooked, the human waste, and everywhere the fragrance of summer flowers. It seemed every garden grew hydrangeas, star jasmine and peppermint.

My brother had told us to wait for him at the horse station

near the *torii* of the Suwa shrine at the end of the road from Himi, near the confluence of the two rivers. He would meet us there and take us to his parents-in-law's house. Of course he did not know the exact time of our arrival, and there was no sign of him. The shrine itself stood in a grove of trees high on the slope. It was hot and humid; from the huge cedars came showers of cicada songs. Outside the *torii* was the usual crowd of pedlars, acrobats, medicine salesmen, street vendors and would-be guides. Their shouts and cries echoed around my ears making my head swim.

The horses stamped their feet and shook their heads, anxious to be free of their loads. We had managed to stay ahead of Daisuke since the morning, but now he pushed his way through the porters who were hovering hopefully around us.

'I know your brother's family well,' he said, waving flies away with one hand and clutching his medicine box with the other, while turning his back on anyone who seemed likely to ask him for money. 'Let me go to the house and tell him you've arrived. Wait here. O-Tsuru-san; move into the shade.'

Makino bought two cups of tea from a street seller. 'We'll never be rid of that fellow,' he grumbled, his eyes flicking around the scene, taking everything in. 'Hey, look at that. What a brilliant idea!'

An itinerant drug pedlar carried a large folding chest which contained a contraption to boil water so he could dispense samples of some powder or other dissolved in hot water. Its name was written in Dutch letters which I could not read.

Makino went off to try some and was deep in conversation with the pedlar when my brother arrived.

Tetsuya had lost some hair and put on weight; he looked more like our father than he used to.

'We met Hayashi-san on the road,' I explained after we had greeted each other warmly. 'Makino-san, my brother is here.'

Makino managed to get away from the pedlar, whose sales pitch became ever more persuasive. He bowed to Tetsuya, saying, 'We did meet once, on that unfortunate day. It is very good of you to assist us.'

'Not at all, not at all. You didn't see me at my best before. I've never been so frightened in my life,' Tetsuya admitted.

The horses were unloaded and porters hired to carry our luggage. Daisuke looked as if he was going to follow, but Tetsuya forestalled him. 'Thank you, Hayashi-san. I hope we see you again soon, but goodbye for now.'

'I'm afraid you have to be brisk with him,' he said to Makino. 'He's a good man, but once he starts talking he can waste half your day.'

I smiled to myself at this summing-up of Daisuke, but neither my husband nor I answered. Daisuke was irritating, but he had only been kind to us.

Our little procession set off through the narrow streets. At every corner there were glimpses of the glittering blue sea surrounded by the deep summer green of the mountains. The harbour was huge, deep and sheltered. No wonder it had been a hub of trade for centuries.

'What was that medicine called?' I asked Makino as Tetsuya strode ahead with the porters.

'*Uruyusu.*'

'Does that mean something?'

'I don't know. Ask your brother. He speaks Dutch, doesn't he?'

'What was it made of?'

'A bit of this, a bit of that. Mainly *daiō*, I suspect, a bit of China root, maybe some opium. Rather like the Cure-All.'

We both laughed. How distant those days seemed.

'I don't want to be a quack like that ever again,' Makino said. 'At last I can study real surgery and be of some use in a battle.'

'You did well enough at Ōda,' I said.

'Not really. There is so much more to learn.'

We finally came to the school where Tetsuya had studied for years and where he now lived as part of the family, having married his teacher's oldest daughter. It was called the Kusunokijuku after the huge camphor tree that grew on one side of the garden. It was a large building with many small rooms down one side for the students, a modern dispensary with all the latest equipment, where alembics steamed and two young men were chopping leaves and rolling pills, separate rooms for consulting and operations, a lecture and study room with many textbooks, some in Japanese and some in Dutch, on the shelves and in piles on the floor. On the wall of this room were pictures of the gods of medicine – Hakutaku, with his gently smiling face, his six horns and nine eyes, Shinnō, looking more stern, and a chart of human anatomy. Various instruments were also displayed. Tetsuya took down a microscope and showed it to us reverently.

'Siebold gave this to my teacher,' he said. 'He gave many presents to the Nagasaki doctors. They practically worship him, you know.'

'Have you ever met his daughter?' I said.

'Yes, I have, several times, when she was living in Nagasaki. As a matter of fact we attended Pompe's first dissection together.'

I tried to suppress my extreme envy as we were shown the rest of the house, the large kitchen, the living rooms for the family and the extensive garden with a well and many curious small shrines. There was the same smell as in our parents' house of boiling medicines, camphor and mint, but there was a lurking odour that was less pleasant.

'What's that smell?' I said to Tetsuya, hoping I wasn't offending him.

'What? Oh, it must be the ammonia pit. I hardly notice it any more.' Far from being offended he was quite proud of it. 'We make our own ammonia. I'll show you later. The pit's behind that wall. The neighbours complain about it, but really it's medical science. They should be grateful!'

'What's your method?' Makino asked.

'Dead animals, cats, dogs, ox heads, that sort of thing. That's what the shrines are for – thanks for the animals' lives. We bury their bodies until they are well rotted and then extract the fluids. Have you studied any chemistry?'

'Not enough,' Makino replied.

'The Dutch doctors teach it as the basis of all medicine.'

Makino was quite silent for the rest of the day, even when we met Tetsuya's new family. Yoshio Gongorō was a widower and Tetsuya's wife, O-Kimi, had run the household for many years. She was a few years older than my brother and had a brusque, direct manner, but she seemed to be genuinely fond of him and they already had one child, a big healthy boy of about nine months. Dr Yoshio was related to the famous Nagasaki family who had been physicians and Dutch scholars for years.

No one noticed Makino's silence but me. Dr Yoshio loved to talk; he was a little deaf and was in the habit of lecturing – his students, his son-in-law and now us. I didn't mind; I was tired after the journey and besides I could not hear enough about Siebold, especially from someone who had sat in the same room as him, heard him speak, watched him treat patients and helped him in his research.

The baby was playing with a stone amulet, holding it up to his mouth. It looked like the sort that was meant to alleviate deafness. Dr Yoshio saw me looking at it and laughed.

'One of my neighbours brought it back from Owari for me.'

'Father scolded him,' O-Kimi said, deftly retrieving the amulet when the baby dropped it. 'We are not supposed to believe in the power of such charms.'

'Well, look at it,' her father said, taking it from her. 'It's a stone. How can it possibly affect my ears which are flesh, blood, cartilage, membrane – part of an intricate system? Unless you hit me on the head with it or jam it in my ear hole!'

'If people have faith in charms it seems they can help them,' I ventured.

'Possibly in cases where the mind is affected,' he allowed grudgingly. 'But generally everyone would be better off if these old superstitions were eradicated. Putting a picture under your pillow or in your wallet will not save you from smallpox. But vaccination will. People must learn to trust modern medicine. Presumably you practise vaccination in your domain?'

'Yes, for many years,' I replied.

The baby began to cry and his grandfather placed the stone in his hands. 'Good for soothing children, but not much more.'

He turned to Makino and addressed him for the first time. 'What is your main interest?'

'Surgery, particularly in the field,' Makino replied.

'Eh? In the field?'

'Makino-san served with the *shotai* during the recent fighting in Chōshū,' Tetsuya explained loudly. 'He is here to study battle injuries and how to treat them.'

'Then the Dutch hospital is the place for you. Pompe and Bauduin are both army doctors. They were trained in the Military Medical College in Utrecht. Europe's been fighting wars unlike anything we've ever seen, with ferocious weapons. I suppose they'll come here in the end and we'll be able to kill each other in all sorts of new ways.'

We went on to talk about the Dutch in Nagasaki. Because his family had been connected with them for so many years Dr Yoshio knew everything about their history. He reminded us that the factory at Dejima had always had a doctor stationed there and many of these individuals, Willem ten Rhijne, Engelbert Kaempfer, Carl Pieter Thunberg, had had a lasting impact on our doctors and scholars. Philipp Franz von Siebold, who came to Japan in Bunsei 6 (1823), was the most famous. People flocked from all over Japan to study with him and watch him carry out treatments.

'He was a wonderful man,' Dr Yoshio said. 'There was something about him, a liveliness and warmth that drew people to him. Nothing was too much trouble for him. He seemed tireless.'

He told us about the school Siebold built at Narutaki, saying Tetsuya should take us there, and then we talked about the disastrous end to Siebold's stay in Japan. He accompanied the Dutch *kapitan* on his visit to Edo, where he met many more physicians and scholars. In Nagasaki he had had his students write reports for him on all aspects of Japanese society, he ordered paintings and models and many translations of books. He was a voracious collector of antiques, works of art, books – and maps. In Edo he managed to obtain maps of Japan from a Bakufu official, Takahashi Kageyasu. On his return to Nagasaki Siebold sent presents to Takahashi and others, together with a letter referring to the maps, and these fell into the hands of the Bakufu. Through a series of accidents, Siebold's ship was delayed long enough for his luggage to be searched. The maps were discovered along with many other forbidden items.

'He had to give up his precious maps,' the old man said. 'But knowing him I expect he copied them first!'

'Tell them what Siebold said,' O-Kimi prompted him.

'He was told it was a crime for foreigners to possess maps of Japan, so he replied, "Then I will become Japanese and there will be no crime!"' Dr Yoshio laughed till he wheezed. 'Imagine that – he thought anyone could become Japanese just like that!'

'What happened to Takahashi?' I asked.

'He died in prison. Some other people were executed, I think. Siebold was told he was never to return. He left a wife and child here. He didn't see them for thirty years. We were all terrified. I was only a young man then, barely twenty years old. There was a real crackdown on foreign learning. Siebold's students scattered, some went into hiding. Everything went very quiet until Mohnike arrived. He was another great man. He taught us how to vaccinate against smallpox, and brought the vaccine from Batavia. And the stethoscope – you may not have seen these but we use them here. Since then it's all been much easier. Pompe came and built the hospital – Dr Makino can go there tomorrow and arrange his studies – and now we have Bauduin. What a blessing Dejima turned out to be! The Dutch called it their prison, but for us it has been a window on the world.'

'And did Siebold ever see his wife and daughter again?'

Tetsuya said, 'He came back to Nagasaki a few years ago. The ban on him was lifted. O-Ine was working as a doctor then. She had her own clinic. When her father left the first time several of his students looked after her and educated her.'

'Looked after her in more ways than one,' O-Kimi said.

'What do you mean?' I asked.

'She had a child. She was living in the household of Ishii Sōken, part apprentice, part maid. People say he forced himself on her but who knows…'

'How terrible,' I said, truly shocked. 'She was his student, his teacher's daughter.'

'Perhaps she should have stayed home with her mother,' Tetsuya said.

'But she wanted to be a doctor!' I was aware that my voice was growing shrill.

'My sister helps my father a great deal,' Tetsuya said to Dr

Yoshio. 'She would like to be a real doctor.'

There was a note of disapproval in his voice that irritated me but I said nothing.

'Maybe O-Tsuru-san will help us in the dispensary,' O-Kimi said. 'There is always so much to do and the students are hopeless. They would much rather see patients than weigh out ingredients.'

I wanted to say 'So would I!' but I knew I would have to agree.

'O-Ine and her father didn't exactly get on when they met again,' O-Kimi said. The baby had fallen asleep against her knee.

'Problem of language really,' Tetsuya said. 'Her Dutch wasn't very good and he'd forgotten any Japanese he ever knew. They sorted it out in the end.'

'Is he still here?' I asked.

'He went to Edo and then back to Germany, I believe. His son by his German wife learned Japanese and is an interpreter in Edo.'

I wanted to ask much more but Dr Yoshio announced he was going to bed, and so the conversation ended.

'I don't even speak Dutch,' Makino confided in me later. We were assigned one of the small student rooms; it was stifling and the smell from the ammonia pit seemed even worse in the still night. At least the mosquito net was fairly new and had no tears in it and the bedding was clean. We spoke in whispers even though we were alone, aware of the students on either side.

'You can learn. Look how quickly you learned from my father.'

'I was younger then and much more motivated.'

'Don't tell me you are not still ambitious.'

'Your brother has been here for years, learning Dutch, apprenticed to Dr Yoshio. I could never catch up with him. They say Dutch is really difficult too.'

'Tetsuya will help you. He has textbooks, even dictionaries. He can translate for you.'

I tried to encourage my husband and eventually he fell asleep. I lay awake for a long time, the events of the day and the words of the evening's conversation going through my mind. How strong O-Ine must have been to continue with her studies after being abandoned by her father and raped by her teacher. I wondered if it was her father's foreign blood that gave her strength and courage. There was something about him that fascinated and appalled me. Men took wives in any country they found themselves in and had children, as easily as they took precious objects they had no right to, but abandoned them, it seemed, more carelessly.

My husband was going to study at the Western hospital while I repaid our obligation to my brother's family by making pills and weighing powders. O-Ine stood outside society in a way, by virtue of her education and her father's blood, but I was enmeshed in a web of obligations, to husband, brother, father. I had cut free once, but I did not think I was strong enough ever to do it again.

'Be patient,' Makino said next morning when I told him something of my feelings. 'I will do my best to obtain permission for you to attend lectures once I feel established myself.'

'Of course you must not do anything that will damage your prospects,' I said meekly.

He gave me a sharp look, suspecting sarcasm. I busied myself helping him dress in his best clothes – I had laid them out under the futon the night before to get the creases out – and trying not to strain his already frayed nerves. He could not eat, and when he left he was so pale I feared he might faint on the way.

The work of the Yoshio practice started early in the morning and went on all day. Though on a larger scale it was similar to the routine in my father's house, and once I had accustomed myself to it, learned where ingredients and utensils were kept and how Dr Yoshio and his daughter liked everything done, I found it easy enough. From the dispensary I could hear the patients describing their symptoms, Dr Yoshio's questions, his brief lecture to his students and then the diagnosis and prescription. While I weighed out ingredients and learned how to use the modern pestle and mortar and the pill-formers, I entertained myself by saying my own diagnosis and prescription under my breath. Once when Dr Yoshio's differed from mine I was shaking my head, and looked up to catch O-Kimi's disapproving expression. I felt the blood rise in my cheeks. Soon afterwards she corrected me about a measurement. I had used the wrong-sized spoon.

'Please be very careful. The amounts have to be exact,' was all she said, but I heard the message clearly enough. *Don't presume to know anything about medicine. You are not nor will you ever be a real doctor.*

Makino and Tetsuya returned from the hospital at the end of the afternoon. My husband had recovered his colour and his appetite. He took off his formal clothes and we walked together down to the public bathhouse while he told me about his day. An interpreter translated the lectures and he had been able to follow everything. Tetsuya spoke fluently to the Dutch doctor and the connection with him made everything easy. Tetsuya had translated many books for the hospital library and everyone had a high regard for him.

'It is the most marvellous opportunity for me,' he said earnestly. 'I must not waste it.'

'Of course you must not,' I said, resigning myself to years of grinding and mixing. Maybe one day I would be allowed to graduate to making ammonia. I could cut up dead animals. That would be interesting.

'I'm sorry to say there are no women among the students,' Makino said. 'I made a point of asking. There are some female nurses but they don't seem to be a very respectable class of women.'

'Maybe they need a Florence Nightingale,' I said, wondering if Florence Nightingale had a husband. Probably not. Briefly I saw myself reforming the nurses, but I did not really want to care for patients in that way. I wanted access to their bodies to satisfy my curiosity about how they worked. I wanted to look inside them one way or another, to cut them open.

'Do you know the first thing we were told today?' Makino said, coming to a halt at the bathhouse entrance. It was a popular time and the street was full of customers. I noticed blind masseurs calling out for clients, mothers with children, workmen and porters naked except for a loincloth. The distinctive smell of Nagasaki cooking with its Chinese spices and herbs wafted through the air.

'Apparently Pompe repeated it all the time. *The patient must always come first.* The Dutch doctor said if you do not believe this with your whole heart you should look for another profession.'

'I'm sure that's what my father has always believed,' I said, and I recalled my dream of Ogata Kōan. I felt a little uncomfortable, aware that I still did not really have their compassion for others.

'It made me question my motives,' Makino confessed. 'I thought of your father too. I fall far short of him. But when I remember the poor lads in the *shotai* I realise I did want to put them first, and even though I recognise my deficiencies in this area I believe I am in the right profession.'

He said this so seriously, standing there in his shabby *geta*, clutching his towel, his skinny legs emerging from the light cotton *yukata*, that I was torn between exasperation and affection.

'You don't want to change your mind now,' I said.

'I just hope I am capable of the effort required.'

Makino devoted himself entirely to this effort, at the hospital all day and studying until late in the night. I read the same books as he did and helped him memorise the new vocabulary in Dutch and Japanese. The hospital syllabus included physics, chemistry, physiology, pathology, internal medicine, eyes, surgery, obstetrics, forensics – all the way through to clinic management. Makino was practising with tourniquets, bone pinchers, thermometers and the stethoscope. He studied anatomy from replicas of the human body called *Kunstlijk*. We were learning things for which we had no words – until recently these words had not even existed in our mother tongue. Each one had to be freshly minted. Even the methods of teaching were new. Most of our teachers had always taught by rote, and students had to memorise vast slabs of text, but the Dutch doctors expected more independent thought and more analysis. Once he had learned Western numbers Makino had no difficulty with mathematics, for he had always done arithmetic in his head without relying on the abacus, but I found the numbers hard, especially the large ones, for we counted with a different system after ten thousand.

The Dutch language seemed impenetrable. Tetsuya spoke it well but now he was learning English at the language school that had been established by the Bakufu not far from Sakuramachi.

'English is the language of the future,' he told us. 'It is spoken throughout Britain and North America and everyone in Europe is learning it now.'

Maybe we did so badly with Dutch because we both felt we should have been learning English instead. Makino would have liked to go to the English school too but there was simply not enough time in the day – *hours in the day* I should say, for along with everything else Makino and the other students had to follow Western time, with its strict division of the day into hours of equal length. Lectures began at *eight o'clock* in the morning and lasted for *four hours*. Our old way of marking the passage of time through day and night began to seem vague and unreliable. Tetsuya lent my husband a small watch like the one he had given our father. I thought it was well named, for it demanded that you watch it throughout the day.

There were already many English and Americans in Nagasaki. Their flags flew on the ships in the harbour, sailors drank in the bars and even began to frequent the pleasure quarters of Maruyama. An American, Verbek, taught at the language school, and everyone knew the most famous British merchant, Thomas Glover.

In fact Mr Glover was to be the first foreigner I ever spoke to, and that came about through Inoue Monta. Katsura and Shiraishi had spoken to us in Shimonoseki about our domain's need to rearm, and in the seventh month of that year, the first year of Keiō (1865), Katsura sent Inoue with Itō to Nagasaki to buy arms from Glover. They came under assumed names, posing as samurai from Satsuma. Weapons were to be purchased from Glover, in Satsuma's name, with the assistance of Sakamoto Ryōma. Despite the failure of the meeting between Katsura and Saigō, the two domains were growing closer.

Monta came to call at Dr Yoshio's house. It was one of the days of rest near the end of the seventh month. Most of the students had gone with Dr Yoshio on a shrine visit. Makino had stayed behind to study and I was as usual making pills, close enough to the entrance to recognise Monta's voice when he asked for us. I hurried out to greet him, but he made a sign that I should say nothing, and when the maid had gone, said, 'I can't talk here, but come and join Itō and me.'

He named a tea house in Nishibama, said, 'Ask for Yamada Shinsuke. See you there,' and disappeared again.

It was still very hot, though as the eighth month grew closer there was a slight hint of autumn in the air. I was eager to go out for we had hardly seen anything of the city. Makino agreed reluctantly.

'We can't really refuse,' he said. 'I wonder what they want from us.'

'What do you mean?'

'Well, I don't suppose it's just a friendly get-together to talk about old times.'

Monta was already in the tea house when we were shown into a private room. I forget the name of the place, but it was built over the water and was pleasantly cool. He greeted us and then remarked that we both looked very tired.

'It's been hot,' I replied. 'And we have been working hard.'

Monta himself looked well despite the scars, which were still a little inflamed. It was less than a year since the attack. He seemed to have regained his old restless energy. There was no sign of Itō – Yoshimura Sōzō, as Monta told us we must remember to call him. Monta occupied himself with ordering sake and side dishes from the maid, which involved a certain amount of flirting on both sides.

The sake arrived at the same time as Itō and another man whom I recognised instantly, even though his hat was pulled down to hide his face. I was more prepared for the resemblance this time and I knew it was Sakamoto.

'We met briefly in Shimonoseki a few weeks ago,' he said as he removed his hat, but neither Makino nor I addressed him by name, not knowing if he was still calling himself Saitani.

Itō greeted us with great warmth and at once started reminiscing about old times – the battles at Ōda and Edō and our voyage to Hagi. They both had to explain the whole campaign for Sakamoto's benefit, using the sake flasks and cups as models for the *shotai*. The Tosa man's eyes glittered with envy, for at that time he had never been in a fight.

Inoue related his adventures while he was in hiding in Beppu, his encounters with a gambling boss and how he thought an old samurai was planning to marry him to his daughter.

'We were in the *onsen* and he asked how I got the scars. Jealous husband, I told him!'

Lowering their voices they talked about *geiko*, Takasugi's lover, O-Uno, and the woman who would become Itō's wife, O-Ume. After a few cups of sake my husband relaxed and joined in with stories of his own of weapons used and the wounds they caused, amputations he had done in the field, the men saved or lost, our pressing need not only for arms but also for medical supplies.

I said very little and the men ignored me. I had gone into something of a reverie, recalling how I had sat in a tea house with Genzui, Katsura, Takasugi and Shinsai, and how much more interesting it had been to be a man among men. Finally Monta broke into my thoughts by saying to me, 'That's all arranged. Let's go to Mr Glover's house now.'

'What's arranged?' I said.

'Your husband's going to explain what you need to Mr Glover. You can come too – he likes meeting Japanese women. And we'll pick up the painting on the way.'

'The painting?'

'The Chikuden. What's it called? Something about plum blossoms. Katsura went to your house to see it and your father said you'd brought it with you. Katsura thought you might present it to Mr Glover as a sign of our appreciation.'

He glanced at my astonished face and laughed. 'It's the Chōshū spy network. You didn't think you were going to outwit us, did you?'

'I wasn't trying to outwit anyone! But the picture belongs to my father.'

'That's all sorted out. He was going to give it to Katsura anyway.'

There was nothing I could do or say, except tell Makino where the painting was and wait for him to bring it back to the tea house before we made our way to Minamiyamate.

'What did I tell you?' he whispered to me. 'I hope that's all they want.'

It already seemed excessive to me.

Mr Glover had built his house on the southwestern side of the bay looking out over the harbour. It was called Ipponmatsu. The sun had set when we arrived and the sky was luminous and pearly. The grey-painted house reflected this colour, and seemed bathed in it. The garden was spacious beneath the old pine that gave the house its name, and beautiful with a mixture of local and exotic flowers heavy with scent in the evening air. But the wide open views across the harbour made me almost dizzy and I felt as though the whole world was peering in at me.

Monta told me that this sort of house was called a bungalow and the English built them wherever they came to live in the East, in Hong Kong or Shanghai – and now there was one here. I thought it a completely Western creation, but in fact like the garden it was a mixture: the roof structure was traditionally Japanese and the house had many Japanese attributes. And Mr Glover had a Japanese wife.

Mr Glover was tall and well built with a luxuriant moustache. At first I was so smitten by shyness that I hardly dared look at him, but he seemed to be the right size for his house and I thought his piercing eyes beneath the thick eyebrows would not be dazzled by the views.

His wife brought tea, sake and whisky. I had never tasted whisky and was keen to try it, but found it too strong and fiery. After one drink Makino and I both turned to sake. Inoue and Itō downed glass after glass of whisky.

'We got into the habit in England,' Itō said.

They both spoke English to Mr Glover, though he understood quite a lot of Japanese. For a while the conversation went along in both languages, as they translated for the benefit of Makino, Sakamoto and myself. It was mainly talk of their mutual acquaintances, the employees of Jardine Matheson who had helped the five young men go to London, what the others were doing there and when they planned to return. Glover told us about the Satsuma students he had helped leave for England in one of his ships just a few weeks before.

'Satsuma always follows Chōshū,' Monta said.

'Yes, we were there first!' Itō said.

'Satsuma sent many more students, nineteen or so, and they seemed very well organised,' Glover observed in Japanese, well aware of how this mild praise would irritate the Chōshū men.

'Typical Satsuma, copy and overkill,' Monta muttered.

'But we are going to be friends now,' Itō reminded him. 'Isn't that right, Sakamoto-san?'

'There is no other alternative,' Sakamoto said quietly.

'You should listen to Sakamoto-san,' Glover said. 'You both know what he says makes sense.' He pointed out that Chōshū and Satsuma had a lot in common, they had experienced the devastating power of Western weapons at Shimonoseki and Kagoshima, and they had similar reasons to resent the failing but still repressive Bakufu.

'The enemy of my enemy is my friend,' he said, filling up the glasses. 'Let's drink to that!'

We all raised our glasses in a Western-style toast and chorused, 'To my enemy's enemy!'

When he had finished his glass, Mr Glover said, 'What's the news of Takasugi?'

'He went to Shikoku with O-Uno,' Monta replied. 'There's

been a bit of opposition to opening Shimonoseki, and he seemed to be in some danger.'

'Look after him. He's one of your greatest assets.'

Itō told us how he and Takasugi had been to see Mr Glover earlier that year. Takasugi wanted to go to England but Glover had persuaded him he was needed in Chōshū.

Monta took this opportunity to broach the real purpose of the visit. 'We need Takasugi, no question about that, but above all we need more weapons.'

'I am sure that can be arranged,' Glover said. 'The Bakufu has forbidden sales of arms to Chōshū, but we will deal through Sakamoto's company, and will make out the bill of sale to Satsuma. Everyone is in agreement on that. Saigō Takamori has given his permission and the weapons will be delivered to Shiraishi in Shimonoseki. He already trades with Satsuma.' He smiled in genuine delight. 'Very neat. Everybody wins. Just the sort of business I like.' He put out his hand and the three men shook it one after the other. It was the first handshake I had seen.

Makino had carried the painting from the Yoshio house. It lay beside him on the carpet, still wrapped in the silk kimono, with an outer covering of hemp, tied with red cords.

Now Monta said, 'Katsura-dono has sent a gift as a sign of our domain's deep gratitude to Mr Glover. Mrs Makino brought it from her father's house. O-Tsuru-san, would you unwrap it for Mr Glover?'

'O-Tsuru? That's my wife's name,' Mr Glover said, beaming.

I smiled but said nothing as I began to unknot the cords. I had never dreamed when my fingers had fastened them that I would be undoing them in these surroundings. I would not have been able to imagine that such a place existed. But when the painting was unrolled and I saw it in the lamp-light, its silvery tones echoing the colour of the walls, I was not sorry that it would hang here.

'It is called *Fragrant Plum Blossoms, Unknown Shadow*,' I said, and told him what I knew of the artist, Tanomura Chikuden, and his life.

Mr Glover was silent for a few moments as if awestruck – he knew enough to appreciate such a gift – before he began to express his thanks.

Monta was as gratified as if he had owned the picture himself. 'Mrs Makino is the daughter, sister and wife of doctors. She knows a great deal about medicine and surgery. She and her husband have a few things they need.'

'Let me know what you want and I will order everything for you from London or Hong Kong,' Glover said without hesitation.

'They will send you a list,' Monta said, smiling in satisfaction.

Mr Glover then began to question my husband about his studies at the hospital and his experience in battle. Ōda and Edō were fought once again, this time with whisky glasses. Monta appealed to me at one stage for verification of the number of casualties, and Mr Glover looked up in surprise.

'Mrs Makino was present during a battle.'

'She helped look after the wounded,' Itō explained.

'As a doctor or a nurse?' Mr Glover enquired.

'Something of both,' I said. 'Not quite a doctor, but more than a nurse.'

He did not fully understand. 'You have female doctors in this country?'

'Not really.' I tried to explain. 'But sometimes doctors' daughters help out. We learn a lot, we treat patients, we know how to make up medicines.'

'My wife is a very skilled doctor and pharmacist,' Makino said. 'At home she works alongside her father but it's different here in Nagasaki. Despite the example of Kusumoto Ine, Siebold's daughter, there are no female doctors, and my wife cannot be accepted by the hospital as a student as I have been.'

'She certainly wouldn't be accepted as a student of medicine or anything else in my country,' Mr Glover said. 'But if she were a nurse, that would be different.'

'Like Florence Nightingale,' I said.

He laughed. 'So the great lady's fame has even reached Japan! You should learn a lesson from her, Mrs Makino. Vastly more men died from disease than were killed by weapons in the war in Crimea, and in the recent war between the North and the South in America disease is the greatest enemy, especially dysentery and typhoid. If you want to save the lives of your countrymen, emulate Miss Nightingale and set up a nursing system with cleanliness and hygiene your first aims. Clean up the streets, get refuse cleared away and dig proper latrines.' Glover had reverted to English for this speech and was getting quite carried away. Itō and Inoue were having trouble keeping up.

'Did you not encounter disease in your recent civil war?' Glover addressed Makino, switching back to Japanese.

'Compared to the war in America it hardly deserves the

name,' Makino replied. 'It was small scale and short-lived. It was still winter; we had little disease apart from coughs and colds.'

'What about gangrene?'

'There were no cases in the civil war. But after the bombardment of Shimonoseki there were some deaths from what must have been gangrene.'

'Well, war is changing,' Glover said, filling the whisky glasses again. 'Railways can carry many more men and matériel to the battlefields; the telegraph transmits information instantly. And weapons become ever more efficient. New rifles, Enfields, breech loaders, a new field gun called the Gatling – that would suit your small-scale encounters. And handguns, like this Colt.'

He brought out a small pistol with a polished wooden handle and a revolving cylinder. 'It's a six-shot,' he explained. 'Very handy in a tight corner. Much better than a sword. You don't have to get so close!'

'We like our swords,' Monta said smiling. 'We like to see the enemy when we kill him.'

Glover looked at his scars and shuddered. 'Brutal weapons,' he said. 'It's not surprising you fellows scare the hell out of the foreign community.'

Sakamoto had been silent for a long time. Now he said, 'We will switch to guns and become civilised like you.' He picked up the Colt and studied it. 'I like it,' he said quietly. 'It would defeat any swordsman.'

Shortly afterwards Makino said we should go. It was getting late and we both had to be up before dawn. We left the others to conclude their negotiations. Mr Glover accompanied us to the entrance and arranged for one of his servants to show us the way home. Then he held out his hand in the Western way to say goodbye.

'I can't thank you enough for the picture. I hope you will come and see it when it is hung.'

I wanted to be a modern woman, so I made myself take his hand. It was surprisingly hot.

Thank you,' I said. I didn't mind leaving the picture there. It was a beautiful setting for it and I couldn't help liking Mr Glover, he was so open and enthusiastic. And in return we would get the supplies we needed.

'Good luck with your studies, Dr Makino. You have chosen a noble profession.'

Makino rubbed his hand on his robe as we walked after the servant, following the light of his lantern.

'What did you think of him?' I said.

'He must be making a great deal of money,' Makino replied.

'He's very charming.'

'I couldn't help thinking it's ironic that we'll be treating wounds caused by his weapons with medicines supplied by him.'

'But we'll have the best weapons, and anyway we won't be looking after the enemy.'

'Glover's probably supplying them too. And if he isn't, someone else will. If it's not the English it will be the French or the Russians. Anyway, the Dutch doctors teach that we should look after enemy prisoners with as much care as our own wounded.'

'That hardly makes sense,' I replied. 'Wouldn't it be easier just to kill them?'

'They are humans like us. And if we fight the Bakufu army they are our countrymen.'

In those days when people used the word *country*, they usually meant their domain or province, so for a moment I didn't understand what my husband meant.

'We have to start thinking of ourselves as one country – Japan,' Makino explained. 'One nation under the Emperor. We don't want to fight a terrible civil war like the one in America – hundreds of thousands of men killed or left with disfiguring and disabling wounds. They talk about it a lot at the hospital. We must not inflict that on our country.'

I thought about his words as I lay restless in bed, my head spinning and my stomach sour from the whisky. Strange visions passed before my eyes, mocking me like a crowd of goblins: Mr Glover, so charming, so ready to sell arms or medicines, it didn't matter to him; my need to be taught compassion by my husband the Accountant; and the war between my domain and the government. It hung over us like the unknown shadow. It could not be avoided, but no one knew when it would start.

PHOTOGRAPHY

Inoue and Itō returned to Chōshū but we had no news from them or from anyone else for the rest of the year. My parents sent letters, but they were all of family life and my father's practice. They did not dare write about politics. In any case there was little to write about other than that the Bakufu preparations for war dragged on and on. The letters made me want to go home. I was exhausted by the gruelling routine of work and study, by being at the bottom of the social hierarchy in Dr Yoshio's house and at the command of everyone. At least at home I could help my father and treat my own patients. I missed Michi. Even though she was not my daughter yet I yearned for her. I did not want her to be too old when she came to us, for she would grieve for her mother and be unhappy. But it seemed my duty to my husband, and the obligation I was fulfilling on his behalf kept me trapped in Nagasaki.

Everyone was on edge. The number of foreigners in the port grew weekly. There were brawls and quarrels every night. The people of Nagasaki were torn between their desire to make money from entertainment and trade and their fear that they faced the foreigners with no protection from the Bakufu. People complained that law and order were breaking down in the same breath as grumbling about spies and informers everywhere.

It rained incessantly through autumn and winter. Nagasaki was not as cold as Hagi or Kyōto but the wind off the sea was chilling and the flimsy houses, built to cope with the heat of summer, became icy. O-Kimi was as careful with charcoal as she was with everything else, and the feeble warmth from the braziers did little to heat the inside of the building. I had chilblains on toes and fingers, my hands were always chapped, and the damp air made me cough at night, keeping me awake.

The preparations for the end of the year were even more exhausting. The whole place had to be swept and scrubbed, all the books had to be made up, the stock taken, before the New Year. On the first day we were able to rest a little, and plenty of spiced sake and rice cakes were provided for us, all the students and the rest of the household, but the dust from the cleaning had aggravated my cough and I spent an uncomfortable day.

The year was the second of Keiō, 1866. When Makino and I talked about the coming months it was clear that he had decided he would return to Chōshū as soon as war began – less clear was when that would be. In the meantime he doubled his efforts to make the most of the time left in Nagasaki.

Towards the end of the second month I had a visitor who brought some real news. It was the artist Eikaku, whom I had last seen in Mitajiri before I had run away with Shinsai. He came to the Yoshio house on what felt like the first real day of spring. There was a gentle breeze from the east and the cherry blossoms were beginning to open, their petals all the fresher for the winter's drenching.

I was both delighted and appalled to see him: delighted

because of my abiding fondness for him, appalled and alarmed because of how much he knew about me. He was completely unpredictable, there was no knowing what he might reveal. I did not want to think of that episode in my life. I did not want to remember Shinsai. But just the sight of Eikaku in his flamboyant paint-stained clothes awakened the grief that always lay dormant.

'Doctor!' he greeted me, making my sister-in-law's lips tighten. 'What's been happening to you? You look terrible. Have you been sick?'

He slipped out of his sandals and stepped up into the house. 'She doesn't look after herself,' he said to O-Kimi. 'I suppose she's been working too hard. She's too devoted to her patients. You must take care of her; she's an irreplaceable gem.'

He pushed past O-Kimi, saying, 'Fetch us some tea, there's a good woman,' and settled down on the matting with a huge sigh and I believe a surreptitious fart. 'That's better. What a terrible journey. The sooner we get the railroad like a civilised country the better, in my opinion. But how would they get up those fearful hills? I suppose tunnels are the answer, to penetrate through the very heart of the mountain.'

I interrupted him before he could expound any further on the problems of the railroad.

'Why are you here?' I sat down next to him. I had been working since before dawn and to sit still for a moment and have a cup of tea, for O-Kimi had gone meekly off to the kitchen to bring hot water, seemed very appealing.

'Photography!' Eikaku announced. 'It is the art of the future and I have to learn how to do it.'

I knew the word and I had noticed photographs in Mr Glover's house. I had also seen photographers around Nagasaki, pointing their wooden box-like apparatus towards ships in the harbour or a shrine festival or a street scene, standing motionless for many moments, their heads and shoulders draped in black cloth. Sometimes boys threw stones at them and women crossed the road to avoid them. People believed photography stole something from your essence and made you sick.

Pompe had given lessons in photography when he had been in Nagasaki, and I knew its basis was in chemistry, like medicine. Makino had told me that many doctors were interested in photography as a way of recording patients' bodies and symptoms.

All this ran through my head while we waited for O-Kimi to return. Eikaku took out a tobacco box and lit a pipe with a spill from the brazier. I was longing for a smoke and starting to wonder if my sister-in-law was going to bring tea or not, so I went to see where she was, fetching my own pipe on the way.

She waylaid me outside the kitchen.

'Shall I call your brother? Or should we get the police?'

'What for?'

'The madman. He is mad, isn't he?'

'Only mildly. And not always. He has cycles. He seems quite sane at the moment. He was a patient of mine in Shimonoseki.'

Her expression suggested that little else could be expected either from Shimonoseki or from me.

'I'll give him some tea and then I'll take him out,' I said.

'But what about your work? Who's going to do that if you're off with some madman?'

My brother appeared at the end of the passage where the washbowl stood and heard her raised voice.

'What's the matter?' He came towards us, wiping his hands.

'A lunatic has come to see O-Tsuru. It was bad enough having that suspicious man coming to the house, but this one – really! He was so rude!'

'Oniisan, he's quite harmless. He's an artist – and famous too. He says he wants to study photography. Where shall I tell him to go?'

Tetsuya had been blinking his eyes rapidly at his wife's tirade and he now seemed grateful to be able to answer my question factually.

'To Ueno-san, I suppose. It's not far, on the Nakajima River.'

'I'll go with him, if it's all right.'

'I suppose we can spare you for a little while. But will you be safe?'

'Of course I will,' I replied, so sharply that it made me start coughing. As I struggled for breath I thought Eikaku was far less likely to do me harm than the daily drudgery of the Yoshio household which was ruining my lungs and which my brother never thought to comment on.

I took the hot water and tea myself and with my pipe tucked under my arm went back to the front room, where Eikaku was rubbing his feet.

'I don't suppose you'd give me a massage, Doctor? I'm aching all over.'

'Maybe we can find someone for you,' I said, for Dr Yoshio

had several blind masseurs he sent patients to. 'Now drink some tea while I have a smoke and then we'll go and see Mr Ueno.'

'Ueno Hikoma!' Eikaku exclaimed. 'That's the man!'

'You've heard of him?'

'Oh yes, he's famous. I've even read some of his writing.' He struck a pose and declaimed, '*The Technique of Photography*. Do you remember the photographer at Maeda? Oh no, that was the second attack, you weren't there. Anyway, he's a colleague of Hikoma. His name is Beato. I wanted to talk to him but it was the middle of a war, not the best time.'

'But what about your painting?' I said. 'What about your depictions of hell?'

'Oh, photography will show a vaster hell than any of my imaginings,' he replied, filling his pipe again.

'Well, tell me the news,' I said, as he puffed silently. 'Did you come straight from Shimonoseki?'

'I went first to Dazaifu to pay my respects to our dear friends, Prince Sanjō and the others.' Eikaku had lost none of his admiration for the noblemen who had been forced to leave Chōshū as part of the settlement after the Bakufu's first campaign.

'I hope they are all well.'

'Your poor patient died, you know? The other five remain together, an inspiration to us all. They are well enough for exiles and prisoners. They are impatient – but they will not have to wait too much longer.'

'Don't talk too loudly,' I said, for I was sure my sister-in-law would be trying to listen to us.

'This I will whisper,' Eikaku replied. 'This is for your ears only.' He leaned towards me and said in a tiny voice, 'Katsura signed an agreement with Saigō Takamori in Kyōto. Satsuma will not join the Bakufu and will not attack Chōshū. They have made an alliance against the Tokugawa.'

I lit my own pipe again. So it had finally happened. Whatever his failings, whatever my personal dislike for him, I had to admire Katsura for this achievement.

'I suppose Sakamoto had something to do with it,' I said as quietly as Eikaku.

'I believe so. They would have talked themselves to a standstill but he pushed them into signing. Then the next day the poor fellow was attacked in the Teradaya in Fushimi.'

'He's not dead?' Shock made me speak too loudly.

'Sshh.' Eikaku held up his hand. 'No, he was wounded, but not fatally. Luckily he had a pistol. Takasugi Shinsaku sent it to him. He sent a fan and a poem too, but it was the pistol that saved his life. And his mistress, O-Ryō. She ran up the back stairs and warned him. That's dramatic, isn't it? Miyoshi Shinzō was with him. You know him – he's a friend of Shiraishi's. That's how I know all this, from Shiraishi.'

'Where is Sakamoto-san now?'

'Saigō Takamori whisked him away to Satsuma to recover. He married O-Ryō and took her with him.'

'Just like a play,' I said.

Eikaku puffed away, looking at me shrewdly.

'I suppose you don't want to talk about your own drama?' he said.

'Only if you have news of the other actor,' I replied after a moment.

'I've never seen him again nor heard of anyone who has.'

'Then let's not speak about it,' I said, but seeing Eikaku had brought back all my memories of Shinsai.

'Come on,' Eikaku said. 'Let's go and see Mr Ueno. I hope it's not too far – my feet are extremely sore.'

As we left the house I thought I saw Hayashi Daisuke at the corner of the street. Despite the warm spring air he was wearing a hat pulled low over his eyes, and to my surprise, though I was sure he had seen me, he ducked away down an alley to avoid crossing paths. I was more relieved than anything else for I did not want to waste time in one of his endless conversations and I thought no more about it. I was more concerned with telling Eikaku about an idea I'd had while working with the pestle and mortar in the pharmacy and listening to Dr Yoshio's diagnoses. So many of the ailments were comparatively trivial and could be cured by prepared medicines of one sort or another – but none of the patients knew which one to choose out of the hundreds available.

'We could make charts,' I told Eikaku, 'matching symptoms, diagnosis and medicines. But they would need to be illustrated in such a way that even uneducated people could comprehend them. People don't understand what's happening inside their own bodies. They see themselves as part of the world of the *kami*, influenced by black magic or spirit possession. My charts would free them from superstition.'

'Superstition is not such a bad thing,' Eikaku replied. 'And magic and possession are perfectly real.'

'But if people understand their bodies and and their processes they will know how to treat their own illnesses.'

'It sounds very rational and sensible, and therefore does

not interest me in the slightest,' Eikaku said, dismissing my idea with a wave of his hand.

'You could paint boils and suppurations,' I pleaded. 'Rashes, injuries, deformities, and all the internal organs in various states of health or decay.'

'Maybe I could take photographs.'

'But I need colour. The inside of the body is brightly coloured. Think of all those shades of red and pink. You love those colours!'

'It's true that photography shows only black and white,' Eikaku said. 'But colour will soon come – how can it not? And even now many people hand-colour photographs afterwards.'

I recalled his single-mindedness. Once he had an idea in his head there was no shifting it.

'Well, maybe one day,' I said. 'While I'm here I've no time for anything anyway.'

'What are you doing here?' Eikaku said. 'You don't seem to be having a very good time.'

'I'm working in Dr Yoshio's household – he's Tetsuya's father-in-law – while my husband studies at the Western hospital.'

'Have you any interesting mad patients like me?'

'I don't have any patients at all. I'm just helping out in the pharmacy.'

Eikaku said nothing for a few moments as we crossed over the stone bridge in front of the great flagged stairway that led to the Suwa shrine.

'No wonder you look exhausted,' he said finally. 'Why are you doing it?'

I found myself getting angry. 'I'm a woman. It's what women do. We have no lives of our own. We just look after men. Like your sister, who devotes herself to you so you can paint.'

'My sister is dead.' He stopped suddenly and gazed down the river towards the harbour. 'She died a few weeks ago. That's partly why I came away. I was getting depressed. The house is so empty.'

'I'm sorry,' I said. 'I liked her very much.'

'Yes, the general opinion is that she was a very good woman, much too good for me.' He nodded his head once or twice, lips pursed. He gave a deep sigh, then resumed his brisk pace.

'Why don't you run away?' he said. 'You did before.'

'That did not turn out well,' I replied. 'My husband wanted me to come back and…well, he is my husband. His work will be important and useful. He serves our domain and I serve him.'

'It's all a mess,' Eikaku said, but cheerfully. 'Whatever way you look at it, human life's a mess.'

'We are all hoping for a new world. Will we see that? Will things change?'

Eikaku snorted dismissively. By this time we had come to the Nakajima River and we turned left to follow it upstream. The Ueno studio stood on the slope, set back from the riverbank, which had been built up with stone walls. The river, swollen by the winter rains, raced over boulders, chattering to itself like a living being. Broken branches, uprooted reeds and other debris were strewn along its edges, sometimes almost as high as the top of the wall. The river smelled of mud and manure and beneath that I caught a familiar stench like the one that hung around the Yoshio house. Mr Ueno was obviously making his own ammonia.

We were met at the gate by a servant in short jacket and leggings who asked us to wait just inside as the master was taking a photograph.

'Maybe we can watch?' Eikaku said eagerly, and we went quietly forward, stopping by a small deutzia shrub which partly concealed us. At the front of the house, the southern side, a strange room had been constructed with no roof and only one wall, painted white with a wooden panel along it at waist height. The floor was covered in a carpet-like material. A woman stood patiently, propped against a small chest. Her face was powdered white and she held herself rigidly still. On the other side was the photographer, his camera on a stand pointing at his subject. We all stood frozen. I was holding my breath as if my slightest movement would spoil the result.

After what seemed like a very long time the photographer emerged from his black tent. 'That's it,' he said. 'You can move now.'

The servant ran forward and helped the woman extricate herself from a neck brace that had been holding her head still. She turned her neck and shoulders carefully. 'Ah, I'm stiff,' she said. Then she saw us and called, 'Mr Ueno! Customers!'

The photographer turned towards us. He was a thin man with a lively, intelligent face.

'You've come to have your photograph taken? It's a good day for it – as long as the sun stays out. I have to work outdoors – the sun is the only light bright enough. But you'll have to wait while I deal with this picture.'

'Can we watch?' Eikaku said, but he spoke to Mr Ueno's back as the photographer hurried inside.

'It can be dangerous,' the servant said. 'Mr Ueno doesn't allow anyone to watch – some photographers have set fire to themselves or blown themselves up.'

'How wonderful,' Eikaku murmured.

The woman, who must have been Ueno's wife, asked if we would like to wait inside and we followed her into the house. In the entrance hall various props for photography sessions were stored – neck and arm supports and Western-style chairs. She showed us into the waiting room and we sat down on the tatami.

'Could we see some of the master's work?' Eikaku asked.

She said she would bring some prints and left the room for a few moments.

'This new method is so good,' she said when she came back, 'he can make several copies. But you have to develop while the collodion is still wet so it's always rather a rush. The old way, the daguerreotype, you could only make one.'

'Like a painting,' Eikaku remarked. 'But that is so old-fashioned. Photography is so modern.'

'Is the gentleman an artist?' she asked, looking at his paint-stained clothes.

'I have been. But after photography – will I ever paint again?'

A doubtful look crossed her face as she began to unwrap the pictures.

'My husband does not take students,' she said. 'We already have enough apprentices among our own family. But he is always looking for clients. You see, there is not much work yet, and the materials are very expensive.'

'Oh.' Eikaku sat for a moment looking downcast. 'But I have come all the way from Shimonoseki!'

'Really?' Mrs Ueno tried to divert Eikaku's attention to the photographs. 'This gentleman is from Shimonoseki, I believe.'

Three men sat on the ground, all with serious expressions, staring downwards. Now I knew the procedure it was clear they were trying to keep still. Eikaku looked at them, pouting.

'Good heavens! It is Itō!' he exclaimed. 'Doctor, you know him. Itō Kyūzō from the *honjin*.'

I recognised him – I had often seen him at Shiraishi's. And I knew the man in the middle of the group too. It was unmistakably Sakamoto Ryōma.

Eikaku of course did not know him by sight and I did not want to mention his name. I could not take my eyes off the photograph. I was amazed at such a likeness. It was almost like seeing a ghost.

Mrs Ueno showed us the other pictures: a woman in geisha costume, a Western sailor, landscapes and street scenes. I told Eikaku I had walked down that street, stood on that bridge, visited that shrine. It made me feel curiously excited as though these colourless images made my existence more real.

Then came another portrait of three men. My eyes fell on Takasugi in the centre, his hands, a fan in one of them, resting on his thighs, his long face 'more like the horse than the rider', his eyes half-closed. Next to him stood Itō Shunsuke, looking pleased with himself as usual, and kneeling on Takasugi's other side a young boy whose name I did not know.

'These men are also from Chōshū, I believe,' Mrs Ueno said, 'though I couldn't tell you their names. Well, half of them use assumed names in Nagasaki anyway.'

She left to fetch the tea. I quickly turned back to the first photograph.

'This is Sakamoto-san,' I whispered to Eikaku.

'It is? What a fine-looking fellow.'

We both gazed at the picture. I was thinking of the skirmish in the Teradaya and the wounds Sakamoto would have received, how they might have been treated, where he was now and if he was recovering.

'Well.' Eikaku sighed. 'It is a miracle.'

'And these, I know these men too. This is Takasugi Shinsaku. He has an illness not unlike yours.'

Eikaku peered at the photograph. 'I bow to you, my fellow sufferer,' he said. 'And who is this good-looking young man?'

'That's Itō Shunsuke.'

'Mmm. He has the face of a womaniser. They both do.'

'They both love women.'

Mrs Ueno came back with a tray of tea things and I asked her when the photograph was taken.

'About a year ago, I think. You can see the floor covering is quite new.'

A year had passed. Takasugi and Itō were a year older, the boy would have grown into a man, yet in the photographs they remained the same. I searched through the pictures again, scrutinising every face. The idea had suddenly come to me that Shinsai would be among them. I was no longer certain that I remembered what he looked like. It was desolating. I saw how photographs might be exciting and consoling and at the same time unbearably sad. They were indeed like ghosts.

While we were drinking the tea the room grew darker and suddenly we heard the sound of rain on the roof. There was a scurry of running feet and a clattering as the outdoor furniture was hurriedly shifted inside.

Mr Ueno came to the door. 'I'm sorry, the weather's turned against us. Can you come back another day? It would be a pleasure to take a photograph of yourself and your wife.'

'Oh, she's not my wife,' Eikaku said. 'And we don't want our photograph taken – that is, I've no objection but unfortunately I have no money. I've come, all the way from Shimonoseki on foot, to ask you to teach me the art of photography.'

'I'm afraid that is quite impossible. I don't take any students, and besides you are too old.'

'Too old?' Eikaku echoed in surprise.

'Yes, photography is a young man's profession. Only young brains can assimilate all the knowledge of chemistry that is required and only young hands have the necessary dexterity and swiftness. My wife tells me you are an artist. Stick to what you know, my dear sir, that's my advice to you. Now I must leave you. I have a great deal of work to do. But please have some more tea before you go.'

Mr Ueno had a charming manner, but it was obvious he was a man who never did anything he did not want to. Eikaku drank his tea in silence. I thought he had accepted the situation, but it turned out he was planning his next move. When the rain eased and we left, after apologising to Mrs Ueno, I went down the steps to the riverbank. When I turned back there was no sign of Eikaku. I ran back up the steps to find him squatting on his heels just inside the gate.

'What are you doing? Come on, we have to go.'

'I will stay here until he accepts me as a pupil,' he said calmly.

'Don't be silly. You aren't in some sort of medieval drama. He isn't a spiritual master in a remote mountain retreat.'

'He is a master, a genius.'

'Well, maybe. But he's a businessman. He explained his position. You can't just force yourself on him.'

'My resolve and fortitude will win him over,' Eikaku declared.

'They'll win you a beating!' I had no idea what to do. Eikaku was deaf to my arguments and far too strong for me to lead away, but if I left him here he probably would get beaten up or even arrested.

No matter how I pleaded he would not budge. I wondered if I should run to the hospital and seek my husband's help. But Dr Yoshio's house was closer, and even though I dreaded his response I went there to get Tetsuya.

However, when I arrived I was the one who was arrested. I spent the rest of the day in the Nagasaki magistrate's office, where I was questioned at length by two officials about why I was in Nagasaki, why I had gone to Mr Glover's house, who were the men I went with and finally who was the artist now encamped in Ueno Hikoma's gateway and refusing to move. I answered more or less truthfully, told them about my husband's studies, that we needed medical supplies and had gone to Mr Glover to discuss importing them and had taken a present, a painting, from my father. The men had been from Satsuma, as far as I knew – they had offered to introduce us. As for Eikaku, he was unfortunately not in his right mind, but if treated gently and looked after he would return to his senses.

At first I assumed it was because of Eikaku that I had got into trouble, but he had known nothing of the night I went to Ipponmatsu with Inoue, Itō and Sakamoto. Someone else had been watching me and reported my every movement.

'I think Hayashi Daisuke is an informer,' I told Makino and Tetsuya when I was released into their care late that evening. 'He's been spying on us all the time we've been here.'

'You drew attention to yourself,' my brother said. 'My wife was right. We should have prevented you from seeing those undesirable men.'

'You won't call them undesirable when they are the next government,' I said, irritated by his patronising attitude.

He looked around nervously, even though we were already some way from the gateway of the magistrate's building. 'That's exactly the sort of thing you shouldn't be talking about. You've been lucky – but you've caused me a great deal of embarrassment. My wife is very angry and Dr Yoshio is appalled. We rely on the goodwill of the officials. We cannot risk upsetting them.'

'I'm very sorry,' I said meekly, and I was sorry even though I did not think it was my fault. I was dismayed too at letting Makino down, frightened he would be sent away because of me, angry at Daisuke's betrayal, and on top of everything anxious about Eikaku.

We heard the next day that he had been removed from

the Ueno house and taken to a kind of asylum run by an acquaintance of Dr Yoshio who specialised in caring for the insane. I begged to be allowed to visit him, but one of the conditions of my release was I was to be sent home to my parents' house and until then I was to be kept indoors. I was mortified, even more so when it became obvious Makino would have to escort me home.

Tetsuya teased me, saying they would have to build an inside cell for me as was the custom for samurai under house arrest.

'I wish you could have seen Dr Inuda's place, though,' he said. 'His treatment is very effective. Maniacs are given purgatives and kept in a special excreting room. After a couple of days when they have voided everything they calm down; then they are kept in more pleasant surroundings.'

Poor Eikaku! I had never tried any treatment like that. I could see how it might be effective, but it seemed extreme.

'Then what will happen to him?' I said.

'He'll be sent back to Shimonoseki, under restraint, I imagine.'

That meant in a prisoner's bamboo cage. It was pitiful to think of.

'At least I'm not being sent home in a cage,' I said that night to my husband. 'I'm sorry that you have to leave with me.'

I was exhausted and close to tears.

'Don't worry,' he replied. 'You know I've been ready to leave at any time. This way I'll be back in Chōshū before the war begins.'

We made the journey back to Shimonoseki by land but when we arrived, around the middle of the fourth month, we found Takasugi had sailed from Nagasaki in a steamship which Mr Glover had sold to him complete with crew. He had agreed to pay more than forty thousand *ryō* for it, without the domain's permission, and named it the *Heiin-maru* after the year we were in.

'I could have brought you with me,' he said when we met him at Shiraishi's place, but we had not even known he was in Nagasaki. He was alight with excitement at his achievement and the prospect of the coming war. His ardour was not dampened in the least by the bad news that Shiraishi had to report: a premature attack by some impatient soldiers of the Second Kiheitai on the Bakufu post at Kurashiki had been punished by the execution of nearly fifty of the participants; the domain bureaucrats did not want to pay Glover for the steamship; the Bakufu army was reported to outnumber Chōshū's forces by four to one.

It was strange to meet him in the flesh again after looking at his photograph so many miles away. He did not look well; apart from his manic state I was convinced there was something more. He complained of the heat, and did indeed look feverish, but there was no point suggesting he should rest or take any treatment. The only thing he was prepared to do at this moment in his life was fight.

'I hope you will stay with me, either on board the ship or with the land army,' he said to Makino.

Makino bowed. 'I have to take my wife to her parents' home and then I will come back here.'

'You will not assist your husband?' Takasugi said to me.

How tempted I was to reply that I would! I would sail into battle with Takasugi and Makino and all the other daring and dedicated men. I looked at my husband. If he had given the smallest sign he wanted me with him, I would have gone. But I could tell from his face that he did not.

'I have been ordered to go home; I suppose I have to obey. Anyway, my father is not well and my parents need me.'

'Well, make sure you don't fall into gloom there. You know war is the best cure for that.'

'If you win,' Shiraishi said.

'We cannot lose,' Takasugi replied.

The medical supplies promised by Mr Glover had already been delivered to the Kokuraya, and before we left for Yuda I helped my husband go through them and divide them up for each field of battle. Chōshū was surrounded by the Bakufu army and would fight on four fronts in what would be known in the domain as the Four Borders War.

Now it seemed what my father had planned all along was going to happen. I would work alongside him, and my husband would join us when he returned from the war. I had had many ambitions to work among men as their equal. I had been caught up in the turbulence of the times. Now I had come to rest where I had started. I looked back at my mistakes and at all I had learned, and wondered if I had even the beginnings of wisdom and compassion.

It was a difficult time. Food was scarce and there were riots as the price of rice shot up. There was a great deal of resentment against the government for the executions of *shotai* soldiers, yet anxiety at the prospect of defeat was greater so no one dared to appear dissident. Negotiations to avoid war had been dragging on all year, but the Bakufu demands were too great and Chōshū never had any real intention of submitting – they mainly wanted to delay the start of the war and make the other side seem like the aggressor.

At home we had another cause for anxiety. My father's breathlessness had grown worse. He often seemed more sick than his patients. He and I both knew he had heart failure and that there was no cure, but we did not discuss it. I was just grateful to be with him in what might be the last months of his life.

Another ultimatum was issued by the Bakufu; the days passed without compliance. In the sixth month they finally launched their attack.

We had very little news at the time, though I tried to glean all I could. Every night I took out the old white fan, and touching the feathers to my lips tried to picture my husband, tried to see the wounded and how he was treating them. But even while the war was taking place all around the encircled domain, another chapter of my life opened, one that had nothing to do with battles and the dying. My sister came from Hagi bringing Michi with her.

The child was four years old and immediately enchanted

us all. My father and I marvelled at her command of language and her abilities of concentration. My mother said, 'She is like a mixture of you and your older sister. She has your curiosity and Oneechan's sweet nature.'

'You don't think I'm sweet-natured?' I said. 'That's all the thanks I get for coming home to look after you.'

'There you are,' my mother replied. 'Your sister would never have spoken like that.' But she smiled as she said it and I knew I had not offended her. Indeed my teasing seemed to lift her spirits and I tried every day to make my parents laugh. I told them about our adventures in Nagasaki, the Yoshio household, the ammonia pit and the animals' shrines, photography and Ueno Hikoma, Mr Glover. I had to confess I'd been made to give him the Chikuden painting in part-exchange for medical supplies and thousands of rifles.

This transaction made my father very thoughtful for a while. 'Well, Katsura-san wanted it,' he said. 'We could not deny him.'

'The sacrifices we make for a new world,' I said lightly.

Father was watching Michi playing on the floor with some paper animals Mother had found for her. She was talking to them quietly but seriously in some complicated game she had made up.

'What sort of world will she grow up in, I wonder,' he murmured.

'One where she will go to university and become a real doctor,' I said. 'One where women will have education and freedom like men.'

I was not the only one who thought like this in those heady days. Everyone had new ideas about the future, how the world would be made new. The old order was crumbling. A lid had been lifted from a boiling pot and everything came bubbling, spluttering and steaming out. Our dreams could not be contained and for me Michi stood for the future.

She was an outgoing and self-possessed child. Mitsue said she would have no trouble adjusting to her new life. They had been talking to her about it for weeks, how she would live with her grandparents and her aunt and uncle would be her new mother and father. I explained that her new father was away looking after soldiers in the war, but he would be home soon.

'Will I be the only girl here?' she said.

'Yes, you will be my only little girl. I hope you won't miss your brothers and sister too much. We will take you to visit them. Hagi is not so very far away. And I will teach you to write so you can send letters to your mother.'

'But you will be my mother?' she said.

'Yes, you will have two mothers because you are so adorable.'

Michi seemed quite accepting of the decision that had been made for her, but the night before Mitsue was due to return home I began to have terrible misgivings. I had no idea how to be a mother. It seemed wrong to take the child away from her own family, especially her mother who clearly loved her so much. I even began to think Mitsue was a much better person than I was. I tried to put all this into words but my sister did not want to listen.

'Please, Tsu-chan, we've made the decision. It's the right one, I'm sure of it.'

'She's going to miss you so much. What will I do if she frets?'

Mitsue was silent for a moment, then she said, 'She will have a better life here. We must not let our feelings get in the way of that. You will give her an education she would never get at home. She will learn how to be strong, how to stand up for herself like you do. And she will come to love you and Makino-san like her own parents. Not another word, I beg you.'

I heard Mitsue weep that night, but she must have shed all her tears then for she left next morning with dry eyes and a cheerful smile. Michi's lip trembled and her eyes filled with tears, but we distracted her with a visit to the cat and her three kittens, my mother got out the snakes-and-ladders board and some other old toys, and when she was tired of playing she came and helped me pick herbs in the garden.

She attached herself to me immediately and there was something about her unquestioning trust that cracked my heart open. I began to love her deeply. For the first time I understood what it meant to love another human being more than myself.

All the men we knew were away at one or other of the fronts, in Hiroshima, around the island of Ōshima, north at Iwami or across the strait at Kokura. The weather was terrible: the first typhoon of the year swept up the country from west to east bringing heavy rain. Michi was made uneasy by the wind and could not sleep so I brought out the fan and began to tell her stories. Just as my mother had told me, I said the fan was magic and that with it you could see what was happening in other distant places.

'There is your father,' I said. 'He is on a ship with Takasugi-*dono*.'

'Who is Takasugi-*dono*?'

'A great hero. Can you see him? The ship is the *Heiin-maru*. She is only small but see how fast she flies over the waves!'

The little *Heiin-maru* was sailing from Shimonoseki at night towards the island of Ōshima, which had been invaded by Bakufu forces with their huge flagship, the *Fujiyama-maru*. She sailed through the darkness towards the lamplit warships, fired a broadside at them, raking them with her Armstrong guns, and disappeared back to Shimonoseki before they could retaliate or even start up their engines.

I did not tell Michi of the burning houses on Ōshima, the women and children killed, the *jizamurai* tearing off their robes and disguising themselves as farmers. We heard about that later from O-Kiyo.

'They were begging the farmers not to call them *danna-sama*,' she said in disgust. 'They're a boastful lot at the best of times. All hot air. Then when the enemy turns up they pretend they aren't samurai. Disgraceful!'

My father laughed. He was no longer well enough to go to the Hanamatsutei but it cheered him up to see O-Kiyo and hear her news. 'At least the island is back in Chōshū's hands,' he said in satisfaction.

O-Kiyo brought a print of a *kawaraban* which was circulating in Yamaguchi. It made the fight look like a battle from the days of the Warring States, when Mōri Motonari joined forces with the Murakami pirate fleet. We all gazed at it in excitement and I thought of Eikaku, wondering where he was, if he was still confined in the asylum in Nagasaki.

'Tell me about my father and the war,' Michi begged every

night, and with a mixture of O-Kiyo's news and the magic fan I wove my stories.

After Ōshima war broke out on the Sekishū front, where Murata Zōroku, the former village doctor, advanced as far as Masuda, taking most of Iwami. Next I saw the Geishū front where the Ii contingent from Hikone were scattered, their red uniforms torn off and left behind. I saw the Chōshū fleet sail for Kokura, the *Kigai-maru* among them.

'Look, there is Sakamoto Ryōma,' I said to Michi, 'in command of the *Otchū-maru*.' I saw five men take a small boat to attack the mighty *Fujiyama-maru*, using the tide to carry them there and back again. I saw Takasugi's strategy repeated over and over again: the lightning attack, often on two fronts simultaneously, and then the pull-back, but always with the result of each attack penetrating deeper into enemy territory. I saw Chōshū soldiers cross mountain passes at midnight, the years of drill and training now paying off, to attack an unwary enemy at dawn.

I saw Bakufu soldiers weighed down by antique armour and fighting with inadequate guns. I saw their commanders in their distinctive *jinbaori* picked off by Chōshū marksmen. I saw them set fire to their own castles at Hamada and Kokura and flee.

'Here is a Kokura elder, insisting on seeing the commander Ogasawara Nagamichi. He forces his way into the room only to find it empty. Lord Ogasawara has fled to Nagasaki. He has heard the news that the Shōgun, Iemochi, the overall commander of the army, is dead.'

'Iemochi is dead,' Michi repeated.

NOMURA BŌTŌNI

Keiō 2 (1866), Autumn, Age 60

The islanders bring food every day, ignoring the threats of the guards, who are mainlanders and therefore do not know anything. Occasionally one of the grandmothers will stop and berate them, asking them if they have no human feeling and what possible harm an old woman who is a nun and a poet can do to them. The grandmothers have immense stamina in grumbling and scolding – all their lives they have been shouting against the wind which never stops blowing on Himejima – and it means nothing to them to stand and assault the ears of the guards with a fifteen-minute torrent of abuse.

The guards, young men from Fukuoka, are embarrassed by the grandmothers' accusations because secretly they agree with them. The old woman seems harmless and all of them would much rather not be here overseeing her imprisonment. They don't even understand what crime she has committed. They have been ordered to bring her to Himejima, build a cell for her and keep her here, and that is what they are going to do. But none of them wants to be answerable for her death. They found the winter harrowing enough and she is three times their age. So they try to pretend they don't notice the villagers visiting two or three times a day, bringing a bowl of hot soup or tea, some millet porridge or grilled fish, which they hand to the poet through the bars.

Bōtōni can only understand one word in three: the dialect is obscure and the old women mostly toothless, but she is grateful for their defence of her and even more grateful for the food they bring and the warm clothes. She would not have survived the winter without them. The hut she is confined in is tiny and completely unprotected from the icy gales.

They also exchange a few precious words. Bōtōni assures them she is well – surprisingly she is still in reasonable health, though the lack of exercise and the damp have brought on a painful inflammation in her knees and fingers; she can hardly stand and she would not be able to hold a needle now if she were allowed such a thing. The villagers tell her about recent events: a whale stranded on a nearby beach, a baby born, a fisherman lost off the rocks.

As well as draughts the cracks in the walls let in moonlight and the fragrance of plum blossoms. Often ideas for poems come to her, but she is only rarely allowed brush and ink. Paper is scarce on the island and she does not want to use up her precious stack of cards. Sometimes she takes a piece of charcoal or writes with a twig on the dirt floor and once she scratched her finger and used her own blood, but mostly she composes the poems in her head. They don't stop coming; they rustle around inside her mind like the mice in the thatched roof. When the cold keeps her awake all night she listens for the mice and the poems and both help her to feel less lonely.

She does not pity herself, nor does she resent her exile.

In fact she is proud of being here, although she is quite surprised anyone would think her such a dangerous criminal. Her only regret is that she has not done more for the cause of the Emperor, whom she reveres. After all, she has only corresponded with a few young men – Saigō, Shinsaku and poor Hirano who was executed in Kyōto after the abortive uprising at Ikuno – and given them shelter when they had nowhere else to go. It's true that she has listened to their incendiary political ideas, for which she has a great deal of sympathy, but she has also written poems and said prayers with them, rather harmless pursuits.

However Fukuoka like so many domains has had its own small-scale internal strife. Its conservative government has seen the change of government brought about in Chōshū by the *shotai*, a highly suspect militia of mixed ranks, and has decided to eliminate its opponents, thus demonstrating its support of the Bakufu in the second campaign against Chōshū. The north Kyūshū domains have been nervously watching their powerful neighbour across the strait. War has been imminent for the last twelve months. No one wants to end up on the losing side, but few have any doubt about the outcome. The Bakufu army is one hundred and fifty thousand strong. Chōshū with a mere ten thousand men is virtually surrounded and will have to defend itself on four fronts. Everyone is hoping Chōshū will be taught a well-deserved lesson and things can go back to the way they were.

The guards hate Chōshū and would like to take part in its humiliation. The villagers don't care one way or the other. They dislike Fukuoka and Chōshū more or less equally and they have barely heard of the Emperor. They just don't think an old woman should be incarcerated, and they continue to look after Bōtōni as best they can.

So everyone's relieved when a ship arrives at the end of summer flying the Fukuoka crest and carrying a small group of men who have orders that Bōtōni is to be handed over to them. Maybe the guards don't look at the flag very carefully or scrutinise the documents as closely as they should, but even if they had challenged these men they wouldn't have stood a chance against them, armed as they are with modern weapons and an air of swaggering confidence as if they have just won a great victory.

At first this victorious attitude makes Bōtōni's heart quail, for she has no reason to suspect they are not from Fukuoka, which can only mean Chōshū is defeated and she is being taken back to the mainland to face execution. When the gate is opened and she is taken outside the bright sunlight dazzles her and she can hardly walk. Her cell suddenly seems most precious and the villagers, who are surrounding her, wailing, most dear. Even the guards cause her a pang – she does not want to take her leave of them.

It is only when they are on the ship and have cast off the lines and raised the anchor, when the leader turns to her with a grin and addresses her using the term peculiar to Chōshū: *boku* – your manservant – which Shinsaku uses too, that she realises she has been rescued. In the midst of his victories in the Four Borders War Shinsaku has not forgotten her. She falls to her knees, weeping with emotion, thanking the soldiers, and Shinsaku and the gods. The men tell her the news, as they raise the Chōshū flag, that Chōshū is victorious on all fronts, the Bakufu army has been defeated, and the war is over because the Shōgun, Iemochi, is dead.

The soldiers look after her as if she is their own beloved grandmother. They have prepared a cabin for her and urge her to rest, but she cannot bear to leave the deck. As the sails spread in the southwesterly wind and the ship scuds along towards Shimonoseki, Bōtōni gazes in the direction of the northeast, where a new Japan is being born.

MY FATHER

With Iemochi's death in Ōsaka the war came to an end. In the ninth month peace was negotiated by Katsu Kaishū. Makino came home on a mild day in the tenth month, well into autumn. Persimmons were glowing orange on the leafless trees. They were the only fruit we would have: the apricots and peaches had been destroyed by the typhoon, the wind stripping the fruit from the branches. Michi was picking the last fresh herbs in the garden. Hachirō had made her a small bamboo basket and tiny dolls out of Chinese lantern flowers. She laid each leaf tenderly in place, around the dolls, talking under her breath all the while. She was wearing a lined blue kimono tied with a red sash. Her little feet were in *tabi* and *geta*. Makino's eyes followed her while we talked. He had fallen under her spell as completely as the rest of us.

'What will happen now?' I said. Another lull seemed to have fallen on the country. Chōshū had beaten the Tokugawa army decisively on all four fronts. They were better equipped and their morale was much greater; Murata and Takasugi's strategies of attack and retreat had been brutally effective, but the Bakufu had contributed to their own defeat by their failure to cooperate, their lack of real fighting spirit, and their frequent decisions to abandon the battle and flee for home.

Iemochi's death provided a convenient excuse to call a halt to hostilities until Keiki was installed as the next Shōgun. In the meantime everything was in suspense.

'It seems Satsuma is determined to fight Keiki,' Makino replied. 'They held back from joining in the campaign against Chōshū – they were under orders to attack Hagi, but they stood by the alliance made between Saigō and Katsura and refused to send troops. Now Chōshū has gained immense prestige and Satsuma want to prove themselves too. I saw Inoue in Shimonoseki and he says Keiki is looking for troops and weapons from the French to restore the Tokugawa.'

'I suppose he will have to be stopped and so there will be more fighting.'

'Almost certainly. Even if Keiki gives in, Aizu and other Tokugawa supporters never will.'

'And you will be involved?'

'I can't abandon the lads now. We are so short of medical staff in the field as it is. On the Aki front they could not keep up with the casualties, and when we withdrew from Kokura we had to bury the dead there.' He fell silent, reliving it all. 'These new rifles cause terrible injuries. If only one side has them, victory is quick and casualties low. But when both sides are armed equally then neither has an advantage; the battle drags on with many more dead and injured.'

At the end of that year Keiki became the fifteenth and last Tokugawa Shōgun, and on the twenty-fifth day of the twelfth month the Emperor Kōmei died, apparently of smallpox, though there were rumours that he had been poisoned. There could be no hostilities during the mourning period, but it did not put an end to the unrest in the country. The New Year saw another astonishing rise in the price of rice – the bad weather and the war had ruined the harvest – and there were many riots and smashings of goods and property.

We heard news of them, but it was as if they were taking place in a distant country. Two days after New Year my father said one evening, 'I don't feel so well.' His face was pale and he was sweating, even though it was bitterly cold. My mother spread out the futon so he could lie down. He thanked her, the last words he spoke. Before I could kneel beside him to take his pulse he was dead.

He was fifty years old. He had led an admirable life. He had helped many people, eased their suffering, saved their lives. He left children and grandchildren and a host of friends. But none of this consoled me. I could not believe he had truly departed. I saw him everywhere: in the garden, kneeling in his consulting room, under the gambling tree by the gate. I woke at night hearing his voice. I thought about him all the time, with deep regret and remorse. I owed everything to him. Not only had he given me life, he had taught me almost everything I knew. He had indulged my passion for learning, he had let me work alongside him, he had allowed me to choose my own husband. I felt I had abused his patience and affection. How glad I was he had never known the truth about me and Shinsai. If it had not been for Michi I believe I would have slipped back into the state I was in in the first year of Genji, three years before, when I almost cried myself blind.

It was Michi's first experience of death; she had come to love her grandfather and she cried with my mother and me.

But for her sake we both tried to mask our grief, to teach her that death is no more than the other side of life.

My father's friends and colleagues came to his funeral and celebrated the fact that he had lived among us with many cups of sake and tears and laughter. But the presence of so many reminded us all the more painfully of those who were missing: my father, Lord Sufu, and, of course, my uncle.

It must have struck my mother too, for some time later, just before the ceremony of the forty-ninth day after my father's death, she said to me, 'Do you think we should hold funeral rites for Shinsai?'

No one had spoken of him for so long. Even my father had stopped mentioning his name in the months before he died.

'I don't know,' I said in confusion. 'No, I don't think so. He may not be dead. I don't know.' I did not understand myself. I believed he was dead, yet I could not bear the thought of a funeral. I sought an escape in tears, and my mother cried too, so we did not speak of it again.

As the weeks passed there were many decisions that needed to be made. Makino and I were expected to take over the practice, but he was committed to the army if hostilities broke out again and I was not sure I could handle it on my own. My father had not accepted any new students since his health began to fail, and there were really too many patients for me to see alone. I wondered how many patients would still come if there were no male doctor ostensibly in charge. It was not a good time to leave, but my mother expressed a desire to make another pilgrimage; she wanted to go to Ise before she died and she wanted me to go with her.

TAKASUGI SHINSAKU

Keiō 3 (1867), Spring, Age 28

Shinsaku is dying. It is taking a long time and he is thoroughly weary of the slow inexorable progression of the disease that is killing him. He has survived the winter and hoped that spring would make him feel better, but he has accepted now that there will be no recovery. For some weeks he has been unable to read or write. He can hardly talk to the friends who visit: in fact he does not want to see them. It is not that he is depressed – though he has been, deeply; he just wants the whole thing to be over.

He has been moved again from the little house he named the Tōgyōan into a place owned by one of the Shimonoseki merchants who has been a faithful supporter of the *shotai*. At the end of the previous summer when Chōshū defeated the Bakufu and the Shōgun Iemochi died, Shinsaku had to withdraw from the naval campaign when the illness suddenly became much worse. He had suspected for some time that he was not well – the cough, the lassitude, the night sweats – but the sudden rush of blood that filled his throat and dripped from his lips meant he could no longer hide it from himself or anyone else. When he returned to Shimonoseki the doctors confirmed that he had consumption.

At first they spoke of a cure and persuaded him to follow their regimens. The weeks passed quite pleasantly – the house was near the garden where the *shotai* who had died in battle were buried and where Yoshida Shōin had his last resting place. Shinsaku liked to go there with O-Uno, to offer thanks to the dead for their sacrifice and drink sake in front of the graves. He made her promise she would do the same at his grave, bring geisha and musicians and dance and sing. He meant to cheer her up, but it only made her cry more wretchedly.

Many of his friends came to visit: Monta, Shunsuke, the three wild boys together again. The parties were the same as they had ever been, except for the one thing that no one talked about – that he was dying. He drank more than ever; the alcohol eased his chest and alleviated the coughing though it also gave him headaches and loose bowels. Now he hardly drinks at all.

One or other of the women is always by his side. He knows one is his wife and one his mistress, but sometimes he can't tell them apart. They seem to have reached a tacit agreement not to meet face to face or to talk to each other, but otherwise they cooperate. One changes the bedding, the other does the washing and airs the futons in the sunshine. One leaves to get some rest, the other slips quietly into her place.

There is another woman too, the poet. Up till a few weeks ago they were still composing poems together, but now he is too tired. She is a calming presence in the house; she mediates between Masa and O-Uno, takes messages between them; at other times she prays, fasting, for his recovery and for victory against the Bakufu.

He does not think he will live that long. He doubts he will last till the next boys' festival; the house will have fluttering carp banners to celebrate his son but he will not see them.

Both women have a claim on him that they are not going to relinquish. Masa is the mother of his son; she lives with his parents and they think highly of her. But O-Uno has shared his life in a different way; she has seen not only the poet but also the creator of the *shotai*, the daring strategist who brought down the conservative government and sank the Bakufu's ships. She came with him in exile, she loves him. It is she who brings branches of flowers into the sick room – the first flowering plum, his favourite, and this week early cherry blossoms. She is hoping he will wait for the irises.

But it is not the women who occupy his thoughts as he hovers between waking and dreaming. He gives them only cursory consideration, mainly when they come to wash or feed him. He cannot lie down, lest the blood drown him, but sits propped against a back rest, which is padded with quilts and cushions. This week the bush warbler has started to sing and its urgent call fills him with regret that he will not see another spring. Is it really only three and a half years since Lord Mōri gave him the command to form the *shotai*, only two years ago that he rode through the snow to Kōzanji and called out to Prince Sanjō to bear witness to the warrior spirit of the sons of Chōshū? He remembers the cups of sake the prince immediately supplied as though they were all taking part in a medieval drama: the farewell toast for the loyal warriors departing for battle.

Yet the campaigns he has fought have been far from medieval. They have had a character all their own, that he was forced to invent, always fighting against overwhelming odds, outnumbered by as many as twenty to one, so he had to perfect the sudden unexpected attack and the equally swift retreat.

Now half dreaming he sees himself on the deck of the *Heiin-maru*, less than a year ago. He loved that ship, how swift and responsive it was! What a moment when he saw that the strategy he had formed in his mind was working, when the Bakufu fleet was thrown into confusion and panic by the night-time assault! He had known intuitively that the very length of time the Bakufu had taken for its preparations had made it ponderous and inflexible. It could not move its huge land army quickly, or even control half of it. It knew nothing of naval warfare. These intuitions inspired him; they were like conceiving a poem, taking something out of the air that had not existed before and turning it into words or actions that would never be forgotten.

He had been too weak to put on armour in the last sortie but had made a virtue out of it, lounging in his night clothes on deck because he could hardly stand, drinking to suppress the coughing and the fever, boasting that the enemy was a sneak thief who deserved no formalities. The men had cheered, and taken courage from his languor. It was only after the victory that they noticed he was near fainting, and then came the rush of blood that could not be disguised.

Now the endgame is about to unfold and he will miss it. He will never know the outcome unless his spirit is able to watch from the other world. He has been told about the agreement between Satsuma and Chōshū; it means the fall of the Bakufu is inevitable. And then? He has no idea what will happen afterwards. Someone once accused him of thinking too much about *afterwards*. Who was it? Ah, yes, Kijima, that night in Ōsaka.

His thoughts rest for a moment on Kijima, shot in Kyōto at the Forbidden Gate. And Genzui, who died the same day. How brief the years between Genzui's death and his own! He feels a moment of envy for those who will survive: Katsura, Inoue and Itō, Satsuma's Saigō Takamori, Ōkubo Toshimichi.

It makes him smile to think of them: they are an unlikely band – runaway Kogorō, the incorrigible pair Monta and Shunsuke, the vain Saigō with his love of food and big women…are they really going to overthrow the Tokugawa, restore the Emperor and build a new Japan?

He is smiling as his eyes close.

The end is less peaceful as his body struggles to the last. Many times the onlookers think he has drawn his last breath, and then his lungs fight to breathe again, great ragged gasps that shock his eyes open. He does not see them but gazes into some other world. Finally a paroxysm of coughing racks him, blood pours and in the middle of the haemorrhage his heart stops.

EE JA NAIKA

In the fourth month news came of Takasugi Shinsaku's death. He had passed away surounded by friends, and the women who loved him: his wife, Masa, O-Uno, and the poet Nomura Bōtōni, and was buried in Shimizuyama, the resting place of the earliest Mōri lords and of many of the Kiheitai. Makino went to the funeral and came back to tell me the burial ground was full of irises, purple and white. After plum blossoms they were Takasugi's favourite flower. His last words had been to exhort his companions *to act while you can, before the darkness closes in, to act...*

His nickname had been *Thunder, lightning, wind, rain.* His boldness had snatched Chōshū from despair and defeat, and his death before the final victory seemed even more cruel. It was ten years since I had first seen him at my sister's wedding, when I had heard him sing. I grieved for him deeply.

The rains began, shrouding the hills in mist. Trees and eaves dripped constantly and mould sprang out on everything. Makino was restless, irritable with the patients and with me. Takasugi's death had added to his sense of urgency. The war would start without him; his colleagues would advance, they would receive the promotions that he deserved, they would outstrip him in skills and technique. He missed his life as an army doctor and his fellow soldiers in the Kiheitai. I wanted him to go, but I had promised my mother to accompany her to Ise when the rains were over, and one of us had to keep the practice running.

It was still raining in the sixth month when there was a call at the gate one evening. I thought it was a patient and went hurrying out. Two figures in straw rain capes and broad-brimmed hats stood beneath the gambling tree. I recognised the shorter one immediately: it was Eikaku. He had lost a great deal of weight and seemed very subdued; like his companion, he was soaked through. It was not cold, despite the rain, but he was shivering.

'Eikaku-san,' I cried. 'Come inside!'

'Doctor,' he replied, 'I am sorry to cause you so much trouble but I have nowhere else to go.'

I hurried them both into the house, calling for Hachirō and O-Kane to take Eikaku to the bath and find him some dry clothes. The other man removed his straw cape and hung it with Eikaku's under the eaves. I handed him a towel to wipe his face and hands.

'Your brother sent me,' he said with a hint of apology in his voice. 'Imaike-san was released from the Inuda treatment house and Dr Itasaki wanted to spare him the discomfort of being transported in a cage. Dr Inuda thought it would undo all that had been achieved. I've been one of Dr Yoshio's students for several years and I volunteered to accompany Imaike. He himself wanted to come here. Your brother thought you might be able to care for him for a while.'

'I see,' I said. Of course I could not turn Eikaku away – but what would my husband and my mother think? The young man's face was familiar, but Dr Yoshio had many students and I couldn't say I really remembered him.

'My name is Kitaoka Jundō,' he added. 'I am originally from Isa.'

Isa, the famous medicine town that Shinsai and I had pretended to be from.

'I know you are a skilled pharmacist,' he said. 'I observed you in Nagasaki. I thought... Tetsuya-san suggested, that is... I don't know how you feel about taking on a student for a while. The thing is, I have wanted to return to Chōshū for some time.'

'I would have to discuss it with my husband,' I said. To take two more into our household would strain our resources.

'Of course,' Kitaoka said. 'But it is you I want to learn from.'

He was a few years younger than me, thin and by no means prepossessing, but as he said this he gave a shy smile and I felt a twinge of recognition. Throughout my life I have met certain people and felt instantly that a bond has always existed between us. People say it is from a past life and maybe it is. There was an instant bond between Kitaoka and myself, not a sexual attraction, but more like the affection between a teacher and a student, an aunt and a nephew. I thought of Nomura Bōtōni and Takasugi and their intense friendship of the mind. By now everyone knew the story of how Takasugi had sent a ship with armed men to rescue the elderly poet when she was in exile on a remote island, and we had all heard the poem she concluded for him when he was on his deathbed:

To live an uninteresting life
With interest
Is up to one's mind,
How interesting!

Kitaoka did not do anything quite so dramatic, but his arrival rescued me nonetheless. His help in the dispensary and with the patients meant I could go to Ise, and Makino would be free to leave whenever he wanted.

Makino rapidly made this calculation himself and was happy to accept Kitaoka. He was less enthusiastic about Eikaku. But my mother rather to my surprise quickly became very fond of the artist. She was used to looking after my father, and Eikaku filled her need to care for a man. He shared her love of popular fiction and drama and liked to listen to her read aloud. She even brought out *A Country Genji*, and we listened again to the adventures of the dashing Mitsuuji, and I reflected how the young men I knew – Monta, Itō, Katsura, Genzui, Takasugi, had led real lives that were no less dramatic. Genzui and Takasugi were no longer with us, but who knew what still lay in store for Monta and the others?

Eikaku submitted to my mother's attentions in matters of haircuts, shaving, clean clothes and regular meals and began to look more like a normal human being. He appeared neither overexcited nor depressed. Dr Inuda's treatment seemed to have had a powerful effect on him. He did not mention photography and expressed no desire to paint. I wondered if it were not too high a price for him to pay for a return to sanity.

As soon as he heard about the planned journey Eikaku

wanted to come with us. He had many reasons – to give thanks for his recovery, to see the paintings and carvings in the great temples in Nara and Kyōto, and to make the pilgrimage to Ise.

'Before I die,' he said in his new calm voice.

'You are not going to die,' I chided him. 'You are not old yet!'

'I am forty-five,' Eikaku replied.

It seemed like a good idea to take him: I did not trust my husband to be patient with him in my absence; a man, even one of unreliable sanity, would be a good companion, and Eikaku, as I knew from our previous journey, was interesting and stimulating to travel with. And maybe seeing great art and visiting sacred buildings would inspire him to paint again.

Makino reluctantly agreed – we were all still having to get used to the idea that he was now the head of the household and in theory should be consulted on everything. Now he had Kitaoka's help I was not worried about him. I was more concerned about leaving Michi. I thought about taking her with us, but it seemed foolish to expose her to the dangers of travelling. She said goodbye happily enough, consoled with the promise of presents from Kyōto, but after I had hugged her she stood back and patted her arms in a gesture just like my father's. I was the one almost in tears. My pain at the parting made me determined not to stay away too long.

It was the seventh month and extremely hot, yet it seemed half the country had been seized by the impulse to travel to

Ise and Kyōto. The roads thronged with people, the boats and inns were all crowded; they were like a stage on which everyone was acting out their own drama: women like my mother freed by widowhood, village groups sponsored by their local shrine, runaway children and teenagers, itinerant musicians, acrobats, jugglers, salesmen of all types, prostitutes, beggars, *rōnin* looking for an army to join. There were pack-horses laden with rice or silk or fish manure, there were lepers and other sick people hoping for a miracle; the towns stank of waste in the humid air, but the forests were full of gentians and bell flowers.

We walked to Mitajiri and took the ship to Ōsaka. From there it was another walk to Nara, where we rested for a few days looking at the temples, the pagoda of Kōfukuji, Tōdaiji and the Great Buddha. At every famous view Mother was able to quote a line of poetry or recall a noble hero. Every tree, every shrine, even the dust of the road under our feet, was imbued with meaning for her, and she drank it all in as if it were the finest sake. Every day she recovered more of her old spirits and I could see the healing that was taking place in her.

Finally we began the journey on the pilgrim road through the mountains to the sacred shrine where Amaterasu o mikami, the sun goddess, and Toyouke no o mikami, the god of the earth, are enshrined. Over the centuries millions of people had walked this route to Ise and many hundreds were doing it now, alongside us, all around us. Their faces shone with sweat from the heat and from the sacred sake everyone was drinking, and their eyes shone with fervour, not only for the gods but with their hopes for a new world.

At the inns and on the road rumours flew, settled here and there, intensified and transformed and flitted on, like the butterflies and huge dragonflies that fluttered among the dark trunks of the forest cedars or like the swallows that darted to and fro in the evening air outside our nightly lodging places. We heard that Satsuma was determined to fight the Bakufu; that Saigō Takamori and Ōkubo Toshimichi were sending troops to Ōsaka; that Tosa domain was trying to intercede to settle things peacefully; that the last Shōgun, Keiki, was preparing to fight, no, on the contrary he was on the point of handing power back to the Emperor – the new young Emperor, son of Kōmei. The Tokugawa regime was finished.

It was as if a whole society had been torn into pieces and hurled into the air – the shreds fluttered and gleamed in the light of the sun but no one could see how they would fall. I was gripped by excitement and emotion. I hardly slept and was moved to tears or laughter by the slightest stimulus. Everyone, it seemed, was in the same state. Even Eikaku began to shed his unnatural air of calm. He became more opinionated and argumentative; he and my mother strove to outdo each other in their knowledge of the historical and artistic significance of everything we saw. We had started our journey in a quiet and sombre mood, but now we were all three full of energy and optimism.

At our inn in Ise the maid told us things had quietened down a little but the week before amulets had fallen from the skies and the crowds had been seized by some divine impulse. Everyone started dancing and singing crazy songs that all ended with the refrain *ee ja naika*: Ain't life great?

'They make up rhymes about anything – Chōshū, Keiki-*sama*, the price of rice, Ebisu-*sama*, the best sake or tea – *eejanaika, eejanaika.*' She demonstrated, dancing and laughing. 'People put on fancy dress, they come out in the streets disguised as animals or birds or insects. Men and women swap clothes and men blacken their teeth.'

Eikaku's eyes gleamed. 'I wish I had seen that. If only we had been here!'

'Who knows, it may break out again,' the girl said. 'Though my master says it will destroy his business if it does. The crowds demand free food and sake. They trash any place where they are refused. But I think it's fun. Last time I joined in dancing and singing until I dropped from exhaustion.'

'Where do the amulets come from?' my mother asked.

'No one knows! They suddenly start falling from the sky!'

I had a vision of a nimble priest climbing a tree and throwing the amulets down – but surely people would notice such a fraud?

'What a mystery,' Eikaku said with a deep sigh.

There were touches of mystery at Ise, in the ancient shrines, constructed with simplicity from unpainted cypress, innocent of decoration, deep within the even more ancient forest. But it was also a place where commerce thrived. The shops and tea houses were full of souvenirs, specialities such as breath fresheners, charms to alleviate everything from indigestion to impotence. Eikaku was delighted with the contrast between the spiritual and the mercantile. My mother and I wept like mountain springs, but we laughed as often as we cried.

On the way to Kyōto my mother's mood continued excited

and cheerful. My feelings suddenly changed. It was three years since I had waved goodbye to Shinsai at Yamazaki, three years with no word of him. Everyone assumed he was dead, burned beyond recognition in the *dondon* fires. But when I tried to pray for his spirit in Ise I did not believe he was dead.

It unsettled me, and I could not share my feelings with anyone. I wished I had not agreed to include Kyōto on my journey. I did not want to remember that year of madness and passion. At night my face and body burned with a mixture of shame and, I admit it, lust and longing.

We stayed at a small inn on the opposite side of the Kamo River from Mrs Minami's shop, not far from where the old Chōshū residence once stood. A wall had been constructed around the site but the mansion had not been rebuilt, though most of the city had been and new houses were springing up everywhere. New businesses were appearing too. Just down the road from our inn was a photography studio. I believe it was the first in Kyōto. I didn't want to awaken Eikaku's mania for photography, but I was gripped by the desire to have a picture of my mother. There were no portraits of my father painted while he was still alive (the one we have was done by Eikaku some years after Father's death, following my mother's instructions: the clothes are accurate but it is not really a likeness). I was captivated by the idea that a photograph was more than just a record; it preserved something of the essence of the sitter.

My mother did not need much persuading. To her it was part of the new world that Kyōto represented. Her only regret was that her clothes seemed so unfashionable and there was no time to have new ones made, even if we had the money. She had to be satisfied with a new hair comb from Yoshino, made from lacquered cherry wood.

Eikaku wanted to visit the shrine to Tenmanjin at Kitano and was easily persuaded to go on his own while we, I said, would do some shopping. When he had left, my mother and I took the opportunity to slip down the road to the studio. Like Mr Ueno the photographer worked outside using the light of the sun. We had to be there at midday, the courtyard was airless, the light dazzling. We had two photographs taken, one of my mother alone, the other of the two of us. When we went back inside the shop my head was swimming. The photographer disappeared into the darkroom at the back and his wife asked us to take a look at some prints to choose the size we wanted.

She placed them on a small table and my mother and I knelt to look through them. The first was of an old man with a white beard. The second was of Shinsai.

Neither my mother nor I could speak. Shinsai's eyes stared up at me with their familiar bold look, his mouth curved in the slight smile I knew so well. I wanted to press my lips against his and kiss them as I had so often.

'When was this taken?' I said, my voice like a stranger's.

'These are all from last year. I don't know exactly when. I'll ask my husband. Do you know the gentleman?'

'He looks like my late husband's brother,' my mother said in a trembling voice. 'But we thought he was dead.'

'I'll ask my husband to come,' the woman said, and left the room.

I picked up the print. I could not help myself. I looked

and looked at it, then, clasping it to myself, stood up.

'Tsuru!' my mother exclaimed, staring at me. For a moment she looked bemused, but then realisation came into her eyes. 'Dear heaven,' she said. 'It cannot be true. Tell me it is not true.'

She rose unsteadily to her feet. She had gone completely white. Somehow she was able to make some excuse to the photographer who had come back into the room, leave some money and promise to return for our pictures. Gripping me by the arm as though I might escape at any moment, she hustled me out into the street. I could feel her shock and anger, and together with the heat, the noise and the crowds, it made me turn faint. I thought I was going to vomit. I felt a nauseating lurch as everything wheeled around me and darkness loomed before me and swallowed me.

When I came round I was lying on the floor of our room in the inn. Mother, kneeling next to me, was sponging my temples with cold water, Eikaku was frantically waving a fan. The room was dim and cool and I no longer felt sick. I wasn't sure what I felt: part of me was rejoicing, *He's alive, he's in Kyōto*, part of me was lamenting, *Mother knows. I am so ashamed*. How could I continue living with her? How could I go home?

My anguish must have shown on my face. Her own features contorted with grief. 'My poor child, my poor child,' she wept. Even now she looked for ways not to blame me.

Later when Eikaku had gone out to buy some food she said to me, 'I was always afraid this would happen. I could see he was too fond of you. I was so relieved when he went away. I thought you would be safe once you were married. Oh, he should have left you alone. I will never forgive him. Why isn't he dead like we all thought he was?'

'I am so happy he is alive,' I said. 'Where is the picture? I want to look at him again.'

My mother told me I must have dropped it in the street, but I was sure she had destroyed it.

'We will leave tomorrow,' she said. 'We must go home. We must not run into him here. Tsuru, promise me you will not try to see him.'

'Of course I will not,' I said. 'It is all over. I have my husband, my daughter, our work...'

I would have given them all up in that moment for the chance to lie with him one more time.

I could eat nothing. Mother and Eikaku watched over me with sympathetic tenderness as though I had suffered some terrible bereavement, but I feigned sleep and eventually exhaustion overtook them and I could tell from their breathing that they had fallen asleep. As the night wore on I realised what I must do. I either had to find Shinsai and kill him or I had to take my own life. I could see no other way to be free. I had thought I had recovered from my madness, but seeing his face had made me realise I was as ensnared as ever. I rose silently and took the nearest clothes – Eikaku's – and his traveller's hat. I found my travelling medicine bag and in it my scalpel, wrapped in cloth. As I felt its heavy shape with my fingers I thought we would both die. It would be like a double suicide, a fitting end for our distorted passion.

The first cocks were crowing and the sky was paling. I went first to Mrs Minami's house, striding out in my male attire, recalling with a feeling akin to pleasure the freedom it gave me. Eikaku's hat covered my hair and I pulled it right down over my shaved eyebrows. Even though I had not blackened my teeth since we had left home they were still stained, but I resolved not to smile and to cover my mouth when I spoke.

The old goods shop was still there, seemingly unchanged. I called at the door, then struck it, and after a while heard Mrs Minami's voice saying, 'Who's there?'

'It is Imaike, the doctor. You remember me – I lived here three years ago.'

She opened the door and slid the shutters back. 'What do you want so early? Are you in trouble again?'

'Itasaki – the man I was with before – is he here?'

'No, he hasn't lived here since you were here together.'

I was sure she was lying. I pushed past her into the entrance hall. 'I know he's alive,' I said. 'I know he's in Kyōto. Please help me find him.'

Mrs Minami shook her head. I thought she was going to push me out and close the door on me. She did push me towards the door, but as she did so she whispered in my ear, 'Try one of the tea houses on Kawaramachi, near the Tosa mansion. He might be there.'

'So you've seen him?'

'He came back to pick up some things, after the fires. Your medicine box, his clothes...But I really don't know anything else about him. Please don't stir up trouble. Kyōto is a dangerous place these days.'

I walked back along the familiar streets to the Kamo River. It was quite light by now and the sky in the east was a brilliant deep yellow. There were already many people around, for although it was the eighth month it was still very hot and in the capital working folk started the day at dawn. A slight mist hung over the river and waterbirds were calling, the sound mingling with the shouts of porters as they began loading boats on the canal and the first cries of morning street sellers, peddling fresh tofu, eggs, spinach and other vegetables and sweet fish from the river.

My mouth filled with saliva at the smell of food, though I thought I would throw up if I tried to eat anything. I crossed the Shijō bridge and then the canal, taking a small lane towards the Tosa mansion. The streets were getting busier but the tea houses I passed, the Takeya, the Kikuya and so on, were not yet open. When I got to the Sanjō bridge I turned to the left and caught sight of the trees surrounding Honnōji. I thought I would go and sit there for a while, maybe drink some water there for my throat was parched and my eyes aching.

I washed my hands and face at the cistern inside the gate and rinsed out my mouth. Then I sat for a while under the great shady trees listening to the birdsong and the chanting of the monks and the sound of gongs. How peaceful it seemed, while beyond the gates the whole country was poised on the brink of war.

Eventually in that peace I came to my senses. What was I doing? Of course I was not going to kill Shinsai, or myself. I was not going to kill anyone. I was one who tried to save life not destroy it. I thought of Ogata Kōan, who had spoken to me in a dream; I remembered my gentle father who disliked death, and I saw Michi, my daughter, as I had last seen her.

I would go back to the lodging place, put on my own clothes and go home to her.

There was a rustling in the leaves above my head and something came fluttering down, landing on the moss beside me. I picked it up: it was a rectangular piece of paper with large characters written on it, words symbolising good fortune and many blessings.

I peered upwards, expecting to see the nimble priest of my earlier imagining but there was no one above me, just the tangle of branches and two crows perched high over my head. Yet the paper amulets continued to fall one by one around me. Others had noticed them by now and were scrambling to pick them up. Within moments a crowd had gathered, exclaiming and shouting. As I stood up, still clutching my paper blessing, I found myself surrounded. Someone started singing, 'Ain't life great! Ain't life great!' and everyone took up the refrain.

Eejanaika, eejanaika! The crowd flowed out from the temple grounds and into the street, carrying me along with it. I no longer had to worry about my disguise for I saw many women like me in men's clothes, and men in women's, their faces white, their lips red, their teeth black. How did it all happen so quickly? Where did they all come from? It was as though everyone had been waiting for this opportunity to burst free of years of constraint and restrictions, of being told what to do and obeying one's elders, obeying one's masters, and always doing the right thing.

'To hell with it all!' the crowd sang and shouted as they danced through Kawaramachi, helping themselves to food and drink, grabbing pieces of fruit, rice cakes and crackers, bean-paste buns, sushi, raw fish, oysters, shrimps, cups of tea, bowls of sake, cramming them into their mouths, swilling them down, and singing, singing, singing their defiance of the old regime which was crumbling around us.

Someone thrust a flask of sake into my hand. 'Drink, oniisan, oneesan, whichever you are. Who cares! Life's great, isn't it?'

I was very close to our inn but there was no way to get out of the crowd. All I could do was stay on my feet and be carried along by it, singing with my companions, 'Ain't life great!' But as I was borne past the inn entrance I saw Eikaku run out, wearing my kimono, his hair piled on his head and secured with my mother's new comb.

'Eikaku-san,' I cried; my voice was lost in the hubbub of the crowd. However, he saw me and he threw himself into the throng as if into a river to be carried along with it as I was.

We were swept into Sanjō Avenue towards the bridge. Here the crowd was joined by all the rogues, beggars, acrobats and musicians who frequented the riverbank, but no one wanted to leave the shopping district with its source of free food and drink, so as if possessed by one mind everyone turned along the bank of the canal heading south. There were many unloading docks and warehouses and at every bridge part of the crowd siphoned off only to flow back at the next bridge, laden with more casks of sake.

Just opposite the Tosa mansion with its long white tile-roofed walls was an alley that led to a tea house Shinsai and I used to go to, the Hisago-tei. I was on the outside of the crowd and I could see Eikaku level with me across the milling heads on the canal side. He was waving a banner someone had thrust into his hands and shouting. I waved back at him, and then I realised he was calling to me and gesticulating, jabbing his free hand in the direction of the Hisago-tei.

I turned my head and saw Shinsai in the entrance to the alley. Our eyes met over the heads of the crowd. I began to fight my way towards him, but as I did so I saw two men appear behind him. They wore samurai dress and swords. There was something purposeful and ruthless about them that contrasted completely with the riotous nature of the crowd. I thought I recognised one of them – it could have been the man I handed a flyer to on my first day in Kyōto, the man who had searched Mrs Minami's shop while I counted the same cups over and over – but I could not be sure. All those figures blended into one dispenser of death. I tried to shout a warning. Shinsai, thrown off guard by the sight of me, turned, drawing his sword too late. Their swords were already in their hands, already inflicting the lethal strokes.

There was a simultaneous cry of shock from many throats, for the blood sprayed out over the crowd and a space opened up before me as people scrambled to get away. I saw as if with microscopic vision the assassins sheath their swords and run back up the alley. I saw Shinsai on his knees, his hands reaching vainly to his throat, as I had seen in my vision. I knelt beside him and caught him as he slumped, trying to staunch the pulsing flow, but the artery in the neck was severed.

He said, 'Imaike-kun,' so I know he recognised me, but that was all he said before he died.

The crowd surged around us, and over us, dancing and singing, *eejanaika, ain't life great!*

SAKAMOTO RYŌMA (1835–1867)

Keiō 3 (1867), Eleventh Month, Age 32

It has been raining all day. Ryōma is not feeling well. He thinks he might have a fever, his throat is sore and he is aching all over. He has caught a cold or maybe influenza. Lately the nights have heralded the bitter Kyōto winter. Last night he could not get warm despite the extra quilt from his landlady. He has been shivering on and off all day. The owners of the Ōmiya suggested he move to the upstairs front room. It has a low roof and is quieter and warmer. He was reluctant at first; ever since he and Miyoshi were trapped in the Teradaya and had to escape through the *shōji* he prefers rooms with more than one way out, but he has decided to take the risk. The capital does not feel dangerous right now. Crowds have been thronging the streets in outbreaks of singing and dancing, helping themselves to food and drink from shops and tea houses. He has been out among them; the atmosphere is rowdy and chaotic, but good-natured and above all optimistic. Everyone believes change is coming; they are drunk on sake and hope in equal measures. He has shared both, in excess perhaps, all the more intoxicated by his secret knowledge that he has been a key instrument in the transformation.

The Tokugawa shōgunate is over. Keiki has agreed to hand the power of the Shōgun back to the Emperor. When he heard the news a few days ago Ryōma wept. It's given him a new respect for Keiki. Many expected the last Shōgun to fight to the end, but in his year as Shōgun, he has made admirable efforts to reform and strengthen the government; he has cosied up to the French, acquiring resources and support from them, and is purchasing arms from the Americans. This has annoyed the British immensely as they are backing Chōshū and Satsuma. But Ryōma never believed Keiki wanted the shōgunate enough to fight for it, even though he has the support of many domains: all the north and east, the stronghold of Tokugawa loyalty, most notably Aizu. Now Ryōma is sure the moderate approach of his own domain of Tosa will prevail. Keiki will resign as Shōgun but will keep all his lands and will have a place in the new government. His presence will curb the ambitions of the Satsuma and Chōshū factions – sometimes Ryōma regrets his role in bringing the two great domains together; he is afraid they will become a force no one can control. He is still close to Saigō Takamori, who was so good to him after the Teradaya affair, but to be honest there is no one in Chōshū he really cares for since poor Shinsaku died. He fell out with Inoue and Itō after their friend Kondō Chōjirō was driven to suicide, for planning to go to England, by Ryōma's associates in the Kaientai, as if that was his fault, and though, like everyone else, he finds Katsura Kogorō charming, he doesn't really trust him.

He pours a little tea from the kettle which is steaming on the brazier. He would like to sleep but there is too much going through his mind: his own plan for a reformed government, all he has learned about international law and trade during his time in Nagasaki, the forms of government practised in Western countries, strange new words – *republic, democracy, parliament*. Japan must have something like this, but the change of government must take place without bloodshed or civil war.

His only experience of war was when he sailed the *Otchū-maru* in support of Takasugi Shinsaku during the battle off the coast of Kokura the previous year. He would not have missed it for anything. It was an essential experience, one he believes everyone should have – but once was enough! He was glad to *have fought*. He loved talking about it afterwards and describing the encounter in letters with illustrations and maps, but the actual fighting had been confusing and uncomfortable. He did not want to lose another ship, having just gone through a protracted legal struggle for compensation after one of his sank in a collision with a ship from Kii, and he hated the idea of men under his command being killed.

'I would never make a general,' he says to Nakaoka Shintarō, who has just come up the stairs. Shintarō is a Tosa man, one of his oldest friends, and Ryōma trusts him completely. 'I don't like soldiers dying.'

Shintarō laughs. 'I've read that soldiers prefer to fight under generals who will risk their lives – they think they have more chance of surviving.'

'I must be more of a merchant than I like to think.'

'In the blood?' Shintarō teases him, for Ryōma's forebears were merchants and he often goes under their name, Saitani.

'I like the way the British conduct trade – it is like warfare but within a framework of rules.'

'They break the rules all the time, or only apply them to themselves and their kind.'

'Maybe, but it is still a system to hold everyone to account. We have nothing like that. Law and punishment both depend on the whim of the powerful.'

He sneezes several times in a row; the cold is coming on heavily now.

'The landlady is sending up some hot food,' Shintarō says. 'That will do you good.'

Several Tosa men, captured by the Shinsengumi, are still being held in prison in Kyōto, and Shintarō has plans to negotiate their release. After they have discussed this they talk in a desultory way about *eejanaika*, the hopes of ordinary people and their demand for a renewal of the world (Shintarō is a village headman's son); they wonder what Keiki will do next, and they reminisce about the last few years, Shintarō's experiences with the Shōkenkaku group in Mitajiri and then as a captain with the *shotai*. He has seen far more fighting than Ryōma; he was wounded at the Forbidden Gate but escaped capture, and fought on Chōshū's side in the Four Borders War. He is probably one of those commanders who don't worry about risking men's lives.

Ryōma is feeling lonely and a little depressed. He closes his eyes and tries to doze. The rain is drumming on the tiles and sluicing down the drains. How far away his homeland seems now. He wishes his wife O-Ryō was with him, wonders about getting some girls in but decides he is not feeling well enough. And O-Ryō would not like it, he thinks with affection. She was so upset when he went to the geisha houses in Shimonoseki. She is a brave girl, though a little bossy. She thinks there is nothing she can't do. What was that place in Kagoshima where there was something women weren't supposed to touch? And O-Ryō went right ahead as if daring the gods to punish her. He is trying to remember the name when they hear footsteps on the stairs.

'That will be our supper,' Shintarō says.

They are both unarmed, their swords resting in the rack by the door. At the Teradaya Ryōma and Miyoshi were prepared – but there is no O-Ryō here to run up the stairs and warn them. They were saved then by the pistol, the gift from Shinsaku, which alarmed the swordsman enough to keep them out of reach – but there is no pistol. Ryōma misses them both, his wife and his weapon, in an agony of regret. He does not want to die now on a rainy night with a cold. How can he leave the world before it is made new? How can it be renewed without him?

The regret is short-lived and lasts only for the moment it takes for the assassins to leap across the room. They are using short swords, he realises, that are not hampered by the low ceiling. Someone has betrayed him, but even if he can guess who, he will never be able to tell anyone. Then he remembers. It was the Sacred Halberd at Mount Kirishima. O-Ryō was told women should not touch it, but she did touch it, and now the gods are punishing them. The swords send him swiftly into the darkness from which none return to share their secrets. Shintarō will linger for a few days but he is unable to identify the murderers before he follows his friend into the next world.

We buried my uncle at Tennōzan, where I had said goodbye to him before he set off for the Forbidden Gate with Kusaka Genzui. We never found out the names of the men who killed him, or the reason, or what Shinsai had been doing during the years he was in hiding. Not long afterwards Sakamoto Ryōma and Nakaoka Shintarō were assassinated in the Ōmiya, just on the other side of the Tosa mansion in Kawaramachi. When I heard this news I thought perhaps Shinsai had been mistaken for Ryōma, or perhaps he was targeted by the same people, whoever they were: some said the Mimawarigumi, some the Shinsengumi, or agents from Satsuma or even Chōshū. I thought Shinsai must have gone back to his work as a spy in Kyōto, and when Katsura and the others had claimed not to know anything of him it was because he was more useful to them if he was believed to be dead. But when he outlived his usefulness would they really have had him killed?

I could not ask Katsura, or Monta or Itō, for I did not see them until the fighting in what would be called the Boshin War was over, and then only from afar, for they had become the new rulers of the nation; they had more pressing concerns.

Makino went away to the war, followed the *shotai* as they

fought their way north, and tended the wounded at Toba-Fushimi, at Ueno, Aizu-Wakamatsu and all the way up to Ezo. He wrote whenever he could. He worked with the English doctor William Willis and sent me letters describing all he had learned about amputations in the field, the use of chloroform, and setting broken limbs, illustrating the procedures with sketches that I tried to follow in my practice, though it would be a long time before Western anaesthetics were available.

That new year became the first year of Meiji – a new era and a new world, marvellous in many ways but not the new world we had dreamed of.

I stayed in Yuda with my mother and my daughter, with Eikaku and Kitaoka, Hachirō and O-Kane. We were a strange household perhaps, but I was happier than I had been for many years. Shinsai's death had lifted the burden I had been carrying, composed of guilt, longing and hope, and healed a festering wound. I no longer looked for him every evening under the gambling tree. I knew where he was, sleeping peacefully at Tennōzan.

One result of our pilgrimage was that Eikaku took up painting again and finally agreed to illustrate my medical charts. It led him to a new interest in sketching from life and we acquired many animals and birds, fish in tanks, frogs, lizards, lobsters, beetles and other insects, and even an octopus at one stage. Michi loved all these creatures, but she was also fascinated by the way they were put together, and any that died were carefully dissected. Eikaku recorded their organs, their veins, muscles and skeletons. We made ammonia from the corpses and then created shrines for them where we offered our prayers and thanks.

I had many patients, all the usual illnesses and mishaps of village life: children with croup or worms, old men with stricture of the chest, women with abdominal dropsy, cases of malaria or measles, farming accidents. Supplies were scarce and our herbal garden became even more important. Kitaoka took over most of the work in the dispensary. Even though he was a good doctor most people wanted to see me. Somehow I had acquired a reputation and had gained their trust.

A year or so passed like this. We heard the fighting was finally over and the *shotai* were returning home. We had a new national government which included Katsura, now called Kido Takayoshi, Itō, with the new name of Hirobumi, and Monta, who was now called Kaoru, along with Prince Sanjō and the Satsuma commanders, Saigō Takamori and Ōkubo Toshimichi. Suddenly the country swarmed with foreigners who had come to build a new and modern Japan.

In Chōshū preparations were made to welcome home the victorious *shotai*, but for most of them there would be no celebration. Our old lord's son, Sadahiro, who had also changed his name, to Motonori, selected just under half from the five thousand who came back from the war. The rest were told to disband and go home.

After the years of fighting and sacrifice, the underpaid and underfed soldiers met this decision with disbelief. They tried to approach the governor's residence in Yamaguchi to plead their case. Many disappointed farmers seized the opportunity to express their own grievances. Chōshū had toppled the Bakufu with courage and perseverance, but they had received nothing in return. Their leaders had given themselves new names and fancy new ranks and had disappeared to Edo, or Tōkyō as it was now called.

The protest was treated as a mutiny and suppressed brutally. One hundred and thirty men were executed at a place called the Holly Tree, and my husband, Makino Keizō, died there. He was trying to go to the help of Sasaki Shōichirō, one of the leaders who had been with the Kiheitai from the start, who had fought at Kokura with Takasugi and who had been negotiating with the domain officials for an amicable outcome.

'Sasaki could not believe his own government would execute him,' Eikaku said mournfully. He was extremely affected by this bloody end to the Kiheitai and was painting a picture of it. 'He fought against being made to kneel, not out of fear or cowardice but because he believed there had been a misunderstanding. They battered him to his knees with an iron club. Your husband went to help him and they smashed his skull.'

I did not need to take up the magic fan. I knew what it would show me: Makino's look of shock as he realised he had miscalculated, that he was dying by mistake, that the world was not ruled by reason but by random acts of madness.

I could not bear it: the waste of all his skill and learning, his hopes and ambitions. He had come through the war unscathed and had no doubt saved many lives, only to end up being killed by his own side so close to home.

I did not love him as I loved Shinsai, but I grieved for him a hundred times more.

Eikaku's picture shows him running forward, arms stretched out towards Sasaki, who is holding his hands over his head as the iron bar descends. Behind lies a pile of bodies, a river of blood spreading from them, while their heads are neatly lined up along one side. On the other side is the trunk of the holly tree, its branches casting a dark shadow into which Makino is about to fall.

It is a great work of art and I think Kido Takayoshi would appreciate it. I plan to give it to him if I ever see him again.

SHIRAISHI SEIICHIRŌ (1812–1880)

Meiji 10 (1877), Spring, Age 65

In the fifth month of 1877 Kido Takayoshi dies after weeks of serious illness. When Shiraishi Seiichirō hears the news of Katsura's death (he has never been able to think of him by his new name) it puts him in a melancholy mood. He cannot sleep that night; it is already very warm and his mind keeps returning to the past. It has been a terrible few months, with the Hagi rebellion in the tenth month last year, the execution of Maebara Issei, one of Shōin's original students, and the suicide of Shōin's uncle, and now the war in Satsuma in which Saigō Takamori has become involved. He is afraid his old friend Saigō will be added to the long list of the departed for whose spirits he prays daily at the shrine.

How has it happened that the old allies are now fighting on opposite sides? But hadn't he foreseen it in the old days at the Kokuraya, when he and Rensaku talked about bringing Satsuma and Chōshū together? Poor Rensaku! He committed suicide after the defeat at Ikuno. It's been nearly fourteen years, but Shiraishi misses him more not less with the passing days. He was always full of good ideas. Maybe if Rensaku had not died they would have been able to keep the business together. He himself has lost everything. He is not sure how it happened: competition from foreign merchants, the growth of Yokohama and Kobe, the new steamships that did not need to wait for wind and tide at Shimonoseki. *And maybe I was too distracted*, he thinks. *Everything changed while my attention was elsewhere. Once I was able to handle so many different things at once, like a plate spinner running from one to the other: rice for Satsuma, wax from Chōshū, arms for Katsura, money for Takasugi, then suddenly I could not do it any longer, and one by one the plates began to totter and fall. Now I am old and I have nothing to show for it.*

He gave away all that money to support the *shotai* without any pecuniary thoughts or hopes of repayment. He enjoys his shrine duties and is grateful for the modest living they provide, but it is galling to have ended up here, when he recalls his activities in those exciting days when everyone was hoping for a new world. Sometimes he rereads his old diaries to remind himself how many famous people came through the Kokuraya, but it is depressing to realise so many of them are dead.

Though he tries to view events with detachment they still cause him pain. Once he thought progress would come about through harmony, a shared vision which everyone worked together to achieve. And they *had* done that for a few months, a few years, when everyone had selflessly thrown themselves into the struggle and brought about what was to be a wonderful restoration: the Emperor resuming his divinely ordained position, head of the nation and mediator between heaven and the people.

Yet now he sees that progress is a more brutal and vicious affair. Country people fear that the foundations of the railroad and the telegraph will be mixed with their blood. Shiraishi is too sophisticated to believe this is literally true, but he pictures progress and the modernisation and Westernisation that accompany it as huge machines which human beings are thrown into, or fall under, to be crushed. Progress is a crucible reducing his old world and distilling it into some new chemical compound.

It is tragic, he thinks, that incidents like the Holly Tree and the Hagi rebellion have occurred in Chōshū. The plight of the *shotai* and the samurai class is pitiful. They were told they were victors, yet they ended up worse off than before, some of them literally starving. They lost their hereditary stipends, were given a handout and told to apply themselves to business. Yet few had any skills or commercial sense and there were no opportunities for employment. Take the scheme to grow summer oranges in Hagi: so many were produced there was a glut and you could hardly give them away. His own business failed despite his years of experience – what hope was there for these half-hearted beginners?

And so came the pathetic, courageous attempts to demand justice. When words were met with indifference or contempt the aggrieved resorted to arms – only to be suppressed brutally. Maebara had been one of Shōin's students, had fought in the Four Borders and the Boshin wars, had been a friend and colleague of Katsura and the others for years, yet they ordered his execution. Shiraishi knows they will deal as ruthlessly with Saigō.

It will soon be light. The birds have begun the loud chorus of an early-summer dawn. It is the hour when he usually gets up, restokes the kitchen fires, sets water to boil, washes his face and hands, makes his first prayers and begins to sweep the wooden floors of the verandas and halls. But after the sleepless night he is slow to start the day. He wants to sleep again and in his dreams return to the past when the young men were all still alive. Suddenly the easy tears of an old man well up in his eyes and he finds himself weeping.

HITOTSUBASHI KEIKI (1837–1913)

1900, New Year's Day, Age 63

Tokugawa Yoshinobu, whom everyone calls Keiki, the fifteenth and last Shōgun of Japan, can often be seen riding his bicycle through the town of Shizuoka. He is what every abdicated leader should be. He leads an exemplary life with his various women and children, dogs and horses, occupying himself with many hobbies: hunting, archery, photography, and brewing French coffee, to which he is addicted.

When he was twenty-three, in 1860, the Tairō, Ii Naosuke, was assassinated in a bloody attack by men of the Mito domain, who then committed *seppuku* in an honourable feudal way. Now he is in his sixties and a new century has begun. His country has changed beyond all recognition. Sometimes he likes to imagine what his father Nariaki would say were he to return now. In all the plans and intrigues of those distant times, none of them had the least inkling of what the future would really be like. Japan has become a world power; it has caught up with the Western nations, and could even outstrip them. Keiki feels he can congratulate himself, not only for surviving but for becoming what he always knew he was capable of being – a thoroughly modern man.

THE SURVIVORS

Itō Hirobumi (Shunsuke)

After 1868 Itō became one of the leading figures in the new government. He joined the Iwakura mission to the US and Europe in 1871 and visited Europe again in 1882 to study Western constitutions. On his return he helped create the Meiji constitution and became Japan's first Prime Minister in 1885. From 1905 to 1909 he was resident-general of the protectorate of Korea. Generally sympathetic towards Koreans, he was not in favour of annexation, but that did not prevent him being assassinated by a Korean student in Harbin in October 1909.

Inoue Kaoru (Monta)

Inoue initially worked in the foreign ministry for the new government, but then became deputy finance minister in 1871. He tried to stabilise the desperate financial situation by land-tax reform and the end of the stipend system. He returned to the foreign ministry in 1879 and worked constantly towards revision of the unequal treaties Japan had signed with the Western powers. He was criticised for his excessive pro-European ideas and for his connections with business and industry, in particular with the Mitsui company. He died in 1915.

Yamagata Aritomo (Kyōsuke)

After fighting in the Boshin War Yamagata studied Western military systems in Europe and was involved in military reform in Japan. He was the driving force behind the introduction of conscription and the fostering of samurai spirit within the armed forces. He served as Home Minister and Prime Minister and in both capacities clashed with the popular-rights movement. Until his death in 1922 he remained the focus of conservative policy.

Sanjō Sanetomi

Prince Sanjō returned to Kyōto in 1867 and went on to hold high positions in the Meiji government, including Lord Privy Seal in 1885. He died in 1891.

Saigō Takamori

Saigō was one of the leaders of the Imperial forces in the Boshin War and with Katsu Kaishū negotiated the surrender of Edo castle without bloodshed. He remained in Japan to run the country while other leaders were away on the Iwakura mission, but strongly supported the idea to invade Korea and when he was overruled resigned from government and returned to Satsuma. He committed suicide in 1877 after the Satsuma rebellion.

Ōkubo Toshimichi

Satsuma samurai Ōkubo is considered with Saigō and Kido Takayoshi to be one of the three giants of the Meiji Restoration. He accompanied the Iwakura mission and on his return opposed the invasion of Korea. He had to suppress the rebellions of 1874 and 1877, putting him in direct conflict with his old comrade Saigō. He was assassinated by discontented samurai in May 1878.

Thomas Glover

After the Restoration Glover continued to live in Japan and became involved in many industrial and business enterprises for which he was awarded the Order of the Rising Sun (second class). He died in 1911 in Tokyo.

Nomura Bōtōni

Bōtōni lived in Hofu after Takasugi's death, where she spent her days fasting and praying for victory against the Bakufu. She died in 1867 shortly after the return of power to the Emperor.

Ōmura Masujirō

After his successes in the Four Borders War Ōmura became one of the leaders of the Imperial forces in the Boshin War. He worked with Yamagata on plans to reform the military and introduce conscription, but was assassinated by conservative samurai in 1869.

ACKNOWLEDGMENTS

My deepest thanks go to:

Asialink for the fellowship that first took me to Yamaguchi prefecture and introduced me to the history of Chōshū.

Arts SA for a mid-career fellowship that enabled me to return to Japan many times.

Shuho-chō for inviting me to stay in their Cultural Exchange House for three months in order to research this novel.

The Friends of the Cultural Exchange House for introducing me to local history and landscape.

Santo Yuko and Mark Brachmann from the Shuho Council Office for all the trips to museums and galleries and help with borrowing books from the Yamaguchi libraries.

Maxine McArthur, Mogi Akiko and Mogi Masaru, Yamaguchi Hiroi and Hosokawa Fumimasa, Matsubara Manami and Kori Yoshinori for friendship, hospitality and encouragement.

Randy Schadel, Dr Ayame Chiba, Dr Ellen Nakamura and Dr Robin Haines for reading the manuscript and for their comments.

The samurai-archives forum members for many interesting discussions on Bakumatsu history.

Lonny Chick for the invaluable and entertaining exchange of ideas, books and resources.

Kimura Miyo for inestimable and endless help in tracking down vital books, articles and obscure facts and with translations.

Staff at the Alexandrina Library in Goolwa and the National Library of Australia.

My agents Jenny Darling, Donica Bettanin and Sarah Lutyens.

Among the many books I read I must mention above all Albert Craig's *Chōshū in the Meiji Restoration* and Thomas Huber's *The Revolutionary Origins of Modern Japan.* I am immeasurably indebted to these authors as to Ichisaka Tarō, whose book *Takasugi Shinsaku wo Aruku* was my guidebook around the historical sites of Chōshū. For a full bibliography please visit my website www.lianhearn.com

A Q&A WITH LIAN HEARN

Tsuru manages to fit an awful lot into what is still a young life. Was it important to you to show what a young woman could achieve in those times?

The book covers the years 1857–67, some of the most turbulent and action-packed in Japanese history. Tsuru's life, as well as being a more or less straightforward story of a young woman caught up in these times, is also an embodiment of them. So everything that happens to her in microcosm is a reflection of what is happening in the larger world around her. I deliberately chose the doctor's family as the imaginary characters of the story: in traditional Asian medicine, curing individual bodies and curing the state are closely entwined, while the revolutionaries of the nineteenth century used Western metaphors of vaccination and surgery in their struggle to restore "healthy" government. Many of the Chōshū loyalists came from medical families. Tsuru's story would have been unusual in the real world, but not impossible; I chose to write about a young woman partly because Japanese history is typically very masculine. Women are usually portrayed in subservient roles, if at all. By placing Tsuru in a doctor's family in Chōshū, I was able to bring her into the company of many of the major historical characters and allow her to witness events.

In mid-nineteenth century Japan, perhaps in reaction to the realisation of superior Western technology, as well as shock at the sheer physical size of Western men, there was a great deal of unease about gender identity: hence cases of cross-dressing similar to Eikaku in the book, outbreaks of spontaneous dancing and dressing up, teenagers absconding from their masters, women who ran away from home and led lives usually restricted to men. All of this adds to the vibrancy of the story.

The relationship between Tsuru and her uncle is quite controversial. What made you choose for her to fall in love with him? Or was it something that happened naturally?

Times of great social upheaval loosen many restrictions and allow people to act out hidden or forbidden fantasies. And this is also something fiction does rather well. I don't see the point of writing about conventional relationships or simply meeting the expectations of the majority of readers. There should always be a transgressive, unpredictable element. So when I was writing – and I don't follow a synopsis: I start writing and discover what is going to happen – I could sense the attraction between Tsuru and Shinsai and then the plot came to a place where their love affair made sense both in reality and as a symbol of the disruption of normality. They have been brought up in the same family; they are very close in age; they become almost comrades in arms – but of course the affair cannot last – do they ever expect it to? However it gives them both what they need at that moment in the middle of war.

What is it about Japan that inspires you? Have you ever thought of living there?

I find Japan intensely interesting and the more I learn about its culture and history, the more it fascinates me. I don't spend too much time asking myself why this should be: all humans have hobbies or passions or obsessions: this is just one of mine. I love being in Japan and I would like to live there but I don't like the Japanese summers and I think the bureaucracy would drive me mad.

Why is this particular period of so much interest to you?

I'm always asking myself why it isn't of more interest to everyone. The Meiji Restoration was a major event in world history, up there with the French Revolution, or the American Civil War, shaping the twentieth century and leading to the Pacific War, yet most European and American readers have never heard of it. A country that had been quite isolated with a semi-feudal form of government, reshaped and reinvented itself with relatively little bloodshed and so avoided colonialisation and communist-style revolution. Of course, what it ended up with was a less than ideal form of government but that's part of the complexity of the story. Add to this some remarkable characters – brave, intelligent, foolhardy, flawed. How could you not be fascinated? The politics are extremely complicated and often confusing: it was quite a challenge to unravel events and I enjoyed that part of it enormously.

What do you enjoy reading? Are there any authors that particularly inspire you?

I read a huge amount and am inspired by many authors. Last year I was very impressed by two biographies by David Bellos on French writers Romain Gary (whose novel *The Roots of Heaven* I fell in love with as a teenager) and Georges Perec (I also read *Life: A User's Manual* last year and adored it). And I discovered Ian Pears and read three of his historical novels: I like his technique of telling the story from several points of view and letting the reader fill in the gaps and work out what is going on. It's very satisfying.

Your research is detailed and meticulous: how did you set about it?

I wanted to give readers a sense of what it might have been like living in a world so different to our own. I first had the idea to try to write about the Meiji Restoration in 1999 when I was just starting *Across the Nightingale Floor*, so this book has been a long time in gestation. In 2002 I spent three months in a small village in Yamaguchi prefecture, living in a former doctor's house, and visiting all the locations mentioned in the book. Over the next few years I immersed myself in the political and social history of the period as well as the development of medical practice in the mid 19th century. The medical side was not so well covered, so required a bit of digging out, but there are many books and mooks in Japanese on lifestyles in the late Edo/early Meiji period, mostly with detailed illustrations. As well as museums and art galleries there is a tradition in Japan of maintaining old houses as they were – you can go and sit on the floor and imagine yourself back one hundred and fifty years ago. There's a bibliography on my website www.lianhearn.com for anyone who is interested in further reading.

You use a first person past tense narrative for Tsuru's story but switch to a present tense third person for several historical characters. What was the reason for this?

It is rather a fragmented approach I know, but I wanted to convey the many elements and personalities that made up the period known as the bakumatsu – the fall of the Bakufu – and this seemed to be a way of indicating the chaotic unfolding of events during those years, especially as many of the people involved, Sufu Masanosuke and Kusaka Genzui for example, died tragically before the change of government. Others like Shiraishi Seiichirō and Nomura Bōtōni, though relatively minor characters, played a significant role. I thought if I gave all of them the attention they deserved, the book would stretch to thousands of pages, but I could not leave them out. History does not occur as a neat narrative – it is only afterwards that the storyline is imposed on it. So there is always going to be conflict between 'history' and 'novel'. I felt this needed to be recognised in some way.